To Sylvia

DEAD HUNT

SMART WOMEN, DUMB LUCK

LINDA LOVELY

Linda Lovely

PUBLISHED BY LHI

SENECA, SOUTH CAROLINA

Interior Design by LHI
Cover Art by Christy Caughie, Gilded Heart Design

ACKNOWLEDGEMENTS

A special thank you to FBI veterans Ann and Chuck Middleton for their expertise and patient help answering questions about agency titles, structure and protocol. Any errors related to the FBI and procedures are mine—along with willful bending of a few facts to satisfy plot requirements. I'm a big fan of the FBI, and Ann and Chuck are terrific representatives.

I'm grateful to my husband, Tom Hooker, for suggestions on early drafts and to Beta reader Fara Driver for her insights. As always, I'm indebted to all my critique partners Maya Reynolds, Robin Weaver and Ashantay Peters, Donna Campbell, Danielle Dahl, Howard Lewis, and Jean Robbins.

I'd also like to thank Christy Caughie at Gilded Heart Design for creating an eye-catching cover for Dead Hunt.

A final shout out to Deborah "Dab" Holt, who won the Wetumpka, Alabama, "Murder on the Menu" auction to have a character named for her in my next novel. Dab, thanks for being a good sport and letting me assign your name to a flirt whose personality I'm sure bears no resemblance to your own.

NOTES

This romantic thriller is set in Upstate South Carolina. I placed the fictional Blue Ridge University in the equally fictional Leeds County, which I located near the real Greenville County and the beautiful foothills of the Southern Appalachian mountain chain.

A lot of action takes place in wilderness areas. The spectacular Foothills Trail described in the book is real. The trail runs along the North Carolina Border and includes old growth forest and unparalleled plant bio-diversity. The petroglyphs referenced in the novel are real, too, though I tampered with their location. More than 600 petroglyphs are carved into rocks near Pinnacle Mountain. Lake Jôcassee and Devils Fork State Park are real, too, and definitely worth visiting.

Now for more made-up names and locations. To the best of my knowledge there is no town of Shelby, no Onward militia group, no His Way University, no Cougar Mountain, no Beaver Falls access point. I'm sure I'm forgetting to mention other locales, groups and institutions I invented because I didn't want to damage the reputation of real entities. However, there is nothing fictional about the beauty of the South Carolina region I describe in the book. It is blessed with natural treasures, excellent universities, and many people of good will.

DEDICATION

For my nieces Tammy and Brenda—
Two of the smartest women I know

ONE

In five minutes, Carl Oldfield would be dead.

L.J. smiled, pleased with the irony. The nosy reporter would die like he lived—clueless.

Concentrate. Don't get ahead of yourself. He pushed the oversized dark glasses snug against the bridge of his nose and tightened his grip on the white cane. A man with a seeing-eye dog walked by. *Perfect.* He merged into the slipstream of blank-eyed figures, confident he'd breeze through the security checkpoint's x-ray machines and metal detectors.

"Go right on through, sir," the officer said. "The elevators are straight ahead."

"Thanks, son," L.J. answered. "Have a nice day."

He silently applauded the organization for the blind. It took clout to snag the Hart Senate Office Building's ninth-floor conference room. The gathering met his needs perfectly. Even the weather was cooperating with his game of blind-man's bluff. An icy rain-sleet mix prompted a sea of raincoats, scarves and hats, making him just one more anonymous trench coat with a dripping hat brim pulled low. The wig and fake moustache almost seemed overkill.

Clicks from dozens of canes echoed in the soaring atrium. It sounded as if the blustery wind had blown in a swarm of hapless cicadas. He tapped his white cane on the marble floor, adding one more discordant note to the invasion of rain-spackled supplicants.

He concentrated on holding his head rigid. No blind man would crane his neck to study the towering sculpture dominating the atrium. His gaze roamed behind his black glasses.

Linda Lovely

Where the hell was Charles? He'd given the senator's nervous aide two simple tasks. Escort the meddlesome *Washington Post* reporter from Senator Yates' office on schedule. Engage the target in conversation beside the elevators until Oldfield's fate was sealed.

With one poke, the tip of L.J.'s cane would induce a massive heart attack. By the time the journalist collapsed, L.J. and his deadly cane would be nine stories up, listening to sightless lobbyists plead with deaf congressmen.

Given the pudgy Oldfield's three-pack-a-day habit and fondness for MoonPies, nobody would think twice about the forty-five-year-old's demise. Even if the death raised questions, no one would suspect L.J. of providing the fatal catalyst.

L.J.'s heart stuttered as he neared the elevators. Taking a deep breath, he told himself his nerves were normal. He was a businessman, not an assassin. His partner had made long-distance arrangements to eliminate the procurement officer. He should have done the same, but Oldfield pissed him off. He wanted to give the prying slob a personal send-off to hell. The self-righteous liberal prick was just like the journalists who'd hounded his father to the edge of insanity after that traitor-bitch bankrupted his family.

Dammit. Some goddamn broad was chatting up Charles and Oldfield. He didn't need a witness.

As the woman gestured, her voluminous raincoat ballooned like a spinnaker sail in a stiff breeze, keeping her shape a secret. He could only gauge her height—almost as tall as Charles, maybe five-eight. As he drew closer, L.J. spied wisps of glistening auburn hair peeking beneath her rain bonnet. His gaze traveled down—tailored slacks, no-nonsense, low-heeled pumps.

She shifted and her freckled face sprang into view. Recognition hit him like a body blow. *Riley Reid.*

The interloper doffed her rain hat and tossed her shiny curls like a bedraggled spaniel. What if she recognized him? He wanted to scream. *Get the hell away.*

Her lively hands danced as she spoke. He doubted she'd shut her trap soon. Like all women, she liked to yammer, share her smug opinions. She was screwing up his careful plan.

The woman was chummy with her companions. Charles worked for her uncle, Senator Yates. Oldfield had interviewed her dozens of times when the reporter worked for the *Greenville News* and she was in the FBI's Greenville office.

She knew L.J., too. Thank God he'd added the wig and moustache. He slowed his pace.

Do I stick with my plan?

Time to decide. He'd reach the yakking trio in seconds. He couldn't walk any slower without attracting attention—a molasses anomaly in a fast-paced kaleidoscope. The deadly cane slipped in his sweat-slicked palm. He tightened his grip.

Tap. Tap. *Goddammit.*

Tap. Tap. Wish I could poke her, too.

He inched forward. Oldfield had his back to him. The woman was focused on the journalist.

He believed in risk-reward analysis. A murder committed in front of a former FBI agent definitely bumped up his risk factor. He bit the inside of his lip and tasted blood. He smelled wet wool. His own heartbeat thundered in his ears.

A crowd bunched near the elevators. Blind people milled around, bumping into things. *I won't stand out.* Reward outweighed risk.

He pressed a lever. Like a serpent's tongue, a needlelike sliver of metal flicked out of the cane's tip. He felt a tiny jolt as the needle point punctured Oldfield's leg. L.J. retracted the tip. He'd moved a yard past Oldfield when the reporter emitted a pig-like squeal. L.J. resumed his innocent tap-tapping on the marble. Two yards away. Tap. Tap. Three.

He sidled up to a blind woman super-glued to the man patting her arm. As L.J. waited for the elevator, no one yelled.

Home free.

* * * *

The reporter's wisecracks about Blue Ridge University turning into a modern-day Sodom and Gomorrah punched Riley Reid's on button. She realized she was talking with hands a-flutter and caught Oldfield's grin. She laughed. The journalist was up to his old tricks, good-natured baiting, and she'd fallen for it.

Riley forgave Oldfield. She felt wired, alive, having spent the day with Nexi Ketts and Kate Johnson. The trio called themselves the "Smart Women, Dumb Luck Club." Dumb luck had brought them together. The "Smart Women" tag was a joke, poking fun at themselves, since their supposed "smarts" seemed to go missing when it came to family relationships and men.

When the fates aligned to bring them together, the ladies made the most of it. This time they all had reasons to be in D.C. Nexi had a forensic accounting gig, Kate was checking out a nearby university's doctoral program, and Riley was attending a conference focused on security.

Oldfield cocked his head. "You seem…well, happier. Not sure I ever saw you laugh when you were with the FBI."

"I am happier." Riley grinned. "Always appreciated your jokes, but surely you know smiling is against agency regs."

At lunch, Nexi and Kate had made a similar observation, teasing Riley about losing her wooden FBI "mannequisms." Their jests held a kernel of truth. As an FBI agent, Riley fought the urge to move more than an eyelash when she spoke. Now she felt free to reveal her emotions—frown, shrug, wag a finger, raise an eyebrow.

A small knot of blind people passed by. Her gestures would be meaningless to them. She thought of all the wonders sighted people take for granted. No sunrises. No smiles.

"Have you read this?" Oldfield's question stopped her woolgathering.

Oh, crap. Now there was a smile she didn't want to see— Wolf Valdes's hundred-watt grin plastered on the book jacket of his erotic thriller. Oldfield fanned himself with the best-selling novel. "Hot, hot, hot."

Riley's smile froze as her gaze fastened on the author's bedroom eyes. Her one-time lover's popular novel constantly reminded her of her transgression. She felt a blush creep up her neck as she imagined Oldfield reading the fictionalized account of her steamy interlude with Wolf Valdes. *Wonder if he's reached page 158?*

The journalist waggled his eyebrows. "I may not write for the *Greenville News* any more, but I still keep tabs on South Carolina happenings. I'm considering doing a piece on Professor Valdes's troubles at Blue Ridge University."

Oldfield chuckled. "Lot a good it did Valdes to publish *Firelight* under a pseudonym. The minute that publishing screw-up put his photo on the book jacket, he was outed. I hear your faculty conservatives want to tar and feather him."

Riley shrugged and flat-out lied. "The drama's blown over."

She didn't want the reporter nosing around and digging up the morbid connection between her family and Wolf's relatives. Riley's mom didn't need her son's death rehashed. Her mother did a fine job of picking at that scab all by her lonesome. Good lord, could it be twenty-six years since Jack died?

Linda Lovely

Oldfield shook his head. "From what I hear, it's still a juicy story. BRU's self-appointed morals police are plotting to terminate Valdes." He cupped a hand around his mouth and whispered. "Wish all my homework was this much fun. I give *Firelight* five stars."

Oldfield stuffed the volume deeper into his nest of papers. "Do you miss the FBI?"

Riley sighed in relief at the change of topic. "No, keeping three thousand students safe is challenge enough. Young people are a tonic. They're so enthusiastic, full of life."

She didn't comment on the irritant of seeing Wolf strut around *her* campus with coeds panting in his wake. Nor did she mention that some faculty barely tolerated her, believing security measures ran counter to intellectual freedom.

She glanced at her watch. Two minutes and she'd be late. In her FBI days she'd faced down drug dealers and crazed neo-Nazis. Still her uncle, the senator, intimidated her.

She offered Oldfield a farewell handshake. "Gotta run. My uncle gets heartburn when people are tardy."

The reporter's body jerked. His fingers spasmed, nearly crushing the bones in her hand. A strangled cry escaped his lips. His eyes scrunched shut; his face contorted.

"You okay?" she asked. "What's wrong?"

Oldfield's grimace relaxed slightly, but his color wasn't good.

"Just a twinge." He panted. "Felt like someone branded my leg with a hot poker. My doc says it's past time to quit smoking and start dieting. Same load of crap he hands everyone over forty."

The reporter's expression didn't jibe with his nonchalant quip.

"You look shaky. Why don't you come to my uncle's office and sit a spell."

6

"Nah, I'm fine."

Before she could utter another word, Charles grabbed her elbow. "Better catch the next elevator if you want to be on time." The aide sounded stressed.

What's his problem? In the ten years she'd known Charles, he'd never touched her. Never touched anyone. Now his fingers dug into her arm as if she were a fleeing felon. His insistent tug pulled her toward the elevators.

"Nice to see you," she called over her shoulder. "You know those doctors aren't always full of crap. Take care."

An elevator door tried to close then hiccupped open. A man gently took his blind wife's elbow and guided her to the left. "Mae, honey, your cane stopped the door from closing."

When he spotted Riley and Charles, the husband stuck out his hand to interrupt the safety beam. "There's plenty of room."

The blind woman sighed. "Sorry. Am I in the way?"

"You're fine, doing great," her husband said.

"Give yourself time," added a stranger, waggling a white cane. "Took me a year to get used to feeling my way with this cattle prod."

The fourth passenger kept silent. Black glasses hid his eyes. A hat brim shadowed the small wedge of visible features. His chin burrowed deep in a heather scarf. His moustache and bushy sideburns—something peculiar about them—drew her attention.

Her eyes fixed on the blind stranger. Riley automatically noted the minutia, the ingrained habit of observing details remained strong. *If that fellow could see, I'd apologize for staring.*

She faced forward as the doors closed and the elevator shot up to Uncle Ed's eighth-floor offices.

* * * *

L.J.'s hammering heart made him wonder if Oldfield would be the day's sole heart attack. Thank God the Reid woman didn't glance back when she stepped off the elevator. What prompted her to stare at him like she was prepping for a police sketch artist? Did she decide he looked familiar? Knowing her, she'd brood on Oldfield's death. Maybe connect him. *Damn her.*

When L.J. came up with the university portion of his plan, he considered sidelining the security director early in the game. He decided against it—even though the uppity bitch begged to be smacked down. Time to revisit his decision?

Her unexpected appearance in D.C. tipped the scales. They weren't in her favor.

TWO

Uncle Ed's bear hug left her breathless. "Riley, what a treat."

"Glad you could fit me in." She smiled as her uncle consulted his watch.

He prized punctuality almost as much as he hated squandering tax dollars. The military had a love-hate relationship with the senator—a hawk who kept a sharp point on his pencil.

"Sorry I'm in a rush," he apologized. "Have to fly out at nine for a blitz tour of Middle East hot spots. It's one of those days I wished I chaired Agriculture instead of Armed Services. I'd get home more often."

He snapped his briefcase closed. "How's your mother?"

"Thrilled you're giving the commencement speech at our alma mater. So is Jennie."

The senator frowned. "I hope so. I don't want to steal the spotlight from my daughter. It's her college graduation."

Riley perched on the edge of a prickly, cane-backed visitor's chair. She assumed it was chosen to encourage occupant brevity. "Don't worry. I saw Jennie yesterday. She thinks it's 'way cool' her father will be on the dais. She's a gem."

Uncle Ed smiled. "Parents never tire of folks bragging on their kids." He leaned over to jot a last-minute note on his desk calendar. "What about you? Ready for graduation?"

"Not completely." Riley chewed her lip. "You're not our only high-profile dad. We're coordinating three security details and expect seven thousand for the ceremonies. Work's pretty hectic."

The senator looked up. "Seven thousand. Really?"

A knock interrupted. Charles poked his head inside. "I thought you would want to know." His normally unctuous voice took on a funereal tone. "Carl Oldfield just had a massive heart attack. He's dead."

"Oh, my God!" Riley shook her head in disbelief. "Right after we left?"

"Apparently," Charles answered.

"Dammit, I knew the man was in pain. I should have insisted...found him medical help. Maybe he'd still be alive."

Senator Yates shook his head. "A massive heart attack? No, Riley. Nothing you could have done. I liked Oldfield, too. He was a stand-up guy."

THREE

Wolf Valdes hustled down the hall. Forty minutes late for the At-Risk Committee meeting. Couldn't be helped. A failing student had stopped to ask about make-up work and came unglued. Hated college. Terrified of his dad. Wolf couldn't just say "have a nice day" and trot off.

He opened the door, scanned the faculty lounge. One free chair next to Riley. Okay, he'd risk freezer burn.

The security director glanced his way, then dropped her eyes to her notes. No nod. No smile. Understandable. If she hadn't known before that *N.Y. Times'* profile that her sworn enemies were his kin, she knew now. The story hit newsstands the week he joined BRU's faculty. It dwelt on his close ties with his Cherokee relatives. The name of Wolf's cousin had to be seared into Riley's brain. For years, her mother and uncle took every opportunity to publicly label Hank a murderer and his acquittal a travesty, reverse discrimination at its worst.

Wolf circled behind the occupied chairs. As he took a seat in the cramped quarters, his leg grazed Riley's. She jumped like she'd been tagged with a live wire.

"Wolf, we waited to talk about Ellen Wingate, since you're her advisor." Dr. Sparks shuffled through a fat file. "Anyone who read the poems dedicated to her roommate could understand why the roommate's parents freaked."

Wolf opened a folder. "No question. The dark imagery reflects Ellen's turmoil."

The poems intermingled images of love, physical torture, and death. Ellen's literary endeavors had added her to the At-Risk Committee's watch list, an eclectic roster of troubled youngsters ranging from bulimics to bullies. Faculty on the At-Risk Committee worked with BRU's mental health professionals to try to intervene before any students came to harm.

Wolf frowned. "Ellen's very young. Confused. Feels guilty about her sexual orientation. After her roommate was yanked out of school, Ellen told me she'd lost her soul mate. I convinced her to see a counselor, sat with her while she phoned for an appointment. She swears she isn't suicidal."

"Sounds like the situation's in hand." The vice chancellor turned to another faculty member. "Ryan, what can we do about James Alexander? His pranks are escalating."

Wolf's gaze slid to Riley. She looked up from massaging her bum knee. Their eyes met. He felt the electricity. Heat lightning. Nothing would come of it. Though unable to tamp down his desire, Wolf knew any relationship beyond frosty formality was fantasy.

Yet a little make-believe hurt no one. Wolf's editor had asked him to add more sizzle to his manuscript. So he'd picture the security director when he started revisions. He imagined sliding a hand between her primly locked knees. The gun on her hip a delicious prop for a dominatrix-flavored daydream. Riley pointing a gun at him and ordering him to "stick it up."

Her real-life voice shut down his fantasy. Something about commencement. The meeting ended. He stood, turned, and found himself face to face with Riley. He smelled her cinnamon-scented shampoo. Her full lips parted as if she invited contact. Close enough to lean in for a kiss.

Wolf spun away. *Get a grip.* Save your fantasies for your fiction.

FOUR

Riley Reid's office resembled a walk-in closet. Big title, small digs. Hoping to coax a pop out of her cranky knee—the souvenir of a bad takedown—she rolled her chair sideways, clearing a spot to stretch. Too many hours at the danged computer.

Riley glanced at the clock, surprised to see eight p.m. The demands of next Saturday's graduation meant sixteen-hour days.

She raised her arms, twisted at the waist. Five days after Carl Oldfield's heart attack, she couldn't stop thinking about him. *Why didn't I realize he was in trouble?*

She touched her palms to the floor. The alarm's unexpected blare almost toppled her. She steadied herself and grabbed her Glock.

"Where is it?" she called to the officer manning Blue Ridge University's 24-hour communications center.

"Code Red by the lake. Ted's closest. Should be there inside a minute."

"Tell him I'm en route. Alert EMS. Did the caller say anything?"

"No. Just punched Big Red. No idea what we're dealing with."

The emergency call kiosks scattered around the rambling campus all featured red buttons to summon help. No student had ever activated Big Red as a prank.

In less than five minutes, her Honda slalomed into the parking lot next to Ted's patrol car. A siren wailed in the distance. The street light's sodium yellow washed over the scene. Ted crouched beside a slender body; blonde hair splayed across the grass, long legs, shapely and bare. Dread quickened her heartbeat. *God, please don't let her be dead. Not another Amanda.*

Riley ran flat out. With every jarring step, her knee sent a stab of pain.

The girl moaned.

Thank heaven, she's alive.

Ted looked up, his eyes worried. "Two knife wounds. One to the thigh, the other to the arm." He spoke in a monotone.

The coed's pasty, stricken face jarred her. Ellen Wingate looked just like the photo in her "at-risk" file. Heart-shaped face, dimpled chin, shoulder-length blonde hair.

The girl's eyes fluttered open. Cornflower blue irises. Dark pupils that reacted to the light. Good, no concussion. The kid looked about ten. Fresh tear tracks stained dust-caked cheeks.

Riley knelt. "You'll be fine, dear. The docs will fix you right up. Don't worry."

She held the girl's slim wrist, took her pulse while Ted grabbed a butterfly fastener from the patrol car's standard issue medical kit. Her pulse was steady but fast.

Ted glanced over. "He grabbed her from behind."

Riley studied the cuts as the officer applied bandages. She'd seen enough knife attacks to decipher the graphic language of entry and exit wounds. The injuries weren't consistent with the girl's story. If she'd been grabbed from behind, the attacker would have slashed from front to back.

"The bastard came alone, hid in the bushes." Ted waved toward a copse of scrub pine. "Ran into the woods at least ten minutes ago. Took her that long to crawl to Big Red."

He gentled his voice as he looked down at the girl. "Our young lady did great. Just needs a little patching up."

Riley brushed a strand of silky hair from the coed's cheek. "You're Ellen Wingate, right?"

The coed seemed puzzled a stranger could pull her name out of thin air.

"So much blood," the girl whispered. "Never guessed there'd be so much blood."

The words sharpened Riley's unwelcome suspicion. Car doors slammed and three more campus security officers jogged toward the scene.

"After I speak with these officers, I'll call your parents," Riley said. "Bet they're here by morning."

"No. Don't. Just Penny. Penny Derr. My roommate."

She patted Ellen's hand. No point interrogating a suspect in shock. *Goddammit.* She hated to think of the confused teen as a suspect. Guilt tinged the anger she felt at the situation.

Why didn't we see it coming? Carl Oldfield's face popped into her mind. *Too late again.*

She directed the new campus cop arrivals to look for a weapon. Before she could get back to the girl, EMS came, treated her gashes, and loaded her in an ambulance.

Once the first responders whisked their charge away, Ted asked, "What now? Call the sheriff? Maybe get a K-9 unit to search the woods? Bet it's the same bastard who murdered Amanda Coffey. Damn Mexicans."

The accusation jolted Riley. "Ellen identified her attacker as Hispanic?"

"Yeah, he was *Hispanic*." The campus cop spat out the ethnic label like a curse.

His reaction startled her though she'd heard plenty of grousing about the swelling ranks of illegal immigrants in nearby Shelby, a farming community on the far fringes of metro Greenville. Shelby had yet to be absorbed by the city's amoeba spread.

She frowned. "The girl actually *said* the man was Hispanic? She described him?"

Ted looked down. "Well, I asked if the man could be Mexican. She nodded yes."

"You coached her? You know better." Anger made her voice hard. "No officer on this campus is going to substitute stereotypes for solid police work."

She'd fought with her own mother about ethnic stereotyping. Got nowhere. No way would she allow any of her thirty officers to equate Hispanic heritage with guilt.

"I doubt there was an attacker—of any nationality," she said. "Ellen's a troubled young woman. I suspect she inflicted those wounds herself."

"What?" The officer sounded incredulous. Ted had accepted Ellen's story at face value.

Amanda Coffey's unsolved murder had poisoned the atmosphere. Two months ago, the grad student, who lived two blocks off campus, had been stabbed sixty-six times and sexually assaulted post-mortem. The violent loss terrified students. A faceless killer magnified fear.

"I'm afraid Ellen staged the attack. She's right-handed. Probably stabbed her right thigh first then reached across to slice her left arm." Riley demonstrated the moves. "No defensive wounds. Her injuries don't jibe with an attack from behind. Did you find a knife?"

"No." Ted's forehead furrowed. "Doesn't that prove someone attacked her?"

"Not necessarily. Ellen's bright. She'd make the attack look real. Probably stabbed herself at the shore, tossed the blade in the lake."

They turned in unison toward Shelby Lake's inky shoreline. They could see the silhouettes of two officers scouring the area.

"We'll search. Given shock and blood loss, she couldn't have thrown a knife far."

Ted's troubled look told her he hated her theory. "We do nothing tonight?"

"Oh no, we follow protocol. I might be wrong."

Riley suddenly thought of Nexi. For a dozen years, people had been convinced her friend had attempted suicide before the truth surfaced. *Don't jump to conclusions.*

She took a deep breath. "Pete already alerted dorm proctors. You help seal the area, search for evidence. I'll call the sheriff, but not on a police band. Let's try to determine the truth before the press goes bonkers with some crazed slasher story. If it turns out Ellen cut herself, I don't want the media hounding her."

Ted shook his head. "God Almighty. She's a good-looking kid. Got the world by the tail. Why would she stab herself?"

"Love," Riley answered, her voice soft. "Love lost."

She didn't mention Ellen's lover was a female roommate. No sense fueling Ted's heartburn. Twenty years as an MP had rigidly fixed his moral compass.

Ellen had landed on BRU's watch list a week ago, when the roommate's parents learned about the girls' lesbian affair and handed Dr. Sparks a stack of Ellen's dark poems.

Riley headed to her office. She wanted to do exactly what Ellen begged her not to do. Phone her folks. She recalled the girl was younger than most freshmen. But how young? If she'd come of age, right-to-privacy issues would limit what she told the parents.

She pulled Ellen's file. Good, still seventeen. Riley skimmed further. *Crap.* The teen's mom was in rehab. Maybe Wolf could call the dad. Based on his comments in the At Risk meeting, he had some rapport with the girl. Would Ellen's father feel less queasy discussing his daughter's sexual proclivities with a man?

Why did it have to be Wolf? Her stomach clenched.

Linda Lovely

Thinking about him made her cheeks flame. Today she'd caught him watching as she massaged her knee. When their eyes met, his gaze reminded he'd once caressed every part of her body. Her mind conjured up an image of Wolf's athletic build and their lovemaking at the most inopportune times. The vivid memories could make her whimper with remembered pleasure.

Yet, even without their poisoned family trees, Wolf would have been off-limits. Her ex-husband had taught her well—passion was a cruel temptress, an overture to pain. She fisted her hands, lifted her chin. Never again would she be played by a user. Wolf's rakish charm, erotic scribbling, and Facebook banter made him easy to peg. Beneath the professor's hard-to-resist packaging, he could easily be her cheating ex-husband's emotional twin.

Don't think of him as Wolf. He's Dr. Valdes, academic colleague and pain in the butt. This is about Ellen, not you.

As she reached for the faculty directory, her gaze flicked by a bouquet of roses from John. A reminder of her screwed-up love life. Why did John persist? They had zilch chemistry.

Concentrate. She was asking Wolf a favor. Might be waking him. Involuntarily she pictured him sleeping au natural, kicking free of the sheets to answer the phone.

Annoyed at her recalcitrant subconscious, she glanced again at the roses. Too bad I can't think of John that way. I need to tell him. No point wasting roses on me.

Riley'd dated John for three months. Two months too long. No spark, and he bored her. Since her mom doted on the long-time family friend, Riley procrastinated about calling it quits.

She shook her head. *Focus on the task at hand.* She rehearsed her opening, testing the timbre of her voice: "Dr. Valdes? Sorry to call you at night . . ."

Riley took a deep breath and punched in Wolf's number.

FIVE

Prodded by a looming deadline, Wolf slipped into a writing groove. His editor wanted more sizzle? Time to revisit his first encounter with Riley—history that packed enough heat to make him squirm.

His fingers hovered above the keyboard. How to describe the heroine? He didn't assign Riley's physical traits to any of his heroines. Her freckle-splashed face was closer to cherub than sensual siren, and though her curly hair hinted at wild abandon, the cropped style would not inflame most men's fantasies.

Wolf's lips curled into a half-smile. What the hell made Riley sexy? Those cat eyes for starters. The left iris was hazel-blue, the right, hazel-brown. The subtle difference captivated. He didn't dare borrow such a unique descriptor for his fiction. Besides, it wasn't the shape or color of her eyes that drew him. It was how they blazed when passion battered down her self-control.

He'd been involved with other women, but he'd never forgotten Riley. One whiff of her spicy scent and he was back on Hilton Head Island, inhaling her fragrance and tasting the honey and salt of her skin. *Perfect.* That was the sensual image he needed. His breath quickened as he typed, vivid memories inspiring make-believe tumult.

Wolf could swear Riley remembered their chemistry, too. Visual hints lingered. Like today when they practically rubbed noses. Her full lips parted, followed by a quick intake of breath.

Too bad their fling was a one-time explosion. All they'd ever share. No way to double back to a time of blissful ignorance. Now he knew Riley was Senator Yates' niece. Now she knew his cousin had played a starring role in her older brother's death.

Dammit. Wolf's mental meandering shattered his focus. He pushed back his chair, stood, and picked up the yo-yo atop his desk. He flung the custom yo-yo with controlled violence, executed a flawless Brain Twister, segued into Buddha's Revenge. As the yo-yo arced above his head, the string tangled. *Damn.*

He unknotted the mess, wishing he could untangle his feelings as easily. The tidal pull of sexual chemistry often came first. But you needed to like and trust each other for it to last. He got it. The kick in the butt was he'd sensed they were in sync— personalities meshing as flawlessly as their bodies.

Before… Before either one of them took a bite out of the damn apple. Sometimes knowledge sucked.

He'd overheard Riley's mother nattering at a faculty-alumni function. She did little to disguise her animosity toward all people of color. Had she felt that way before her son died? If Riley shared her mom's views, she hid it well. Didn't matter. Riley had to know her mother would disown her if she was ever seen with him.

He slammed the yo-yo down on his desk. This tight-ass town is getting to me. Fundamentalist preachers. White bread conformity.

The phone cut off his mental rant. Peeved, he glanced at the receiver. Just what he needed, another interruption.

The phone rang a fourth time. Why didn't the damn machine pick up? Had to be a student. One so panicked over a thesis he'd dreamed up a whopper of a sob story.

No kidding, your roommate visited a porn site and infected your computer with an STD? And it crashed your hard drive and destroyed your term paper?

Wolf counted himself lucky the whiner hadn't waited for him to climb into bed. Easier to put one over on a groggy instructor. He barked a hello.

"Dr. Valdes?"

Riley. Her voice always retained its alto promise, deep and sensual. If other women were babbling brooks, she was the Gulf Stream.

He tried to erase his fantasy Riley and concentrate on the flesh-and-blood security director. This was no social call. The woman would only phone him for a campus emergency.

Double crap.

SIX

As the patrol car jounced along the rutted road, L.J. reread the newspaper article. With each bounce, the penlight on his key chain highlighted another heavy-handed adjective — "intelligent ... probing ... resourceful." He snickered at the embellishment. The *Greenville News* trotted out every journalistic honor Oldfield earned during his five-year stint on staff. Yet the article devoted only one sentence to the dead reporter's gleeful escape to the *Washington Post*.

Flipping to the obits, he revisited the notice of Harold Beck's death. Relatives hadn't scrimped on the paid eulogy for the Department of Defense procurement officer. He sniffed. A waste of money for a DoD drone.

"Two down," he muttered.

"What?" the driver asked. "You say something?"

"No." He switched off his penlight and stared out the passenger window. The octopus arms of tree branches scratched at the car door. The overgrown logging road made him claustrophobic. "How long?"

"Couple a minutes. Then we walk."

L.J. nodded and returned to his thoughts. Disposing of Beck and Oldfield had been easy. The men weren't celebrities. No one except family or coworkers gave a shit. The next deaths would be different. His blood seemed to heat as he contemplated the days ahead. Art, his partner, had dumped the scheme's messier aspects in his lap. But the man understood they'd both go down if the boat capsized.

The car lurched to a stop. L.J. climbed out and his feet sunk in reddish goo. "Shit." He glared at the globs of clay sullying the mirrored finish of his shoes. The deputy had arrived at his home early and insisted there wasn't time for L.J. to change clothes.

What a waste. He'd paid fifteen hundred dollars for the semi-brogues, made of two-hundred-year-old Russian reindeer hide cured in seal oil. Ruined.

"Come on," Nick said. "Put on that hood. We need to hurry."

Following the deputy along the forest trail, he smelled the men before he saw them. Five days ago, he'd pretended he was blind. Tonight he wished his sense of smell would vanish. The men, all dressed in grimy camouflage, reeked. He made no offer to shake hands. Recruiting these losers was a distasteful but necessary part of his agenda.

As he stepped into the clearing, a shotgun roared and a panicked doe crashed through underbrush in the woods opposite. The thrashing noises continued, grew fainter. Two men sauntered in from the woods, one still tucking his dick in his pants. His companion raised the shotgun in triumph and laughed. "We were taking a leak. Guess seeing our big peckers startled that deer. Pretty sure I hit her."

L.J.'s disgust mounted. No one suggested they track the animal, put her out of her misery. His dad, a hunter, had taught him it was wrong to wound an animal and let it suffer. You corrected your mistakes, accepted responsibility. What was that saying about lying with dogs? Well, his new bedmates had fleas, and they made his skin crawl.

The men seemed antsy. Nervous fingers idly scratched butts, picked teeth, and hitched up pants. They'd been waiting on him to start the festivities. Nick's sharp elbow found his ribs, directing his attention to a beefy hunter. He could barely see through the slits cut in the scratchy hood. What had Nick used to make it—a feedbag?

"Ready for a game of Mexican jumping beans?" Nick called to the marksman.

"Yeah, let one loose." The answer came as an excited growl. The man leveled his .35 Whelen and pulled the rifle's mahogany gunstock tight against his padded vest.

"It's Benny's first time," Nick whispered.

He turned to the rifleman. "Don't miss and hit the little creep. You're supposed to scare him, not kill him. Too much work to bury him."

"I hear ya." Benny put the scope to his eye. In the flickering firelight, his bushy eyebrow squirmed above the eyepiece like an obese caterpillar.

A tall man in stained fatigues dragged a shriveled figure into the center of the clearing. L.J. thought the prisoner might be an amputee until he spotted the man's trussed left leg. Rough twine bound his ankle to his upper thigh like an entrant in a potato-sack race.

More twine secured the captive's wrists behind his back. One corner of a red bandana gag hung from his mouth like a panting tongue. L.J. almost chuckled at the comic image until his gaze locked on the scarecrow's terrified eyes.

Nick's busy elbow jarred him again.

One more poke and I'll shoot him.

"We've found a surefire way to make a bean-o jump," Nick sniggered as the guard abandoned his tottering charge and hotfooted for cover. Five men formed a semi-circle behind the shooter and began to catcall.

"Hop, hippity-hop."

"Hop. Hop. Hop."

A gun bolt slid into place. The peg-legged captive's head jerked at the metallic clack. A frantic hop flipped him one hundred and eighty degrees. Without his arms to help balance, he had less chance of staying vertical than a whore on a Saturday night.

Like his dad, L.J. saw no sport in a hobbled clay pigeon.

Benny pulled the trigger as his prey began another pathetic jump. Carrot-colored dust rose in a miniature tornado when the bullet twanged near the man's feet. The rifleman toyed with him, prolonging the jitterbug.

The agile prisoner moved as if he'd mounted a demonic pogo stick. He hopped forward two feet. Another leap earned twelve more inches of distance from the rifleman. Desperate to reach the trees, the target was gaining ground. L.J. felt like rooting for him.

The rifle discharged another bullet. The raggedy prisoner fell to the ground.

One of the onlookers sauntered to the body. He kicked at the crumpled bundle with his boot, knelt.

"Good shooting, Benny. You scared the piss out of him, but didn't put a single hole in him."

The man grabbed the prisoner's shirt to drag him out of the makeshift arena. He slapped the man's face until he came to. "We're gonna let you go. Better run all the way back to Mey-hi-co, padre. Tell your buddies what's in store if'n they take more of our jobs. Now get! Next time one of them bullets will knock more than the pee out of you."

Nick nudged L.J. "One more bean to process. You're a good shot. Wanna take a turn?"

"No." The hood was stifling, but L.J. wasn't about to doff the sack and reveal his identity. "Let's go."

He didn't speak on the hike to Nick's cruiser. The gravel road they'd driven up petered out a half mile from the Onward camp. L.J. flinched as more gunshots punctuated the forest's lullaby of tree frogs and wind-whisked pines. He shared a concern with these bozos. America's bloodline was under attack. Statistics suggested whites would become a minority before long. But these fair-skinned idiots were no argument for racial superiority.

He felt slightly winded by the time they reached the car. In the clearing, moonlight shone on the Leeds County Sheriff's insignia. Painted in South Carolina's official state color, indigo blue, it stood out boldly against the car's white shell.

He opened the passenger side door, then glanced at his feet and asked for a rag.

"Jesus, you still worried about those fancy shoes?" Nick snorted. "With the money you pull down, you could buy enough shoes to fill a football stadium."

L.J. realized his boyhood friend had no inkling a man might shell out more than fifty bucks for a pair of shoes. Nick popped his trunk, rooted around, and tossed him a rag. It smelled of gasoline. *The shoes will have to go.*

"So, whatcha think?" Nick asked.

L.J. considered the men he'd seen. Stupid white trash.

"How come they didn't insist on seeing my face?"

"Hell, you gave them fifty thou, and I vouched for you. They don't care if you're the freakin' Lone Ranger. If you keep the cash tap open, they'll let you wear a mask and shout 'Hi, ho, Silver.'"

L.J. rubbed his cheek, itchy from contact with the hood. "I hope the FBI will believe these clowns are capable of hatching a plot." He couldn't afford for Miss Know-It-All and her old pals to look past the puppets and realize he pulled the strings.

Though he'd not seen the security director naked, he had no problem imagining the lithe body hiding beneath her crisp trousers and utilitarian blazer. He pictured her helpless. Trussed like the hopping migrant. The rough twine biting into her porcelain skin. Leaving angry red welts. The unbidden image pleased him. He found the thought of Riley Reid at his feet—at his mercy—thrilling. Too bad he'd given another man the pleasure of dealing with her.

He shook his head to jar the tempting vision from his brain. "Wonder if we should kill these clowns when it's over?"

"Why?" Nick's question carried a hint of whine. "They don't know who you are."

L.J. started. He hadn't meant to speak out loud. Careless.

"Buddy, they know who *you* are. Dead men don't talk."

SEVEN

Relief flooded Riley. Talking to Wolf on the phone was easier than face-to-face. She could pretend he was a stranger. Almost.

"You really think Ellen stabbed herself?" he asked.

"I do. The wounds don't jibe with her story."

Wolf held the silence a beat. "Suppose her injuries are self-inflicted. Will you prosecute?"

"Of course not." *What kind of tight ass do you take me for?* Shocked, she realized his opinion mattered. "I don't want to crucify the girl. But locals are angry about illegals taking jobs, not paying taxes. Accuse a Latino of attacking a coed and you might as well put a match to gasoline."

"I agree," Wolf said. "Her story could stir up a hornet's nest. Ellen's a good kid. She'll tell the truth once someone explains the facts of life."

"Will you call her dad?" Riley held her breath.

"Sure. If he decides to come, I'll even meet his plane."

"Uh, thanks." Riley didn't know how to wind down the conversation. "If you sense bringing in the father's a mistake, discourage a visit. I'll make sure Ellen wakes to a friendly face. Call me after you talk with the dad."

She hung up. Her gaze lingered on the photo of Amanda Coffey taped above her desk. The grad student's picture served as a daily reminder of the unsolved murder.

She kept a copy of the sheriff's files, too. Though the case belonged to the Leeds County Sheriff's Office, she pored over the paperwork, rereading reports and officers' notes whenever she could. She'd never met the attractive brunette, who lived off-campus. But Kate, Riley's Smart Women, Dumb Luck buddy, had been friends with the coed. Kate was a senior when she'd recruited Amanda, a freshman, to work weekends with her at a soup kitchen.

The murder case frustrated Riley. There'd been no sign of forced entry. Deputies quizzed every apartment resident. Only one lady noticed strangers around the time of Amanda's death. She'd watched a well-dressed, middle-aged couple drive off in a two-tone car. Unlikely sexual psychopaths.

Amanda's apartment was just two blocks from campus. How did the killer get inside? No jimmied lock. No open window. No sign of struggle. Scotty hadn't beamed the killer inside.

Riley rotated her head from left to right, front to back, to ease the knotted tension in her neck. Not the time for a cold case rehash. Not with graduation three days away. She stifled a yawn and pulled out the latest report on security and crowd control measures for graduation.

Focus. Read ten more pages and you can go home.

EIGHT

L.J. stared out the floor-to-ceiling window in his office. On a sunny day, he could see Blue Ridge University's piney-green border and the glimmer of its central lake. Now, at ten p.m., the campus appeared as a black blob on the horizon with a few pinpricks of light.

He loosened his shirt collar and returned to his desk. A burning sensation in his chest told him he'd pay for tonight's indulgences. He'd slugged down two whiskeys the moment he returned from the god-awful Onward initiation. Then he'd picked up a cheeseburger and fries at a fast-food dive while he drove from his home to the office.

The evening bore no resemblance to his normal routine. Last night was far more typical. He'd entertained two Army generals and their wives, fawning over the horse-faced women and their unimaginative husbands.

On reflection, he wasn't certain which group he'd rather hang with—the Onward idiots or the military windbags. But filet mignon and a fine Merlot sure rested easier on the stomach.

L.J. rummaged around for the Pepcid AC bottle in his top drawer and dry-swallowed a tablet before sinking into his executive chair's consoling leather. Swiveling to face his computer, he called up the email. He'd tinkered with the phrasing ten times. Still too long?

A threat needed punch, shock value. *The hell with it. This will do.*

He clicked the mouse and the message vanished. The untraceable email would appear to originate in Sweden and ping-pong around the Eastern Bloc before materializing on computers at five colleges. He doubted anyone would read the threats before morning.

Which college would be first? Geography meant nothing with cyber deliveries. Too bad BRU's security director would be benched for this game. Taunting her might have been fun.

Fun? He smiled. Yes, he *was* having fun.

During his fifty years on the planet, he'd worked hard to restrain his dark urges. How he'd wanted to pummel the woman who gave him birth. Didn't deign to call her mother. She'd screwed his father but good. He'd used his brains rather than his fists to make her suffer.

Sure he'd beat a few whores who asked for it. Recreation, not high stakes. Now he enjoyed the same power as the generals he glad-handed. Power over life and death. Intoxicating.

Once again he'd found a way to impose his will without risking any part of his anatomy or even his reputation. Better to play the conductor and lift his baton to signal each section of the orchestra. He stood and stretched, a long day.

He smiled again. Couldn't help it. The thought of Riley Reid in pain gave him pleasure. Another know-it-all woman didn't know her place.

Why hasn't that damn goon called with an injury report?

NINE

A loud thud vibrated through the basement facility, shattering Riley's concentration. The front entrance? Running footsteps gave a staccato beat to unintelligible shouts.

What now? She headed for the hall.

A kid brandished a computer printout. The boy's wispy moustache quivered. His eyes were wide; his pupils dilated. High on drugs?

"They're going to kill us!" he yelped.

Pete gripped the boy's shoulder. "Who's threatening you?"

"Not me. The whole school. I was sorting university emails."

Riley joined Pete as the agitated student thrust a printout toward them.

"Calm down. Give us a chance to read." She held the flimsy recycled paper so Pete could scan it with her.

> *Your school is a consort of the Devil! You willingly aid the unholy conspiracy of drug dealers, pimps and perverts invading America!*
>
> *You send our young to study in Mexico where they become brainwashed apologists for a flood of filthy illegals. You snatch scholarships from Christian Americans to offer handouts to the satanic hordes.*
>
> *Renounce these sins or pay! Continue to serve the Devil and we'll turn your school into a funeral pyre! Your deadline is midnight Friday.*

Riley spotted Onward's signature. Goose bumps raced up her arms.

"Onward?" Pete's voice wavered. "I've heard of them—some hate group—but I can't remember any details."

Riley frowned. "Their followers claim to be foot soldiers for Jesus, heeding the call: 'Onward, Christian Soldiers.' They're neo-Nazis, and they hate everybody."

The kid's eyes widened.

"It's probably a hoax," she added quickly. Stupid to discuss Onward in front of a frightened student.

"What's your name?"

"Darryl Thomas. I graduate Saturday. Are these maniacs talking about bombing commencement?"

"Take it easy, Darryl. You'd be amazed how many fake threats we receive."

His darting gaze said she'd failed to dial down his panic.

"Prank or no prank, we have three days to locate the sender and throw him in jail."

Darryl shook his head. He wasn't buying.

"We won't risk anyone's safety. Dr. Harris will do what's best." She invoked the chancellor's kindly grandfather image. "No call for panic. First, let's find out if this note's for real." She locked eyes with the boy.

"You're not going to warn people?" The student's voice rose.

"Of course, we will. Our officers will begin a campus search immediately and alert dorm proctors. I'll call the FBI. They'll dispatch a terrorism task force, bring in specialists to search for explosives. But I need you to keep quiet about this email until we piece together more information. We don't need a media circus."

Riley rested her hand lightly on Darryl's arm. "I was an FBI agent for fourteen years. Spent two of them building a case against extremists like Onward. If this is real, the FBI will nail them. Nothing bad will happen."

Darryl's breathing slowed. His patchy moustache stopped twitching.

That's when the hairs on the back of Riley's neck began to quiver. She sensed another presence. Someone had slipped into the anteroom beside the outer door.

Her eyes slid over the silhouette. A man. At least six-four. Well built. Hand in pocket. Had he come with Darryl or was the kid a well-scripted distraction?

Shadow man stepped into the light. Wolf.

Her relief was transitory. *Crapola.* The professor might as well have "Liberal" as a middle name.

With her luck, he'd scream police state and demand freedom of information. The perfect end to a day from hell.

TEN

Riley nodded at Wolf. "Good evening, Dr. Valdes. I thought you were going to call me after you spoke with Ellen's dad."

"Haven't phoned yet. Didn't mean to startle you. It seemed a bad idea to interrupt."

She turned to Pete. "Take Darryl to the break room and buy him a Coke. Maybe he can tell us more about email routines. Once you get him settled, alert our dorm proctors and our officers about the situation. We've had enough drills. They know the search protocol."

Pete put an arm around the young man's shoulder to steer him down the hall.

"I'm sorry, Dr. Valdes, but I can't talk now. I need to contact the FBI."

"I'll wait." Wolf pre-empted her planned "beat-it" spiel and claimed one of six vinyl chairs bolted to the wall. He picked up a magazine from the potpourri of time wasters on the entry coffee table.

"Suit yourself. I don't know how long I'll be." Her inflection implied hours.

Actually, Riley figured her FBI alert would take five minutes. Until nine months ago, she'd been the FBI's Supervisory Special Agent (SSA) in Greenville, a Resident Agency that handled all FBI cases in the Upstate. Greenville reported to the Columbia Field Division. She knew the routines by heart. But Wolf's presence ruffled her. She fibbed because she needed all her brain cells firing in synch.

She connected with Jeff Wilson, the new Greenville SSA. He wasted no time on niceties. "I should be there in thirty. I'll get a K-9 search team out there tonight. Can you give a consent search on the computer hard drive? I don't want to waste time getting a warrant. Our cyber guys should start work tonight."

Riley pictured the wiry agent. His voice sounded syrupy as if he were still trying to wake up. "No problem on the consent search. Anything else you want me to do before you get here?"

"Yeah, hold the kid who downloaded the email. I'll take his statement. You know the drill. I'll have a bomb squad do an initial sweep. Contact Columbia and Quantico. Get a start on querying databases in other offices. Maybe we'll get a hit on Onward activity or similar school threats.

"You know your vulnerabilities better than we do, so we'll coordinate with you. How about an early morning meeting at your place, say seven? You provide the coffee. I'll alert our Joint Terrorism Task Force and key locals. Columbia and Quantico might send folks, too."

"Okay, thanks. See you in a few."

Leaving a voice message for her boss took a minute more. She considered stalling. Would Wolf leave if she procrastinated until Jeff arrived? She was in no mood to debate law enforcement tactics with a lefty. Of course, he knew how to keep silent. He'd left her bed without a word of explanation. Was it because she'd mentioned her uncle? Had that clued him he was sleeping with the enemy? Or had he known all along, and screwed her for laughs, always planning to exit like a john?

"Oh, hell, might as well get this over with."

Returning to the reception area, she tried to read Wolf's expression. The professor made no bones about his views on institutional transparency. Given he'd just heard her order a student to keep his trap shut about a threat to rain death and destruction on the university, she expected at least token umbrage. Instead the corners of his mouth twitched up. A suppressed smile?

Her pulse perked up when she looked at his face, a handsome, startling medley of heritage. High cheekbones, straight blue-black hair, café au lait skin. His almond-shaped eyes were a malachite green veined with smoky whorls. An agitated sea.

She knew Wolf's striking looks came courtesy of his grandparents. Book reviewers loved to trace his genealogy. His paternal Irish grandmother wed a Cuban who fled the island after learning he was on General Batista's hit list. Wolf's maternal Irish grandfather married a Cherokee. The name "Wolf" was the English translation of his great-grandfather's name.

She forced her eyes from his tempting face and cleared her throat. "Let's go to my office." She walked briskly. Within two strides, she sensed him behind her. Whenever he was near, she slid into bat mode, internal radar reading his position and relative proximity.

Riley claimed her duct-taped swivel chair, a comfortable if shabby island of personal space. Building renovations had forced her department to relocate. At the moment, security was shoehorned into the auditorium/theater's basement.

Wolf dropped into a cheap, molded visitor's chair and scooted forward, breaching her invisible buffer. Since her desk faced a casement window, her chair sat naked in the compact space. A few more inches and their knees would kiss.

She met his gaze. His eyes twinkled, sunlight on magnolia leaves. *God, he is smiling.*

"I know. It's not funny." His voice was husky. "But I can't help replaying a conversation when we met. Seem to recall you fretting any post-FBI job would be a bore."

She lowered her gaze. "Yeah, well, wouldn't be my only mistake."

She lifted her head and saw him wince. Bulls-eye.

Riley couldn't fathom why Wolf still ogled her when his novel made it clear she'd passed her "best-used-by" date. Though he was thirty-eight, just a year younger than she was, he obviously preferred younger women. He'd cast a college-age sexpot for her role in *Firelight*.

Two years had passed since they met at a Sprint triathlon and Riley, newly divorced, succumbed to a lustful impulse. A fling—exceedingly hot, totally harmless. Wolf taught at a Vermont college. She'd reasoned she'd never see him again. Truth be told, she'd seduced Wolf.

Still, titillating readers with a highlights reel of their weekend seemed almost as insulting as his departure. Wolf's book failed to mention his "hero" slunk away in the middle of the night. With his novel, he'd used her a second time. No money on the nightstand either outing.

Wolf shifted in his chair. "I came over on impulse. Thought you might want to listen in on my call to Ellen's dad. Then we could decide how to play it. You're good at reading people."

The compliment unsettled her. She seemed incapable of reading the professor.

"Look, I'm sorry." He stood. "My timing's bad. You're up to your eyeballs."

Riley bit the inside of her cheek. *Stop acting like a teenager*.

"It's been a bad day. Please sit down. Use my phone. I'll grab an extension. One crisis at a time. Onward isn't threatening to bomb us tonight. And just in case Onward's fibbing about a deadline, we have a search underway for anything suspicious."

Wolf flashed a heart-stopping grin. "I wouldn't mind hunkering down here in an emergency." He arched an eyebrow. "It pays to have the law on your side."

"Never imagined you as a law-and-order fan, given how your fictional characters engage in sexual activities illegal in several states."

Damn, why did I say that? I'm joining in his game.

Wolf's grin widened. "I wondered if you'd read my book."

Riley felt a flush of heat crawl up her cheeks. "Let's make that phone call."

Eavesdropping on an extension, she marveled at the professor's finesse. In minutes, Ellen's dad shared confidences as if he were speaking with a life-long friend.

When the call ended, Riley moved to the doorway. "Nicely done. Would you call in the morning with a take on Ellen's mental state? I'll time my visit accordingly."

She paused, leaning against the doorjamb. "Try to keep Ellen's father from quizzing her on details. I don't want her to repeat her story. It'll make it tougher for her to recant."

"Will do." Wolf moved closer. Before she could back away, he tucked one of her curls behind an ear. His touch triggered heat. She flinched.

"You may be right to keep this Onward thing quiet tonight," he added. "But word will leak—always does. Either Darryl will blab, or Onward will copy the media. Hell, a note may be waiting on some news editor's desk right now."

She nodded. "I'll ask the FBI's blessing to go public come morning, but Dr. Harris needs to be the one to break the news."

"Good. Knowing the FBI's on board should dampen the rumor mill. Amanda's murder has everyone on edge. It won't take much to create full-scale panic."

After he left, she flicked off her office light, tired of hearing the fluorescent's sputtering death throes. The room's descent into gloom made her appreciate the full moon. Its beams danced on her gun, hanging in its holster on the old-fashioned hall tree.

How romantic.

She massaged her temples to clear her befuddled brain. No luck. A vintage memory kept repeating in a continuous loop.

Her fingers danced along Wolf's skin, the color of toasted almonds. His muscles were fluid and disciplined. His body hard and toned.

She felt giddy, guilt-free, satisfied. Until that moment, Gary, her cheating, scumbag ex, had been her sole lover.

Wolf turned on his side, fumbled for the nightstand's light. "I like to study the terrain before I compete. We dashed across the finish line before I fully reconnoitered the course."

The lamplight tinted their bodies gold and revealed his predatory smile.

"I'm better at long-distance than sprints," he said. "Let's take our time this go-round."

Riley writhed as his velvet tongue sashayed its way from her earlobes to just below her belly button.

He paused and looked up with a mischievous grin.

"I'm disappointed," he murmured. "No neat round bullet holes. No jagged knife scars. Don't you have a single memento of your FBI hitch?"

She laughed. "Just a bad knee. But it's still strong enough to do this." She pinned his head in a scissor grip. A position he quickly exploited.

Thinking about his perfect name, she chuckled. "My, what a big, long tongue you have, Mr. Wolf."

His rejoinder was gleeful. "All the better to . . ."

"Stop," Riley said out loud. "It's been two years. Get over it."

The phone rang and she noted the caller ID. Good, she needed to talk to her boss.

ELEVEN

Riley pulled up a chair beside Pete. "How are things going by the lake?"

"Leeds County crime techs are finishing up. No footprints other than the girl's. Everyone's okay with keeping the incident under wraps till we chat with our victim tomorrow."

Relief swept over her. Maybe Ellen's situation would resolve itself quickly. "Darryl's still here, right?" she asked.

"Yeah, Alex is babysitting him at the computer lab. The kid seemed jazzed about talking to the FBI." The communications officer turned to face her. "I'll bet you a sawbuck that kid won't keep his mouth shut. He told me he phones his folks every day. What is it with these helicopter parents? He'll blab to them before sunrise."

She snorted. "Mom and Dad were lucky if I called twice a semester. When I did, they knew I'd run out of money." She grinned at the memory. "Usually they said 'no' before I even asked. 'Course, we didn't have cell phones, and we were charged for every call."

"You went to school here, right?" the officer asked.

"Yep. Mom's alma mater. My uncle, grandfather and great-grandfather are BRU grads. Mom would have disowned me if I'd picked another school. She hoped BRU would counter the influence of Dad's boisterous family. Prayed I'd acquire Southern gentility by osmosis."

Pete playfully punched her arm. "Bet your mom's still praying."

"Not exactly. She's given up hope I'll master decorum. Now she just prays I won't scandalize her Sunday school class."

Like cavorting naked on a golf green with Wolf. Our second night.

Linda Lovely

"Oh, dang. I'm supposed to drive Mom to the doctor's tomorrow. I'll have to cancel."

And she'll grill me. I could tell her John Hunter wants to see me. That'd get me off the hook.

Her mom loved John the Gentleman. Too much of a gentleman. He treated her like fragile china when she was closer to Corelleware—heat resistant, unbreakable, utilitarian.

Now her Mom was china—easy to shatter. She'd never been the same since Jack's death. Whatever glue once held her together had become increasingly cracked and brittle. Poor health didn't help.

With her dad and big brother gone, Riley felt obligated to look after her mom. Emphysema upped her susceptibility to nasty infections. That was the reason Riley always gave for resigning the FBI rather than accept a transfer to Washington D.C.

"Hey, earth to boss. Anything else to do tonight on this Onward email?"

She snapped her attention back to Pete. "The FBI will call the investigative shots, but we need to beef up campus security."

She stood and paced. "The FBI will help with an immediate bomb sweep, but given that our bad boys gave us three days' grace, a bomb could be in transit, awaiting Saturday delivery."

"Yeah, what's with these terrorists?" Pete asked. "It's obvious they're targeting graduation. Why give us time to prepare? They know we'll search. Beef up security."

She frowned. "Good question, and I have plenty more. Any thoughts on how they might attack? A bomb's the first thing that comes to mind. But maybe they've gotten their hands on rockets or anthrax or assault weapons. Who knows?"

42

She grabbed a pencil. "I know Wednesday is your day off, but can you come in at seven tomorrow morning? I'd like you to sit in on the meeting with the FBI."

"You bet. Should I call in anyone else?"

"Bill. He has SWAT team experience and knows how to assess security weak points."

Pete tugged on his earlobe. "Did you talk to Chancellor Harris?"

"No, I gave a full report to Vice Chancellor Sparks. Don't know whether he'll roust his boss tonight or not." She stood. "I asked for a nine o'clock tomorrow with both men. By then I'll have a better take on the threat and the FBI's plan of attack."

Given the administration's love affair with meetings, she had a hunch what portion of tomorrow she'd squander in yak fests. Hours wasted analyzing and re-analyzing the same teaspoonful of information.

The outer door opened. Jeff had estimated his arrival time perfectly.

She introduced the FBI agent to Pete. "The computer lab's only a block away. You up for a walk?"

While the cool night air made Riley shiver, she welcomed the sudden quiet.

"Do you miss the FBI?" Jeff asked. "I still can't believe you resigned."

Oldfield had asked the same question.

"Sure, I miss it. But you know agency policy. Turning down a transfer is a career killer."

Riley reminded Jeff that she'd wanted to stay put to look after her widowed mom. "This university job was kismet."

"I guess." Jeff didn't sound convinced.

Riley knew her answer hadn't satisfied. Agents rarely left the bureau before they put in twenty years and qualified for retirement, usually between age forty-eight and fifty. Leaving early meant zip benefits, and resignations carried a taint of disloyalty.

A large trust fund established by Grandfather Yates took the financial sting out of Riley's forfeiture. And there'd been another motivation, a clean break from Gary. Ever since her ex-husband led the daring capture of a terrorist group, he was Mr. FBI and could do no wrong. She didn't need to work inside an agency that worshipped the man who'd betrayed her.

She turned the conversation back to the threat. "You think Onward's serious or just spewing bile? Any local suspects?"

Jeff shrugged. "These clowns could be serious. I took a quick look at the latest intel. Our experts estimate the militia's membership at a couple hundred, divided among ten chapters. Larry Burnette, the founder, hails from Alabama. Nobody knows his whereabouts. He killed three people during an armored car robbery before he disappeared."

"Is there a local unit?"

"Yeah. Upstate South Carolina has a cell. No confirmations on numbers. No source to lean on. It's frustrating as hell."

She bit her lip. "Jeff, there's something off about this threat. If Onward wanted to target a heathen campus, there are higher-profile targets. And what terrorist group gives three days' warning? Do they know how much time academic committees need to make decisions?"

Jeff chuckled. "They obviously lost their terrorist cheat sheet. Rule number one: don't claim responsibility before the fact. Rule number two: don't give your enemy time to think. Twenty-four hours is tops for an 'or else' deadline."

She opened the door to the computer lab. "Hope you can trace the email."

As Riley listened to Jeff question Darryl, she wondered if the FBI agent felt more confident than she did about catching the morons quickly, before the deadline.

Since campus security became her charge, she'd been plagued with nightmares about the bloody havoc one homicidal maniac could inflict. A psychopath with an automatic weapon could rack up horrendous body counts. Onward made her lone gunman nightmare seem unimaginative.

How long could they wait to send everyone home? Come morning, she'd ask the administration to set a timeline for closing the university.

Jeff finished his interview, and the officer who'd been babysitting Darryl, unplugged the computer that downloaded the threat. The campus cop hoisted the processor to his shoulder.

"My car's out front. I'll give you two a lift back to Riley's office."

* * * *

At ten after midnight, Riley closed the door to her office. Wednesday, May 6, had officially dawned. Her communications officer gave her a little, two-finger salute as she walked past his desk. "Hope you're headed home, boss. You going to get gussied up to greet the FBI? You're gonna wear a dress, right?"

She laughed. "Not unless you wear one." Her officers had never seen her in anything but tailored black pants and a black blazer. Only the blouse or knit top beneath the jacket changed color. She shared Johnny Cash's fashion mantra—black simplified life.

Re-entering the chilly spring night her stiffened knee caused her to do a Frankenstein impersonation. The notion that her stiff-legged shadow might scare the bejeesus out of some sleep-deprived undergraduate amused her. Could it be eighteen years since she'd pulled an all-nighter for finals? Had she been as hyper as these kids?

Kids? Gawd, I'm morphing into my mother.

Linda Lovely

For the second time in the space of three hours, she sensed someone lurking in the shadows. She felt certain it wasn't Wolf. Her adrenaline kicked in.

Halfway to her car, she put her hand on her gun.

TWELVE

L.J. stabbed at the numbers on his disposable cell, his anger channeled into his fingertips.

Why hadn't the hired goon called? By now he should have phoned with a blow-by-blow of Riley Reid's injuries. Though he hadn't met the ape, he'd seen video of him using a pointy-toed boot to kick a vagrant senseless.

After two rings, the tattooed testament to evolution's hiccups answered.

"What's happening?" L.J. demanded.

"Hey, man, I'm freezing my freakin' balls off."

The slurred words prompted L.J. to wonder if the idiot was skunked. "Have you seen the security director?"

"She went out once, but a big bruiser tagged along. She had two men with her when she came back. You didn't pay for no mob scene." The thug snorted. "I ain't about to wait all night for the bitch to leave the damn building by her lonesome."

Did the jerk-off think he was entitled to overtime? How about a 401k or sick leave? L.J. wanted to leap through the telephone and feed the foul-mouthed felon his own freakin' balls.

"If you want the rest of the money, stay put. She's bound to leave soon."

After the call ended, an idea tempted L.J. If the security director procrastinated a few more minutes, he could watch the attack. Live theater.

Thanks to almost nonexistent traffic, he needed less than fifteen minutes to reach the campus, park the car a few blocks away, and hide near the building.

A sharp wind reminded foothill dwellers that spring flowers meant nothing. The mountains providing the campus with its postcard backdrop were capable of delivering a knockout punch of frost in late spring, often following days of eighty-degree temperatures.

He'd changed into a navy running suit. The thin nylon felt icy against his skin. He tugged the dark knit hat further down and stamped his feet to warm them. Thick turf muffled the sound.

He crouched a hundred feet from the main security office door. The full moon dictated the location, making him easy to spot if he skulked closer. A magnolia's dense foliage offered inky shadows and good cover. The cloying scent of tea olives tickled his nose. *Damn allergies.*

Though he knew his *employee* hid on the eastern fringe of the parking lot, an overgrown patch of azaleas swallowed the man and his "hog" in a black hole.

What the hell is keeping her?

L.J. heard the door to the security offices groan open, the aged timbers complaining like some querulous old fart. The security director shambled toward her sensible Honda with a zombie's gait. It was like watching a schlock horror flick.

Midway between the building and her car, she paused. Her head swiveled toward the bushes a second before the Harley roared to life.

* * * *

Riley heard a twig snap and turned toward the azalea thicket bordering the parking lot. A motorcycle engine rumbled. Tires squealed. A helmeted monster barreled toward her.

No time to draw her Glock. The man raised his right arm brandishing something slender and long.

A sword? A length of pipe? God almighty!

The assailant moved too fast. He'd land only a single blow. Dive and roll.

Riley paused for a second that felt like eternity. She needed to time her move. Too early and the biker would adjust, run her down. Too late and he'd bash her head open like a ripe melon. Now?

The motorcycle's headlight blinded her. She smelled oil and burnt rubber. The heated air vibrated. *Go!*

She sprang. Her damaged knee buckled. Her left shoulder smashed into pavement, imploded in pain. The biker landed a blow.

His weapon glanced off her exposed ribs. Shards of white-hot pain. Her concentration splintered.

"Help!"

The engine's din trumped her muted cry.

"Freakin' bitch, get ready." Her attacker's slurred words ran together.

Is he drunk?

"Poppa's comin'," he screeched. "Poppa's gonna learn ya what a proper beatin' means."

Riley raised her gun. Shock and nausea slowed her reaction. *Dear Lord. Too late.*

Her attacker executed a half doughnut, spinning round for another pass. Tires squealed. The huge bike bore down on her again.

She coiled and rolled. Not fast enough. Whomp. His second strike landed. Pain radiated from shoulder to gut. Her muscles spasmed in protest. Bile rose in her throat.

He's using a broom handle. Hard. Solid.

The fact that her brain continued to process data amazed and somehow comforted her.

The thug's second hit paralyzed. Riley marshaled all her willpower to stave off unconsciousness. She longed to drop her gun, wrap her arms around herself, and sob. Instead she tightened the grip on her Glock. A deep breath brought instant agony. She drew her elbows tight to support her ribs and arm.

The biker appeared to lose balance. His bike weaved into a skid. His broad back formed an inviting target.

Riley aimed through unspilled tears.

The sound of the gunshot disoriented her. The motorcycle wobbled, then crashed. Metal screeched. Sparks flew as the downed bike skidded across the macadam.

When the Harley stopped, the world seemed to stand still. The rider didn't move. Didn't utter a moan.

The crickets reclaimed their rights to the night's soundtrack.

THIRTEEN

L.J. froze, his heart galloping, icy sweat trickled down his back. Unlike Onward's shooting gallery with its trussed prisoners, this show was akin to a gladiator match. The unrehearsed violence turned him on. Watching was almost as good as sex.

The goon was dead. His neck shredded. Too much blood to live.

Good riddance.

He'd taken every precaution to prevent the thug from fingering him, but dead meant no loose ends. Unable to question the freak, the police would have no motive. Because of the Onward email, they'd search for a connection. There wasn't one. L.J. had made certain of that. The cops would eventually pigeonhole the two-time felon as a whacko, chalk the attack up to steroid rage.

L.J. watched Reid shuffle toward the security officer standing next to the smoking carnage. She cradled her left arm, pushing it against her rib cage. Her body appeared on tilt, and she limped. Not enough damage.

He'd ordered sufficient injury to keep the woman bed-bound for a week, minimum. However, he'd set limits. No rape. No murder. No mutilation. He needed her alive for his plan. He'd felt clinical ordering the attack. Now he ached to force his will on the woman.

Time to exit.

L.J. pulled down his knit cap and raised the collar of his running suit, leaving only his eyes and nose exposed. He glided noiselessly between shadows. He'd parked far enough away that his vehicle wouldn't earn a glance from any cops responding to the attack. He could justify his presence—late exercise.

A block from the scene, he cut to the sidewalk. Just ahead, a man ran flat out, his long strides eating up the distance between them. *Is he after me?* No, the runner headed toward the commotion. *I'll huff and puff. Look winded. Just another jogger.*

Picking up his pace, L.J. risked only a brief glance as the runner streaked below a streetlight. A tall man, dark-skinned but not black. Mixed breed? The nighttime athlete's intense stare made L.J. feel like a frog pinned for dissection.

As he reached his car, L.J. braced himself on the trunk and sucked in air. He felt light-headed. *Maybe I should start jogging.*

The car alarm chirped as he touched his key fob. Once inside, the new car smell revived him. Cocooned in his leather cave, he felt back in control.

And aroused. His dick was painfully hard. How he'd love to hook up with one of the women who got off on punishing sex. He'd deliver. Give the slut what she deserved.

He mentally recast Riley Reid in the slut's role. *Even better.*

L.J. heard sirens and buckled his seat belt. Not the time or place. Suppose a deputy ordered him out of his car and saw his tent pole. Wouldn't do to have a cop peg him as a pervert after a nubile coed. Not his type. Too independent. Selfish bitches.

Like his mother.

Like Barbara.

Like Riley Reid.

His tongue snaked over his lips as he pictured the security director in the role of trembling submissive.

He put his car in gear. Forced his mind back on business. One small cog in his plan had slipped. Disappointing. But the machinery would grind on. If the security director poked around, he'd tweak his plan. If she bollixed things, he'd invest some discretionary funds to arrange a new mishap.

FOURTEEN

Unable to sleep, Wolf decided to jog the winding campus path. He'd reached the turnaround for his four-mile circuit when he heard a motorcycle's roar.

Did someone scream? He couldn't be sure. The gunshot was unmistakable. A thunderous crash sent him sprinting toward the melee. Twenty yards out, he spotted a smoldering hunk of metal. A body practically floated in blood.

His long strides closed the distance. The parking lot's halogens spilled light on the corpse. Nearby Riley slumped, doubled over, against a car. His stomach clenched. A male officer sat in the driver's seat, elbows on his knees, his face buried in large, bony hands. Pain? Grief?

What the hell had gone down?

* * * *

Confused, Riley stared at her gun, certain she hadn't pulled the trigger. Was her brain on the fritz? She watched Ted move toward the felled assailant, gun drawn. Riley climbed to her feet and crab-walked toward the biker's still form.

"Looks like you beat me to the punch. Is the creep down for the count?"

Keeping his weapon trained on her attacker, Ted pulled back the man's leather jacket to feel for a pulse. The body no longer had a recognizable neck. "Dead."

The officer's hands trembled. His tone went flat, as if he wanted to strip the death of its violence. "Caught an artery." He turned to Riley. "You hurt?"

"No. I'm okay."

The Harley's fat front tire spun like an abandoned merry-go-round. Wisps of smoke puffed from the wreckage, forming miniature clouds in the crisp night air.

Ted raised the face shield on the biker's helmet. "Seen him before?"

Riley sidestepped the pool of spreading blood to study the corpse's bloated face and fish-belly complexion. His mouth gaped open, revealing what appeared to be stage-three gum disease. The few remaining teeth looked like an old hound dog's—dingy, yellow and worn.

"Never had the pleasure." She shivered. "I'd remember that face."

Ted shook his head. "What in God's name brought this joker here tonight? I thought maybe he was one of your old collars."

The officer stared at his weapon. "Hard to believe—twenty years as an MP, and I never fired my gun. I come to a quiet college campus and kill someone."

"You beat me by an eyelash," Riley said. "I'd started to squeeze the trigger."

Ted seemed rooted to the spot. She eased the gun from his hand, laid it on the ground several feet away. She took his radio and reported the homicide. While she spoke with a deputy, she kept her eyes on Ted's face. He looked physically ill.

"You going to be sick? It's okay. But let's move away from the body." *God, I wish I'd fired first. This is going to haunt Ted.*

Riley had killed one subject in the line of duty and understood how taking any life pried a piece from your soul. Justification helped but never erased the doubts.

"It'll be fine. We'll dot every 'i.' It's crystal clear how it went down."

She steered Ted to her car, the battered shepherding the broken. She unlocked her Honda, told Ted to sit in the driver's seat. Sirens screamed in the distance.

"The sheriff's sending the crime techs over from the lake," she said. "They were just packing up. EMS and an ambulance are en route."

Ted looked at her and frowned. "You're bleeding. You better take that ambulance."

He handed her a cotton handkerchief and motioned to scrub her cheek. Men of his generation still carried handkerchiefs. She swiped the cloth across her face and felt the sticky residue. *Yep, I'm bleeding. But in drips and drabs, not buckets.*

"I don't need an ambulance. After the officers finish, I'll drive to the ER. Have them x-ray my arm and ribs. Might have cracked a few bones. The bloody nose and scraped cheek are my own fault. Never try a swan dive on asphalt."

Ted shrugged. "You're the boss. Don't go loco trying to prove how tough you are. You definitely shouldn't drive."

Riley heard heavy breathing and pounding feet and bit back a smart-aleck retort.

"What happened?" Alarm laced the newcomer's shout.

What the hell? Wolf? She didn't want him to see her banged up and shaking. Her second thought felt closer to a wish. She craved his strong arms, wished he'd take her home.

Dammit. Homicides aren't the only things that haunt you.

* * * *

Blood trickled from Riley's nose. Her skinned left cheek looked red and raw. Wolf wanted to hug her, but he was afraid to do more than touch her shoulder. "Are you hurt?"

"I'm fine. Ted shot the guy before he could mow me down. Third time might have been the charm."

She stifled a gasp as she straightened. Riley's two-tone cat eyes usually made him think of kaleidoscopes. Tonight they radiated pain. She was hurt and too damn stubborn to admit it.

"That man attacked you?"

She nodded. Wolf studied the dead biker. Prison tats decorated the man's sausage-like fingers. "Some crook from your past?"

"No." Riley shook her head.

Random violence? Wolf doubted it.

Leeds County sheriff's deputies appeared amid a flurry of blue and red strobes. Once they determined Wolf wasn't a witness, they banished him to the sidelines. Riley shambled over to personally shoo him away.

He shook his head. "That officer said you shouldn't drive. I'll take you to the hospital."

"That's not necessary. Besides I don't know how long this will take."

"Doesn't matter. I'm staying."

Riley shuddered. He could tell every movement triggered a stab of pain. She dumped her car keys in his hand. Good thing she hadn't fought him. If someone hired this monster to attack her, the danger might not be over.

At the hospital, the doctor, a Reid family friend, treated Riley and released her into Wolf's custody. "She's lucky," the doc said. "Only minor cuts, a few bruised ribs, and a sprain."

Wolf glanced at Riley, surprised she wasn't raising Cain about someone talking about her in the third person. Her blank expression said she was present in body, not mind.

"I put her left arm in a sling to reduce shoulder strain and loaded her up with pain killers. She'll be out like a light, probably before you get her home."

The physician handed over a bottle of pills. "I guarantee she'll want more when she wakes."

FIFTEEN

Wolf's wristwatch alarm chirped. Morning already? He sensed pressure on his chest, warm breath on his cheek. Alarmed, he jerked, knocking a framed picture off a side table. Lucy yowled in protest. Riley had mumbled the name of her cat—black as a panther but not as svelte—last night.

"Sorry, kitty." Having parachuted to safety, the cat arched her back in a display of pique. "You scared me more than I scared you. Forgive me?"

He rolled over and came eye-level with the big cat. She studied him with disdain, then relented and rubbed her fur against his bare arm. Lucy's meows grew louder.

"Okay, I get it. You want something."

Wolf followed the cat to the back door. When he opened it, she shot out, a black streak disappearing into greening foliage.

"Glad someone's feeling perky. Don't disappear, or Riley will have my head."

He sauntered back to the couch and picked up the photo he'd knocked over. Decked out in cap and gown, Riley waved a diploma. Her mother and her uncle, Senator Edwin Yates, flanked her. Leaders of the enemy camp.

Wolf knew how they'd feel about his presence in Riley's home. His Uncle Ray and his cousin Hank would feel the same way. Did Riley share their bitter hatred? Wolf and Riley were both in their early teens when Hank was tried for the murders. So neither had sat in the courtroom during the trial. That meant they heard only one version of the testimony, how their kin reacted to the "not guilty" verdict.

He replaced the picture and stretched. The pullout sofa featured the standard torture bar perfectly centered to break a man's back. He felt like a jumbo pretzel.

Still he was glad he'd stayed. The drugs made Riley loopy. He couldn't have left her alone. She even giggled, too far gone to protest his sleepover. In fact, when he put her to bed, she invited him to join her. Too bad there'd be no rain check once she regained her senses.

When he tucked her in, she'd pulled his head close and whispered. "Promise you'll wake me by six." Her eyelids fluttered. "Gotta chat with the FBI and the chancellor."

Wolf tiptoed into her bedroom. Morning sun poked through the lace curtains, creating intricate patterns on the bed's apple-green comforter. Riley was nearly invisible. Only a few auburn ringlets peeked from under the covers.

He quietly closed the door to the bathroom. The scent of her soap lent encouragement to his standard first-of-the-morning hard-on. *Wonder if Pavlov ever studied dicks.*

He splashed water on his face, leaned down to drink from the faucet. The metallic taste on his tongue suggested he'd been chewing staples. He coveted her toothbrush, wished he could brush his teeth. That's when it dawned on him. A single toothbrush.

Good. The joker who sent roses to her office didn't have toothbrush privileges.

Wolf zipped his running suit and sat on the toilet to lace his shoes. He glanced at his watch. One minute to six. He hated to wake her. He gently pulled back the comforter and brushed a curl off her forehead. Slowly he trailed his fingers across her soft skin. She looked so innocent, a cuddly —if banged up— lamb.

A Bible verse popped into his mind. "And the lion shall lay down with the lamb." *Maybe the wolf should lay down with the lamb.*

Forget it. Minus the drugs, she'd never be interested.

Wolf reached out to tap Riley's uninjured shoulder when he noticed his book on her nightstand. As he picked up *Firelight*, it fell open to page 158. An underlined passage described the hero ravishing the young blonde's lush body.

A single word was scratched in the margin. Big, black exclamation points marched behind it. The curse wasn't one he'd ever heard her utter—in polite company or otherwise.

His description of their lovemaking had incensed Riley. Why? He'd altered his heroine's looks so no one would ever guess Riley was his sensual vixen. Had anger and hatred erased her memory? How good it had been?

He brushed his lips against the cheek she'd roughed up during her concrete slide. "Wake up, sunshine. Time to sniff out mad bombers and do whatever else you law types do."

Her eyes blinked open. She looked confused, then pleased. Her smile proved fleeting.

"What time is it?" she asked, all business.

"Six on the dot."

"I have to hurry." She sat up and gasped. Clasping her side, she slid back under the covers.

"Go slow. I put pain pills on your bathroom sink. You might want to pop one. Can I do anything for you before I leave?"

Whoa. Did she just check out my hard-on?

"No," Riley said, her answer firm. "Thanks for driving me to the hospital and babysitting."

Wolf kissed her. This time it wasn't a brotherly peck. He threaded his fingers through her untamed curls as he lifted her head off the pillow. Her generous lips were warm and supple. When his tongue gently prodded, she seemed to welcome the breach. For an instant, she joined him in the first tentative steps of a sweet oral tango.

He lowered her head to its pillow nest. Her curls licked the pillow like dark flames. Though his tingling lips argued against it, he stuck with a disciplined retreat, his fingers grazing her warm skin as he pulled back.

"Wish I could stay, but I want to be on time to pick up Ellen's father."

At the doorway, he turned. "I'll call later. See if you need anything."

When he opened the front door, the rotund cat sauntered inside. How many times had the black cat crossed his path?

Glad I'm not superstitious.

* * * *

Riley's body sent urgent messages. The pain—which should have been the headline—was barely a footnote. Even before Wolf kissed her, she noticed the erection tenting the silky nylon of his running suit. The mint taste of his tongue made her nipples salute. Warmth cascaded down her body, as if a sunbeam pierced a dense cloudbank to focus its rays on her chilled flesh.

Damn him! One kiss and I'm panting. Her whole being remembered what followed his kiss.

A flash of memory cut through the gauzy haze of last evening. His warm hands meandered down her thighs as he slid off her slacks. She heard his chuckle when he found her flannel nightie—the one covered with goofy moose heads—and pulled it over her head.

Oh, God! He undressed me, and I asked him to sleep with me. Alcohol had nothing on pain pills as an uninhibitor.

It took all of Riley's discipline to reorder her thoughts as Wolf vanished from her doorway. Remember, how it ended. Think about your mom.

Family history aside, she would never allow herself to be charmed by another Gary, another player. The unwanted memory surfaced. The hurt of learning her husband of fifteen years was a serial fornicator, boinking a long line of other women for fourteen of those years. *Forget Wolf. You're just horny.*

The familiar black cloud of injured pride choked out the warmth of Wolf's smile. Gary's legacy. He'd left her for his last fling. A woman he'd made pregnant. A mistake he couldn't hide. Riley felt humiliated and stupid. Such a clever FBI agent— she couldn't even detect her own husband's philandering. She tossed aside the covers. *Get real.*

SIXTEEN

Riley walked into her office at 6:45 a.m. Five minutes later, Gary Jacob's six-foot-three-inch frame filled her doorway. Her stomach somersaulted as her emotions spiraled into freefall.

It had been two years and two months since she'd been eyeball to eyeball with her ex. She'd seen him plenty on TV though since the Bureau capitalized on his media sex appeal.

Packaged head-to-toe in a snowy shirt, crisply creased slacks, and shiny wingtips, he looked unchanged. A runner's build. Dazzling white teeth. Lying blue eyes.

He smiled. "Hello, Riley."

His face morphed into its "earnest" veneer. She could classify his mercurial expressions faster than he could quirk his brows.

Gary took two steps toward her desk. She rose from her chair. He stopped, uncharacteristically cautious, awaiting her reaction.

Her brain screamed, "What the hell?" She clamped her mouth shut and waited. The man hadn't dropped in to toast the good old days.

Her silence compelled him to speak. "Thought I'd arrive a few minutes early so we could have a private moment. Give you a chance to get over any discomfort."

Her ex paused dramatically. He always did when he played his audience. Drum roll, Riley thought. Here it comes.

"I've come down from D.C. to take charge of the Onward case."

She bit her tongue. Didn't trust herself to speak. You son-of-a-bitch! And I thought last night was a nightmare. I'd rather tangle with a psycho biker.

At least the biker hadn't blindsided her. She'd seen him coming. Gary was more devious. Her husband had sex with her eight hours before announcing he'd knocked up another woman. Oh, and he needed a divorce. Sorry. He still loved her, but—well, he hoped they could part friends.

As long as she remained in the FBI, Gary was impossible to forget. The agency garnered good press when he nailed a Chicago terrorist cell with a weapons cache large enough to decimate the Loop. Gary's victory earned him a promotion to Assistant Special Agent in Charge of the sprawling Chicago office. An up and comer.

Why the hell was he in South Carolina? Had he been demoted? She could only hope.

As Riley stared at the intimate stranger, Gary dropped his head. His manicured nails ran through his thick blond hair. *No balding, damn.*

When he finally returned her gaze, he frowned at her bruises and sling. Did he think she'd gone a round with an abusive boyfriend? He didn't inquire.

"I hope you can put aside any ill will," he managed. "You're a pro. I'm sure you've built a top-notch security force here."

"Can the crap." Her response popped out just shy of a bark. "I'm not thrilled to see you. But Lord knows I'd collaborate with J. Edgar Hoover's paranoid pit bull to nail these bastards."

Gary's lips twitched. He didn't respond. She didn't blink. "Thought you were in Chicago."

"Transferred a month ago to D.C. Section Chief, Domestic Terrorism. When I heard about BRU, I asked permission to serve as on-scene commander. I want to see how our task force approach works. And, well, I wanted to see you."

His eyes locked on hers and held. "BRU isn't the only school under the Onward gun."

"What?"

A knock interrupted. Though the door stood open, Pete rapped on the doorframe to advertise his presence. He knew the meeting was personal. Though she'd kept her maiden name and no one mentioned her divorce, Pete and his cohorts had undoubtedly researched her the minute they learned she'd be their new boss.

"Sorry to interrupt," Pete began, "but Jeff Wilson and company are here. Bill, too. Patty set up the faculty lounge upstairs."

"Thanks. This is Gary Jacob, head of Domestic Terrorism. A bigwig. We have the FBI's attention."

Pete moved forward to shake hands. "Glad to meet you, sir. I'm Peter Barnes."

The interruption let Riley bottle her emotions. *Why does Gary want to see me*?

"Agent Jacob just told me another college has been threatened." She locked eyes with her ex. "Tell us about the other school? Is it nearby?"

"Two more targets—one in Florida, one in Maryland. Onward emailed identical threats to all three schools."

Pete reacted first. "Holy crap. Are these guys for real?"

Gary's phone buzzed. He walked away to answer it.

* * * *

When Riley entered the faculty lounge, Sheriff Hendricks hurried to pull out a chair at the head of the table. "I heard about last night's attack. You're one gutsy lady. Think that biker might be connected to Onward?"

The assembled men stopped pouring coffee to listen.

"It crossed my mind." She gave Hendricks a thoughtful look. Though his physical appearance fit the roly-poly caricature of a small-town sheriff, he was a sharp cookie.

"Coincidences are always suspicious. But why would Onward target me? Your deputies ran the biker. Been out of prison two days. Not much time to hook up with Onward."

"I'd like to hear the whole story," Jeff interrupted. "What happened after I left last night?"

Though any link between the biker and Onward seemed iffy, Riley's concise report prompted suspicion—law enforcement types don't trust coincidence.

Since Gary had yet to reappear, Jeff handled the introductions, beginning with a cyber specialist from Quantico. He then ran down the home team roster for the Joint Terrorism Task Force. In addition to Sheriff Hendricks, the team included three officers from the South Carolina Law Enforcement Division (SLED), and representatives from the Alcohol, Tobacco & Firearms (ATF) and Immigration Control and Enforcement (ICE) agencies.

Finally, Riley introduced Pete and Alan.

With roll call complete, Jeff updated everyone on the FBI's paltry Onward intelligence. The SLED officers said their files contained little more than rumors about the local chapter. No member names.

The door to the meeting room opened and Gary strode in. "The count's gone up. Onward has threatened at least five campuses. Pretty grandiose ambitions."

"Are the new targets in the South?" Riley asked.

"No. Connecticut and New Jersey. Five schools, five states. Onward appears to be picking on private, well-respected colleges founded by Protestant denominations—Methodists, Baptists, Presbyterians."

Bone tired and in pain, Riley felt scratchy. "What, no Catholics, Jews, or Mormons? Maybe we can sue for discrimination."

A few of the men at the table chuckled. Gary wasn't one of them.

"What else do our schools have in common?" she asked.

"Spanish cultural programs, international student exchange programs, and you operate in communities with sizeable populations of illegal immigrants. But what college doesn't these days? Plus you all have Saturday commencements."

Her headache escalated to jackhammer mode. "Graduations are tempting targets. Lots of people gathered in one spot."

"Why would Onward threaten schools outside its natural geography?" the sheriff asked. "Picking schools hundreds of miles apart presents logistical nightmares." He paused for a second. "Unless they're trying to spread us thin while they concentrate on one target."

Gary interrupted. "Maybe 9/11 inspired them to plan multiple, same-day strikes."

Riley discounted that theory. Unless FBI intel was horribly wrong, Onward lacked the manpower and organizational skills to carry out multi-state attacks. BRU was the only truly Southern campus. She feared the sheriff had nailed it. Her university was the logical target. The others were smokescreen.

While Riley's primary duty was to secure her campus, she wanted in on the investigation. Would Gary object? See it as a turf war?

"I have friends at the Southern Poverty Law Center. Any problem if I pick their brains? Maybe my old sources can tip us about Onward members they deem capable of mass murder. I'll write up anything I find for the team."

She looked at Jeff and her ex for a go-ahead.

"I don't see a problem," Gary finally said, "as long as you share any leads immediately."

"Fine." She managed a polite smile. She needed Gary in her corner. He could access resources she couldn't touch.

SEVENTEEN

Wolf instantly recognized the genetic link between Ellen and her dad—fair hair, widely spaced blue eyes, slender nose.

"Mr. Wingate? I'm Wolf Valdes, your daughter's counselor."

The man offered a firm handshake. "Call me Steve."

As they left baggage claim, Steve wasted no time on small talk. "How's my daughter? Tell me about the attack."

Wolf reported on the girl's health, waiting until they'd fastened their seatbelts to suggest the wounds might be self-inflicted.

"It's my fault, isn't it?" Steve's troubled eyes spoke of guilt. "I left town as soon as we divorced. Ellen must think I abandoned her. That's what's turned her off men."

Wolf shook his head. "I'm no psychologist. But beating yourself up won't help Ellen. She fell in love. Yeah, with a woman. Maybe she's wired that way. Maybe it's youthful experimentation. The who really doesn't matter."

He locked eyes with Steve. "She was desperate, hurting. Forget the lesbian stuff and your guilt. Tell Ellen you're in her corner no matter what."

Steve scrubbed at his cheek. "Okay. Got it."

"Good man. The fact you're here may be all your daughter needs to make a fresh start."

A tense silence followed. "You live in California, right? What do you do for a living?"

The question flipped an animation switch. Steve's eyes lit and his shoulders lifted as he described his work as a computer security guru for one of the industry giants.

The father's energy drained away when Wolf parked the car. "I'm nervous."

Wolf nodded. "Want me to go in first? Let her know you're here?"

"Yeah, please."

Ellen's complexion appeared only a shade darker than the starched white sheets. Wolf pulled up a chair beside her bed to explain her dad had taken a red-eye flight to be at her side. Her eyes brimmed with tears. *She's fragile. Go easy.*

"Did you know I'm one-quarter Cherokee?" he asked.

Ellen looked puzzled at the turn in the conversation.

"My Cherokee great-grandfather—my namesake—was a priest. Though the Cherokee don't believe priests have supernatural powers, these men serve as the tribe's vessels, filled with sacred knowledge by their elders. They're taught to heal the sick, ward off evil, bless crops."

The girl relaxed. *Stories are good medicine.* Wolf leaned forward.

"When the elders decided my great-grandfather was ready to join the priesthood, they buried him alive, covered his grave with leaves, and set them on fire."

"What?" A hint of color crept into Ellen's cheeks.

"Scary, huh? The story gave me the willies as a child." He smiled. "They poked a hollow cane through the sod so he could breathe. Still I marveled at his bravery—and trust. Smothering soil. Total darkness. And he accepted it."

Ellen whispered, "I could never do that."

"Not sure I could either," Wolf agreed. "But Grandmother told me her father claimed that light and air had a new quality once he rose from that grave. The experience brought color and joy to everything that followed. It gave him a taste for life."

He stood and smiled down at Ellen. "We don't have to be buried alive to have darkness swallow us. It's what we do when we climb out of the blackness that matters."

She looked up with pleading eyes. "You know, don't you? There was no attacker."

"It's okay," he whispered. "May I tell the authorities? You don't want someone wrongly accused, do you?"

"Oh, no," she sobbed. "But I lied to the police. They'll send me to jail."

"They won't," he said. "I promise."

Witnessing the father-daughter reunion that followed buoyed Wolf's spirits. They hugged and cried. In a weird way, he envied Ellen's emotional train wreck. The girl obviously had great capacity to love. She'd be fine.

He rolled his eyes at his sappy musings. Day in and day out, bachelorhood suited him. He ate cold pizza for breakfast. Fished for salmon in Alaska. Wore T-shirts frayed to perfection. No complications. No fights.

He liked ladies. Let's amend that—he loved them. During each relationship, he remained monogamous. When relationships ran their course, the women often remained friends—sometimes friends with benefits.

Maybe that's why Riley intrigues me. I walked away long before I was ready.

Something drew him to her. Something besides imaginative sex and her keen sense of humor. Too bad he'd never had the chance to find out what that something might be.

EIGHTEEN

Riley's head throbbed. She'd been bounced on asphalt, forced to team up with her scummy ex, and now Dr. Harris and Dr. Sparks were obsessing about word choice. When they'd asked her to help polish an FBI-approved statement, she figured five minutes. Ha! Thirty and counting.

She understood Chancellor Harris's jitters. His words would go out via radio, podcast, email, text message and phone. Riley thought two jiggers of rum might help more than wordsmithing.

"Let me try again." Dr. Harris cleared his throat. "Campus security is working closely with the FBI. The email may be a hoax. But, if it isn't, these professionals will track down this hate group before anyone is harmed." The tremor in his voice channeled fear.

Sparks tried to calm his boss. "That's fine, Henry. Go on."

Dr. Harris glanced at his notes. "Today is the last day of final exams for spring semester so most of our students are headed home. However, we will tighten security, lock down the campus, and impose an eleven p.m. curfew to protect those who remain on campus."

Harris looked up, seeking approval. When Sparks nodded, the chancellor continued. "I make you two promises. First, we will keep everyone informed. Second, the safety of our university community will always be our top priority in every decision."

Sparks shot his boss a thumbs-up. "Good, Henry, but remind folks that Onward has declared war on all higher learning."

Sparks jotted a note, and Dr. Harris's lips moved as he silently read the new closing.

With the dress rehearsal complete, Riley was eager to get going. Dr. Harris was stalling.

She felt miserable and grumpy. Dressing for work, she found her classic black blazer wouldn't fit over her sling. She felt hot and self-conscious dressed in a stoplight red sweater.

Her cell phone vibrated. Patty, her admin. She excused herself and walked to a corner of the conference room. "What's up?"

"A patrol just spotted a phalanx of the enemy headed your way. Doris Hillman and Reverend Jimmy are in Doris's Rolls Royce with the WHYG-TV van on their heels."

"Arrghh. Thanks for the warning."

She'd expected the media to swoop in. But why were Doris and the preacher leading the parade? Had they learned about Onward's threat and come to point fingers?

Doris had sued BRU for control of the Hillman Foundation created by her granddad seventy-five years ago. The stock he'd donated, now worth $300 million, served as the university's primary financial artery. The lawsuit claimed BRU had violated its verbal contract with Doris's Bible-thumping progenitor, who expected his endowment to be used to promote Christian values. Doris wanted to transfer the entire Foundation to Reverend Jimmy Long's ultra-right His Way University.

When Ms. Hillman and her smarmy televangelist ventured on campus, they usually headed straight to the chancellor's office to be filmed before the building's fluted columns while they painted BRU as a den of iniquity. Security officers had a standing BOLO—be on the lookout—for the holy terrors.

Dr. Harris walked to a window. "Good heavens, they're headed inside."

The chancellor opened the conference room door.

"Where's Dr. Harris?" Reverend Jimmy's booming bass overrode the chirpy protests of the ninety-pound coed on receptionist duty.

"Right here." The chancellor matched the preacher's volume and outrage. "What's the meaning of this ... this assault? My office is always open, but I expect the courtesy of an appointment."

Quivering double chins signaled Dr. Harris's discomfort, his fight against his ostrich tendencies. Riley mentally applauded his moxie. She edged out the door to stand beside Harris and Sparks on the second-floor landing.

"My, my, the complete cabal." The preacher scurried halfway up the curved rotunda stairs and pivoted to gesture at the TV crew below.

Riley knew the reporter, Brad Able. While she maintained friendly relationships with most members of the Fourth Estate, this slug ranked below slime. Riley noticed a green light blinking on a shouldered TV camera. *Uh, oh. Live and livid.*

Reverend Jimmy pointed at the BRU triumvirate. "These godless traitors know Blue Ridge University is in grave danger. Yet they hide their shameful secrets at the peril of students. Another example of the cancer eating away at BRU's moral backbone."

The televangelist lasered his wrath on Riley. "Last night that *woman* ordered a student, Darryl Thomas, to hide the fact that young men and women attending BRU are in imminent danger. Fortunately her intimidation didn't stop him from confiding in his parents."

What a loose-lipped idiot! Couldn't you wait for daylight, Darryl?

For one wild moment, Riley considered putting a bullet in the rose-encrusted plaster ceiling to stop the reverend and let Dr. Harris claim the floor.

The preacher sucked in a deep breath. "An hour after that travesty, this woman who was hired to *protect* people, killed an unarmed man—"

Out of desperation, Riley clapped her hands. Hard. A jolt of pain boomeranged from her wrist to her damaged shoulder and back again.

"Dr. Harris would have made his announcement by now if you hadn't interrupted. Let him speak."

The chancellor fumbled with the paper, swallowed twice, and began reading.

The instant he finished, the reporter yelled, "Will you comply with Onward's demands?"

Dr. Sparks picked up the ball. "Student safety will guide all decisions. We're sure officials at the four sister universities threatened by these terrorists will do the same. Hate groups like Onward are anathema to every *legitimate* institution of higher learning."

He glared at Jimmy. No need to actually identify the preacher's institution as a cow-patty college. However, the recipient of the scorn appeared unfazed.

"Miz Reid," the reporter yelled, "what about the allegation you killed a man?"

"False." She answered, her tone flat. "Early this morning, a motorcyclist attacked me using deadly force. A fellow officer yelled a warning. The biker's continued attack forced the officer to shoot. The Leeds County Sheriff's Office investigated."

"Was your attacker a student? Any connection to Onward?" Able asked.

Dr. Sparks intervened. "No, he was not a student. Sorry, no more sound bites. The FBI and the sheriff are investigating these matters. It's inappropriate to comment further."

Riley's gaze snagged on Doris, who huddled a foot behind the preacher. The heiress was dressed in a rich person's version of sackcloth. Gray silk. Muted lipstick. Salt-and-pepper hair pinned in a bun so severe it yanked her eyelids into an Asian slant. Her potato face was a notch lower than plain. But one thing was clear. She was gaa-gaa over Reverend Jimmy.

Her personal savior or something more?

Doris wasn't dumb. She'd been a B+ student when she and Riley were BRU undergraduates.

What makes her buy into Reverend Jimmy's claptrap?

Suddenly Doris stared straight at Riley. Her look pulsed with hatred.

Riley figured she knew why. You idiot. I'm not going to blab about ancient history.

Twenty years before, Riley saw an unglued Doris lunge at a coed with scissors while she screamed "Whore!" at the top of her lungs. Doris blamed the girl for stealing her boyfriend.

The attack took place in the dorm's communal showers. Riley and a friend separated the squirming naked bodies. After the dorm mother forced Doris to get professional counseling, the victim—only bruised—agreed not to press charges.

Riley broke eye contact with her former classmate. She followed Sparks and Harris back inside the conference room. Once the door closed, the chancellor collapsed in a chair.

"Well, wasn't that fun? Even if this threat's a prank, it's a PR nightmare."

Sparks waved his hand as if he were shooing away a fly. "This will blow over. Surely Doris and Jimmy realize they go too far if they align themselves with maniacs threatening to kill students."

BRU's chancellor took off his wire-rimmed glasses and polished them with his silk tie.

"That preacher is an expert at twisting the word of God to tap into a wellspring of hate," he grumbled. "I still cringe when I think about those depositions. They used every trick to make it sound as if BRU professors *encourage* homosexuality, abortion, and pornography."

Sparks sighed. "I attended the Valdes deposition. Jimmy's attorneys must have memorized every sexual passage in his book. Hell, many of our own alumni think *Firelight* is porn. Have you read it? The sex scenes could singe your eyebrows."

Riley held her tongue. How would her bosses feel if they learned her gymnastics helped inspire the incendiary prose?

Dr. Sparks walked to the window. "At least this Hillman Foundation mess will be over soon. We have a court date in three weeks. Just wish we'd drawn a judge appointed *after* the Civil War. Judge Jones is eighty-five and right of Attila the Hun."

Dr. Harris's sausage-sized fingers rubbed his chest. Riley wondered if she should dispense some of her pain pills. The way things were going the campus infirmary should restock.

NINETEEN

BRU's administrators seemed cheered that other colleges faced the same threat. Riley understood. They weren't in this nightmare alone, and it made it harder for the reverend's PR hacks to portray BRU as uniquely evil and marked for divine retribution.

Multiple threats also made hounding Onward to hell the FBI's top priority. Gary's presence was good and bad news. Yet if BRU had to be threatened, Riley would rather it was the solo target. Issues would be simpler, clearer. The FBI's focus wouldn't be splintered.

At the morning roundtable, her ex announced he'd made BRU his operational base. His desire to camp in South Carolina puzzled her. In his shoes, she'd pick any campus but Blue Ridge. Was saving her alma mater his way of making amends?

Since their first moments together, there'd been no personal exchange. Riley had avoided the temptation to make snarky inquiries about his wife and kid. In turn, Gary hadn't asked if someone occupied his old side of their king-sized bed.

She was surprised Director Stewart permitted Gary to gallop to the rescue. Their marital history was no secret, and the FBI normally made certain personal baggage didn't clutter agency business. Gary must have perfected his brown nose routine or called in some chips. Why?

As she walked past Patty's desk, her admin clamped a pudgy brown hand over the phone's mouthpiece. "You're Miss Popularity. It's Senator Yates' secretary."

"Ask her to hold." Riley hurried to her desk. She'd been expecting her uncle's call.

"Riley Reid here"

"I'll tell the Senator you're free." Unaccustomed to being put on hold, the senator's secretary sounded peeved.

"Hello, Riley." A politician's mellow baritone. "I've been briefed on the terrorist threat by Director Stewart. He said Gary's heading the investigation. You okay with that?"

"No problem. I've moved on. So has he."

"You're right on that score. Gary and wife number two didn't last long. You knew they divorced, right? Bet he wants you back."

Riley snickered. "Wants me back? He didn't want me when he had me. But thanks for the heads up. I won't ask about his wife or Jacob Junior."

"Uh, Riley, the little boy died. Thought you knew. It happened a few months before the marriage blew up."

The news felt like a punch in the solar plexus. Her mind had manufactured a dozen catty zingers about the perfect family. "Gary must be hurting. I can't imagine losing a child."

She instantly regretted her choice of words. Neither Riley nor her uncle spoke for a moment. The Senator had lost a child. Twenty-six years ago his son, Will, and Riley's brother, Jack, plunged off a mountain road to a fiery death. Wolf's cousin Hank had driven the car that hounded the scared teenagers up the mountain.

The senator cleared his throat. "I called Jennie. My daughter's more worried about today's psych exam than terrorists. You know kids—bad things only happen to other people."

Riley had lunched with her young cousin over the weekend. She pictured Jennie hunched in concentration, chewing on a No. 2 pencil as she parsed exam answers.

"I'm glad Jennie's unconcerned. Finals are all any student should worry about this week." She rubbed her forehead. "I'll do anything I can to help the FBI round up these bozos. If that means playing nice with Gary, I will. Thanks for telling me his situation."

"Where do you stand on canceling commencement?"

"No decision yet. I'm toying with a change of venue. The note threatened to turn *our* campus into a funeral pyre. Maybe their plans specifically target our layout and facilities."

Senator Yates sighed. "I hate the break in tradition, but safety trumps ceremony. How's your mother? Has this threat unnerved her?"

"Oh, no! I planned to tell Mom about the threat before she heard it on the news. Too late."

The schoolmarm voice of her uncle's secretary intruded. The woman sounded as if she might smack the senator with a ruler if he didn't hang up and take an *important* call.

"The boss tells me I have to run," he said. "Call if you need anything. *Anything*. Nancy and I are like all the parents of BRU students. Frightened. So call. Okay?"

"Yes, Senator," Riley replied.

"Senator? What happened to Uncle Ed?"

"When you're offering governmental assistance, you're Senator. When you're dishing up peach pie, you're Uncle Ed."

He chuckled. "Fair enough. Call me."

Riley's fingers flew over her keyboard. There was a reason she'd been at her desk last night when all hell broke loose, and it had nothing to do with terrorists. She still had a Clery Act report to review and file.

Named for a coed raped and murdered in 1986, the Clery Act required colleges to disclose crime statistics on or near their campuses. Riley treated the report with the gravity it deserved. She re-checked stats on student identify theft—a burgeoning problem. Satisfied with the report's accuracy, she emailed it to Patty to proof and process.

Reminded again of Amanda Coffey, the BRU coed killed two months earlier, Riley stole a glance at the picture of Kate's friend. Not even six degrees of separation. Riley ran a finger across the photo's pebbled surface. *I haven't forgotten.*

Her subconscious had stumbled across a clue but couldn't dredge it up. A comment by Kate or another of Amanda's friends? Some artifact in the murdered coed's apartment? After the police processed the crime scene, she'd escorted the parents to the victim's Spartan quarters.

Focus on live students for now. Keep all of them breathing. Should they cancel commencement? Mailing diplomas would guarantee everyone's safety. Yet the administration was loath to go that route too quickly. The email might prove a hoax — someone appropriating Onward's name as a scare tactic. Even if Onward was behind the threat, it didn't mean the group intended to carry through. Maybe their goal was simply to create chaos and gain exposure.

There was another issue, too. If BRU caved, how many more disgruntled nuts would issue threats, hoping to disrupt college exams or commencements elsewhere?

Riley leaned back, steepled her fingers, and closed her eyes. She pictured stadium entrances and exits. What would she do if she wanted to kill people? If she wanted to make a grand statement?

Think like Onward. A sniper attack was out. No pizzazz. No mass murder.

What about loading a vehicle with explosives and ramming an entrance? Crude, but effective. Riley made a note. They could stop that type of assault.

Some scheme to deliver death from above? A private plane or a hijacking? She'd coordinate with Gary. Gather info on private planes at local airstrips.

"Even your frown becomes you."

Riley jumped at Gary's voice. She hadn't heard her ex enter. "Mind if I close the door? I'd like a word in private."

"Of course." She watched him lower his elegant body into the single visitor's chair. He looked even more handsome than she remembered. Riley wished she could switch off the flashback videos. A laughing Gary frolicking in the surf on their honeymoon. A grim-faced stranger telling her he needed a divorce.

Gary was too close. Random thoughts skittered through her mind, including a vow to rearrange her office. She'd positioned her desk to see out the high casement window. Her recent visitors convinced her she'd rather have her back to the window and her scarred pine desk as a room divider and barrier.

"Riley, I didn't say everything I wanted to this morning. I'm not sure what you know. My son died last year, and my divorce from Penny will be final next month." He swallowed.

"I'm sorry, Gary." Her voice was little more than a whisper. "I mean it. It must be horrible to lose a young child."

"I'm not looking for pity. I just want you to understand. I'm a different person. I'm so sorry I hurt you." He bowed his head to avoid her eyes. "I realize how incredibly selfish I was. Everything was about me. My career. My needs. My ego." He shook his head. "After Tommy died and Penny asked for a divorce, I was a mess. I saw a therapist and took a good hard look at myself."

He glanced up and met Riley's eyes. "Can you forgive me?"

She blinked. Startled. Unprepared. Not the conversation she expected. "That was long ago. It's over. I've moved on."

He stood and walked toward her. Riley froze. Was he going to offer more personal revelations? Sympathy for the loss of his baby warred with her discomfort at being cast as his confidante. *Let's get back to the case. Please.*

Her ex-husband cupped her chin, tilted her head up. His kiss was a whisper. His breath stirred the air beside her ear. "Riley, I want you back. I need you. Will you give me another chance?"

Another chance? For the two of them? Riley was too startled to reply.

Gary seized on her silence. "I'm not the same man." His hands imprisoned her face. His thumb stroked her cheek. "I realize now what I lost. I love you, Riley."

Finally her body worked. "No." She found his hands, pulled them away. "No. I'm sorry. We can't go back."

He frowned. "Is there someone else?"

She pulled free. "Don't go there. You have no right. We're professional colleagues. Period."

She turned to her desk to straighten a sheaf of papers. She didn't want Gary to see her face. Didn't want to look into his eyes. "Anything new on Onward? Any leads?"

Silence. She looked up. He was gone. *What did he expect?*

Patty, Riley's good-natured assistant, materialized in the doorway, her lopsided grin an ivory beacon in her ebony face. "Your mother asked for Riley Yates Reid. Want to take it, or shall I tell her you'll call back?"

"Riley Yates Reid? Holy camole! She's steamed! That damned Brad Able."

No doubt her mother had caught Able's TV report. Riley had hoped to deliver the news about the biker and Onward with a tad more finesse. Out of cowardice she'd left a message on her mom's answering machine saying she couldn't play chauffeur. "Sorry to make you reschedule your doctor's appointment, Mom. Have to deal with a work crisis."

To avoid the third-degree, Riley phoned when she knew Miz Pearl would be out for her "morning constitutional." Her mother took pride in her ability to engage in light exercise even though she had to wheel her portable oxygen concentrator wherever she went.

"Are all the officers here and ready for the briefing?"

Patty nodded a yes.

"Then tell Mom I'm in a meeting. I'll call back as soon as I can."

TWENTY

Wolf's beeline from front door to refrigerator took twenty seconds. Twin Blue Moons called to him from the top shelf. He grabbed a beer, snatched a container of leftover Kung Po chicken, and shoved it in the microwave.

He was thirsty, hungry, exhausted, and pressed for time. Under ten minutes to call Riley, check messages, and eat. He groaned when her voice mail picked up. "Yeah, yeah," he muttered. "You're out of the office or on another line. My message is *very* important. Yada, yada."

He paced while he waited for the recorded voice to peter out. Finally a beep. Wolf briefly recapped his visit with Ellen. He hung up as the microwave beeped. *Idiot. You told Riley everything she needs to know. No reason for her to call back.*

It was past time for them to talk. Really talk. He'd never explained why he walked out at Hilton Head. She'd never asked. When they were introduced at a faculty meeting, she pretended they'd never met. He wanted to clear the air, say his piece.

Wolf plunked his leftovers on the kitchen bar and punched in a code to retrieve phone messages. Forking a mouthful of overheated rice, he scorched his tongue. *Damn it all to hell!*

The agitated voice made Wolf forgot all about his Chinese takeout. Tom Jenkins, his favorite graduate assistant, sounded beyond upset.

"Hey, Dr. Wolfman, I had to let you know. A bunch of thugs—Aryan Brotherhood types—cornered Rosie this morning. They were shoving her around, calling her a wetback ..."

Wolf heard a choked-off sob.

"Oh, man, Rosie's hurt real bad. She broke away, jumped in front of a pick-up. She's in a coma. Doctors don't know if she'll make it. They wouldn't let me see her. Said I wasn't family. I couldn't just sit in the waiting room, doing nothing."

The line went silent. For a minute Wolf thought Tom had hung up. The grad student's voice came back shaky but belligerent. "I'm going to nail those assholes. Onward's threat has been all over TV. Has to be the same bastards."

A pause. "I'll join up, get the goods on them. Make them pay."

Wolf heard a click. Tom was gone.

"Damn fool!" Wolf cursed. Those freaking Nazis were serious.

He pictured perky, saucy Rosie. Pressure built behind his eyes. Senseless brutality. Rosalind Perez came from Puerto Rico. Tom and Rosie planned to marry as soon as they finished their degrees. Wolf had treated the lovebirds to Sunday brunch a week ago.

"Goddammit!"

While he shared Tom's rage, fear for the grad student tempered his anger. The twenty-two-year-old spoke with a hill country twang and his skin was pale enough to mingle with the Onward crowd. But he had no idea how dangerous his undercover scam might be.

Wolf dumped his uneaten lunch down the garbage disposal. He phoned his department secretary, told her where to find his final exams, and asked her to locate a proctor to monitor his class. "I'm sorry. It's truly an emergency."

He had to find that hot-blooded numbskull before he got killed.

Riley'd worked undercover. Maybe she could help.

TWENTY-ONE

Riley hustled her banged-up body to the auditorium-theater commandeered for the full staff assembly. Taking the podium, she looked out over a predominately male audience. Most officers were in their fifties or early sixties, ten to twenty years her senior. All seasoned professionals—ex-cops or retired military police, many with SWAT experience.

Thank God for small favors.

The officers cheered. One shouted, "You oughta see the other guy!"

Self-conscious, she brought her hand to her skinned cheek. She didn't mind the bawdy give and take. Got past that at Quantico. Men had their own way of showing respect. Something she'd earned by running the usual macho gauntlet. She held her own on the shooting range, and her martial arts skills were better than her typing. More importantly, she knew not to act like a know-it-all. When she arrived on campus, she listened to the veterans, accepted their advice.

She cleared her throat. "Let's get started."

Riley introduced Jeff and Gary, sneaking a glance at her ex's stony expression as she said his name. After welcoming the outsiders, she ceded the podium to Jeff. He kept his spiel short, stating facts, and asking for full cooperation. Gary described cyber efforts to trace the email's origin and the work underway to scour databases to identify Onward suspects and put them under court-ordered surveillance.

When Riley reclaimed the microphone, she stressed her priority—making BRU as secure as possible. She encouraged her officers to brainstorm.

"About fifteen hundred students have already completed finals and checked out of the dorms. That leaves two thousand on campus. Given that today's the last day for exams, our population will nosedive tomorrow.

"But we still have a big challenge. Our campus sprawls over six hundred acres with a perimeter of unpatrolled woods. BRU has always prided itself on its relationship with the community. Onward is forcing us to be less neighborly. We'll station a guard at the gate and check IDs. Only students, faculty, and staff will be allowed entry. Known vendors and contractors must be escorted. As of this moment, we're closed to the public."

Riley took a swig of the bottled water Patty had placed by the podium. "No new, unknown service personnel — landscapers, sanitation, food service, etc. — will be admitted. Period. Guards will inspect every incoming vehicle and package."

A hand rose in the audience. "Do we have enough manpower?"

"The FBI, SLED and the sheriff's office will help. But we're still understaffed so all leaves are canceled. We'll post new work schedules this afternoon."

Riley paused. "We *are* private. Check IDs on anyone suspicious. If there's any doubt, ask them to leave. No ID, no entry. Don't take any guff."

A black officer raised his hand. "How do I decide if a person's suspicious?" He grinned. "There are lots of scraggly-looking Caucasian students."

A nervous titter of laughter rose from the audience.

"True enough." Riley smiled. "We're not talking ethnic profiling. Onward appears to be well funded. That means it could recruit folks from any ethnic group."

A hand shot up in the front row. "Was the thug Ted shot last night with Onward?"

She chewed her lip. "No obvious connection, but I'm not a big believer in coincidence. The Harley was stolen, and the assailant carried no ID. The sheriff got a hit on his fingerprints. He was just released from prison."

She took a sip of water. Sounds of scuffling feet and muffled coughs filled the void. "If you believe Onward's email, the attack will come after midnight Friday—their deadline. It doesn't take a genius to guess the implied threat is Saturday's graduation."

A mumbled chorus of "damns" echoed in the auditorium.

"At two p.m. Saturday, we're expecting seven thousand people to applaud their children, grandchildren, friends and lovers who are graduating. Parking logistics and VIP security requests were already driving us batty. Now we need to revisit all arrangements. A last-minute venue change is a possibility. Call Pete and Bill with any ideas. It's Wednesday. We're running out of time."

She looked into the first row of seats and locked eyes with Ted. "I want to take one more moment of your time to salute Ted Sharp for his quick thinking. Ted, I owe you my life. Thank you."

Riley started clapping. Ted's fellow officers gave the blushing veteran a standing ovation. As she turned, her eyes met Gary's. She couldn't read his expression. Wistful? She looked away.

* * * *

L.J. stared out his window toward the BRU campus. Warmed by the bright May sunshine, the floor-to-ceiling glass radiated heat. The instant his cell phone chirped, he picked up. He didn't say hello.

"Gotta be quick," a voice whispered. "Not much privacy. You were right. The FBI is all over this, including some FBI honcho name of Gary Jacob. Looks like the bitch will make changes in security. Might even switch graduation locations. She suspects a link between the biker and Onward. No proof. It's only her gut. Someone's coming. Gotta go."

L.J. slipped the phone back in his pocket and smiled. He knew Gary Jacob was the Reid woman's ex-husband. Could prove a distraction.

Still Jacob might put a monkey wrench in his plans. The temptation to engage in a private game of cat-and-mouse with the security director had become irresistible, a compulsion. He'd already cast Riley Reid in the role of mouse, and cartoons to the contrary, such games rarely spelled victory for the rodent.

TWENTY-TWO

Riley groaned when Patty dumped a two-inch stack of printouts on her desk.

"Sorry. I attempted a first-level cull, but wasn't sure what you wanted."

"Neither am I." A tiny throb behind her eyes hinted of coming attractions. *Time to pop another pain pill?*

"Patty, would you please set up a meeting on commencement security with Pete and Alan for eight a.m.? Block out two hours."

Given the Onward threat, Riley hoped this year's celebrity parents would opt out. As a respected private school, BRU often attracted the children of high-ranking officials and well-heeled, sometimes controversial, public figures. Two of this year's VIP dads had recently received death threats. One was a fertility specialist experimenting with cloning in a third-world clinic. The other was a CEO who bankrupted his company's employee pension fund with a stock manipulation scheme.

Patty jotted a note on her steno pad. "Two calls rolled over to voice mail while I was visiting the ladies' room. One from Dr. Valdes." The admin sighed theatrically. "That man is one fine specimen. Though I usually prefer dark cocoa, he makes milk chocolate look yummy."

Riley laughed. "Oh, yeah? Want me to share that verdict with your hubby?" Wed for thirty-five years, Patty and Charlie had five children and twelve grandkids.

"No, ma'am." Patty giggled. "You don't tattle to Charlie, and I won't tell your mama on you—which reminds me you'd better call her."

Riley played back her messages. John Hunter was first up, miffed that he'd had to hear about the biker attack and Onward via a newscast. "Thanks heavens the FBI has taken over. I'll come over tonight, grill us some steaks. Make damn sure no one else tries to kill you."

What made him imagine she'd scurry home once the FBI cavalry arrived? The assumption she needed his protection made her teeth ache.

Okay. Unclench. You're in a bad mood. You'd be torqued if he offered to kiss your feet.

She smiled at the preposterous image. She'd tell John—diplomatically—she had other plans.

Wolf's message started out as a mood lifter. Ellen was in good health and spirits. The reunion with her dad a success. Then he delivered the bombshell. "Ellen confessed she stabbed herself."

Riley ground her teeth. *I told Wolf not to question her. Damn!* What if the kid decides she's been wronged and waffles on her story down the road? There was a right way to handle these bombshells. Questioning the girl alone wasn't it.

She vented with a few under-her-breath mutters before she called her mom.

"Good morning, Reid residence," her mother answered.

Riley rolled her eyes. Her mother believed Southern ladies always kept the silver polished, the beds made, and answered the phone in a fashion that said good manners ruled this home.

"Hey, Mom." Riley twirled the cord on her desk phone as she pictured her mother in her customary sweater set and pearls. "Sorry I couldn't take you to the doctor's. Did you cancel?"

"No, Riley Yates Reid, I did not cancel. John Hunter was kind enough to escort me. I didn't call to talk about *my* day. I saw that TV report."

Her mother's emphysema offered a tiny respite in the form of a wheeze. But Riley knew the oxygen-refueling pause wouldn't end her tirade.

"Why didn't you tell me you were mauled last night? For heaven's sake, am I the last to know your life's threatened? I can't believe you didn't come home. That you spent the night alone."

Riley knew how quickly her mom's disposition would head south if she knew Wolf had slept on her couch.

"Mom, TV blows everything out of proportion. I'm fine—a few scrapes. No big deal."

"Riley, I was married to a detective. He never brought his work home, but I understood the danger. I'm old, not senile. Your attacker was shot to death. It *is* a big deal."

Okay. Time for a little conversational two-step.

"You're right. I should have called. It was the middle of the night. No point waking you to fret about something that was over and done. Now, how did John end up taking you to the doctor? You didn't call him, did you?"

"Of course not." Pearl huffed in indignation. "John came by to visit his father. He took Lewis out for a bit of fresh air. I ran into them when I walked to the mailbox. We chatted and John volunteered."

Riley pictured the encounter. Lewis Hunter dozing in his wheelchair. Miz Pearl spotting the father and son from her window and hustling out to make *accidental* contact with the man she wanted for a son-in-law.

John would have welcomed the interaction. The senior Mr. Hunter's mind was as crippled as his body. He no longer knew his son. Yet John faithfully visited three times a week. His devotion touched Riley. The fact that Lewis's condition was self-inflicted made John's loyalty all the more gallant. John's mother had his father after his dad lost the family fortune. His dad couldn't cope. Put a gun to his head while sitting on the steps of the BRU building named for him. The attempted suicide failed.

The Yates and Hunter families had four generations of history. When Riley's widowed mother returned to the Shelby area, she couldn't resist playing matchmaker for her daughter with the very eligible John Hunter, a man who hadn't let bad fortune ruin him.

Initially Riley enjoyed John's attentions. He was smart. Successful. Respectable. A church deacon. Good looking, too. Fifty-two with chiseled features, brown puppy-dog eyes, and wavy silver hair. Unfortunately they held opposing views on almost every social issue.

Her mother's voice brought her back. "John's worried about you, honey. That TV report came on while we were in the doctor's waiting room. He couldn't believe you were injured and hadn't phoned. He thinks you work too hard and have way too much stress."

He's spot on with that. Still she didn't cotton to John gossiping with her mother. It felt as if the grownups were deciding how to handle a naughty ten-year-old.

"Listen, Mom, I have to run. Your checkup was okay? Need me to come by tonight?"

"No, sweetheart. You go straight home and rest. We'll catch up later."

No matter how trying her mother seemed to outsiders, Riley knew her love was genuine.

She returned to her teetering paperwork pile. Patty's Google search had produced a passel of hits about campus threats and Onward. Like the Ku Klux Klan, this group operated in secret, loosely linked cells. For the fragmented organization to make coordinated threats against five colleges seemed totally out of whack. Could Onward have recruited students on the targeted campuses?

She phoned her friend Barb at the Southern Poverty Law Center for some unofficial intel. As she wrapped up that conversation, Patty appeared and used her finger to draw a line across her throat—a not-so-subtle signal to hang up. Riley rushed a thank you.

"What?"

"Dr. Sparks phoned. A student, Rosalind Perez, is in critical condition at the hospital. He's already made travel arrangements for her parents. She's from Puerto Rico."

"A car crash?" Vehicle accidents were the number one cause of serious student trauma.

Patty shuddered. "A truck mowed the girl down. The sheriff's investigating. It's possible Onward's involved."

"What? My God! How?"

"That's all I know. Dr. Sparks wants you to talk to the deputies and doctors and get the facts before the girl's parents arrive—or Reverend Jimmy launches a new rant."

"Okay." She slipped her cell and car keys into her jacket pockets. "Call if there's another emergency."

As Riley reached the office entrance, Wolf barreled through the massive front door. He slammed into her. She buckled and slid halfway to the floor before he scooped her up. She felt his taut muscles, the rapid thud of his heart. A tangy scent of musk and lime confused her senses.

"We need to talk." Wolf righted her. "It's an emergency."

Riley didn't know whether to laugh or cry. *Get in line.*

TWENTY-THREE

L.J. whistled as he strolled toward Art Whitten's office. He'd shaken off his disappointment about the biker attack. The plan was good. Damn good. It would survive this setback.

He nodded a greeting to his partner's executive assistant.

"Go right in. He's expecting you."

Hunched over a gleaming mahogany desk, Art's balding head bobbed up briefly. His coal black eyes darted to his vice president, then back to his task.

L.J. claimed his customary chair and tilted back to stretch his legs. Art would talk when he was ready. His former brother-in-law liked to provide the occasional reminder that, while L.J. owned forty-nine percent of Whitten stock, he owned fifty-one percent. Controlling interest.

While L.J. didn't actually *like* Art, he admired him. The man took cunning and greed to impressive heights. Plus he never questioned his weakling sister's untimely death, just a few weeks after old man Whitten kicked the bucket. Art knew a profitable alliance when he saw one.

Art shoved aside some papers. "I understand funerals were held for our D.C. friends."

Though the soundproof office was swept regularly for bugs, the men talked obliquely.

"The bodies are ashes now," L.J. confirmed. "Our DoD friend was incinerated in his car crash. The reporter's family cremated him."

Art's eyes bored into L.J.'s. "What about the paper trail that got us into this mess?" His tone left no doubt where he assigned the blame.

Damn you. Art had suggested using the real estate swaps and set an impossible deadline.

Over the years, Whitten Industries had bribed its DoD "friend" — Beck — a dozen times. When a contract worth billions came up, the procurement officer upped the ante. Buying a piece of property from Beck for half a million above market value was Art's brainchild. Though L.J. filtered the deal through three cutout corporations, Oldfield, the busybody reporter, found a tie between Whitten Industries and one leg of the transaction.

"The property transfer records have vanished," L.J. answered. "And the *Washington Post* was shocked to learn its ace investigator left no notes on the scandal he was pursuing."

Nice of Oldfield to keep a complete electronic journal.

The reporter's journal confirmed he'd shared details of his scoop with just one person, Senator Yates. Oldfield wanted to finish fact checking before plunking a full-blown exposé on his editor's desk. As soon as Senator Yates died, all threats would disappear.

"We're ruined if we lose this contract," Art reminded. "We leveraged our projected profits on the Beck deal to finance the merger with Allied Armaments. Our stock will sink like the Titanic if the deal falls through. Even a delay for a half-assed investigation would be catastrophic."

L.J. chafed at the lecture. He understood the consequences — corporate and personal. He fisted his hands. He wanted to leap over the desk and pummel Art. Feel the cartilage in his nose snap. Hear his bones break. Reunite him with his dear departed sister.

They'd worked together for years. L.J. started as Whitten's corporate attorney. After he married Art's sister, he moved steadily up the family company's hierarchy. Normally Art's Little Napoleon blame games didn't bother him. Today L.J. struggled to swallow the words he longed to scream. *If I fry, so will you, sucker.*

When Art broke eye contact, L.J. wondered if he'd gotten a mental whiff of his anger.

"If we . . . *graduate* to the next step, you're certain we'll remain blameless?" Art asked.

"I'm certain. Our surrogate's agenda is light years from our dollars-and-cents interests."

L. J. simply needed to keep all hands rowing in the same direction—a challenge when some Onward knights didn't seem to have two oars to put in the water.

He kept his doubts to himself. No need to step Art through Saturday's bombing a second time. They'd hashed out the details two days ago while sitting on an isolated park bench.

Onward's two bombs would be delivered at 2:15 p.m. The second attached GPS devices confirmed delivery, L.J.'s cell phone would detonate the third, primary bomb. Its fifty-foot kill zone would incinerate the senator along with everyone else seated in the VIP section.

While the punier Onward explosives would do little more than blow up the delivery boys, they'd add to the panic and ensure the home-grown terrorists shouldered the blame. Authorities would have no reason to question who benefited from Yates' passing. A tragic collateral loss.

A smile crept across L.J.'s face. The FBI and the campus cops were focused on Onward. That made Pearl Yates Reid the perfect improvised explosive device. As the senator's only sister, she'd have a place of honor at her niece's commencement. Too bad she had to die. He had a soft spot for the old lady.

Art nodded approval. "You're absolutely sure it'll end here? This is a huge risk."

He motioned L.J. to follow him onto the office balcony and activated a white noise device. The men faced the building's bricks so no one with binoculars could read their lips.

"This wraps it," L.J. assured Art. "Oldfield warned Yates that his staff was compromised, which, of course, it is. Lucky for us the senator selected our mole to look into Oldfield's allegations. When the senator dies, Charles will destroy all evidence."

"How can you be so confident this Charles will do as he promises? What if he has a last-minute bout of conscience when his boss's remains are scraped into sandwich bags?"

L.J. shook his head. "He's desperate. His lover has full-blown AIDS and no health insurance. We're giving him a million reasons to bury this."

"Okay, let's do it," Art said. "They can't hang us twice."

Before L.J. departed, his partner dictated a couple minor changes to the plan. He was displeased BRU's security director remained a wild card. However, he agreed that killing the Reid woman wasn't a viable option. They needed her mother to attend graduation, not likely to happen if the woman's only daughter was on ice in a morgue.

They needed Riley Reid disabled or distracted, not dead.

TWENTY-FOUR

Riley's shoulder felt on fire. The collision with Wolf reinvigorated all the pain-carrying neurons muted by her pills. She cradled her arm to increase the sling's support.

"You have an emergency? Take a number. Let's see, you're ninety-nine."

A second after she barked, she processed Wolf's expression.

"Sorry. I can tell you have a serious problem." She met his stormy gaze. "I'm sure Pete can help—"

"No."

Riley shook her head. "I'm en route to the hospital. A student has been hit by a truck—"

"Rosie Perez. I'll drive. We'll talk on the way."

How in hell did Wolf know about Rosalind Perez? And why was this man suddenly tangled up in all her crises?

Wolf hustled her toward a battered, mud-splattered Jeep Wrangler with an empty gun rack. Not the ride she'd pictured for a dashing professor/novelist. As she slid into the passenger seat, she remembered he'd used her Honda to chauffeur her to the hospital and home. That meant he'd been stranded at her house.

"I didn't offer you a ride home this morning. I apologize. Afraid I was out of it."

"No problem. I live two miles away. A quick jog."

Wolf kept the speedometer five miles above the speed limit and spoke at an equally brisk clip as he relayed his grad student's message.

"Did you try to call him back?" Riley asked.

"Yeah, no answer."

"Your student—Tom—what's he like?"

"Very bright, but he has a temper and a smart mouth. I can't imagine him pulling off an undercover stunt. Some thug will spout off, and Tom will take the bait. That'll cut it. He should be sitting beside Rosie's bed, not playing avenging hero."

Automotive snails clogged the right lane. To the left, a car doddered along at forty-five miles an hour, making it impossible to pass. Wolf punched the horn three staccato beeps. "Always one clown who doesn't get the concept of a passing lane."

Riley turned toward him. "Do you really think Tom can hook up with the terrorists? The FBI doesn't have any concrete leads on the local Onward cell."

Wolf snorted. "They're not asking the right folks. I get an update whenever I go hunting with my uncle. Onward's on a big recruiting kick. Mostly rednecks. Mad as hell about illegal immigrants, gays, blacks, rich Yankees buying up mountain tracts, you name it."

Her breath caught at Wolf's mention of his uncle. No name needed. *Focus on Onward.*

"Have they recruited many locals?" she asked. "FBI intel indicates only a small band of supporters in upstate South Carolina. The local ringleaders are deemed garden-variety blowhards."

Wolf's shrug increased her unease. While the Greater Greenville atmosphere seemed progressive, Riley had eavesdropped on some chilling conversations. Some hatreds festered for decades, just waiting for the right provocation to ooze into a virulent pustule.

"Did your uncle give you any idea how many people belong to the local cell?"

"His guess is thirty hard-core members. Sympathizers worry him more. I doubt he knows where they meet, but I'll ask."

"So how would Tom hook up?"

The slowpoke in the passing lane moved over. Wolf stomped on the accelerator. "If I were Tom, I'd try bars or pool halls near where they attacked Rosie. Pose as someone who lost a job because a manufacturing plant moved to Mexico. Tom graduated from Mount Anna High School. He knows the lingo."

Riley bit her lip, recalling her undercover days and how bile inched up her throat when the neo-Nazis she pretended to befriend spoke about exterminating inferiors. "He's playing a damned dangerous game. No support. No backup. I'll ask the sheriff to put a BOLO on him. Maybe they can pick him up before he finds a heap of trouble."

"No. Don't." Wolf took his eyes off the road long enough to shoot her a warning look. "Uncle Ray told me one more thing. At least one Leeds County deputy belongs to Onward."

"What?"

"You heard right. Didn't surprise me. I grew up here. I'm not saying there aren't decent deputies. But law enforcement can attract bullies, too. Gives them a license to pound people."

She watched his hands tighten on the steering wheel.

"When I was a kid, one deputy loved to taunt me. Said I ought to be called the 'cigar-store injun' since I had a squaw for a granny and Castro's cousin for a grandpa.'"

Riley stayed quiet, unable to imagine an apt response. Instead she focused on Tom.

"Could we charge your graduate assistant with a trumped-up crime? Say he's suspected of stealing student identities. That's practically a cottage industry."

Wolf shook his head. "Won't work. Release his name in conjunction with BRU and someone will Google him. He and Rosie made a YouTube video together."

"Dammit. Everyone surfs the Internet these days. If Onward was responsible for last night's email, some Onward 'knight' knows his way around a keyboard. Without cover, Tom's odds get worse. I hope Onward doesn't do background checks on new recruits."

"Dammit." Wolf groaned. "They might. Especially if a stranger seems too nosy."

They swung into the hospital's short-term parking lot, and Riley gripped the door handle before the engine stopped. "Let's hope Rosie's conscious and can describe her attackers. Find them, and maybe we find Tom."

TWENTY-FIVE

Riley detested hospitals. The synthetic brightness. The chemical odor that invaded every breath. The hushed conversations. Did the floor's acrylic sheen make it easier to mop up blood?

She spotted Deputies Katko and McClure in the waiting room. She'd worked with both men on the Amanda Coffey case. A dozen young people stood in two-and three-person knots. Tear-streaked faces marked them as Rosie's friends.

They shouldn't be here. Rosie shouldn't be here.

Riley caught Katko's eye. He nodded toward a couple of vacant chairs.

"I'm going to speak with that officer," she told Wolf. "Why don't you chat with the students? See if they saw or heard something."

She slunk into a pea-green chair beside Katko. The molded shell proved as uncomfortable as it was ugly.

The deputy didn't wait for obvious questions. "She's clinging to life. The docs give her fifty-fifty odds. Surgeons are still working on her. They treated a collapsed lung and removed a piece of her skull to relieve the pressure on her swollen brain."

"Goddammit," Riley interjected. "Any leads?"

Katko motioned toward a black man, sitting alone, his meaty hands massaging his head as he stared at the floor. "Truck driver's a basket case. Couldn't tell us much. But we found a waiter, who'd been sneaking a smoke when four or five punks dragged the girl into an alley. He didn't see faces just orange caps. Heard one yell, 'Gonna send you stinking wetbacks back to Taco-land.'"

"Good Lord. Is Onward involved?"

"Can't prove it," the deputy grumbled. "Not all of our local bigots are joiners. Could have been your run-of-the-mill white trash getting their jollies."

"What about the orange caps? Are they part of some uniform?"

"Nah. I've seen dozens. Some right-wing conservative group shipped them to mom-and-pop stores as freebies. The gas station by the hospital has 'em sitting by the cash register with a 'FREE, take one!' sign."

"Are these right-wingers tied to Onward?"

"Haven't a clue. The caps have a 'Take America Back' logo. You'll have to ask your FBI buddies about the group. Never heard of 'em before this."

Riley fisted her hands. "No one got a good look at the attackers?"

"Nope. They scattered like cockroaches. Didn't happen in the best section of Shelby. The girl was dropping clothes at a dry cleaner. Half the stores on that side street are boarded up. We're damned lucky the waiter needed a tobacco fix."

"Get any leads from the fiancé?"

Her mention of the fiancé earned her a how-do-you-know-about-him look before Katko shrugged. "The boyfriend's number popped up on the girl's cell phone. I questioned him. Felt like I'd just hung up when he barreled into the ER."

"He didn't stay?" Riley wanted a better handle on the boy's frame of mind.

"No. He was pretty tore up. When he couldn't see his girl, he took off. Said he couldn't stand it."

Riley longed to tell the deputy he'd unleashed a vigilante. But Wolf's allegation that Onward had a pipeline into the sheriff's office stopped her. She trusted Katko, but she didn't know his buddies.

"Thanks for the update. Sheriff Hendricks is working the Onward threat with the FBI. Be sure to fill him in. My gut tells me Onward's to blame. Keep me in the loop, will you? The trickle down doesn't always reach us low-lying mushrooms."

"Sure." Katko stood. "Goes both ways. Call with any campus leads about boys making trouble for Rosie."

Riley touched Katko's arm. "Anything new on Amanda's murder? I keep wondering how the killer got into her apartment."

"That case haunts me, too. Whenever there's time I go back over our lists. Classmates, professors, folks in her church choir, delivery boys. The killer's in there somewhere."

The deputy turned to leave, then spoke over his shoulder. "Docs say it'll be at least twenty-four hours before we can question Ms. Perez—if she makes it."

* * * *

Wolf didn't know any of the students in the waiting room. His gaze fell on a black man, alone and clearly grief stricken.

The fellow stood to stretch. His name—Chuck—was sewn on the pocket of the regional trucking firm's uniform. Even absent that clue, the man's slumped shoulders and hanging head identified him as the driver of the truck that hit Rosie.

Wolf sat beside him. "Hey, man, I heard you did all you could for her."

The trucker looked up as Wolf stuck out his hand. "Wolf Valdes. Rosie's one of my students."

"I swear to God I never saw the kid." Chuck seemed eager to talk. "Never had a chance to put on the brakes. When I got out . . . oh, God, her body was all broke."

"But you called 911 right away."

"It seemed to take forever, though the cops say it was only minutes."

"Did Rosie say anything?"

"No." Chuck looked at the floor. "She couldn't."

"What about the men? See any of their faces?"

"Nah, man. Wish I had. The bastards ran when I got out of the truck. All I saw was a flash of orange and their backs as they took off. They were young. I could tell from how they ran. Wore jeans and T-shirts. But I saw their arms . . . they was white."

Wolf wondered if there was anything else he could ask. "Did they yell anything, maybe call to one another as they hightailed it out of there?"

Chuck's forehead creased. "Now that you mention it, one yelled something. I'm not sure but it might have been Smith or Smitty."

Wolf spotted Riley walking his way. He stood and patted Chuck's arm. "Take it easy, man."

He fell into step beside her. "Learn anything?"

"Rosie's odds are fifty-fifty, and there's no proof Onward's involved. A waiter heard the boys taunting her, calling her a stinking wetback."

"Damn," Wolf growled.

"How about you? Pick up any tidbits?"

"The trucker only saw the backs of Rosie's attackers. But he says they were young and white. All wore orange ball caps."

"Okay. Let's get back to campus."

He touched her sleeve. "Don't you want to see Ellen first?"

TWENTY-SIX

How could I have forgotten Ellen?

"Of course," Riley answered. "You know her room number, right?"

The private room was two floors down. The door was open and sunlight flooded the white-on-white space.

Color had returned to the blonde's cheeks. Ellen giggled. The middle-aged man sitting on the edge of her bed smiled. Father and daughter watched a wall-mounted TV. Ellen's laughter died the moment she saw Riley. In contrast, Wolf's appearance earned a fleeting smile.

Riley introduced herself to the father and said she needed to ask Ellen a few questions. Panic crumpled the coed's face.

"Can't this wait?" The father scowled as his gaze raked over Riley's purpling bruises.

"It's okay, Steve," Wolf intervened. "Ms. Reid didn't earn those black-and-blue marks in a barroom brawl. She's quite peaceable, only here to help."

Apparently Wolf's word was gold. Wolf led Steve to a corner of the room, and Riley walked to Ellen's bed. "Professor Valdes is right. I want to help."

The girl didn't look convinced.

"Listen, Ellen. No one will press charges. I just need to understand what happened."

The girl haltingly repeated her confession. Riley patted her arm. "It's okay."

She glanced at the men. Wolf had his arm draped around the shorter man's shoulder.

"I can't begin to thank you," Steve said. "If I can ever do anything for you, call me Maybe I can hack into the CIA files to get material for one of your novels."

The good mood proved infectious. In the past twenty-four hours, the professor had climbed several notches in Riley's estimation. She doubted—no, she knew—she couldn't have accomplished half as much without his help.

Ellen begged Wolf to do one of his "routines." Kids flocked to his lectures for two reasons—a hope he might read an erotic passage from his novel and his humorous skits. The professor surrendered and conducted a mock literary debate between Robert Frost and Edgar Allen Poe. He changed his voice—and scrunched his features—to play both roles.

Ellen giggled, and Riley grinned.

As they left the building, she touched Wolf's arm. "You were great. Really great."

Wolf stopped, spun Riley around, and gripped her shoulders. He lowered his head, bringing them eye-to-eye.

"This past year you've done a superb job of pretending we're total strangers. No history." His iron grip and blazing eyes squelched the scream bubbling at the back of her throat.

"If you didn't figure it out on Hilton Head, by now you know why I left. Once you said you were Senator Yates' niece, I had no choice. That meant you were Jack Reid's sister. You were still going by your married name when we met. I had no clue."

Riley's pulse thundered in her ears. "You snuck out, you coward. How do you think I felt, waking to an empty bed? We'd spent two days making love. I'd told you my husband threw me over for a pregnant girlfriend. You knew I was vulnerable."

"What could I have said?" Wolf released her. "I figured you'd rather not know you'd slept with the enemy. Your mother and uncle have made it plain what they think of my family. Dirty, lying, stinking lowlifes. Murderers. The stress of Hank's trial killed my aunt. She died less than three months after my cousin's acquittal."

Her breath came in staccato puffs. Anger floated in the air, contagious. "Your last name was Valdes. You taught at a college in Vermont. I had no idea Ray Youngblood was your uncle, or that Hank Youngblood was your cousin. I had to find that out from the *N.Y. Times*. You owed me the truth."

"Truth? What do you know about truth? Your uncle almost sold his lies to the jury. Your brother died because the senator's son was a bullying asshole."

Riley's heart thumped wildly. She slapped Wolf so hard the contact jarred her whole body. He spun away.

"Wolf," she called.

He kept walking. She hurried after him. Her bruised ribs punished her with each step. This conversation wasn't finished.

* * * *

By the time he reached his Wrangler, Wolf regretted he'd snapped and called her dead cousin an asshole. Not exactly the resolution he'd hoped for.

But he couldn't let go of his rage. His cousin eventually moved two-thousand miles away to escape Senator Yates' influential reach. Acquittal hadn't protected Hank from good-old-boy backlash. He couldn't even get a tooth filled. Amazing how South Carolina dentists had full patient rosters when Hank Youngblood called. And Ray. His uncle became a virtual hermit.

He heard Riley's footsteps. Did she want to slap him again? Call him worse names than coward? Though sorely tempted to leave the passenger door locked, he pushed the button on his key fob twice. She climbed inside.

He put the key in the ignition.

Riley reached over and touched his hand. "Wolf, I knew the truth about my cousin." Her voice was soft. "Dad was a Chicago detective. He flew down to South Carolina when Jack died. Wanted to find out for himself what happened. Dad blamed Will Yates as much as he did Hank Youngblood. It all came out in the trial. Will insulted your cousin's date. Then, after Hank decked him, my cousin Will retaliated with a baseball bat. That pretty well made the car chase inevitable."

Wolf turned toward Riley. "But your mother and uncle—"

"Couldn't accept the truth. Their sons were seventeen. I loved my older brother." A tear meandered down Riley's cheek. "But I never bought into mom's or Uncle Ed's hate."

Wolf nodded. "Hank wasn't blameless." He paused. "Did your father share his opinion with your mother and uncle?"

"Yes. It opened a huge family rift. If Dad hadn't been killed on the job, Mom might have divorced him. I kept quiet. Mom didn't need more grief."

Wolf searched her face. "So what would you have done, if I'd told you the truth on Hilton Head?"

"I don't know. Probably I'd have walked away. But I can't seem to forget that weekend." She took a deep breath. "That doesn't mean we'll ever end up in bed again. Our family history is only one reason. I'm through with Casanovas."

Her cheeks flushed. "I read your book. You weren't even thinking about me in that bed. You were picturing your fictional Kayla and her honking big tits."

Wolf started to laugh. A big, booming laugh. He couldn't help it, although he could tell his reaction re-ignited Riley's desire to beat the snot out of him. Her multi-hued cat eyes narrowed to slits.

"Hellfire, Riley." He grinned at her fury. "Kayla's a cliché. I invented her because I wasn't about to share you with anyone else."

He reached across the seat, pulled her against his body, and kissed her.

She pushed him away, creating a small space between them. "Wolf . . ." Her voice quavered, though he sensed anger was no longer the fuel. She stared at her fisted knuckles. Her nails dug red crescents into her ivory skin.

"I told you about my ex-husband." Her voice roughened. "We were married fifteen years. He was monogamous for one."

She lifted her head to meet his gaze. "Don't get me wrong. I'm not shopping for a husband, or expecting a pledge of undying love. But neither do I view making love as meaningless aerobic exercise."

The silence lengthened. Wolf decided she'd said her piece. Then he noticed her teeth worrying her lip. The tell signaled she had more on her mind. "What else? You're holding back."

She lifted an eyebrow. "You didn't meet the real Riley Reid on Hilton Head. I was hurt. I wanted to lose myself. I did. In ways I never imagined. That weekend meant more than I intended. It scared me."

Wolf kept his gaze locked on her. "I thought you law-enforcement types were supposed to give the accused the benefit of the doubt. Innocent until proven guilty. You convicted me without a trial."

He sensed she was preparing to argue. When they met, her willingness to challenge him excited him. Not now. He reached his hand across the divide and gently placed two fingers against her soft lips.

"Don't jump to conclusions. Besides, I should be allowed to defend myself. Maybe take a lie detector test or offer character witnesses."

"You're making fun of me." But the corners of her mouth hitched upward. "Okay, maybe we both deserve a trial. But rest assured, if you call character witnesses, I won't go easy. I'm a trained interrogator."

He watched her amusement evaporate. The light faded from her calico irises. Her gaze carried the punch of a sudden cold front. It took a second for Wolf to realize she was staring beyond him, out the window. A man's knuckles rapped on the car door and a pair of calculating blue eyes assessed Wolf. Then the man's gaze riveted on Riley.

"Riley, I need to speak to you in private." Though polite, the words were an order, not a request. "Ride back to Blue Ridge with me. We'll talk on the way."

Riley turned to Wolf. "I'll only be a minute. Don't leave without me."

She climbed out of the Jeep.

What the…? Wolf stared as the man briskly circled the car. He latched onto Riley's arm—the one outside the sling—as if he had every right to control her, possess her. Wolf wanted to pummel the guy. His muscles tensed. He cracked his door open, ready to jump out.

Riley's tone stopped him. Her voice was dry ice, simultaneously fiery and freezing. Instinctively he understood she wanted to handle this alone.

"What are you doing, Gary?"

Gary? Her ex-husband. What the devil was he doing here?

The man maneuvered her farther from the Jeep. His broad back blocked Wolf's view of Riley's face. The couple's exchange became muffled. Only agitated whispers reached his ears.

Should I confront him? No, don't be a sexist jerk. But by God, he'd look better with a smashed nose and blackened eyes.

Wolf slumped unhappily in his seat. Riley and Gary shifted positions, giving him a clear view of Riley's face. Her body language communicated no sense of danger.

A moment later she yanked her arm free and walked back to the Jeep. She slid inside and slammed the car door.

"Let's go." Her seatbelt snapped shut with the fury of a bear trap.

Wolf closed his door and started the engine as the pissed stranger glared at him. *Tough, buddy. She's with me. At least for the moment.*

Wolf had to find out why Romeo was prowling about. Hadn't he done enough damage?

TWENTY-SEVEN

L.J. parked two blocks from the security director's home. The afternoon was bright and cloudless. Mirrored sunglasses hid a quarter of his face, the trendy, wrap-around frames providing a benign mask.

The uncharacteristic cold snap was losing its grip. The weatherman predicted temperatures climbing into the seventies by late afternoon. While the forecast made his cashmere topcoat overkill, the garment hid his build. The cost? A thin patina of sweat on his forehead.

Though hardly dressed for a stroll around the block, he figured any nosy neighbor would dismiss him as an insurance salesman. He strode past a meticulously restored Victorian. Renovation crews made a tidy profit in the gentrified neighborhood.

Enormous azalea bushes edging his target's deep porch cast a convenient umbrella of darkness as he slid a key into the front door lock. The cost of the key and security pass code had been minimal. He'd made nice with Miz Pearl and rummaged her pocketbook when she visited the powder room. Bless old ladies and their zippered purse compartments.

As the alarm's warning chirps sounded, his fingers flew over the keypad. A comforting silence descended as he punched in the fifth number. The irony wasn't lost on him. Tsk. Tsk. A security chief should know better than write down her digital code for anyone, even her mother.

L.J. consulted his watch. Two-thirty and the lady of the house rarely arrived home before six. Still he'd restrict his visit to sixty minutes.

He shucked his topcoat, set his briefcase on a side table, and extracted his tools. He glanced at a photo given a place of honor. Graduation day with Senator Yates and her mother. *An omen?* He had to give her credit. She didn't trade on her family connections. Of course she'd grown up in Chicago as a Reid, far removed from the Southern aristocrats populating the Yates family tree.

L.J. tugged off his leather driving gloves and tossed them on his coat. He studied the senator's smiling face. He'd always welcomed L.J.'s campaign donations, but now the politician was ready to play Mr. Tidy-Bowl, intent on cleaning out DoD toilets and flushing him into the sewer.

He slipped on skin-tight surgeon's gloves and flexed his fingers. Much better.

L.J. had a bachelor's degree in electrical engineering. Household wiring was a piece of cake, and he loved electronic gadgetry. He targeted the wireless Internet connection first. In under eight minutes, he arranged for every keystroke sent or received to create a phantom twin on his screen.

He treated his next project as a game of hide-and-seek. Where to conceal video feeds? They needed to be hidden yet poised to capture conversations. Since police would be summoned, the devices had to go undetected during a pro forma household search. Of course, the cops wouldn't be looking for sophisticated spyware.

Now for the fun stuff.

He opened the door to the basement, and a black fur ball shot past him. "Damn cat," he muttered as his heart rate slowed. Then the notion dawned—a dead pussy could be a highly effective postscript. One small furry sacrifice for greater psychological harm.

"Here, kitty, kitty," he cooed as he switched on the stairwell light. The stairs squeaked in complaint. The basement—somewhat rare in vintage Sunbelt homes—felt

damp and chilly, a good fifteen degrees cooler than the first
floor.

While the upper floors had been retrofitted with granite
countertops and cosmetic nods to twenty-first century style,
there'd been no renovations below. Open stairs teetered on the
cusp of rickety. The old treads spongy.

The stairs led to a low-ceilinged, cobwebbed space. A
switch controlled the stairwell bulb. In the cellar itself, pull
strings controlled each of the three bare bulbs that lit specific
areas.

L.J. yanked the string dangling from the first socket, then
the second. The water heater and an HVAC unit lined the back
wall. To the side, a moldy workbench showcased a jumble of
old hand tools. A rusted saw lay on top.

"Here, kitty. Damned cat's like the woman. Uppity." The
feline would turn up.

L.J. tripped the breaker to the water heater. One icy shower
and she'd come down to check. He grabbed the saw. Two-thirds
of the way up the stairs he stopped. Sawing the old wood
proved hard work. Sweat plastered the dress shirt to his back.

Recalling one of his father's old sayings— "The fall won't
kill you. But the landing might."—he checked the landing zone.
Nothing lethal. The descent would be painful, not fatal.

After unscrewing the light bulb above the booby-trapped
tread, he substituted the burned-out one he'd brought. At the
top of the stairs, he flipped the light switch to its off position
and left the door ajar. Maybe Miss Puss would slink out of
hiding once he moved away.

He stopped briefly at the refrigerator then headed to the
bedroom. His tongue moistened his lips as he rummaged her
neatly folded underwear. He frowned in disappointment. No
silk. No bikini underpants. No lacy bustiers. Only cotton
panties, utilitarian bras, ribbed white socks.

No wonder her husband left. Bitch had no imagination.

Again, a vision of Riley seized him. She cowered on her knees—nude—pleading. His initial reasons for sidelining the security director remained. Alongside them, a new itch. He longed to punish this woman, break her will.

L.J. recalled the look on his wife's face as the heart attack stole her life. He hadn't actually *killed* his spouse. Just withheld the tiny nitroglycerin pill as she sucked air and her face turned cartoon shades. What crime? She was weak. It was nature's way.

He shook his head. Riley was fit. *But not as fit as me.* How would her face look when she admitted that truth?

L.J. glanced at his watch. Ten minutes left. Enough time to corral the damn cat?

TWENTY-EIGHT

Wolf started the Jeep and kept silent until he merged into I-85's northbound traffic. "Let me take a wild guess. Gary's your former husband, right? Why's he here?"

He glanced sideways. His passenger sat ramrod straight, her face a stiff mask.

"Gary heads the FBI's Domestic Terrorism Section. He's on-site commander for the Onward investigation."

"Is the FBI that stupid? Surely they could have sent somebody else. How can they expect you to work with him?"

"Easy. Gary has excellent credentials. Stopping Onward is all that matters. We can put our feelings aside for a few days."

"Bullshit. If you two weren't ready to duke it out, you were giving a pretty good imitation."

"Just clearing up jurisdictional boundaries. Gary was upset I didn't call him the minute I heard Onward might have played a role in Rosie's assault. He thinks all this may tie together, provide leads."

"And your answer?"

"I wanted to assess relevance before wasting FBI and task force resources on a wild goose chase. I reminded him I'm not some schlock rent-a-cop. I'm a trained operative."

"Well, I'm no 'trained operative,' but I could tell Mr. FBI had more than Onward on his mind. He looked daggers at me. The man has feelings for you. Possessive, husband-type feelings. He's jealous. What did he do, assume I was your boy toy?"

The corners of Riley's mouth twitched upward. "He didn't *assume* it. I told him you were my lover."

"You what?"

"I didn't think you'd mind. I wanted to make it clear I'd moved on."

Wolf laughed. "Great, just what I need—a jealous ex licensed to use lethal force. It's okay. I bet my gun's as big as his." He glanced at her. "I do own a rifle—a black-powder primitive—but I'm better with a bow and arrow."

He returned his gaze to the road. "I don't want you caught in a lie though. I'd be glad to renew that lover description."

* * * *

Riley couldn't believe he made her laugh. How to answer his tease? Last night, she invited him into her bed while snockered on painkillers. Was she ready to reissue the invitation? Goose bumps raced up her arms. She closed her eyes and fantasized . . . tonight? A flush of warmth ambushed her.

Her cell phone vibrated. She pulled it from her pocket and stifled a groan when she saw the caller ID. John Hunter. *Dammit.* She let the call go to voice mail.

She resolved to break it off with John. Relief accompanied the decision. For weeks her lukewarm feelings toward the man had been edging toward frost. She harbored a sneaking suspicion John would welcome the reprieve—despite the roses. His declarations of affection seemed pro forma. Their break-up would sadden only one person. Her mom kept hinting how BRU's gardens offered a lovely setting for a wedding.

Wolf took the BRU exit from I-85. "Maybe I can help with Onward. I'll visit Ray and find out what he knows."

Riley frowned. "You told me Ray's become a hermit. Is he stable? I don't mean to restart our argument, but could he belong to Onward?"

He snorted. "Ray's not exactly the right color. To Onward, red, as in Indian, is almost as bad as black and brown. Yet those good old boys buy his bows and muzzle-loaders for South Carolina's primitive weapon hunting season."

"Okay. But you didn't answer one of my questions. Is Ray stable?"

"Not entirely," Wolf admitted. "I'm not sure what he'd do if he came across your uncle in the woods. But Ray doesn't hunt trouble, just bear. He avoids people, he doesn't stalk them. We hunt together at least three times a year."

The notion of Wolf toting a rifle didn't trouble Riley. While she wasn't keen on decorating her den with moose heads, her hunter dad had taught her the sport's place in managing wildlife populations.

"You mentioned primitive weapons. What kind?"

"Ray lost his affinity for modern guns after serving in Bosnia. He hunts with black-powder guns or bow and arrow. I prefer a bow."

Riley pictured Wolf's muscled arm pulling back a bowstring, his jade eyes locked on his target. The image quickened her pulse.

They turned onto the short access road to the college. "I should be off the mountain by five, back before six," he said. "Can I come by your house? Maybe one of us will have a lead. If not, we can brainstorm other ways to track Tom."

A rendezvous sounded good to Riley. "Fine, I'll pick up pizza. Anything you won't eat?"

Wolf pulled into a visitor's slot. "You pick the toppings." He shot her a raffish grin. "I'm sure I can find something to nibble on."

"I'm sure." Riley rolled her eyes. She grabbed a fistful of blue cashmere sweater and reeled him toward her for an on-the-lips kiss. Her out-of-character aggression felt wonderfully wicked.

"See you tonight." She waggled her fingers as she left the car. "No snacking before then."

When she exited the Wrangler, the sleek lines of a Mercedes roadster registered in her peripheral vision. She recognized John Hunter's plates.

Oh, cripes. John didn't deserve to find out like this. Nobody did. Riley knew how it felt to be the last to know.

Dread accompanied every step as she walked to John's car. The tinted windows obscured his face until she was close enough to knock on a side window.

John lowered the window. A smile flicked across his face. "On the phone," he mouthed silently. His head swiveled, showcasing the Bluetooth clipped to his ear.

Either he hadn't seen her kiss Wolf, or he was one hell of an actor. Didn't matter. She had to tell him. A clean break.

John patted the passenger seat and motioned for her to join him. She considered doing her own pantomime routine, tapping her watch, shaking her head, trotting off to her office.

Coward, she admonished herself. She circled the car and climbed inside.

TWENTY-NINE

After putting the Wrangler in gear, Wolf paused to admire Riley's backside. Her red sweater dipped just below her waistband, offering a rewarding view of her firm little butt.

She walked toward a Mercedes and tapped on the glass. Huh? The tinted driver's window rolled down.

Even minus the sports car, the man's appearance shrieked money. Fancy haircut. Tanned face. A Bluetooth signaling his importance. Silvered hair suggested he had a decade on Wolf.

Riley climbed inside. Wolf's jaw clenched.

You're as jealous as that asshole Gary. She agreed to see you. Not become a nun.

Wolf frowned as the man's head darted at Riley like a coiled snake. The luxury car's darkened glass made a play-by-play impossible. Still Wolf felt confident he'd witnessed a kiss. Thankfully, it was brief.

Suddenly he realized the inappropriateness of gawking. He increased pressure on the accelerator and exited the parking lot at a stately pace. He felt something more than jealousy. Unease. He'd seen that man before. Where?

What seemed wrong? Yeah, the guy kissing Riley wasn't him.

His mind leapt to the evening reunion and his desire to trade more than leads. He hoped his scouting trip wouldn't be a waste of time. Since Ray had no telephone—land line or cell—calling ahead wasn't an option.

Often Ray sensed he was coming and waited on the front stoop with his Bluetick coonhound. However, the hermit's precognitive powers weren't always switched on, especially if he was off on a "ramble."

He turned onto Highway 11 and spoke aloud. "Hey, Uncle Ray, I'm coming. Keep your butt planted till I get there."

He'd almost reached the cabin when recognition dawned. Mercedes man was John Hunter. BRU had named an auditorium for his father. Another blue-blood family. A chill prickled its way down his spine as he remembered how Sherry, the R.N. he once dated, shuddered when Hunter walked past their table in a Greenville restaurant.

"What's wrong?" he'd asked.

"That man gives me the willies."

It took ten minutes to drag the story out of her.

"I was on duty when he brought this girl to the ER with a broken arm and a black eye. She looked all of sixteen. The way he acted wasn't . . . natural. Said she was a neighbor who got banged up when she fell."

His date sighed. "The girl looked scared to death. She backed him up."

"Did the police investigate?" Wolf asked.

"No report was filed. Probably because of who he was. If there'd been a repeat, someone might have taken a closer look. Never saw that child again. She was hooking. No doubt in my mind. She moved or died. Street kids have short life expectancies."

Should he call Riley? And say what—an ex-girlfriend suspected the guy she just kissed beats prostitutes? Dammit to hell, that's what he wanted to do.

His Wrangler bumped onto the deeply rutted path to Ray's cabin. Wolf made a mental note to check out John Hunter. He'd heard gossip about the family, but couldn't remember details. His secretary would.

It hadn't rained in days and his four-wheel drive stirred up clouds of red dust as the rough-hewn timbers of Ray's porch came into view. His uncle waited on the stoop, and Smokey, his coonhound, howled a forlorn greeting. Two firearms leaned against the stone steps.

His uncle stood as Wolf climbed from the car. "Had a feeling you were coming." Ray handed a rifle to his nephew. "For some critters, you need guns."

THIRTY

John's smug smile suggested he'd missed Wolf's kiss. When he shifted toward her for a kiss of his own, it shocked her. Public displays of affection offended him. Was he trying to compete?

She jerked back as his lips grazed hers. He seemed unfazed by her unenthusiastic response. Could he tell the difference?

"I'm surprised to see you, John. Aren't you finalizing a big merger?"

"Yes. But you were attacked, and you didn't return my calls." His tone intimated she'd failed a test. "I was concerned."

"It's been a zoo. Not just the Onward threat. A student was badly injured off campus. I just came from the hospital."

John gingerly ran a finger along the blossoming bruise on her cheek. Riley flinched. "Is this Onward nonsense tied to the freak who attacked you?" he asked.

"I have no idea what that monster wanted. Nothing to connect him to Onward. Maybe I was just in the wrong place at the wrong time."

Did she believe that? No. But John—and her mom—didn't need to know.

He cleared his throat, captured her hand. "Riley, I love you. I'm confident you'll feel the same way . . . with time. We need to see each other more, spend more time together."

Riley freed her hand. The withdrawal triggered a transformation. John's lips reset in a thin straight line. His brown irises darkened. His eyes looked like the dead glass orbs that stared out of his hunting trophies.

He was used to getting what he wanted. Bur Riley couldn't believe he wanted her.

Her stomach knotted. She didn't want to hurt him. Dating had been weird déjà vu for a thirty-nine-year-old divorcee. Theater, four-star restaurants, Godiva chocolates for Riley and her mother. His attentions provided a semblance of a social life, despite the zilch chemistry.

She'd rebuffed John's attempts to ratchet their relationship beyond a casual goodnight peck. Said she wasn't ready for a physical relationship. So why was he launching a romantic assault now? *Because he saw me kiss Wolf? Does he just hate the idea of losing to another man?*

A corporate lawyer, John said he'd never argued before a jury. Still his approach made her think of rehearsed closing arguments. "Ladies and gentlemen of the jury . . ." His declaration of love exhibited all the passion of a canned script.

She harbored serious doubts about any future with Wolf—was a fling worth crushing her mother? Yet John was no alternative. The more time they spent together, the less she *liked* him. His hovering solicitousness grated. His demeanor suggested he believed his IQ dwarfed hers. Not the makings of a lasting partnership.

And he was a sloppy kisser.

Hell, quit picking at the edges—rip off the Band-Aid.

"John, I'm truly sorry. You're a nice man, but I don't love you." She prefaced the next sentence with an involuntary, nervous laugh. "If Mom were twenty years younger, she'd snatch you up in a heartbeat. But I feel no spark. It's time to admit we'll never be a couple."

He didn't say a word. Shock? Riley's gut cramped. She hated to hurt him, even if only his ego. Still, goodbye was the right thing.

He stared into middle space. His hands strangled the leather steering wheel, causing the bones in his raised knuckles to show white against his taut skin.

He shook his head slightly. "You're not yourself. The shock of that attack. The horrible pressure of your job. You'll change your mind."

She opened the car door.

"No, John," she whispered. "I'm sorry. I won't."

THIRTY-ONE

Despite his training and altitude fitness, Wolf's breath came in pants as he trudged up the cliff behind his reclusive uncle. Deep shade cast by large pines didn't prevent sweat from dribbling down his back. The exertion didn't seem to bother Ray. Wolf hoped he'd be half as fit when he turned sixty.

Wolf considered himself in good — hell, excellent — shape. He'd earned an athletic scholarship to Duke University for track. He'd kept running, too, even after aching joints replaced scholarship rewards. No matter where he lived at the time, he made it a point each year to run the thirty-three-mile Foothills Trail Endurance Race.

Today, factors beyond Blue Ridge topography tested his stamina. He'd slept little last night and eaten a mouthful of rice since sun up. He worried Tom might be beaten to death before he found him. And Ray had ordered Wolf to use his gun to kill if shooting started. His uncle's premonition that he was coming — and why — made him queasy.

Ray left Smoky in a chain-link enclosed dog run behind his cabin. They couldn't risk the company of a coonhound that howled whenever it spied any life form, animal or human.

They darted quickly and stealthily through unmarked forest trails. They'd trekked this backdoor approach to Cougar Mountain, a favorite bear-hunting stand, often. The first time Ray guided him to the area, his uncle pointed at a fragrant pile, and laughed. "Yes, son, bears do crap in the woods."

Ray read scat like shamans read entrails. He could tell how many bears inhabited this chunk of real estate, their diet, age, size and general health.

"I climbed Cougar two days ago," Ray said as they rested in a clearing. "When I didn't see scat—none, zero—I knew something had spooked the bears from their haunts."

He took a swig from his water bottle. "Didn't take me long to find what. Onward bush-hogged a large area. Kept just enough canopy to hide the camp from the air. Though no one was about, I saw plenty of boot prints, cigarette butts, discarded shotgun shells and shredded targets."

They resumed their ascent. "What makes you think they'll return?" Wolf asked. "Maybe they've already abandoned that camp."

"Nope. This is no one-time, shoot-em-up site. They looped camouflage netting over trees. Built a large lean-to. I found deep four-wheeler ruts on the other side of Cougar. Bears aren't the only ones who leave scat."

"You sure these dipwads belong to Onward?"

His uncle shrugged. "No. They're just the only loonies poking about now. There are always fanatics wanting to 'save America' by arming themselves up the wazoo and bullying anyone who says 'howdy' differently."

Ray held up a hand, signaling him to stop. Wolf heard two men arguing. Creeping forward, he peered through foliage at a half-dozen milling males. They looked no different from other hunters—though hunting was off-limits this time of year.

Except for the AR-15s they carried, the men were unremarkable. Solidly built and generally young—twenties and thirties—unrelentingly Caucasian. Their splotched cammies looked worn, not purchased yesterday. Nary an orange cap in sight. That just meant they weren't idiots. Forest flyovers might pick up flashes of orange below the netting. He scanned the group. No Tom. Relief and disappointment.

Two males, both with chins thrust forward, appeared ready to throw punches.

"Grabbing that puta was stupid," barked the bigger, dark-haired man. "Until we do the college, you keep your boys in check. You want to blow this? You think a freakin' Santa Claus is gonna come along next week with another fifty thou for the cause?"

The smaller man scuffed the dirt at his feet. "They was just letting off steam." He unfisted one hand to rake back a clump of greasy hair. The runt was backing down. "The stupid bitch did herself in, running in front of a truck. For cripes sake, a tamale has more brains."

Wolf's grip tightened on his gun. He wanted to smash faces. Break jaws. Grind their teeth to dust. But getting himself and Ray killed helped no one. Only in movies did two black-powder, one-shot rifles trump six semi-automatics, each capable of firing up to sixty bullets in thirty seconds.

"It's your IQ at issue, Dickhead," Dark Hair snapped. "Hard for our deputy friends to play ignorant when the media's all het up about bullies terrorizing college kids."

Dark Hair hawked one up, a tangible exclamation mark. The ejected phlegm wet the dust next to Runt's toes.

"We got a chance to go big time," Dark Hair continued. "Bank some real dough. Get the kind of press to bring in recruits. And your boys get their rocks off hassling some no account chica. Enforce a little discipline, okay?"

"Is the big meet still on for tomorrow?" Runt hoped to change the subject.

"Yeah, lay low till then. Not all the deputies are simpatico. Last thing we need is some badge pointing a finger at one of your idiots and tailing him to the meet."

Ray touched Wolf's shoulder and pointed to a black bear rubbing her broad back against a hickory tree. Only one hundred feet away, the small female—maybe two hundred and seventy-five pounds—hadn't noticed them yet.

Crap. A cub cuddled at her side. Protective moms made larger male bears look like pussycats. Ray signaled retreat. As he'd been taught, Wolf did not turn his back, move with visible haste, or look the bear in the eye. He edged slowly backward, puffing himself up to appear as large as possible.

Sweat popped on his forehead like raindrops on a freshly oiled deck. No one had been killed by a bear in South Carolina in the past hundred years. He mentally repeated the state park brochure copy like a magic talisman.

If the bear started posturing with angry growls, she'd attract the attention of the machine-gun coven. Then they'd pepper the woods with automatic fire and bag two homo sapiens as surprise trophies.

Five minutes passed before Wolf gulped air and rested his own back against a tree. He felt as though he'd held his breath for hours. Halfway down the mountain, well out of Onward's audio range, he looked sideways at his uncle. "Hey, Great Indian Chief, thought you said there were no bears on Cougar."

Ray grinned. "Women of all species are unpredictable. You'd know if you ever married one."

Wolf rolled his eyes. "Did you recognize those men?"

"The guy getting reamed for attacking the girl is Smitty. Buford Smith. Bought a gun off me last year. Not the sharpest knife in the drawer. Doubt he made it past junior high. Last I heard he worked at a plant that bottles spring water."

"Know where he lives?"

"Can't say I do."

Wolf sensed something off as Ray's cabin came into view. It looked as if someone had jammed half a pumpkin on his uncle's door. Wolf shuddered when they came close enough to recognize the door hanger—an orange ball cap with a neatly embroidered legend: "Take Back America."

His uncle yanked the cap off the doorknob and read the note pinned inside. "Sorry we missed you."

THIRTY-TWO

Riley phoned Dr. Sparks to report on Rosie's condition and the attack.

The vice chancellor cut her short. "Sorry, Riley, I'm en route to meet Rosie's parents, and I need to tell you about another, uh, situation." He cleared his throat. "It needs to be handled with . . . delicacy."

Oh great, delicacy. Nine months of interpreting academia-speak enabled her to translate: someone had stepped in it so deep, he'd need a derrick to hoist him clear.

"Reverend Jimmy held a press conference and announced a prayer meeting tonight on the BRU green—"

"He can't. We issued a statement hours ago restricting campus access. We're only admitting people with student or faculty IDs and authorized service personnel."

"Yes, yes, I realize . . . but the original Hillman grant included a stipulation his descendants would have access to BRU whenever they wished. The reverend says his prayer meeting is at Doris Hillman's invitation. Dr. Harris doesn't want a fight over this. The university might be seen as interfering with prayer. . . . With this court case pending . . ."

Three pregnant pauses in thirty seconds. Oh, boy.

Sparks continued. "Denying any type of religious service . . . well, it could give ammunition to the people claiming BRU has turned its back on our Christian foundation."

"We're risking student lives for good evangelical PR?"

She'd moved beyond anger. She needed to protect students from the psychopaths threatening to wreak death and destruction on *her* campus. One coed already died on her watch. Another might not live through the night. How could the administration buckle?

She didn't hide her contempt. "Maybe we should issue our own statement. Terrorists, y'all come. Sure, we'll bend over."

"That's quite enough," Dr. Sparks barked. "Our policy hasn't changed. We're simply making a one-time exception. Mr. Jacob has given the FBI's approval. Agents will mix with the crowd, use the opportunity to potentially tag and bag bad guys."

Good God. Had Gary lost his mind? The situation had FUBAR written all over it. She'd complain to Director Stewart, force Gary to revoke his blessing.

The vice chancellor's clipped tone told Riley she'd pushed her boss beyond displeasure. He expected ladylike debate and demure acceptance. After all, BRU was a cultured institution of higher learning. Well, screw that.

Dr. Sparks cleared his throat. "TV crews are coming. The Onward threat is national news. Far better for the media to broadcast a prayer meeting than a nasty confrontation. If we'd kept Reverend Jimmy out, things might have gotten out of hand."

"*Things* wouldn't have gotten out of hand," she shot back. "Our officers are pros."

"Fine." Her boss spat the word as a period. "Then they'll handle tonight's security professionally and diplomatically. Coordinate with Mr. Jacob."

She forced a calming breath. Her bosses had talked this to death—without her—and decided. She wouldn't change their minds.

She longed to employ a few action verbs to say how she really felt. But Dr. Sparks might fire her. She cared too much to jump ship with the campus as a potential theater of war.

"Okay." She sighed. "When is this religious extravaganza to begin—and end?"

"Reverend Jimmy announced an eight p.m. start, presumably to give TV crews ten o'clock footage. Mr. Jacob said the preacher's media fixation would help us retain our eleven p.m. curfew."

Now that's one bet she'd take. If the reverend stayed one minute past eleven, he'd think God had sent a new plague.

Back in her office, she retrieved Gary's business card. He'd acted like a Tupperware saleslady as he handed them out. Fighting fear-induced nausea, she dialed his cell.

"Are you nuts?" Her words were darts, sharp and piercing. "Onward's threat arrived last night. We've had no time—zip, nada—to beef up security, hire extra guards, probe weak spots in our defenses. And you give the go-ahead to open campus to anyone who claims to have a prayer on his lips? If this is the kind of help you're offering, the FBI should butt out."

"You through?" Gary asked.

Riley hated that deadpan tone. The same pitch he'd used to confess a pregnant girlfriend. Too bad he was out of range for a contemptuous spitball.

"We'll videotape everyone coming through the gates. Agents and sheriff's deputies will join your officers and mingle with the crowd. Our FBI profilers are confident Onward won't act before their Saturday deadline. It would violate their sense of honor."

"What if they're more flexible about honor than you think? What if the three-day deadline was a lie from the start?"

"Riley, think rationally. You're upset because your bosses agree with me. If you're considering calling Director Stewart, forget it. He's in full accord."

She slammed down the receiver, glad she'd called on her landline. Disconnecting a cell call wasn't nearly as satisfying. Would Gary fib about the director's seal of approval? Could be a bluff. Then again, she was a civilian. The director would back his own man.

She choked off her anger. Time to think clearly. How many people might show for this carnival? What kind of screening could her staff do? She'd ask Pete to get details on FBI staffing since she was too spitting mad to call back.

Riley tasked Patty with phoning off-duty officers. Over the next two hours, she worked like a demon to allocate BRU's scarce resources. At quarter past five, her stomach rumbled.

No wonder. I haven't eaten since . . .

She checked her watch. Wolf would arrive at her house in less than forty-five minutes. Should she call and cancel?

She tugged on one of her curls, a sure sign of jangled nerves. She seized a lock of her hair and yanked it. Hard. Get real! Nothing more to do if you stay.

Riley rolled her eyes imagining how Reverend Jimmy would gloat if she fainted from hunger at his prayer fest. A fantastic finale to this day.

Besides Wolf would be waiting.

She needed to return to campus by seven-thirty. That left a two-hour break. She smiled. Eat fast and maybe I can give Wolf's motor a few starter cranks.

THIRTY-THREE

"Oh, Luc-cee, I'm home!" Riley's greeting, a singsong imitation of Ricky Ricardo's call to Lucille Ball, always appeared to delight her cat, a plump and playful Bombay with eyes that gleamed like polished pennies.

She first announced her homecoming that way the day her divorce became final. Her way of poking fun at her self-pity. *Oh, woe is me! A spinster alone with her cat.*

Lucy had seemed entranced—the cat bounded to her side so quickly Riley figured "I'm home" sounded like "mouse buffet" in cat speak. Either that or Lucy had a Latino master in some prior life. No matter. The greeting became ritual.

Riley wondered what Wolf would think if she popped in an *I Love Lucy* DVD. The fictional Ricky arrived in the U.S. about the same time as Wolf's Cuban granddad. However, Riley doubted the South Carolina neighbors greeting Wolf's ancestor resembled Fred and Ethel.

Balancing her purse and the steaming pizza box, she punched in her security code to shut off the alarm. Where was Lucy? She scanned the room.

Maybe she'd found a mouse. Ugh. She hated it when the cat deposited grisly presents at her feet.

She moved to the kitchen and glanced at the clock. Ten till six. A good customer of the Italian Pizzeria, Riley had begged the owner to fast track her pizza.

She turned the oven dial to two hundred degrees, transferred the pizza to a pan, and set the pie on the middle rack to stay warm. Turning, she noticed the basement door ajar. How did it get open? Was Lucy exploring the house's nether regions?

Her fingers fumbled the clammy cellar wall in search of the switch plate. She toggled the rocker. Nothing. *Dammit.* A burned-out bulb.

The doorbell chimed and she abandoned her basement exploration. Her cranky knee and aching ribs jockeyed for most-painful honors as she hurried toward the front door. The moment she saw Wolf's face, she knew he had news. The bad variety.

"Any luck finding Tom?"

With an imperceptible shake of his head, he skipped to the bottom line. "No."

She relaxed a bit. Could be worse. Tom might be dead.

"Come in." She hesitated, unsure if she should hug him.

Wolf decided the matter. He pulled her into him, tilted her head up, and settled a gentle kiss on her lips. He smelled like crushed pine needles. He pulled back, and she instantly missed the heat radiating from his core. Like uranium, he was a powerful—and dangerous—energy source.

"Hey, where's your sling?" he asked.

"My shoulder's feeling better. Don't want to coddle it too much. The doctor said I could start physical therapy next week once the inflammation's down."

She headed toward the kitchen. "Dinner's ready. Let's talk while we eat."

"Good. I didn't want to appear uncouth, but I'm running on two sugar packets in one cup of coffee. The pizza smells great."

"I'm starving, too—and short on time. Have a seat." Her fingers skimmed the back of a wooden chair at the two-person table. "I need to be on campus by seven-thirty—at the latest."

Any trace of a smile vanished from Wolf's face. "Why? What's wrong?"

Riley gave her rendition of events as they shared the pizza. Wolf had polished off a third slice by the time she finished.

"Ordinarily I'm not a prayer meeting kind of guy," he said. "But I'm coming. I doubt Reverend Jimmy's in cahoots with Onward, but the orange-hat goons may take advantage to scout our campus. I can pick out a few of the bastards."

"What?" Riley choked on her pizza.

His voice became a deep rumble. "I know one member's name—Buford Smith, better known as Smitty."

When he finished reporting on his adventure, Riley stood. "I need to call Gary." Her voice vibrated with excitement. "Onward's meeting tomorrow, right? He can raid the camp. If they're stockpiling guns, he can nail them on firearm charges. If we net Smitty, Gary can squeeze him on kidnap and assault charges. With that kind of leverage, the ape might squeal on his buddies."

She smiled. Light at the end of the tunnel.

"Do you suppose Smitty knows who's financing these goons? Who would give these assholes fifty thousand dollars?"

Wolf frowned. Her sudden optimism hadn't infected him.

"It won't be that easy, Riley. We have no idea when this big meeting will take place. Noon, three o'clock, the stroke of midnight? And we're only guessing it's on Cougar. How can the FBI stage a raid there? Sure, Ray and I tiptoed around without being seen—and I'm not even sure of that—but there's no way to hide an assault team."

Riley had more faith in her former colleagues. Gary excelled at tactics. "We'll find a way."

Wolf scowled. "Don't forget your ex has a problem with the locals. At least one deputy's dirty. I heard it with my own ears. With the sheriff wired into the task force, word will leak."

He had a point, but she had to tell Gary. She left the room to make her call.

"Where are you?" Gary's unspoken rebuke implied she should be on campus. A wave of guilt fueled her anxiety as she ended the call. Maybe she should return.

Back in the kitchen, she glanced at the clock. The pendulum—a swishing cat's tail—reminded her time was vanishing. Quarter till seven. She looked back at the clock and the hairs on her neck rose.

The cat's tail.

"What's wrong?" Wolf asked.

"My cat. Lucy. Haven't seen her since I came home." She walked over to check the cat's dish. "She always greets me. When I eat in the kitchen, she practically sits on my feet, waiting to see if I'll drop some morsel."

Wolf stood. "Is she shy? Maybe it's me. Though she didn't avoid me this morning."

Riley carried the paper plates to the waste can. "Lucy's no shrinking violet. She inspects anyone invading her turf."

"Do you have a pet door? Can she come and go on her own?"

"No." She shook her head and shivered. "I have a bad feeling."

Wolf captured her hand, squeezed it. "Let's look together. I'm sure she's just being a cat, aloof and independent."

"Thanks. We only have a few minutes. You scout the living room. I'll head upstairs. Then we'll try the basement."

Riley called softly to Lucy as she climbed. She started with the second bedroom, the one she used as an office. Empty. She turned toward her bedroom. Why was her door closed?

She drew her weapon before she eased the door open.

Riley tightened the grip on her Glock. Blood dripped from the torn bras and panties strewn across her bed. Deep gashes crisscrossed her quilt. The bureau's top drawers dangled precariously, while the bottom ones littered the floor. A condom covered one of the bedposts, and a butcher knife glittered on her pillow.

She tamped down her terror and moved into a shooter's stance. She kept her back hard against the wall as she surveyed the destruction.

"If you're hiding, come out now. Hands up! I'm armed. If I see anything move, I'll shoot first, interrogate your corpse later."

She caught a blur of motion. As she swiveled, her finger stroked the trigger. Her breath caught as she identified the intruder—Lucy.

"Goddammit Lucy, I almost shot you."

"Riley, where are you?" Wolf's footsteps pounded on the stairs.

"I'm fine. Stay on the landing while I check the bathroom and closet."

"The hell I will."

Riley pulled back the shower curtain on an empty tub enclosure. She heard Wolf barrel into the bedroom and yelled to calm him. "No one's here."

That news didn't halt his torrent of curses.

As she reentered her bedroom, Wolf stuck a finger in one of the trails of red goop, raised it to his nose and sniffed. His forehead crinkled. "Goddamn ketchup. Not blood."

She scanned her ruined bedroom. "Whoever was here is gone." She holstered her gun. "He left a message on the bathroom mirror."

Wolf's long strides ate up the distance between them. He pulled her into his arms. Hugged her fiercely. "Let's see."

"Sorry I missed you" was scrawled in her lipstick.

Wolf's strong arms encircled Riley as he rocked on his heels. Their reflections shimmered in the mirror. His green eyes, hers a hazel blend, burned with the same intensity. Somehow the image comforted.

"Any idea who did this?" His voice was soft. "The message echoes the one on Ray's door. But this—" he waved his hand at the chilling chaos "—shouts sexual rage. Have any wacko ex-lovers?"

The question made her snort. "Ex-lovers? Since college, I've had exactly two. One former husband and you. I can safely rule out both of you."

She shivered. "I can't imagine who did this. But he's no dummy. My alarm was on and the door locked. He somehow bypassed security."

"Want to call 911 or some friend on the force? I imagine you know several deputies."

"I'll tell Gary at the rally. No time to deal with this now."

Wolf spun her around to face him. His eyes searched hers. "Throw some clothes in a bag. You're coming home with me. You can't stay here alone. Not tonight."

Riley chewed on her lip, then nodded. "Okay, but your invitation had better be a package deal. If I come, so does Lucy."

Wolf smiled as his hands fell away from her shoulders. He knelt and scooped up the black cat unashamedly rubbing against his pant leg. Lucy purred contentedly. The cat's eyes squeezed shut in ecstasy as his quicksilver fingers combed her fur.

I know, Lucy. Those hands are magic.

THIRTY-FOUR

Wolf tailed Riley to campus, keeping the front grill of his Wrangler a mere car length off her bumper. Absent clues on the motorcycle attack and home invasion, he cast his suspicion net broadly, checking out any drivers who crowded their two-car caravan.

They reached the campus entrance, a protective arch of aged stone and ivy that looked as if it belonged to a fairytale castle. The sun rode low on the horizon, spearing the entry flowerbed with slanted shafts of gold. A uniformed officer, his face stern and sidearm prominent, stepped out of the doll-sized gatehouse that ordinarily sat vacant. Riley powered down her window.

Worry gnawed at him although she was safer on campus. Her bedroom scene seemed contrived. A red herring to shift the security director's attention away from Onward?

His gut said Riley's tormentor knew her. But perhaps his jealousy conjured straw villains. Maybe a weirdo stranger stalked her. Some nut who'd concocted a full-fledged fantasy relationship. It happened.

Her claim of two ex-lovers baffled him. Wolf knew first-hand how much she enjoyed sex, and she'd been single for two years. Hard to imagine she'd remained celibate since their Hilton Head fling. Did that mean she and John Hunter had never made love, or—dammit, was she playing with semantics—maybe he wasn't a "former" lover?

Though Riley ridiculed the idea, Wolf refused to cross her former husband off his suspect list. FBI honchos knew how to bypass alarms, and the man's parking lot demeanor suggested strong emotions. Gary would be roaming campus tonight. He'd keep an eye peeled for him as well as the Onward thugs. While he doubted John Hunter would show, he'd keep that bastard on his radar, too.

He pulled forward as Riley's car shot ahead. After glancing at his windshield parking decal and checking his ID, the guard waved him on. When he reached the parking lot, Riley was pulling Lucy's pet carrier from her car. She made a beeline for the closest uniform.

He flexed his hands, cramped from gripping the steering wheel like a bull whip. He was on Riley's turf now. He watched a female officer take Lucy's carrier and head toward the office.

Riley's matter-of-fact manner impressed him. Her house had been invaded, her bedroom ransacked, and her bruised body must ache like the dickens. One resilient lady.

He opened his glove compartment and extracted the binoculars he kept handy for mountain hikes. He'd have an hour to scan the faces of Reverend Jimmy's congregants before twilight shut down his surveillance. Like the preacher's disciples, Wolf wanted prayers answered quickly. He longed to spot Smitty or one of the other Onward miscreants he'd seen toting guns.

He walked briskly toward a knot of spectators.

"Dr. Valdes, surprised to see you here."

Wolf smiled at his department secretary. "Mrs. Lee, I could say the same about you. Didn't think an upstanding Catholic lady like yourself would associate with Reverend Jimmy."

Mrs. Lee, a pudgy, sixty-year-old, chuckled. "I'm writing a report for our parish priest on how to raise money and crowds."

Wolf and Mrs. Lee razzed each other regularly on a variety of subjects.

"I wanted to ask you something." Wolf's eyebrows knitted. "Now what was it?"

"Hey, you're not allowed to use that forgetful ploy. That's a privilege of the over-sixty crowd."

"I remember. Some gossip about the Hunter family. I can't recall what you told me. I ran into John Hunter the other day, and—"

"You don't want to mess with that one," Mrs. Lee interrupted. "Oh, dear, he's not a friend, is he?"

Wolf shook his head. "Decidedly not." *Okay, what the hell do I tell her?* "A friend mentioned Hunter was dating his sister. Asked if I knew anything about him, given that the Hunter name is plastered on several BRU buildings."

Mrs. Lee looked left and right. "Tell your friend his sister should stay clear of that man. I knew his father, Lewis Hunter, a gentleman. He's the one who paid for BRU's auditorium when he was rolling in it. Old money. Then he lost it all."

"He did? I thought John Hunter was rich."

"If you'll quit interrupting, I'll finish. Lewis Hunter invested in some Ponzi scheme at his wife's insistence. A scammer hoodwinked her with fake credentials. She bought into the con artist's hint that the investment would up her social standing beyond the Upstate's compact circle. She skedaddled as soon as the money disappeared. Left Lewis and her son. Think John was seventeen. Anyway, Lewis took a gun, sat on the steps of Hunter Auditorium, and tried to blow his brains out. Failed. He's paralyzed now and missing too many marbles to play in any game."

Wolf shook his head. "I'm not following. Why does Lewis Hunter's attempted suicide make his son someone to steer clear of?"

"I think the whole event did permanent psychological damage. BRU offered John a needs scholarship but the boy turned it down. Said he wouldn't need a scholarship if his father hadn't been hoodwinked into giving money for a damn auditorium. The boy went to Clemson, a state school, instead."

Wolf almost felt sorry for John Hunter. Must have been a bitch for a teenager to instantly go from rich to poor and from two parents to none. "Surprised he came back to this area."

"Everyone was," Mrs. Lee added. "Joined Whitten Industries, owned by a friend of his dad's. He bought back the Hunter estate where he grew up. Married the boss's daughter. A lovely lady. I watched John at her funeral. I swear he could barely contain his glee. He gives me the willies. I heard she 'fell down' a lot before her death."

He swallowed. Would Hunter harm Riley? No. The kind of man who enjoyed battering females wouldn't pick on one who packed a gun. Why was he seeing her?

"Yoo hoo," Mrs. Lee waved at a friend. "See you tomorrow, Wolf. Have to run. I told Mabel I'd meet her here."

Wolf had taken less than ten steps when Deborah Holt, better known as Dab, practically bowled him over. Her ample chest bumped against him like a shock-absorbing fender. She giggled.

"Didn't mean to knock you down." She tossed her long blonde hair as she tugged playfully on his jacket lapels. "You all by your lonesome? I'll keep you company."

"Uh, I sort of told friends I'd meet them."

She didn't take the hint. Dab was a human Post-It. While you could peel her off, she reattached unless a replacement anchor happened by. Her glue only bonded to males.

She locked onto his elbow with her Western tennis grip. "Great, let's find your friends."

The first time Dab targeted him he'd been flattered. The tennis coach was easy on the retinas. Athletic and built, the bubbly twenty-five-year-old Amazon sent out sexual pulses that scrambled male neurons. Yet once Dab started jabbering about sports and celebrities, Wolf wished he had a remote to mute the audio.

The sexy coach fingered the strap on his binoculars. "What's with these?"

Wolf paused to dream up a fib. "Helping a colleague with research. She wants to document who attends events like this. I'll be working. Won't be good company."

He pried her fingers from his arm. "Look, Dr. Davis is all alone. Bet he'd love your company."

"Okay. Catch you later!" Using his binocular strap as a makeshift lariat, Dab roped him for a goodbye kiss.

Straightening, he saw Riley looking at him. Not with adoring eyes. *Oh, good. This'll convince her I'm not a lecherous reprobate.*

Riley practically sprinted away. She appeared to have a destination—or quarry—in mind? That silver-haired man on the sidelines? Hunter? The hairs on Wolf's neck stood at attention. He replayed the nurse's suspicions about the battered girl Hunter escorted to the ER and his secretary's story about his dead wife.

He focused his binoculars. Good, it wasn't Hunter. Tonight, he'd coax Riley into spilling more information about their relationship.

His instant distrust of Gary made him question his objectivity. Yet he remained convinced Mr. FBI's dog-in-the-manger signals meant he didn't like new males prowling un-relinquished territory.

Chastising himself for woolgathering, he climbed a knoll midway between the perimeter road and the grassy center stage where Reverend Jimmy would preside. As the trickle of arrivals became a steady drip, he searched for Smitty's runty body and skanky hair. One hundred people? A last-minute swell might double the audience by show time.

Only a sprinkling of young men looked like Onward candidates. While he didn't want violence, he felt disappointed. He'd hoped to ID someone from the Onward camp.

With exams over, many students had already left campus for home. They made up less than half the assembly. Wolf couldn't pin a label on the rest of the milling crowd—well-dressed elders, farmers, blue-collar workers, soccer parents, a few faculty members. The non-student population appeared to have only one common denominator: winter white faces, a sea of cauliflower.

A tug on his sleeve startled him. He turned to see Stan Vidler and his girlfriend, Chantelle. Rosie and Tom were close friends with the bi-racial couple.

"Professor Valdes. Did you hear about Rosie?" Stan asked.

"Yes. I'm looking for any putz in an orange hat. For Rosie's sake, I'd love to run into one of those morons."

"We just left the hospital," Chantelle said. "She's critical but stable." The coed gnawed on her lip. "Tom's disappeared. We're really worried."

"So am I," Wolf said.

Stan's chin jutted forward. "Bet he's gone after the creeps who attacked Rosie. He's got street smarts, but he shouldn't fly solo."

Chantelle squeezed her boyfriend's arm. "Those guys are bad news."

"She's right," Wolf agreed. "I've talked to the authorities—"

"Yeah, like they care," Stan snapped.

"Some do," he countered. "Some do."

"Guess that's why BRU gave this hate-monger a stage." Rage tinged Chantelle's tone. "I can predict his spiel: Blue Ridge students—sinners all—have brought down God's wrath."

Wolf nodded. "He'll include faculty in the blame game. While the man's repugnant, BRU champions free speech. Standing here, I've listened to opponents and proponents of intelligent design, gay rights—"

"Free speech?" Chantelle pounced. "This joker doesn't need *free* speech. His church owns a TV studio. If the courts let that Hillman broad hand over her granddad's fortune, he'll own a television network."

Wolf's free speech rhetoric tasted like ashes on his tongue. Chantelle was right. The televangelist used his fundamentalist college—unaccredited—to legitimize his hateful dogma. Tonight he'd coattail on the terrorist threat for the benefit of TV, radio and newspaper reporters.

"Geez, take a look at that monstrosity." Stan pointed at the preacher's media van with its larger-than-life mural of Reverend Jimmy blessing his flock.

Wolf barked a laugh. The countenance of Jesus—midget-sized compared to Jimmy's puss—was relegated to the van's back doors. The holy face split in two when the doors swung open.

"Looks like the reverend gives Christ second billing. You'd think that would make him worry about his own heavenly prospects."

A crew positioned oversized speakers and snaked wires to a portable generator. The heavy lifters wore uniforms with "Jimmy's God Squad" embroidered on their backs. A silver Rolls Royce delivered the reverend.

Wolf focused his binoculars. Like a moth drawn to bright light, the preacher flitted from one spotlight to another. Though his capped teeth gleamed like Chiclets, crow's feet creased the skin around his eyes.

While changing TV channels late one night, Wolf had caught Jimmy in top revival form. Definite stage presence. A

Nordic Elvis with swaying hips that suggested something different from his sanitized lyrics. He'd grown flabby. Any ecclesiastic gyrations would now create Jell-O-esque ripples.

Wolf lowered his binoculars. As dusk settled, the reverend's minions fanned out, dispensing votive candles. The man understood TV. His tailored suit, powder blue shirt and red silk tie would look spiffy on the tube.

He worked the crowd. Grinning, pumping hands, grasping men's shoulders to encourage them to stand tall for Jesus. The preacher had a thing for young girls. Older ladies and plain Janes got arm pats. Every buxom lass got a kiss.

You horny old buzzard.

Wolf caught sight of a trailing Doris Hillman, looking daggers at any sweet young thing who captured Jimmy's eye. Here was one disciple who didn't believe in sharing.

"Time to move closer," Stan said. "My tomatoes might miss from here."

"You're kidding, right?" Wolf had visions of FBI agents wrestling Stan to the ground. "Throw anything, and an officer might think it's a bomb or grenade. This is no time for pranks."

"Don't have a stroke, Doc. I'm speaking metaphorically."

They'd shouldered their way to the second row when Chantelle groaned. "Oh, no. It's Professor Marick."

The stocky man appeared hard on Jimmy's heels. Wolf swore under his breath as his gaze swept Marick's sallow face. The man was a buffoon, an intellectual disgrace. He was also a history professor and tenured colleague.

For years, Marick contented himself with lame lectures on ancient civilizations. Then six months ago, he published an article in a no-name magazine that claimed dark-skinned people were incapable of self-government, though he "graciously" added his research didn't necessarily suggest lower IQ—simply a genetic propensity toward anti-social behavior and an inability to cooperate for the greater good.

The article outraged the BRU faculty, and the administration canceled his classes. Now Marick was a voiceless, well-paid ghost, who occasionally haunted campus.

"All we need now are the Rockettes and Mickey Mouse," Chantelle quipped.

Wolf prayed Marick had a nonspeaking role.

The crowd had swollen to two hundred or more. The preacher helped Doris settle. Then Jimmy tested the microphone.

Near the stage a human hulk chatted with Riley. She looked like Goldilocks standing in papa bear's shadow. Her hands fluttered as she spoke. Wolf smiled. Would handcuffs render her speechless? Hmm, might try that sometime.

Stan slid a protective arm around Chantelle. Wolf wished he could do the same with Riley. He'd wanted to shadow her tonight. She'd warned him off with a give-me-a-break look and a throw-away line— "No offense but, if I need backup, thirty guys with guns will come running to help if I whistle. It's my job."

If their relationship had any chance, he had to respect her professional boundaries. Backing away wasn't easy.

THIRTY-FIVE

Reverend Jimmy powered on his cordless mike. Riley flinched at the high-pitched feedback. The preacher grinned in the spotlight's flared, yellow beam. Not flattering. His teeth looked like he'd been eating field corn and hadn't flossed.

Her head throbbed. She felt testy—with good reason. Some pervert had shredded her underwear and smothered it in ketchup. Fear of right-wing condemnation had prompted BRU to bend over for Jimmy. Her injured shoulder and ribs begged for a narcotic deadening.

Mostly, she was irritated at herself. She'd let emotions evaporate her cool. If a task force leader other than Gary had blessed this campus invasion, would she be equally peeved? She had to let go of old hurts, depersonalize the interaction.

Then there was Wolf. When she spied him kissing the well-endowed coach—a dead ringer for his novel's Kayla—Riley wanted to bop both of them.

Forget it. Get to work.

A piece of paper fluttered against her leg. She picked up a color brochure promoting the reverend's ministry. Jimmy's hooded eyes made her shiver. The flyer pricked at her memory. Why?

She folded the flyer, thrust it in a pocket, and posted herself near the stage. Given the haste in planning tonight's security, her officers were performing admirably. She spotted Gary and walked over to meet him.

Nice and easy.

"I hear you have over a dozen agents here. Any potential suspects or problems?"

"No. It's quiet. Your officers took screening seriously. Searched every backpack and handbag coming through the gates. They turned away anyone trying to slip through the woods."

She nodded, uncertain whether Gary was issuing a compliment or complaint. He'd wanted bad guys to appear so he could net them for questioning.

"Excuse me." Gary turned, pressed a finger to his earpiece. He started talking, and she fled. Nothing more to say.

The preening reverend deserved only cursory attention. He wouldn't overtly condone violence though his presence invited a riot. The faces of students telegraphed their anger. They'd been hammered with Amanda's unsolved murder, the pressure of finals, Onward's threat, and Rosie's attack. Nerves were stretched thin. She prayed the reverend wouldn't blast them as godless, fornicating sinners who deserved hell's punishments.

When Professor Marick materialized, Riley sensed the students' rage build into an almost tangible force. Crap.

The reverend cleared his throat. "Dear Lord, we gather in your name. Let your cleansing light shine down. Evil is holding Blue Ridge University hostage. We ask you to intervene."

Jimmy spread his arms to encompass the assembly. "These students—confused and tormented souls—can be saved. We beseech you, Lord, spare them. Our Onward brethren believe they must wage war to capture eternal peace for this tortured campus. Counsel your fervent foot soldiers to lay down their swords. Command them to exchange Godly wrath for your Son's forgiveness."

Riley could almost hear the grinding of student teeth. Her ears picked up a muted undercurrent of "Screw you."

Keep it short. Make your sales pitch and leave.

Jimmy's nostrils flared. "We know Satan lectures here." His voice boomed. "He teaches it's no sin to murder unborn babies . . . that sex with a stranger has less meaning than a sneeze . . . that homosexuals can enter into holy matrimony. The Devil claims that You, Lord, are not our Creator . . . that mankind was begotten by slime—"

"Hey, you're slime!" a female voice broke in. "Theory proved."

A titter of laughter helped Riley locate the verbal poacher, a red-haired spitfire.

The reverend spoke even louder. "The Devil is here. Braying. No wonder Onward set its sights on BRU. It ached to purify and purge, if necessary, by fire."

His lips curled in a sneer. "Lord, I understand. You used Onward as our wake-up call. You sent a lightning bolt to jolt us from sinful slumber. We must stand up to the abortionists and the gays."

He beat his fist on the podium. "Time to say no to the feminists and Islam boot lickers." Another fist slam. "Time to shout down the atheists who want to strip 'God' from our pledge of allegiance."

His fist crashed down so hard Riley expected the podium to splinter. Her stomach somersaulted as she felt the audience's agitation climb.

Jimmy's followers shouted "Hallelujah" and "You tell 'em!" Outraged students began a different chant: "Reverend Jimmy sucks; we don't give a fuck! Reverend Jimmy sucks; we don't give a fuck!"

A sheen of sweat coated Jimmy's forehead. Was it the spotlight's heat, or did he realize matters were getting out of hand?

"Before a final prayer, Professor Marick, one of BRU's few God-fearing faculty members, has a few words to say. Like me, Dr. Marick abhors violence but understands why Onward lashed out at Blue Ridge University. He bears testimony to the frustration of dealing with educators who turn their backs on our Christian roots."

The professor shot out of his chair. His Adam's apple bobbled a few times before he spoke. "I am not a racist." His first words arrived as an amplified squeak, a dramatic contrast to the pastor's commanding bass.

An alto yell interrupted. "Right, as long as us Spics mow your lawn and clean your toilets!"

Riley's gaze swept over the students and locked on the protestor.

"Bet you'd pay us to abort!" added the man's date, shaking her fist. "No problemo murdering the babies of mud people."

Students cheered. Marick's nose wrinkled as if he smelled rotten eggs. His thin voice droned on. "A tide of illegal aliens pollutes our nation, bringing drugs and prostitution. They steal jobs and commit crimes. They corrupt family values and visit a plague of violence—"

"What about Onward's violence, you little Nazi?" someone shouted.

Riley zeroed in. Anger turned the tall blond heckler's face blotchy. He draped an arm around a pretty black coed, who yelled, "What about our friend Rosie, you goddamn racist?"

A jumbo-sized white man in a flannel shirt and a Braves baseball cap muscled nearer the girl. The veins on his neck bulged in bas-relief. "Shut up, you foul-mouthed little bitch, or I'll shut you up!"

His friends cheered him. "Give 'em what-for, Ernie!"

Wolf wedged between the hecklers and the blue-collar bubbas. Judging by his look of fury, he didn't plan to play diplomat. He spoiled for a fight.

Time to separate the combatants and evict the agitators. She nodded toward the potential powder keg, sending a three-hundred-pound officer to play peacemaker. *Come on, Wolf. Hustle the kids clear. We don't need a bare knuckle free-for-all.*

She spoke quietly into her radio, signaling officers on the fringes to move in. She told one of her techno-gifted officers to silence the proceedings. Time for a final "Amen."

A quick movement caught her eye. A gangly young man wearing an Old West-style duster bent with his back to her, then spun to face her. A long white barrel materialized out of his coat's swirling folds.

Don't overreact. Riley tasted bile. She knew what an FBI agent might do if he thought a nut was about to empty a gun into this crowd.

She ran at the shooter. Adrenaline charged her speed. She frantically waved her good arm to distract the boy's aim. She knew his weapon. A spud gun. Kids used them to blast potatoes—or other fruits and veggies—at short-range targets. Junior engineers fashioned them out of PVC pipe, hairspray, and fireplace lighters. The kids didn't think of their creations as "real" weapons. But like B-B guns, the homemade artillery could wreak havoc and harm.

Her heart thudded. A puff of white smoke preceded a thunderclap of electronic noise. A series of ear-splitting booms rolled over the green. The potato missile decimated the preacher's sound system. People screamed and stampeded.

She dived for the shooter's legs, sent him ass over teakettle. A second later, an officer hauled the kid upright and cuffed him. His science project gun lay discarded in the grass.

"Take him to my office." Riley panted as she sat in the wet grass, cradling her arm. Her shoulder felt as if a crazed band member had mistaken it for a snare drum.

She staggered upright. Jimmy, Marick and Doris remained prone, hands shielding heads. She thumbed on her radio. "Pete, put me on air. Now!"

A second later her voice floated from loudspeakers. "This is the security director. Do not panic. The only people with guns are law enforcement. The blast was a prank. The ammunition was a potato. Proceed calmly to your vehicles—or your dorm rooms. This gathering is over. The situation's under control."

"Under control" was a gross exaggeration. Angry shouts ricocheted as the opposing camps rubbed shoulders in their exodus. When she saw flying fists, she hustled toward the brawlers. A uniformed officer had joined the plainclothesman she'd dispatched.

She was ten feet from the action when Plaid Shirt punched a student. Wolf yanked the bully's arm, turning him 180 degrees. A second later, Gary waded into the mix.

Oh, no!

Gary targeted Wolf, twisted his arm behind his back.

"It's Smitty. He's here!" Wolf yelled. "Let me go, you moron. The guy who attacked Rosie Perez is over there. Let go!"

Riley searched for a would-be Smitty in the crowd. She couldn't see. She glanced back, saw Wolf lower his shoulder and shove Gary to get free. Her ex retaliated. He tripped Wolf, who landed flat on his face.

Smitty—if he'd been here—was long gone.

A TV cameraman jumped in front of her. She elbowed him. "Out of my way." The newsman swayed, then steadied his camera as she stormed ahead.

Great, live feed from BRU! Who needs Wrestlemania?

THIRTY-SIX

L.J. pushed aside the Request for Proposal. No mystery. Whitten had a lock on the hydroelectric project bid. Bribes oiled third-world business, and Whitten had honed kickback skills to an art form. Yet he always took care to ensure RFPs looked legit.

A headache played above the bridge of his nose. L.J. took off his reading glasses and massaged his forehead. He was sick of sitting at a damn desk.

He glanced at his Rolex. Was she home yet? He entered a string of computer commands to view any activity on the spyware he'd placed in Riley's home. Since the bugs were sound-and-motion activated, his private movie began when she opened her front door. L.J. smirked as she called to her cat. Damn but he wished he'd found that fleabag. Maybe next visit.

He frowned at the disappointing camera angle. The video only captured the shiny curls atop her head, then her tight little ass swayed into view as she walked down the hall.

A new optical lead picked up in the kitchen, improving his field of vision. As she puttered, he grabbed a letter opener and pushed back his cuticles. Boring. He fast-forwarded.

Come on, honey, I don't have all night. Can't you see the basement door's open?

L.J. turned his full attention to the monitor when she swung the basement door wide and yoo-hooed to the cat. She read the basement wall like Braille, seeking the light switch.

Now *this* was reality TV.

The doorbell chimed. This time the angle was perfect. He read the woman's face as she hustled to the door. Eyes wide, lips parted. Lust?

A man entered. Riley's face tipped up, then disappeared, swallowed in a kiss. L.J.'s temples pounded. Miss Law-and-

Linda Lovely

Morality had a clandestine lover. Should have known. Women were sluts.

He recalled seeing the interloper's face on a book jacket. A friend told him the man was a professor of some liberal arts crap—religion, philosophy? He wouldn't have remembered his name if she hadn't purred it repeatedly. Wolf.

God, the woman had the hots for this Wolf. Insulting. More proof hormones ruled even the smarter females. Men were meant to control them.

As Wolf described his mountain adventure, L.J. scribbled down the uncle's name.

Finally, jerky movements signaled Riley suspected an intruder. His letter opener tapped against his desk, the cadence increasing as she burst into her bedroom, gun drawn. No scream but her mouth opened like a hooked fish in a silent gasp. Fear shadowed her eyes.

His video thrill proved transitory. Her boyfriend bumbled in and spoiled the fun. So much for theater. The man asked Riley about ex-lovers. She admitted to only two—one being the half-breed. *Whore.* L.J. grabbed his crystal paperweight, aching to throw it. Instead he hefted it in his palm, and examined how it refracted the light. Like a puzzle. Lots of facets.

The decision to vacate her home would end his high-tech peep show. The Indian had to go. The slut had to pay.

THIRTY-SEVEN

"Want a drink?" Wolf asked as he poured himself a generous slug of whiskey.

"No." Riley sank into one of her host's kitchen chairs. "I shouldn't mix booze with pain pills."

Wolf stomped to the refrigerator, shoveled ice into a mixing bowl, and grabbed a tea towel. "A make-shift cold pack is the best I can do. I have plenty of ice. Need one?"

Riley craved the opposite, a warm mug to cradle in her hands, hold against her cheek. Was it an omen? *Fire and ice.* Maybe she and Wolf were too different. "Any tea bags?"

Wolf shook his head. "Cocoa?" he countered, tight-lipped.

"Fine." I can do terse, too.

He set a packet of instant hot chocolate mix beside a mug and put a kettle on the stove. Before sitting, he stripped off his sweater, scooped a handful of ice from the mixing bowl, and corralled the cubes in a tea towel. He clamped the pack to the shoulder he'd injured in the melee. His eyes squeezed shut. Pain or was he just avoiding her?

She wished he hadn't discarded the sweater. A trickle of water escaped the melting ice. It slithered along his smooth, almost hairless chest, a glint of silver on his coppery skin.

She bit her lip. Her fingers had played over the taut muscles and honeyed skin where the droplet meandered. The icy rivulet was about to skirt his nipple. Would the small nub jump to attention as it did when her teeth grazed it?

She flushed and looked toward the stove. She couldn't let Wolf catch her in a lustful stare. Not when all he offered was an arctic demeanor.

She sensed his icy manner was a thin veneer. Fury crackled like a force field through his rigid body. She could see it in his tensed jaw muscles, the way his hand gripped the cold pack like a rock to be crushed. He'd barely spoken. A volcano about to blow.

Two mental video clips kept recycling in Riley's head—Wolf kissing the limber lady jock, and, later, barreling into her ex-husband. He knew Gary was FBI, and he still tried to plow through him on his way to Smitty. Gary's response was over the top, too. After he tripped Wolf, he rammed a knee in his back to hold him in place and cuff him. Wolf wrenched his shoulder in the fall. Cuffing him added a painful insult.

The way she saw it, both men acted like children. Wolf's attitude said he refused to let it go.

Lucy, the traitor, purred and rubbed herself against Wolf's leg. *I should shove Lucy back in her cage and get the hell out of here.*

But where could she go? Not home until she changed her locks. And her mother's condo was no refuge. She didn't want to explain a home invasion. And she couldn't put her mother in jeopardy.

Did being here endanger Wolf? No. She was certain no one tailed them from campus. Besides who could have predicted she'd wind up here? Twenty-four hours ago she'd have howled with laughter at an invitation to spend a night under his roof.

Wolf's eyes snapped open. "That dipwad Smitty was a dozen feet away." His voice was gravel. "I could have tackled him if your Gestapo ex hadn't interfered."

Not exactly news. Once the dust settled on the campus brawl, the Onward thug had vanished—if he wasn't a figment of Wolf's imagination. He hadn't been caught on video.

"Gary was breaking up a fight. You resisted." She folded her arms across her chest. "For all he knew, you were trying to throw a punch."

"I had Smitty dead in my sights." His tone telegraphed angry frustration. "I didn't have time to recite my life history. I needed to catch the bastard."

He shifted the ice pack, and a small groan escaped. "Besides, once I went down, your ex rammed a knee in my back. Hard to talk when you're eating grass."

"You had your chance." She held his gaze. "You could have acted the adult, shooed those students away once testosterone levels began to rise. Then you wouldn't have been in a brawl when you spotted Smitty."

She looked away. "Guess you should have stayed cozy with Boobsie Bubbles."

"What?"

"The tennis coach. Bet she coaches all kinds of sports."

Wolf laughed. "Could be. But I've never played on one of her teams."

"Then why did you kiss her?"

"Hey, I was ambushed. I sicced her on one of my buddies first chance I got." His eyes sparkled. Amusement apparently tempered his ire. "Glad you're jealous. Thought I was alone in that department. I didn't like it one bit when you kissed Moneybags this afternoon."

The teakettle whistled, a referee's signal to end round one.

Riley walked to the stove. Should she tell Wolf that kiss was a kiss off—a clean break with John Hunter? She felt Wolf's scrutiny as she emptied chocolate powder into the mug.

She pivoted toward the table, and Lucy shot across her path. Her right foot stuttered. Her body maintained its forward trajectory. She became fixated on the cup of cocoa.

As gravity took hold, she swiveled. She slid across the bright white tile as if she'd rounded third base and was sliding for home plate. Though her bottom absorbed the brunt of the shock, her tender shoulder and bruised ribs suffered collateral jostling.

"Riley!" Wolf sprang from his chair.

Ice cubes from Wolf's homemade cold pack skittered across the ceramic floor like glittering dice. Hot chocolate sloshed over her extended right hand.

"Dammit! Dammit! Dammit!" she yelped.

He knelt and eased the half-empty mug from her hand. Using the tea towel that had wrapped his ice, he sponged chocolate from her skin.

She rolled onto her good side and curled into a fetal ball to hold in the pain. Her eyes scrunched shut. She refused to cry. God, it hurt!

Wolf's warm breath whispered across her cheek. His fingers caressed her skin.

"Riley, sweetheart, talk to me. How bad is it? Want to go to the hospital?"

"I'm okay." She hated that her voice, issued through clenched teeth, sounded anything but fine. "My rump's well padded."

"Let me help you up."

She sucked in a deep breath, rolled onto her back. "Give me a sec."

He kissed her forehead, pushed a curl back from her face. His finger stroked her cheek. The pain receded. He kissed the top of her ear.

Riley's senses relayed signals that had nothing to do with pain. She opened her eyes. He hovered above her, the bare skin of his torso aglow in the warm kitchen light.

It was as if she'd channeled one of *those* dreams. The one where Wolf floated above, a wicked grin on his face. His malachite eyes watching as he pushed her to the brink of climax, then snatched her back so she would tremble and beg for more. When she awoke from that dream, a staccato pulse thrummed in her neck and a warm flutter between her thighs reminded her of how long it had been since she'd slept with a man.

Wolf leaned in. His lips brushed hers. "I really am sorry." He lifted her chin. "You had the day from hell. I made it worse, not better."

"No, you made today bearable. I'm sorry you got mauled."

Starting below his nipple, her index finger sketched the reverse of the icy droplet's descent. When she reached his shoulder, she tapped her fingernail. "I could ask Gary to kiss it here and make it better."

Wolf laughed. "Trying to slough off the dirty work, eh? I think you should shoulder some of the load."

"Come closer and I might."

"Okay, but if we're making up, you're more banged up than I am—lots of spots to kiss and make better. I need a head start."

He rolled her soft angora sweater upward, unbuttoned her pants, and eased the zipper down. His hand snaked inside the waistband on her panties, tugging them just short of her bikini line. Having gained total dominion over her midriff, he feathered kisses below her ribs. His teasing tongue rimmed her belly button, darting in and out of the indentation in a mock siege.

Heat flowed down her belly. She reached out, wanting to grab a handful of his thick ebony hair to pull him on top of her. Her fingers slid through his silky mane, and he dodged out of her sprained shoulder's limited range.

Keeping his left hand atop her thin slacks, he inched his probing fingers downward, as determined as a heat-seeking missile. He cupped her and slowly massaged.

"Any bruises that need kissing down here?"

Linda Lovely

"No . . . bruises." Each word came out as a punctuation point to a tiny gasp. Riley bucked upward, straining tight against his palm. Moisture gathered as her body signaled its eagerness. The want of Wolf made her tremble.

While his left hand stroked between her thighs, Wolf's right hand nudged her red sweater above her stretchy bra. The brand was Barely There, but Riley knew her tight nipples said Clearly Here. Wolf's tongue traced one of her erect nipples through the thin fabric.

"Well, now, how about here?" He rolled her right nipple between his thumb and middle finger. "Any healing kisses needed in this general vicinity?"

Her nipples grew rock hard. "What could it hurt?" she gasped on an indrawn breath.

He suckled her through the whisper of fabric. Riley arched up, urging him to take more of her breast in his mouth. His talented hands played her like a musical instrument. She didn't know which chord to answer first—the sweet treble or the bold and demanding bass.

"You know I do have a bed." Wolf's voice was husky. "We don't have to make out on the kitchen floor."

"Oh, yes, we do. It's not fair to get a girl all hot and bothered and take an intermission."

Wolf laughed. "Maybe we need a cooling off period."

He moved the ice-filled mixing bowl to his side. Then he swung a leg over her hips and straddled her. He knelt. None of his weight rested on her. Yet his heat sent its scorching demands right through their clothing.

The bulge in his jeans made it look downright dangerous to pull down his zipper. But that was exactly what Riley planned to do.

He hoisted her stretchy bra above her breasts, freeing them, and grabbed an ice cube. Their eyes held as he lowered the cube within a few millimeters of her right nipple. For what seemed an eternity, a drop of ice water clung stubbornly to the melting cube before it cascaded. Riley squirmed as a tingling sensation flooded her senses. Wolf's hot tongue lapped up the moisture.

He carried his promise of fire and ice to her other breast. Riley writhed, climbing to a plateau of pleasure she'd only visited with him.

She longed to sit up, bring her mouth to his. Her bruised ribs kept her prone. "I want to kiss you, feel you." Riley realized her voice belonged to a supplicant, a beggar. She wanted to feel his lips against hers more than anything in the world.

"Not yet." Wolf wore the impish grin of her dreams. "You may be the boss at BRU, but here you have to wait your turn."

He scooted away from her questing hands, and his fingers dipped inside the waistband of her slacks. He tugged with authority. She raised her bottom to assist. He shifted position, removed her pants, and tossed them into a distant corner. On his next sortie, he captured her panties and sent them sailing in another direction.

Again he placed his palm against her mound and held it there as if to absorb the shuddering heat. "God, you're beautiful."

To her surprise, he withdrew. She wanted to cry out, "Come back! This instant!" But the interruption would be brief. She knew Wolf wanted her as much as she craved him.

He fetched his discarded sweater, knelt again, and kissed her on the lips. Then he wadded his sweater into a makeshift pillow and gently lifted her head.

"Comfy? This kissing stuff could take a while."

Her stomach fluttered as he scooted back toward her hips. The balled sweater raised her head, providing an unfettered view of his handsome face and chiseled torso. A pulse throbbed in a vein at his throat as he trailed his fingers along the outer curves of her hips and thighs.

When he reached her ankles, he grasped them, gently tugged her legs apart, and centered himself between them. His eyebrow lifted as he released one ankle and reached for the bowl of ice. "Ready for a little experiment? They say ice is good for injuries, too."

Riley nodded, shivering with anticipation.

He draped her legs over his shoulders. "If you don't like this, tell me to stop."

"Okay." She pressed her palms hard against the cool tile to ground herself. She was so hot she thought the ice might just sizzle and vanish as steam the instant it touched her.

Wolf watched her face as he once again held the ice cube teasingly, a few millimeters above her.

When the first droplet fell, Riley cried out. All her senses on fire. He reached out to the mixing bowl and popped a fresh ice cube between his teeth. He lowered his head. Half his face disappeared, but the memory of his stormy green eyes burned into hers.

THIRTY-EIGHT

Wolf figured the evening's lovemaking was on the wane. That was okay. He'd loved watching Riley in the throes of passion, listening to her contented sighs, her sensuous purrs.

She spooned against him on the tile floor. He hugged her, trying to stave off the goose bumps staking claims on her cooling flesh. He didn't want the closeness to end.

"Remember when we met—the triathlon?" His lips grazed her ear. "Do you still compete?"

Her laugh approached a giggle. "Hope you're not asking me to swim 500 meters, bike thirteen miles, and run a 5K tonight."

"No, I watched you massage your bad knee the other day. Wondered how much grief it gives you."

"I don't *compete* anymore. But I train. After my knee surgery, I asked the surgeon if any activities were off limit. His answer, 'motion is lotion.' He recommended biking and swimming over running. I joined a hiking club last fall. The mountain trails are spectacular."

"I love them, too." He pictured her strolling along a foothills trail, purple mountain laurel billowing around her like a fragrant aura. "When this mess ends, we'll go hiking. Have you ever explored the petroglyphs?"

"Petroglyphs? Like cave drawings? I didn't know we had any near here."

"They're about a mile southeast of Twin Peak. Symbols— mostly circles—chiseled on granite boulders by paleo Indians. At least two thousand years' old. The theory is boys had to make their mark to become men. A rite of passage."

Riley shivered.

"You're cold. Time to tuck you into bed."

Linda Lovely

Let her rest. Come morning he'd give his delectable
houseguest more than cereal to start her day. He scrambled to
his feet, pulled on his jeans. Avoiding her tender shoulder joint,
he slid his hands beneath her armpits to raise her to her feet.

When she was upright, Riley slid her hand inside *his*
waistband. "Yes, I agree completely. Time for bed." Her
lopsided grin showed off trouble-making dimples. "Chop, chop.
Let's go."

She appeared to have something other than slumber in
mind. Her energy reserves amazed him. Who was he to argue?
Neither stopped to pick up her forsaken clothes.

When they reached the stairs, he bowed her ahead. "Ladies
first."

"My ass," she countered.

"Exactly." He patted her bare butt.

"Just wait till you're nude and defenseless." She
punctuated the threat with an evil comic book chortle.

He feigned a cringe of fear. "At your service."

"You bet." She lasered him with a look of mock ferocity.
Her sprightly step belied her battered state and the day's
endless stressors.

In the bedroom, Wolf pulled back the covers. Then Riley
seized control, unzipping his jeans and sliding them downward
as she playfully tapped on his chest. He toppled onto the bed.
Her energetic fingers and darting tongue stoked him to the
flashpoint.

When she requisitioned a condom, Wolf figured he'd retake
command. Her outstretched fingers wriggled in a give-it-here
gesture. She cloaked his length. Her languid finesse made him
think about gartered ladies sliding silk stockings over naked
legs.

Her mouth heated and moistened his second skin. The
tactic hoisted his butt right off the bed. She guided him inside

168

her. His fists twisted the sheets to maintain a modicum of control.

Riley made it clear. She would lead this entire dance number. First a waltz, an agile glide around the ballroom, followed by hip-swiveling rock-n-roll. Then utter stillness. A pause for him to control his raspy breath. And, finally, a sizzling build up to a Calypso beat.

He kept his eyes open, memorizing her wild beauty. Wide eyes, irises that sparkled like cat's-eye marbles. A glimpse of even white teeth and pink tongue behind parted lips. The curve of her arched back as his fingers fastened on her rigid nipples. Explosion.

THIRTY-NINE

L.J. wrinkled his nose. While a new building was being constructed on campus, BRU's English Department had rented space in an empty elementary school the county was trying to unload. Nick had loaned him a pick set to get past the front door's simple lock.

A dark hallway exuded the stale musk unique to old buildings that had hosted decades of sweaty little bodies. His penlight swung across the posted directory: Dr. Wolf Valdes, Room 110. He groped down the corridor.

He picked the lock to 110, closed the door, and splayed his light over the compact space. Scarred desk, twin visitor chairs, sagging bookshelves packed floor-to-ceiling, and a hall tree.

Excellent. A man's jacket hung in plain sight. He stuffed it in the plastic bag he'd brought for loot. He'd pry some threads loose to leave at the murder scene. Then bury the jacket where a deputy could discover it. Once Valdes was framed. Nick could legitimately shoot him—a murder suspect—for resisting arrest.

His gaze swept the professor's desk. *Must be my clean living. Pure karma.* The half-breed used a ceremonial hunting knife as a letter opener. A helpful addition to his treasure sack.

Ten minutes later, he parked around the corner from the professor's townhouse. Though more than a block from the action, he had a clear line of sight for his night scope. Less than five minutes elapsed before the Onward lackeys' jalopy wheezed into position.

He felt as if he watched a silent movie. Unfortunately the scene bore a striking resemblance to a Three Stooges flick. The trio of rubes seemed to wander around the professor's lawn for hours trying to decide where to hoist the effigy.

Pick a spot and get on with it! You're not erecting a Confederate monument.

When they finally retrieved the tri-pod from the car, they slammed the trunk. *Are you trying to get caught?* Low IQ had to be an Onward membership requirement.

He watched the village idiots place gas-soaked rags around their diorama. When they finally torched them, he flipped open his throwaway cell phone and placed anonymous calls to the sheriff's department and the TV station. To ensure a timely response by cops and cameras, his compromised deputy had already firebombed a car nearby.

* * * *

Wolf could no longer feel his arm. Riley's head lay on his numbed bicep. Yet he couldn't bring himself to shift and risk waking her. God knew she deserved some shut-eye.

Courtesy didn't stop his erection from staging a full salute. Patches of her satin skin innocently contacted his chest and thighs, radiating warmth. He tried to slow his jacked up pulse. Her delicious proximity sabotaged his efforts.

His arm began to cramp. *Please. Wake up.*

Watery moonlight from a high transom washed the room a cool blue. Daybreak had to be an hour or two away. Wolf read the digital clock. Three a.m.

Eyes closed, he tried to place himself in a soothing scene. His make-believe waterfall cascaded through mountain greenery. A creek gurgled, a bird sang.

Voices and scuffling sounds intruded. Not part of his imaginary paradise. Whoosh. A flicker of orange flooded the window shade. He tugged his arm free, jumped from bed, yanked aside the shade.

He grasped the symbolism in a blink. No subtlety. Three braced timbers formed a tri-pod. An absurd effigy swung from the apex, a noose around its neck. Dancing flames gave the object a jerky kinetoscopic life.

Wolf's night visitors had lynched a one-time staple of Confederate lawns. The statue's round white eyes and large rouged lips offered a minstrel-show version of a black man. But the vandals had added something more — the cascading feathers of an Indian headdress.

"Goddamn bastards!"

"What is it?" Wide awake now, Riley sprang from the bed.

"Visitors," he growled. He pulled on boxers and rushed to the door. "Stay here. I want a piece of those goons."

His bare feet glided over the polished wood stairs. He saw Riley's Glock atop the hall table and grabbed it. He yanked the front door open and barreled onto the lawn. He raised the gun as his feet traded sidewalk for dew-soaked grass. He ran toward three males fleeing the ring of fire. Two jumped in the getaway car's front seat. The third bubba dove into the rear. His door clanked shut.

The muffler's ragged rumble signaled he was too late. Wolf tried to catch his breath. Damn. Smeared mud hid the license plate. The rusty heap's faded paint job made the color impossible to decipher.

He bellowed in frustration and pointed the gun at the sky. "Here's what's waiting for you if you come back, Dickheads!" He pulled the trigger.

The gun's report rumbled across the suburban neighborhood like receding thunder. Riley called to him. A siren burped. Blue lights swirled. Cops. A van zoomed into the empty space behind the bubbletop.

"Wolf, stop." Riley's voice vibrated with anger.

He lowered the gun and turned toward her. And instantly regretted his impetuous reaction.

Stupid. Stupid. Stupid.

·

Dressed in one of his dress shirts, she wrapped it tight to her body. The shirttails barely skimmed her knees. He hurried toward her, wanting to protect her, to hustle her inside. It wouldn't take a genius to realize she was nude beneath the white cotton.

Riley coughed as the breeze swirled thick, pungent smoke in her face. The noxious smell held a heavy chemical component. Gasoline. The hate-mongers had used gas-soaked rags. Must have wanted the acrid fire to burn long enough for his neighbors to get an eyeful.

The idiots confused their ethnic insults. Cuban ancestors—Latin, not African—deepened the shade of his skin. But the Indian war bonnet worried him. This was no random threat.

He reached Riley midway between the front stoop and the fire-lit effigy and pulled her toward him.

"Drop your weapon!" The command issued from a cop crouched behind an open vehicle door. The man's drawn weapon registered just before the spotlight's glare ruined his night vision.

"I'm placing the gun on the ground." Wolf kept his voice soft. He stepped away from Riley and set the Glock on the grass.

Damn. I hope this yokel doesn't blow my head off.

His heart hammered. He was keenly aware a Leeds County lawman might leap to the wrong conclusion seeing a gun-toting brown man and a half-clothed white woman.

Fear and anger warred for internal control. He gestured at the abomination left by his nighttime callers. "My visitors weren't here to wish me well. I grabbed the gun for defense. I didn't shoot at anyone—just fired into the air to scare them."

"It's illegal to discharge a firearm in public." The officer spoke in a flat, emotionless voice. "Put your hands up and keep them up. You're under arrest."

Un-freakin' believable. Could they really arrest him?

The officer straightened, lowered his firearm and walked briskly toward him. Meanwhile the partner, positioned near the patrol car, lowered his blinding light.

Wolf couldn't see. Red dots swam on an inky sea. His eyesight lacked detail and depth. He blinked. Damn. The deputies weren't the only interlopers. The van behind the cruiser sported a TV station's call letters. It disgorged a cameraman and reporter.

He stole a glance at Riley. She ducked her head like a turtle retreating into its shell. She lifted her good arm to block her face from the cameraman while she clamped the nightshirt closed with her left fist.

Lights flitted on in surrounding townhouses. Wolf winced as he heard the scrapes of doors and windows flung open by curious neighbors.

"Officer, can we please talk inside?" He swiveled his outstretched hands back and forth with his fingers splayed. "Come on, you can see I'm unarmed."

The deputy, now a mere foot away, kicked the surrendered gun farther from Wolf's reach and turned his attention to Riley. "Ma'am, are you okay?"

When she lifted her head to answer, the officer snorted in surprise. "Riley Reid! What in blazes are you doing here?"

"Can we go inside, Phil?" Riley asked. "This gentleman in his skivvies is a professor at BRU. He's no threat to the general peace and neither am I."

"Sure, Riley." Phil holstered his gun, waved his partner forward, and retrieved the Glock.

Sensing gunplay was now unlikely, the reporter and cameraman sprinted forward. "Do you live here?" the reporter yelled. "Is someone threatening you? Did you shoot someone?"

"Dammit," Riley swore as she ducked inside. "It's that slime bucket, Brad Able. He'll think he's died and gone to heaven. A chance to crucify me as a low-life slut. We'll both be fired. Mom'll be mortified."

Her words brought Wolf up short. Someone had hung a crude effigy on his lawn, a deputy just told him he was under arrest, and she was worried about her mom's sensibilities?

Who the hell needs this?

FORTY

L.J. started his Mercedes. What idiots! When Wolf ran outside waving a gun, L.J. almost hoped he'd plug one of the fleeing boobs. An arrest would remove the Indian from the picture. He sighed. Still, he was glad the getaway car got away. A wounded vandal could have been real trouble.

He replayed the image of Riley trotting outside like a surprised whore. Maybe now that her reputation was smeared, she'd reconsider shacking up with Valdes. More importantly, Injun boy now had a personal motive for seeking vengeance against Onward.

L.J. pushed his watch's light display and drove away. Fifteen minutes to meet up with Nick.

He coasted to a stop and turned off the engine. Grabbing the bag with his pilfered treasures, L.J. walked to the waiting cruiser and climbed in the backseat. Nick and his front-seat passenger swiveled to face him.

"Things go as planned?" Nick asked.

"Smoother than a bikini wax job. Who's your sidekick, Nick?"

"This here is Buford Smith. Smitty, meet our benefactor, Mr. Bond. James Bond."

Nick winked at L.J. Smitty dipped his head in a silent greeting. No chuckle at the intro, his lips didn't hitch up in a smile. L.J. wasn't sure if Smitty was scared or plain stupid.

James Bond, indeed. He could always count on his pal's hillbilly humor, even as they herded Smitty toward the gallows. L.J. and Nick had been high school classmates and starters on the state championship football team. Though their lives followed different paths, they stayed hunting buddies, bagging duck and deer together.

L.J. had ordered the deputy to round up Smitty. First they'd scour the mountaintop retreat to remove any evidence that might help the FBI catch the Onward numbnuts before they served their purpose. Then Smitty would be put to his highest and best use—as a corpse decoy.

L.J. paid Nick well to insulate Whitten Industries from direct contact with the sheriff's other bent deputy and the Onward rabble. He regretted his anonymous attendance at an Onward meeting. But Nick had insisted the leaders needed assurance they weren't being set up.

Tonight L.J. didn't need to shield his identity. Smitty would never talk.

No one spoke on the drive. Only the crunch of tires on the graveled fire road broke the silence. Smitty rocked to and fro like a penitent at a revival meeting. His stringy hair looked as if it had been combed with bear grease. Sour sweat poured off the man. When they neared the Cougar Mountain hideaway, the rube finally gave voice to his fear.

"How come there ain't no one else with us?" He stole a quick look at Nick. "You told me we was gonna clean up the camp before some FBI raid. Don't we need help?"

"The three of us can manage," Nick answered. "Mr. Bond and I only need one extra pair of hands. Consider it KP duty for your stupidity with the Latino girl."

"I'm real sorry about that . . ."

"No worry, son." Nick's voice soothed. "Everyone makes mistakes."

L.J. smiled. His childhood friend had a way with cretins.

For the next half hour, Nick snapped orders and Smitty followed them. The menial assignments relaxed the sacrificial lamb—plus the work needed doing. No point in Nick and L.J. doing all the humping when they had willing manual labor.

He couldn't believe Smitty never noticed his hands were the only ones not sporting gloves. Nick crept up on the runt as he bent over to pick up a rifle shell. He grabbed Smitty's fouled hair with his left hand and jerked his head backward. Wolf's ceremonial knife sliced cleanly through the victim's neck. Smitty's blood sprayed like a geyser.

The body quit twitching in seconds. Nick nudged the crumpled form with his boot. L.J. wasn't sure why he bothered—Smitty wasn't a chicken. He couldn't run around with his head practically severed.

"Still want me to give him a haircut?" Nick asked.

"Yeah. Scalp him."

Nick tugged on the dead man's hair for lift and applied the knife's keen edge. A generous hank of Smitty's dingy hair and skin slid free. White skull peeked through the bloody leftovers.

"Good enough." The process reminded L.J. of skinning a rabbit. He held out a large plastic baggie for the deposit. Nick dropped the severed scalp inside.

L.J. smiled. "I know just where to bury this. An anonymous call to your buddies in blue will put the professor in a real pickle."

"You're one mean mother. Hope you never have a grudge against me."

L.J. fixed his boyhood friend with a hard stare. "Me, too."

The deputy looked away. "Reporters are gonna wet their pants when they hear how Smitty bought it. Think the FBI will tell all?"

"Don't care as long as it makes the sheriff and FBI run in more directions."

"Are we leaving the knife here for the Feebs to find?" Nick asked as he wiped the jagged blade on a clump of grass to clean off some of the gore.

"No, it's a family heirloom. He wouldn't abandon it. Toss it in the bag with our toupee."

L.J. zipped the bag shut and set it near the path they'd taken into camp.

Nick grabbed a rake to obliterate the dusty shoeprints around Smitty's body. "Good idea bringing this. Hard to pin a murder on someone when the footprints don't match."

L.J. watched the deputy tidy up. "You have everything straight? Think you can disguise your voice and play the panicked motorist?"

Nick huffed. "Hey, it's not that tough."

"Prove it," L.J. said.

Nick repeated his prepared script three times. L.J. assumed the role of a 911 operator and grilled the deputy. The rehearsed answers sounded uninspired, but adequate.

"Okay. That just leaves your friends, the Onward *knights*. They have another camp north of Twin Peak, right? Have 'em meet you there tonight and give it to them straight—Smitty died from fatal sloppiness. I want their assholes to pucker if they even think about deviating from my orders. Make sure they get it—they lay low until after the bombs explode Saturday."

Nick nodded. "Hey, I get it. Sometimes it sounds like you think I'm as dumb as old Smitty." He tossed down the rake. "Done."

A crackling noise snapped the men to attention. Wind rustling leaves? An animal foraging? Nick crouched and unholstered his gun. He motioned L.J. to head into the woods and circle in the opposite direction, a classic pincher move.

L.J. readied his gun. He tried to move silently, but dry leaves advertised every footfall. Surely they'd hear the same rustling sounds if someone were spying on them. Probably just an animal.

The silhouette of a man appeared, and L.J. trained his gun on the figure. "Stop, it's me," Nick called in a stage whisper. "Point that pistolo somewhere else. No one's here."

"You sure?" L.J. asked.

No longer trying to stay silent, Nick beat the bushes around him with a fallen branch. "Yeah, I'm sure. Let's blow."

L.J. wavered. He had the eerie sensation he was being watched—that the eyes following him were human. "You suppose that Indian's uncle is poking around? Maybe we should pay a visit, put him permanently to sleep. Stage it like his nephew went on a homicidal rampage."

"Nah," Nick answered. "That'd raise more questions. You're the one always preachin' to keep it simple. I know the old coot. Ray might be a danger come sun-up, but once night falls he keeps steady company with Jim Beam. He's dead drunk by now. Forget it. It was an animal."

Bone tired, L.J. blamed his paranoia on fatigue. As they trudged toward the car, he gazed at the heavens. Only a smattering of stars remained visible in the pre-dawn sky.

FORTY-ONE

It was still dark when Riley let herself into her mother's condo. Inside she paused, weighing what would be more likely to trigger a heart attack—a yoo-hoo that roused her mom from sleep or the aroma of perking coffee. Either would tell the seventy-two-year-old she wasn't home alone.

Craving caffeine, she gave the edge to Maxwell House and tiptoed to the kitchen. Lucy proved less considerate, meowing a cranky protest at being jailed again.

Before liberating the feline, Riley closed the kitchen door to keep Lucy semi-confined. The last thing her mom needed was a twenty-pound cat pouncing on her fragile chest. As she released Lucy, Riley stroked her broad ebony back in apology. After she set down dishes of water and kibble, she drew back lace curtains covering the jalousied windows above the spotless sink. Dawn sent tender shoots of yellow into the eggplant sky.

She started the coffeemaker and settled at the kitchen table. Riley glanced at the oven clock: 6:05. Unbelievable. Her emotional roller coaster made it seem as if the world had spun on its axis a dozen times since she made love with Wolf.

She braced her elbows on the polished oak table and dropped her weary head into her hands. Her optimistic dad raised her to look for positives. Were there any? A couple. The officers had shooed the media ghouls away, though only after they captured embarrassing footage. Phil also relented about arresting Wolf for illegally discharging a firearm. But his comment—"Riley, if you vouch for him, I'll let it slide."—didn't exactly improve Wolf's mood.

Once the deputies left, Wolf grew quiet, unresponsive. It was clear he believed racist bias colored the deputies' actions? She had a different take. While the effigy outraged her, Wolf had shown bad judgment, firing a gun in the suburbs. What if his bullet had ricocheted and injured a neighbor peeking out a second-story window?

She tried to persuade Wolf the deputies would put real effort into running down the vandals. They promised to treat the mock hanging as a hate crime, and Phil put out a BOLO.

Problem was neither Wolf nor Riley could give the officers a worthwhile description. No license plate. No year or make of vehicle. Not even car color. The men wore hoods—orange rather than Klan white. While Riley felt certain they belonged to Onward—orange appeared to be a gang color—she had no proof. She couldn't even swear the thugs were Caucasian.

She kept asking why. Why target Wolf? Because he spotted Smitty? If so, they'd exacted retribution very quickly. The timetable and organization seemed improbable.

Phil asked Wolf to guess why he'd been targeted. His answer: "You mean like me being both Injun and Spic—two of your redneck's favorite targets?"

The atmosphere descended further into the crapper when Phil asked if someone might have a problem with Wolf's and Riley's *relationship*—"given how some folks feel about race mixing." For a moment, Riley wondered if her lover might deck the peace officer.

But, dammit, the question had merit. Could whoever trashed her bedroom have spied her kissing Wolf in the BRU parking lot? John Hunter's face popped into her mind, but she scoffed at the notion of the millionaire businessman having any truck with Onward.

If her romance with Wolf triggered the incident, it had to be some white supremacist freak. The deputies floated the idea of a stalker. Maybe. It fit with the break-in at her home.

The kitchen door creaked. She jumped.

"Hi, sweetie. I smelled coffee and figured it was you. When I looked out my window and saw your car, I ruled out a considerate burglar."

Miz Pearl had applied foundation makeup and lipstick and patted her lacquered hair in place before padding downstairs. From the drape of her housecoat, she'd evidently donned a bra, too. Appearances had to be maintained. The nasal cannula that fed oxygen from her mother's concentrator was absent. *Must have had a good night.*

"Hi, Mom. Glad I didn't frighten you. I just wanted to talk first thing."

Her mother frowned. She ambled to the coffee pot, which had just announced its gurgling finale. She poured two mugs and took the chair beside Riley.

"What's wrong?"

Riley hated to see the worry clouding her mother's eyes. Those eyes had once been sky blue. After her brother died, the color began to leach away like pigment in a fading photo.

"Mom, I'm fine. But someone broke into my house yesterday."

Her mother gasped, and Riley reached out and squeezed her hand. "Just vandalism. Nothing stolen. To play it safe I spent the night with a friend."

She paused in her fumbling storytelling. Was her mother following? The woman looked weak and confused, and she hadn't even reached the good part.

"While I was at my friend's house, there was another . . . um, incident . . ."

It took twenty minutes for Riley to spit out her tale and answer questions—the ones Miz Pearl voiced. She knew her mother held back. If she didn't inquire, she wouldn't hear unpalatable answers. Ignoring unpleasantness was one of her mom's prime coping strategies, though she had no problem making other people uncomfortable.

The Cherokee Nation had hired an attorney to represent Hank Youngblood. Once Hank was acquitted, Miz Pearl blamed a corrupt court system. At every opportunity, she voiced her opinion that minorities got away with murder by crying discrimination. Boo hoo.

Years had passed since Riley and her mother fought about those racist views. Her mother wisely quit voicing her opinions in Riley's presence. A truce of silence.

"That name Valdes. Is this man a Mexican?"

"No, mother. He's a professor at the university."

Come on, Riley. Tell her who he is. Just do it.

"Oh, Riley, why didn't you come stay with me? I know it may have been totally innocent, but what will John think? Why you're practically engaged."

The hand that rested under Riley's scrabbled in agitation. Her mother's breathing deteriorated to a wheezy staccato.

"Mom, want me to get your oxygen?"

"No, no. I'm fine."

She gently squeezed her mother's fingers to still them. "I am not 'practically engaged' to John Hunter."

Her mom's lips quivered as if she were about to cry.

Riley didn't relent. "Yesterday I told John I didn't want to date him any longer. He's a nice man. Simply not the one for me."

"Oh, honey, don't be rash!" Miz Pearl sucked in a ragged breath, followed by a wet cough. "Give this more thought. You have a real future with John. You're still young enough for children. Surely you're not letting him go for this Valdes person. What do you even know about him?"

It has to be done. Do it.

"Mom, listen to me. Wolf Valdes is a quarter Cuban, a quarter Cherokee, and fifty-percent bullheaded Irish. He's a very nice man. Like me, he was about thirteen when Jack died. He never met my brother. But he does know Hank Youngblood. He's his cousin."

All color drained from her mother's face. "How could you?" She stumbled to her feet. "I can't look at you right now. I can't talk to you."

Tears ran down Riley's cheeks. "Mom, you have to let go of your hate. I don't know what may happen. But I have feelings for Wolf."

Her mother shook her head and shuffled toward the bedroom.

"If you love me, you'll find a way to understand. He played no part in Jack's death." Riley's last words were spoken to a closing door.

* * * *

Sitting in her car, Riley flipped open her cell phone. Though Wolf had no morning class, she was certain he'd be awake. After seven rings, a mechanical leave-a-message spiel played. Riley hung up. She couldn't say what she wanted to a freaking answering machine.

Had he screened the call? Seen it was her and decided not to pick up? Or was he already out chasing down leads?

Where are you, Wolf?

FORTY-TWO

After Riley left, Wolf couldn't sleep. By five a.m., he gave up, threw on jeans and a long-sleeved T-shirt, and started a pot of industrial-strength coffee. The first mug did nothing to ease his exhaustion. In fact, the high-test brew put a jangled edge on his nerves.

"Screw this." He stomped to the sink and tossed the dregs. Yesterday his students took their last final. He had no classes and was too worked up to sit around and brood. He thought he'd matured enough that ethnic insults no longer burrowed under his skin like painful splinters. Consider the source, and all that.

Wrong. He was spoiling for a fight.

Needing a mission, Wolf decided to pay an early morning call on his uncle. He pulled on hiking boots, grabbed a jacket, and headed for his Jeep. Ray rose at first light no matter how many conversations he'd held with a bottle the night before. Though Wolf didn't know when the FBI would raid Onward's camp, he figured spending the day with Ray would put him close to the action. Maybe the agents would call on his uncle as a guide and he could tag along.

Fear for his missing assistant ratcheted up with each hour of silence. He wished the kid would answer his damn phone. Maybe Tom would be rescued by day's end—if he needed rescuing. Perhaps the brash student had pulled off his pose as a rabid racist. If Tom had been welcomed into the brotherhood, Wolf hoped he'd gained concrete evidence of their planned violence. Empty threats would be worthless in court.

Cool morning mist dallied. The clouds seemed tethered in the mountain valleys. As his Jeep hurtled ahead, Wolf's mood improved. He tuned to a country radio station and sang loudly to "Thank God, I'm a Man!" His stomach joined in, growling for a manly meal.

He pulled into the Gas-N-Go country store less than a quarter-mile from his uncle's turnoff. His mouth watered as he shut off the ignition. The owners offered a sinful selection of doughnuts, including Ray's favorite cream-filled long johns.

Mary, the rotund grandmother who ran the store with her husband, Bob, unhooked the front chain and flipped the store sign from "Closed" to "Open" when she saw Wolf.

"You're up early, and it's not even hunting season."

Wolf stopped in with Ray quite often so Mary knew him well. They chatted about the weather—sunny with a high expected in the eighties—as he filled a bag with day-old sweets. "Them are half-price. Leftovers. Sorry we haven't got fresh. Coffee's not ready neither."

He smiled as she counted out his change. "This'll do fine, Miss Mary. Thanks."

Once he turned down the rutted road to Ray's cabin, the sweet aroma of chocolate and grease sabotaged his willpower and he pulled out the top pastry. He was licking chocolate off his fingers when Ray ran out of the woods, arms windmilling, eyes wide with fright.

Wolf slammed on his brakes and jumped out. Ray practically plowed him over. "Get back in. Now! Turn around. We have to get the hell away. Fast."

"What's wrong? Where are we going?"

"I'll explain—after we grab weapons, food, and camping gear. You put Smoky in his pen. Put out plenty of food and water. Don't know when we'll get back."

Was Ray hallucinating? His uncle went through some bad times after his last tour in Bosnia. Gory flashbacks. Frightening delusions. Maybe yesterday's excitement triggered old nightmares.

Wolf did as his uncle bid. If Ray was in his right mind, he had solid reasons. If his uncle were delusional, Wolf stood a better chance of calming him if he humored him first.

"Smoky," Wolf called to the hound. "Time for breakfast." The dog bayed a welcome, bounded out of the woods, and skidded to his side. He knelt and patted Smoky's head, coaxed him into his run, and closed the gate. He lowered a bucket into the well to bring up fresh water and fetched a bag of Kibbles N Bits from the back porch.

Tasks complete, he entered the cabin. His jaw dropped when he surveyed the jumble of camping gear and weapons piled by the front door. The arsenal included bows and arrows, hatchets, bear traps, knives, and guns.

"We going to war, Ray?" He kept his voice calm.

His uncle fixed him with a cold stare. "Damn straight, son. You've been drafted whether you know it or not. Carry this load to the Jeep, will you?"

Wolf's heart beat faster. *What's going on?* He picked up as much of the weapons cache as he could carry and dumped it in his backseat. Ray was right behind him with pup tents, a camping stove, backpacks, bolt cutters, and a saw.

Ray opened the passenger door and climbed inside. When he spied the bag of fried treats, he shook his head. "Jesus H. Christ. You stopped at Gas-N-Go?"

That cut it. Wolf snapped. "Dammit, Ray, what's the matter? You drunk? Stoned?"

"Wish I were. Mary and Bob will tell the cops you came by. That's the final nail in your coffin. Reliable eye witnesses to place you here round the time of the murder."

"What murder? We're not going anywhere till you make some sense."

"Smitty," Ray replied. "They slit his throat and scalped him. I'm pretty sure they used your great grandad's blade. They're planting the knife and Smitty's scalp to frame you."

Wolf grabbed his uncle's arm. He wondered if he'd have to squeeze each detail out of the agitated vet. "Ray, who are *they*?"

"Nick Monson, a deputy. He slit Smitty's throat. I didn't know his pal, the guy calling the shots. The boss man had wavy silver hair, dark eyes, fancy gold watch. Late forties? Oh, yeah, and a strawberry birthmark below his chin. "

Dread cramped Wolf's stomach. His mouth went so dry he wondered if his tongue could unglue itself to form a word. Ray wasn't hallucinating. The order giver had to be John Hunter. He'd noticed the birthmark when his date had reacted to Hunter in the restaurant.

Is he framing me for murder because of Riley?

No. That was insane.

"Ray, we need to call the sheriff or the FBI. And I mean right now. Any so-called evidence they're using to frame me is circumstantial. Plus you can testify, set things straight."

His uncle's snort was derisive. "Boy, you're dreamin'. They'll say I'm lying 'cause you're kin, or they'll label me certifiably crazy. Besides they don't plan to *arrest* you, you fool. You're gonna be shot *resistin'* arrest."

Wolf stared at Ray, wondering if his uncle intended to counter this insanity with his own brand of crazy. Why all the weapons? Did Ray envision some kamikaze last-stand against authority? That would spell more death, Ray's included.

He grabbed his uncle's arm, forced him to look him in the eye. "I'm not going to hole up somewhere and shoot it out with the law. If that's what you're thinking, my answer is no."

Ray shook him off. "Wrong enemy, son. We're going hunting. I know where Onward's gone to ground. They're meeting tonight north of Twin Peak. There's a clearing. Fairly level. An old logging road runs within a mile of it. That's how the Onward members will arrive."

His uncle's tobacco-stained teeth appeared in a twisted smile. "I'm sure Deputy Nick will show. And, if there's one thing I learned in Bosnia, it was how to make a man talk."

Wolf didn't like the haunted look in his uncle's rheumy eyes or the not-so-subtle hint that Ray's thoughts ran to kidnapping and torture. But he saw no point in waiting for authorities to arrest—or shoot—him. If Ray had a notion how to track Onward, maybe they could extract Tom and find proof Nick had wielded Wolf's knife.

"They're sure to have lookouts," Wolf said. "We won't be able to use the logging road."

"Don't have to. There's another way in." Ray grinned. "When old Murph had his still, he kept chickens roosting in the trees. His own low-tech warning system. We'll cut in the back way."

"Aren't those trails closed to the public this time of year?"

Ray pulled a gooey long john out of the pastry sack and took a big bite.

"Damn, these are good. Hope they're not our last." His tongue chased a smear of chocolate around his lips. "Don't worry. I've yet to see a trail that's closed to me. Now move it."

"Not quite yet." Wolf pulled out his cell phone.

"Don't be an idiot!" Ray grabbed for the phone. "I heard tell these phones have some sort of GPS implants. Don't go giving the law any help tracking us."

"I won't," Wolf answered. "They'll know I was in the neighborhood soon enough. I'll just send a text message, then trash the phone. I have to warn Riley that Hunter's tied to the terrorists."

He paused realizing her phone could be tapped. So what? He didn't care if eavesdroppers heard him identify Hunter. The more people who heard his side of the story, the less likely they'd be to shoot him resisting arrest.

Wolf' flipped open the phone. "If we find any evidence, I need a way to get it to Riley. I sure don't want to draw Deputy Monson a treasure map."

"Who's this woman? You sure you can trust her?" Ray asked.

He hesitated. Should he tell Ray? His uncle would think he was really around the bend to trust anyone with Yates blood.

"I trust Riley to do what she believes is right. But, if they convince her I've killed someone, she may not consider my capture a bad thing."

Ray shook his head. His eyes told Wolf he pitied him. "Do what you must. But you're the crazy one."

After he sent the message, he stomped his phone with his hiking boot. Then he picked up a concrete block by the side of the road and dropped it on the slender tech package. It felt strangely good to obliterate his high-priced toy.

FORTY-THREE

Riley arrived at her office a few minutes before eight. The aroma of freshly brewed coffee cheered her. She poured a mug and headed for the windowless hole her staff mockingly called the executive boardroom, a space furnished with a folding table and five mismatched chairs.

Pete and Alan were seated. She'd never known either man to be late. Riley shut the door. As she joined them at the rickety table, Pete shuffled a newspaper beneath a stack of papers. A blush spread up his neck. *Damn, bet Wolf and I made the front page.*

She attempted a smile. "Pete?" She wiggled her fingers in a hand-it-over gesture. "I'll see it sooner or later. Might as well be sooner."

Should have picked up a copy on the way to work. Just call me Ms. Denial.

The officer plucked the folded newspaper free. Riley kept her expression neutral as she stared at the black-and-white snapshot of Wolf waving a gun and gripping Riley's forearm. The pair had just enough skin hidden for the paper to avoid a barrage of porno complaints. Wolf appeared in boxers; her partially-buttoned shirt teased her thighs. The photo captured a deputy running toward them, gun drawn. The swaying effigy was outside the picture frame. The headline read "Mock Lynching, Gunshots Shatter Suburban Quiet."

At least the editors didn't blast BRU in the headline. Riley skimmed the first paragraph.

Responding to an anonymous tip, Leeds County sheriff's deputies discovered a statue dangling from a noose on the front lawn of Dr. Wolf Valdes' townhouse. The black-faced statue used in the mock lynching wore an Indian war bonnet. An

English professor at Blue Ridge University (BRU) and author of a best-selling erotic thriller, Dr. Valdes is of Cuban and Cherokee descent.

Authorities report that Dr. Valdes and a houseguest, Riley Yates Reid, Director of Security for BRU, ran outside in an attempt to scare off the vandals. Dr. Valdes fired a warning shot as the vehicle departed.

The report made her wonder why the chancellor hadn't demanded her head on a plate. Well, he'll have to fire me. I won't resign before Saturday. Not until the Onward threat is over.

She tried a little levity to put Alan and Pete at ease. "Now you see why I never wear a dress?" She nodded at the picture. "Toothpick legs."

Her officers responded with eye rolls and chuckles, just as she'd hoped.

"Okay, back to business. Have you two solved all our graduation problems?"

"Not all." Pete toyed with his stack of papers and tried to match her nonchalance. "Wouldn't want you to feel unneeded, Boss."

"How about an alternative commencement site?"

Alan cleared his throat. "No dice on the Bi-Lo Center. Ringling Brothers has it booked." The officer fidgeted. "The manager quizzed me about the function and I stink at ad lib. I said we expected seven thousand people. I'm afraid that might give us away."

She frowned. "It'll make him wonder, but I doubt he'll phone the papers. He may gossip, but what are the odds he sips cocktails with Onward goons?"

She lifted her coffee cup. "How many ticket requests so far?"

Pete extracted a printout. "Just over six thousand. Usually we get a fair number of last-minute orders. We did last year."

"Do our attendance figures include faculty and students as well as guests?" she asked.

"Yep, the whole kit and caboodle. Seven thousand seems like a good number unless the Onward mess scares folks off."

"That would be sad." She shook her head. "I'd hate for these cretins to ruin a once-in-a-lifetime day for graduates and their families."

"Well, Clemson's Littlejohn Coliseum is an option," Pete said. "They held graduation last weekend. A buddy in Clemson security thought the school would work with us. We could adopt their security plan, layer in extras. No cobbling something together last minute."

"Sounds like a possibility. Good work." Riley smiled. "I'll ask Dr. Harris to phone Clemson's president. See if we can get a little brotherly cooperation. A venue change might throw Onward a curve, mess up anything planned specifically for our campus."

She scribbled a note. "Any word from the protection details for our VIPs? Have our illustrious dads backed out?" She didn't need to name names. Planning for their attendance had consumed hours of security staff time.

"With the exception of Senator Yates, all our celebs bailed," Alan said. "Their protection teams advised them the situation was too chaotic."

She nodded. "Good advice. Senator Yates is too stubborn. He told me he's not about to let a little uptick in death threats spoil his daughter's graduation."

Repeated death threats had desensitized her uncle. His position as head of the Senate Committee on Armed Services seemed to attract nut cases.

Alan's voice broke into her woolgathering. What in the world had he said?

"Sorry, I spaced out for a moment."

"Assuming Clemson gives a green light, when do we announce the change? It's Thursday. We only have today and tomorrow for prep time. Saturday is D day."

"I'll ask Dr. Harris to make the announcement as soon as Clemson agrees. PR can tackle notifying all graduating students and posting directions and maps on the web."

The door to the conference room flew open. Patty's panicked look telegraphed bad news.

"Riley, it's the FBI. I told Mr. Jacob you were in a meeting. He insisted it's an emergency, and he wants to talk to you *now*."

FORTY-FOUR

L.J. wasn't certain what prompted the urge to drive deeper into the mountains when Nick dropped him at his car.

His speedometer hovered around fifty—twenty miles over the mountain road's posted limit for its rare straight-aways. He smiled as he glanced at the shift knob and flicked the "Comfort" setting to "Sport." His right foot steadily increased pressure on the gas pedal.

Fifty-five. Sixty.

His tiredness evaporated. Images of Smitty's gory death played in his mind. Watching a man die was . . . invigorating.

With the sports car's hardtop retracted, wind combed his hair, and the morning sun sparked off his Rolex. Roadside trees, blushing with spring buds, rushed by in a soft blur of chartreuse and lime. His skin prickled. The dizzying speed jacked his pulse, boosted his high.

A caution sign popped into view—twisting black ink snaking across yellow metal. A series of switchbacks loomed. L.J. mentally gave the road sign the finger. Seconds later a new warning appeared. The first hairpin curve. Only a spindly railing separated his hurtling car from a steep drop. His body tensed. *Screw it.* He'd cling to the ribbon of pavement, defy death.

L.J. loved his Mercedes, an SL Class Roadster. Well worth its one-hundred-fifty thousand sticker price. The sports car could leap from a standstill to sixty miles per hour in 4.2 seconds. "Let's see what you've got!" he screamed into the wind.

Once before he'd pushed the speedometer over one hundred miles per hour, but that had been on a deserted country straightaway. This was different. This was living.

He knew better than to brake as he entered the curve. The squealing tires slid sideways. For an instant, the horizon offered only empty sky. He dragged the car back from the precipice, his knuckles white from a death-grip on the wheel. Coming out of each bend, he eased back slightly before slinging himself into the next curve in the slalom course.

Rounding the final bow in the hairpin marathon, he spotted the glint of sun on metal. His wheels played hopscotch with the centerline. The cop car careening toward him hugged the inside lane. Headed in the opposite direction—down the mountain.

Blue lights swirled. His chest tightened. He swerved, fought for control as the car shimmied. The patrol car slid by with inches to spare, vanishing before the scream of its siren.

Shit, shit, shit!

He sucked in a breath. The cop couldn't turn around. He had no view of the license plate. L.J. crested the mountain and pulled off on the first gravel road. His breath came in staccato pants. He laughed.

He swung the car around, flinging white gravel like wedding rice. Quiet descended. He sat, motionless as a sunning alligator. Ten minutes passed. Twenty. No cops. Looking out his windshield, he studied the peak of a distant mountain. Sun shone on a stone outcropping, making the granite look like a field of snow. He remembered Alaska's spectacular blue glaciers. He'd watched one calve. A gigantic mountain of ice breaking free to brave the roiling sea.

He felt a kinship with that glacier. Before his father's attempted suicide, he'd been strangely unemotional. But there'd always been a fault line, a part of him ready to break free.

He remembered the first time boiling anger consumed him. His mother, the bitch, had talked his father into backing some society pal. A crook. When the scheme imploded, she jettisoned L.J. and his dad to cozy up with another rich dude. He'd

wanted to smash her face. Kick in her ribs. But he wasn't ready
to face the consequences. She'd tell on him. Not a doubt in the
world. So he found another way to punish her. Nabbed the
yappy little dog she fussed over. Paid lots more attention to the
damn dog than she'd ever paid him. She never kissed her son
but she let the slobbering mutt lick her face.

Revenge. L.J. drove the stupid dog to another town and
dumped him. Didn't kill the mutt, but he let her think so. A
perfect outcome. She cried; he laughed up his sleeve.

Then came Barbara. Sophomore year. Pregnant with L.J.'s
son. She killed the baby, aborted it, before he even knew. Said
she wasn't about to throw away her future for a "mistake." He
wanted to punch Barbara, too. But people knew about them.
She'd tell. Another good-for-nothing, disloyal slut.

That night, L.J. picked up a prostitute in Columbia, SC,
screwed her, and beat her senseless. He'd never enjoyed sex
more.

FORTY-FIVE

Wolf nosed the Jeep up to a sturdy steel gate, spray-painted red. "Dammit, Uncle Ray, how do we get around this? Your puny bolt cutters won't do the trick."

While the Forest Service opened "red" roads to hunters and hikers for brief periods, they were generally reserved for law enforcement, firefighting, and rescue operations. Rangers took trespassing seriously.

The gate's metal supports were as thick as Wolf's thighs and sunk in concrete. The steel cross members weren't scrawny either. Even the padlock was encased in a secure cubbyhole, recessed within the steel frame. Massive pines and white oaks crowded the no-nonsense barrier. No side gaps to finesse.

"Do we hoof it from here? Must be eight miles and you want us to schlep an arsenal on our backs."

"Oh, ye of little faith." Ray swung a small key back and forth hypnotist-style.

"How in tarnation did you get that?"

Ray moseyed over to the gate. "Ranger Dennis gave me a key so's I could help with a black bear count. It's a master. Fits all the locks."

"So why did we bring bolt cutters?"

His uncle shrugged. "Never know. Might come in handy. Onward didn't give me the keys to their kingdom."

Wolf stretched. They'd driven for an hour, though they'd probably covered less than fifteen miles. Ray played navigator, directing him through a tangle of rutted dirt and gravel passageways. Without his uncle, he'd be lost, unless he stumbled on a Foothills Trail marker or scaled a peak that brought familiar landmarks into view.

The tangy pine scent invigorated him. Hard to believe this wasn't a run-of-the-mill wilderness outing. He and his uncle had hiked and hunted these woods a hundred times over.

"I'm going to take a little walk," Wolf told his uncle. "Be right back."

Maybe I'm the one hallucinating. Did Ray really say I'd been framed for murder?

He sighed. No. The nightmare was real, and he still wasn't certain what he and his uncle could accomplish playing guerilla warfare. What happened if they actually found the Onward camp?

If Riley tried to phone, she'd undoubtedly hear some "out of range" mumbo jumbo. He doubted Verizon had a canned message for "Sorry this phone was beaten to death."

By now she'd know he was a murder suspect. Would that color her response to his cryptic text message? After his angry performance last night—firing her gun—his fugitive status might not be a surprise.

No explanations were possible now. Time to forget Riley and focus on Onward and evidence. He needed proof some rich executive and a dirty deputy were trying to pin a murder on him.

Maybe. If he took photos of this Deputy Monson at Onward's new camp, he'd have backup. He kept a digital camera in his glove compartment to capture settings for his novels. He'd operate the camera in manual mode. Couldn't risk a flash.

A photo of Monson with Onward members might help convince authorities Ray wasn't telling a whopper to save his nephew. However, proving the deputy's guilt would be child's play compared to the challenge of nailing John Hunter. Would anyone believe his uncle witnessed the rich executive ordering Smitty to be scalped?

He imagined Hunter and the deputy safely immersed in their daytime routines—drinking lattes, making business deals, locking up drunks. His eyes narrowed. He prayed the deputy would visit the Onward camp come nightfall.

None of it made sense. Hunter—and his money—had to be behind Onward's sudden activity. Why? He couldn't picture the millionaire hanging out with these bubbas. Financing an attack on Blue Ridge University seemed idiotic. Even if Hunter harbored a grudge about his father's hefty donations to the school, taking revenge on the institution seemed insane.

What would Hunter get for his fifty thou investment? Chaos? Fear? Misdirection?

Wolf's gait slowed while his mind churned. As he ducked under a tree branch and returned to the dirt road, he watched a whistling Ray double-check their backseat arsenal. The grizzled mountain man's mood swings worried him. Wolf felt he was being sucked into a bottomless sinkhole. No rope in sight.

He assigned James Dickey's *Deliverance* in freshman English lit for its powerful, poetic prose. A Southern classic. He loved the book, but it made him wonder. In Dickey's novel, the hero's hand trembles when he first sights down on a living creature. Buck fever. Wolf had hunted bear and boar, deer and rabbit. But could he shoot a man?

His uncle stared at him. "Son, you're thinking too much. Sometimes you just need to act. Keep moving, and let life sort itself out. Better than sitting still, locked up in fear."

He nodded. No point debating. "How much farther?"

"About two hours."

"You sure they won't see or hear us coming?"

"Nah, we'll park a couple miles from the camp, sneak in the back door on foot."

FORTY-SIX

"You can't be serious, Gary. Wolf is no murderer!" Riley strangled the phone receiver, wishing it were someone's neck.

"I just left the Cougar Mountain campsite. It was deserted, literally broom clean—except for Buford Smith's corpse. I'm assuming he's the Smitty your Dr. Valdes screamed about. Smitty's throat was slit, and he'd been scalped."

"Scalped?" Horrified by the image, Riley took a second to make the connection.

"I see. That's why you suspect the English professor? Because he's one-quarter Cherokee? Give me a break."

"There's more to it." Gary adopted his I'm-the-authority tone. "A frightened motorist saw a man fitting Valdes' description run from the woods. The caller said the wild man was waving a knife and looked like he'd bathed in blood."

"An anonymous call, right? From an untraceable cell?"

"Doesn't invalidate it. Lots of people phone anonymously. Don't want to get involved."

"And just how did the sheriff come up with Wolf Valdes as a match?" Riley wasn't buying what Gary was shoveling. "He's the only six-foot-four male with black hair in the county? This reeks of set up."

"Owners of a Gas-N-Go near the crime scene confirmed Valdes purchased items around the estimated time of death, just after six a.m." Gary plowed on, ignoring her sarcasm. "Your boy had opportunity and motive."

"Motive? What motive?"

"Rage. Payback. Speculation is the professor decided Smitty hung the effigy on his lawn. Valdes knew the camp was one place Smitty might go. I heard him scream threats at Smitty—"

She cut off her ex-husband. "Gee, what was I thinking? Every time I say I want to teach a man a lesson, it means I plan to slit his throat. He's a professor, not Jack the Ripper. Besides Wolf reported the camp's location. He knew the FBI planned surveillance."

Her anger bloomed. "Why would he murder Smitty someplace the authorities would investigate? Valdes isn't stupid. I'll reserve that label for whoever deemed the bloody woodsman phone tip credible."

"I called as a courtesy." Gary's tone dropped to freezer level. "The rest of the team—especially the sheriff—weren't sure how to handle you, given your *relationship* with the suspect. I assured them you'd be objective, wouldn't fly off the handle or try to warn Valdes. Don't prove me wrong."

"You want objectivity—how's this? You see video of your half-naked ex-wife in a lover's arms. Maybe *you* have motive to nudge the sheriff into jumping on Wolf as a suspect."

She listened to Gary's breath. Staccato. Audible.

Finally, he spoke. "There's a BOLO out for Valdes as a person of interest in a homicide. This is a murder investigation—a local matter, outside FBI jurisdiction. The sheriff's en route to question you, to get more info on Valdes. I suggest you get it together."

The phone clicked. No goodbye.

She replaced the receiver and stared into space. Her mind wasn't blank. Just the opposite. It reeled with possibilities. She was dead certain Wolf hadn't murdered Smitty. Not that she thought him incapable of taking a life. She sensed he could kill—in self-defense or to protect someone. If she'd been told Wolf shot Smitty while attempting to rescue Tom, she'd have bought in. But scalping? No way.

Her thoughts turned to Wolf's uncle? Could the hermit have murdered Smitty and called his nephew to bail him out?

The possibility seemed remote. Two anonymous calls. One to send deputies to Wolf's house. Another to ID the professor as a demented killer. A huge coincidence.

She rubbed her thumb along her cell phone's thin silhouette. Should she warn Wolf? No, the sheriff would be here any minute.

"Riley?" Patty stood in the doorway, her plump black arms crossed as if trying to ward off a chill. "Do they seriously think Dr. Valdes murdered someone?"

"It's a mistake," Riley answered.

"Who got killed?"

"Buford Smith, goes by Smitty. The sheriff wants to bring Wolf in for questioning."

"Oh my God—Smitty." Patty shivered. "Smitty's cousin is Billy Swihart, a sheriff's deputy. In high school, my boys tangled with those SOBs—Smitty and Swihart. If Swihart and his pals think Wolf killed his cousin . . ." Her voice trailed off as loud footsteps echoed in the hall.

Sheriff Hendricks' deep raspy voice carried easily. "I need to see the director. Is she in?"

Patty raised her eyebrows and mouthed a silent question, "You here?"

"You bet. Show him in."

Riley switched off her cell. She had no reason to think Wolf would call. Still she didn't want the phone to ring and have the sheriff direct her to answer. She was glad Gary had given her a heads up—no matter his motive. She secured the lid on her roiling anger, relegated her emotions to a backburner.

Sheriff Hendricks entered, and she stood, ready to play the detached professional. He'd clam up if he suspected she and Wolf were lovers. She needed him to tell all.

FORTY-SEVEN

L.J. checked his watch. Five minutes till nine. Not too early for Miz Pearl. He rang the doorbell, stifling the urge to jam the buzzer. This level of impatience felt foreign to him. *What's gotten into me?* Nothing could compel the old lady to step up her tortoise pace.

A minute passed and the door cracked open. "Miz Pearl, hope I'm not calling on you too early." He gave a slight bow and his brightest smile.

Pearl let the door swing wide, her frail body swayed slightly on the threshold. The sun's probing rays did Riley's mother no favors. Dark smudges marred her parchment skin. Her face looked like crinkled typing paper haphazardly erased and smoothed. The haggard woman's seven decades were no mystery. On the bright side, she wasn't sucking oxygen. Things were definitely going his way.

Pearl's pale eyes refused to meet his steady gaze. She'd seen the news or talked with Riley. She knew her daughter was caught shacking up with a relative of the boy who'd chased her son to his death.

Despite her embarrassment, she managed a fleeting smile. He counted on old-fashioned manners and her fondness for him to earn entry into her condo. His opportunities for access were dwindling. Given Riley's housing predicament, she might camp at her mom's.

"Oh, John, I've been up for hours. I wasn't expecting company." She patted absently at her permed hair. "Please, come in. You know you're always welcome."

She led him toward a living room crammed with valuable antiques. A few weeks back, Pearl said she couldn't bear to part with any of the treasures since Riley would want them once she remarried and settled down.

Pearl made no attempt to hide her enthusiasm for him as future son-in-law. She wanted her daughter to wed Lewis John Hunter, IV. Good family stock, despite his father's surrender to despair. Wealthy. Eligible widower.

Since L.J.'s father went by Lewis, John's family called him by his middle name. However, he answered just as often to L.J., a nickname that stuck after a first-grade teacher used initials to distinguish between three "John-boys" in her class.

Pearl motioned to the room's sole easy chair. "Can I get you something? Coffee?"

"Coffee, if you'll join me, Miz Pearl. The Yates and Hunters have been friends for what, a century? I think I'm due kitchen company status. Why don't you let me help?"

Pearl rewarded him with another flicker of a smile. "Coffee it is. You're welcome to a seat at the kitchen table while I make a fresh pot."

Good. One hurdle down. Now all he needed was a moment's distraction to spike her drink. The sedative would knock her out cold in half an hour. He'd already made an impression of her house key. Once Pearl lost consciousness, he'd come back inside, make the switch.

L.J. followed her down the short hallway and pulled out a cane-backed kitchen chair.

"Have you visited your father?" Pearl asked as she scooped out coffee.

"Yes, I just left," he lied.

Who would dispute him? Certainly not his addled dad, or his father's Vietnamese caretaker. Even if Pearl quizzed the live-in nursing aide, the woman's broken English provided an effective barrier.

"Dad's doing well today. We had breakfast together. He still has his appetite even if he can no longer read the paper with his morning coffee."

"I know how hard it is to see him like this." Pearl sighed and poured water into the coffee maker's reservoir. "Lewis was so brilliant and always a considerate gentleman."

Yeah, before his loving wife drove him to put a gun to his head.

He watched Pearl extract dainty china cups and saucers from her cupboard. Couldn't bring herself to use mugs with company. She shuffled over to sit beside him. As the coffee perked, L.J. engaged in requisite small talk. He wouldn't hint his visit had another motive until she started sipping her doctored brew. When the coffee quit gurgling, he jumped up before she could object.

"Sounds like it's ready. I'll pour." With his back blocking Pearl's vision, he slipped the meds in her cup and swirled the powder with the teaspoon of sugar she preferred.

"Here you are," he said. "A little sugar, just the way you like it."

"Why, thank you, John. You're so thoughtful."

He sat and sipped his coffee. She followed suit.

"I have a confession to make," he said. "I stopped by to talk about Riley."

Pearl's pursed lips said she wanted to object, but didn't know how to do so gracefully.

He hurried on. "I'm sorry to make you uncomfortable, but I'm worried about Riley. You heard what happened last night?"

Pearl lowered her gaze. Her thumb rubbed nervously back and forth across the delicate china rim. "Oh, John, we shouldn't discuss Riley. She's a private person. She'd be very angry—"

Linda Lovely

"Please, hear me out. My only motive is to protect your daughter and your family from scandal. If the situation is left to fester, it might affect your brother."

That grabbed her attention. Pearl doted on her younger sibling, the senator. Her expression changed from discomfort to near panic. Her breaths escaped in percussive huffs.

Use some tact. You can't have her gasping for air.

"Perhaps Riley told you she broke off our relationship. While I pray she'll change her mind, I'd never ask you to intervene. That's not why I'm here."

He looked down, feigning embarrassment. "While I was at Dad's, a friend in the sheriff's office called—a deputy who knows I've been seeing Riley. He described what happened at the Valdes home, how the professor fired your daughter's gun, and shouted threats. The deputy told me Valdes is now wanted for murder."

Pearl gasped on cue. "Oh, my! Oh, my!" One hand shot up, covering her open mouth. The other fumbled along the surface of the tablecloth.

L.J.'s hand captured the woman's bony forearm. He squeezed ever so gently. "It's okay. No need to get over-excited. Riley's not linked to this unpleasantness. We just need to shield her. Make certain it stays that way. She must keep her distance until we know if this man's a killer."

Pearl nodded with vigor. She was with him.

"Perhaps this professor's innocent," he added magnanimously. "But, if he's guilty and the press ties Riley to him, she could lose her job. I don't have to tell you about the social toll. If there's one thing that grows faster than kudzu in Leeds County, it's vicious gossip."

* * * *

L.J. climbed into his roadster and waved goodbye to Pearl. She listed to port in the doorway. Her eyelids losing the fight against gravity. She wouldn't be on her feet long.

He drove around the block, out of sight, and shut off the engine. He closed his eyes and meditated to clear his mind. *Wait thirty minutes. Play it safe.*

At ten o'clock, his duplicate key unlocked the deadbolt on Pearl's back door. A soft snore made the old woman easy to locate. She was out cold, sprawled in the living room easy chair. The meds felled her within steps of the front door.

He hustled through the kitchen door and hoisted a brand-new oxygen concentrator over the threshold. The unit resembled a portable suitcase complete with an extended handle and wheels. Its exterior was identical to the concentrator Pearl dragged behind her wherever she wandered. Like Mary and her little lamb. If Pearl needed a toke of oxygen, L.J.'s doppelganger would perform just fine. Only the custom-made replacement had an additional function—an explosive he could trigger from his cell phone.

Having spotted Pearl's concentrator in the hallway on his prior visit, he quickly made the switch and carted the original away. When Miz Pearl attended her niece's commencement, she'd tote an unexpected graduation gift.

L.J. smiled as he re-locked Pearl's back door. What a perfect Thursday morning. Less than forty-eight hours to go. In a way, he dreaded Saturday's arrival. Not the bloodshed. But the aftermath. The calm after the coming storm.

He preferred the storm.

FORTY-EIGHT

"Good morning, Sheriff." Riley stepped forward to shake hands. "Please, have a seat. Gary phoned. I hear the FBI found Buford Smith's body at the Onward camp, and you have a BOLO out on Dr. Valdes as a person of interest."

She forced a smile. "I'll be happy to tell you what I know about the professor. But first, can you bring me up to speed? The incident involves a BRU faculty member, and it may bear on our campus threat."

To her ear, her matter-of-fact recitation seemed credible, a law enforcement pro talking shop, nothing personal. Her directness erased the sheriff's scowl. He lowered his ample body into her visitor's chair. A musical wheeze escaped as his belt vanished between his stomach's accordion folds.

The security director returned to her seat and swiveled to face him.

"Riley, I'm sorry . . ." The sheriff stared at the hat in his hands as he slowly twirled it. "Before I share information, I need to clear up your relationship with Dr. Valdes. There's talk that you are, uhm, involved."

She cocked her head as if she'd heard something outlandish. "Things aren't always what they seem. Dr. Valdes and I both arrived at BRU at the start of the fall semester. Until two days ago, I doubt we'd exchanged a dozen words. I phoned him Tuesday when a student he counseled was injured. Later that evening, Dr. Valdes happened to be jogging when that psycho biker attacked me. He drove me to the hospital, then home."

Riley wet her lips. Everything she said was true. It was the part she left out that made it such thirsty business. She wished Patty would deliver some bottled water.

"Yesterday—Wednesday—Dr. Valdes stopped by my house to update me on the hospitalized student. His visit coincided with my discovery that someone had trashed my bedroom. I should have phoned the police immediately, but I had bigger worries, overseeing security for Reverend Jimmy's shindig. Dr. Valdes offered me accommodations for the night as a safety precaution. Unfortunately, when thugs strung up an effigy on his lawn, I got my picture taken. That's the *relationship*. I barely know the man."

Now there's a true statement.

"Uhm, I don't understand." The sheriff fumbled for words. "Why did you tell Gary Jacob that Dr. Valdes was your lover?"

Riley laughed. "You got me. Gary is my ex-husband. We divorced after he knocked up the most recent in a string of extracurricular women. I wanted to make him jealous. Figured it was a harmless fib." *It was a fib when I said it.*

The sheriff's cheeks puffed out as he loudly exhaled. "Truth be told, I had a hard time picturing you hooked up with some radical who writes dirty books. I've known your mother's family and your uncle forever. All straight arrows."

"Well, Sheriff," Riley said. "How can I help? Where do things stand?"

"Initially we just wanted to question Valdes. Now he's looking more and more like the killer. Deputy Swihart found Smitty's scalp buried with a fancy knife and a bloody jacket. The dry cleaner had pinned a 'VAL' tag on the jacket to ID the customer."

Sensing the sheriff's scrutiny, she feigned curiosity and sieved sarcasm from her response. "Remarkable. Your deputies found the items in a matter of hours?"

Sheriff Hendricks leaned forward. Red blotches warred with his beard's bristly shadow for facial terrain. His black eyes glittered with excitement. If one discounted domestic homicides, Leeds County had few murders to solve. This was his shot at the big time.

"Sometimes wild-assed hunches pay off." Hendricks chuckled. "Swihart had just left the crime scene. He wanted a first-hand look since Smitty was some relation of his. Anyway, he radioed another deputy, Nick Monson, who recalled a history marker that had something to do with Indian lore. What with the victim being scalped, Nick suggested Swihart take a look-see. Soon as the deputy drove in—there's a horseshoe-shaped pull-off so people can read the plaque—he spied freshly dug earth. Real lucky."

Oh, wasn't it. What instincts this Nick has. A real Sherlock Holmes.

"We just executed a search warrant for Valdes's office," Hendricks continued. "The department secretary admits the professor uses a knife just like the one we found as a letter opener. It was missing. A raincoat hanging on a hall tree in his office had the same 'VAL' dry-cleaning tag."

Though she wanted to scream, Riley kept her voice level. Good thing he couldn't see the sweat gliding down her spine. "My goodness, you've made fast progress. How can I help?"

The sheriff asked if the professor might have said anything during their time together about tracking Smitty down.

She shrugged. "Sorry, he cursed Smitty, but I never heard any specific threats."

Next, Hendricks asked about Valdes's campus associates, friends and relatives.

This time, her answers were the whole truth. She mentioned Ray, since the sheriff already knew Wolf's uncle. The probe increased Riley's unease. She didn't know a single thing about her lover's workaday life, any living relatives besides Ray and Hank, or even if Wolf had close friends—male or female.

Sheriff Hendricks stood. "Guess that's all. We posted a deputy at Dr. Valdes's office. Please alert your officers. If they spot the suspect, they should report to us. I don't want your men to detain him. I suspect he's gone off the deep end. Never know about these brainiacs."

Riley escorted the sheriff out. Hendricks had just cleared her threshold when he turned back. "You know I don't believe in coincidences." His eyebrows knitted with concern. "Can you meet a couple of deputies at your house? Nothing's been touched since your intruder visited, right? I'd like a crime scene unit to look around."

"Sheriff, can't we can put that on hold? I can leave my house locked, stay with Mother. I need to focus on security for Saturday's graduation."

Hendricks shook his head. "It'll only take a few moments. There may be a connection. First, Dr. Valdes magically appears in the wee hours of the morning when a biker attacks you. Then he takes you home, and you're not, shall we say, fully alert. The doc gave you pain pills, right? The next day someone trashes your bedroom and there's no sign of a break-in."

The sheriff's hands made a seesaw motion, a pudgy pantomime of the scales of justice. "Add it up. The professor could have copied your key. Plus he turned up when you needed a bed for the night. I can't tell you why, but I think Dr. Valdes set you up."

The blood drained from Riley's face.

No, it can't be true. Wolf would never try to terrify me.

He was with his uncle in the mountains Wednesday afternoon.

Yeah, but can you account for every minute of his day?

Riley swallowed down her nausea and shrugged. "You win, Sheriff. I'll meet your men. But not until lunch time. That's the best I can do. Graduation security has to come first."

When the sheriff left, Riley collapsed. Her mind flashed back to the lipsticked threat on her mirror. *No! This is insane.*

Riley reached for her cell phone, turned it on. No missed calls. She checked her inbox. A text message. She held her breath as she called it up.

Deputy Monson killed Smitty on Hunter's orders. If no new message by Friday, go where boys become men

Riley fought down a scream. *Sweet Jesus.*

Wolf's text message was less than half an hour old. What did it mean? Hunter? Surely he wasn't pointing a finger at John Hunter. Was it code? Some Onward bozo known as The Hunter. And what was she supposed to make of the "where boys become men" line?

Riley knew what she should do. At the rate the roly-poly sheriff moved, he was still waddling down the hall. She should call Hendricks back. Give him Wolf's message. Of course, he'd scoff at the notion that one of his deputies was a stone cold killer. And what about Hunter? A respected multi-millionaire playing The Godfather. She wasn't even sure she believed the accusation—if that's what it was.

In a flash, she understood the message's final clue. Last night Wolf talked about petroglyphs near Twin Peak and suggested they hike there. It fit. Boys journeyed to the petroglyphs to make their mark and become men.

Is he asking me to meet him there? Or is it a test to see if I'll betray him?

The coded message was clever. Wolf knew she'd understand, but the line would likely mystify any stranger—at least for a time. The petroglyphs weren't widely known. The sheriff or the FBI could track Wolf only if she gave him up.

Her heart beat as rapidly as it did in a sprint marathon. Wolf had entrusted her with a secret, with his life.

Holding information back from the sheriff went against everything she believed. Law enforcement was a constant in her life. A legacy from her detective father—an honorable man she respected more than any she'd known.

Riley kept her silence. If she alerted the sheriff, Hendricks would send his deputies—including Monson and Swihart—after Wolf. If they found him, they'd kill him. Riley couldn't afford to trust anyone in the sheriff's department, but she would pass the first half of Wolf's message to Gary. The accusations against Monson and Hunter.

She erased the message, snapped her cell phone shut. Was she nuts? She'd dated John for three months. Spent less than a week of her life with Wolf. Yet she accepted the notion that John might be capable of murder.

Don't kid yourself. You always sensed something was very wrong about Mr. Right—Lewis John Hunter the Fourth.

Riley made her decision. She'd hike to the petroglyphs after midnight. Alone. She wanted answers. Would Wolf be waiting?

She left her office, heading to a scheduled meeting. She had plenty to do before a noon visit to a crime scene—her home.

FORTY-NINE

"This is as far as we drive," Ray said. "The road turns south now. The camp's less than three miles. We walk from here."

Wolf muscled the Jeep off the fire road and into a small break in the trees.

The hermit scrambled out and pulled a machete from the rear of the Jeep. "I'm gonna cut a few branches. Don't want a Ranger helicopter to spot sun glinting off the hood."

Wolf glanced skyward. Though the forest canopy was thick, the leafy lacework provided peepholes to the earth's blue ceiling. The day was bright, the sun directly overhead. His watch confirmed the time: half-past noon.

"What now?" he asked Ray. "Just a quick surveillance, right? You think anyone will be around before nightfall?"

"Imagine they have at least one guard. Since the other camp was compromised, they'll be nervous. But, you're right, won't be many folks about. These boys may be loco but most hold down day jobs."

"So what do we pack in?"

"We'll travel light. Pick yourself out a knife, a bow, and a gun."

Wolf's eyebrows shot up as he watched his uncle stuff two sticks of dynamite in his pack. "My lord, what are you doing with dynamite?"

"A rock slide blocked my creek. I was planning a little reverse engineering." Ray grinned. "Hey, we need to level the odds. They've got semi-automatics. We've got flintlocks, bows and arrows. This'll slow 'em down if they chase our asses."

"A comforting thought." Wolf hefted a gun then decided against it. He picked up his favorite recurve bow and a quiver of arrows. While his uncle could load a one-shot flintlock, fire, and reload three times in a minute, Wolf had never been a speedster with the whole black-powder, ball prep process. If he failed to kill game with that first ball, he never got a second chance. That's why he never hunted with a flintlock.

Wolf preferred his bow. He could fire multiple arrows in the time it took him to prime a primitive gun for shot number two.

He watched his uncle adjust his backpack's webbed straps. "I'll lead and signal silence when we're a quarter mile out. If you gotta fart, do it before we get that close."

Wolf strapped a sheathed knife to his ankle and nodded. "Ready."

Half an hour later, sweat soaked his shirt, and he'd picked two fat ticks off his forearms. However, Lyme disease was the least of his worries.

Ray ducked behind a rotting log and motioned silence. In a flash, he saw what put his uncle on alert. A man toting a gun. His back to them.

Wolf crept forward silently to join Ray in the lee of a giant poplar log. A twig snapped, and the rifleman swiveled, aiming his gun their way. Wolf's gaze riveted on the hand that held the gun. Obvious tremors. *Shit.* Then he turned his attention to the man's face. "Oh, no."

He jumped up, fully exposing himself as his uncle feverishly tugged on his jeans to pull him back to cover.

When the gunman spotted him, Wolf put a finger to his lips, fervently praying his graduate assistant would recognize him before his sweaty finger stroked the trigger.

Tom lowered his weapon and speed-walked toward the interlopers.

Once he came close enough, Wolf whispered, "Is it safe to talk?"

Tom shook his head. "No. There are two more on patrol." His voice was so soft Wolf practically had to rely on lip reading. "We need to move farther away."

Ray led the trio deeper into the leafy sanctuary, away from the camp. Tom grabbed Wolf's sleeve. "This is far enough." Still he opted to whisper. "What the hell are you doing? If they see us, we're all dead."

Red splotches on the student's cheeks and darting eyes telegraphed fear and anger. Wolf grabbed Tom's shoulder and squeezed hard. "Settle down. There's a lot you don't know."

There was no mirth in Tom's harsh laugh. "Yeah, well, I could say the same. These bozos are planning mass murder. A BRU graduation special. They've stockpiled explosives. But I don't know yet how they expect to beat security."

Tom scuffed at the dirt then looked back at Wolf. "Rosie. I'm afraid to ask . . . "

"Last I heard she's critical but stable. Tom, you should be with her, not out here."

The student shook his head. "Nothing I can do for Rosie. I can do something here. Believe me, I'll run like hell once I get enough information to hang these sleazebags."

Wolf wanted to tell his grad student to leave matters to the authorities. But Tom was right. At least one deputy was a murderer, conspiring with Onward. The FBI? Nice idea but the FBI collaborated with the sheriff's office. Contacting authorities too soon could provide an early warning, and the bad guys would cover their tracks. Yet every minute Tom spent in their midst increased his odds of discovery.

Wolf sighed. "What have you found out? Did they mention any colleges besides BRU? Are they coordinating with other Onward cells?"

"No. The other schools are smoke. BRU's the sole target. They're really jazzed about teaching spoiled rich kids a lesson."

"Have you picked up any hints—anything at all—about their plan of attack?"

"Nobody who counts trusts me. I'm too new. I've overheard scraps of conversation about using trikes. I guess they mean three-wheeled motorcycles." The student shrugged. "Nothing makes sense."

Wolf searched the student's face. "You sure they don't suspect you? You can't help Rosie or BRU if you're dead."

"These guys aren't bright. I talk the talk. Was born less than fifty miles from here. They accepted me as a grunt." He paused to moisten his lips. "Whatever they intend, they didn't dream it up on their own. Some outsider is paying big bucks to stage the attack. They're delirious about the money."

Wolf nodded. "I'm ninety-nine percent sure I know Mr. Moneybag's identity. But why? For the life of me, I can't come up with a valid motive."

After they talked a few more minutes, Tom agreed to meet Wolf and Ray at eleven-thirty that night—same spot.

"It ends tonight." Wolf's tone brooked no disagreement. "You're coming back with us. The authorities may not take the word of a fugitive and his hermit uncle, but they'll believe you. Even if you don't pick up more details, we can stop graduation, prevent more deaths."

Tom nodded.

FIFTY

Riley spotted the deputy's cruiser parked outside her home, waiting. She sidled up to the patrol car's back bumper. As she shifted into park, a deputy yanked her door open. The shadow cast by his Stetson smudged his features—except his crafty brown eyes. They glittered in the artificial gloom.

"Riley Reid?"

She stood and extended her hand.

"I'm Deputy Nick Monson."

Riley jerked her hand back. Monson's jaw jutted forward.

Crap! He knows I recognized his name.

"Sorry." Riley cradled her right hand in her left. "Didn't mean to flinch. I had a recent run-in with an eight-hundred-pound motorcycle. There isn't a spot on my body that doesn't hurt."

The muscular deputy stood a head taller than her. He removed his hat to swipe a handkerchief across his sweaty forehead. Gray shot through receding brown hair, and shoe-leather skin bunched around his eyes. Early fifties?

He replaced his hat. "Call me Nick. This here's Deputy Carl Brens."

She nodded a greeting, and Deputy Carl mumbled, "Nice to meet you, ma'am." He looked younger than most BRU students and innocent. *Don't be fooled. Carl could be dirty, too.*

"Let's get this over with." She took off at a near trot, eager to return to work and escape the dirty deputy. "Is a crime scene unit coming?"

"The techs are en route. Should be here any second," Nick replied.

"Should we wait?"

"Nah, we won't touch nothing."

"Fine." She unlocked her front door and positioned her body to shield the house alarm keypad while she entered her code.

"Was your alarm on Wednesday?" Nick asked, clearly the talker in the twosome.

"Yes." Don't volunteer any more than you have to. "The bedroom's upstairs."

Riley led the way. She planted herself in the hall and motioned the deputies inside. "I've seen it. Look in the bathroom, too."

The officers stopped at the threshold to survey the bedlam.

"Shee-it," Deputy Carl swore. "Sorry, ma'am." He ducked his head at Riley.

Nick stayed mute, but Riley caught the hint of a smile before he parked his lips in neutral. She steeled herself to study the manufactured chaos anew. The simulated blood had browned and separated. Today the shredded underwear struck her as childish rather than frightening.

Could this be John Hunter's work?

Odd. She was willing to consider John a party to murder, yet balked at believing he'd do this. Even if his affection was bogus, what did shredding her underwear gain him?

And how could John have entered without triggering the alarm? She'd never given him a key, much less her security code. If it wasn't John's handiwork, whose?

From the hall, she watched the deputies jot notes as they strolled through the bedroom and studied the lipsticked mirror.

"Looks like a pissed-off boyfriend." Nick smirked. "You sure you and this Wolf fella aren't heating up the sheets?" He flaunted a suggestive sneer.

She refused to take the bait. "As I told Sheriff Hendricks, I hardly know Dr. Valdes." She turned on her heel and walked away, assuming they'd follow. "Anything else you want to see?"

"Yeah, so long as we're here, give us a nickel tour and tell us if anything's out a whack."

"Sure." Riley made a point of checking her watch. "I'm in a bit of a time crunch. Could you call the techs—"

The doorbell rang, and she rushed to welcome the two-person CSI crew. She knew the newcomers, and was relieved one was female. While she wasn't naïve enough to believe a lady cop couldn't be dirty, she couldn't imagine Nick recruiting a female accomplice.

After a short conference, the CSI techs scurried toward the bedroom, and Nick asked Riley to continue her busman's tour. She strode from living room to kitchen, the officers hustling in her wake. She sighed. "I see nothing amiss."

Nick motioned toward a door. "Where's that lead?"

Riley frowned. "The cellar. I forgot. I keep that door closed. Yesterday it was open when I came home. I started downstairs to investigate, but the light was burned out. Then I got distracted."

She grabbed a replacement bulb from a cupboard and walked briskly to the cellar entry. "I'll replace the bulb, and we can take a quick look. Not much down there."

She swung the basement door wide. The kitchen fluorescents did little to brighten the cave-like darkness. She ran her hand along the wall to the switch plate to verify the switch was off. She didn't like to screw in a bulb with the electricity on.

Riley started down the steps to the wall sconce five stairs below.

"Miz Reid, I'll be glad to change that for you," Deputy Carl offered. She swiveled to answer him. "Thanks but—"

Her left foot crashed through a tread and her ankle buckled. She swung her arms like a high-wire walker flailing the air to regain balance.

Scrambling for purchase on the railing, she dropped the bulb. A splinter from the wood railing thrust into her palm. She yelped. Her hands clawed the air as her center of gravity shifted. An unplanned back dive.

Glass tinkled. Her tender ribs banged against unyielding wood. She bumped down the stairs like a bundle of laundry on an oversized washboard. Her skull bounced against one tread, then another . . . and another. The pale square of light from the kitchen shimmied and shrank.

Riley ached all over. Her eyelids felt like bowling balls, too heavy to lift.

"Hey, Nick, should I call for an…an … ambulance?"

They didn't know she'd regained consciousness. She decided to keep it that way. She eased her eyelids open a fraction. Through a fringe of lashes, she spotted Nick mucking about near her water heater.

"She's breathing," Nick told Carl. "Just got the air knocked out of her."

"Maybe she's got a concussion…"

Her cheek throbbed against the damp floor. Skewed sideways, her gaze tracked Nick's flashlight as if it were a magnet. The deputy's gloved hand dropped a tiny object. Riley followed its short fall. The object danced in the flashlight's beam for a heartbeat. What was it?

Riley had no doubt. He was planting bogus evidence.

Time to make an appearance.

She moaned theatrically. Didn't take much acting. She fingered a rapidly growing goose egg on the back of her head. The movement didn't leave her nauseous. If she had a concussion, it was slight. *Nice self-diagnosis, Doctor Reid.*

"Take it easy." Carl squatted next to her. "Should we call a doctor?"

"No." She levered herself to a sitting position. "I'll be fine. What happened?"

"Someone doesn't like you." Nick's comment didn't answer her question.

The deputy walked toward her, swinging his flashlight like a pendulum. He stood over her, aiming the flashlight in her eyes. She batted it away.

"Someone sawed through a stair tread from the bottom up so it would give just right," Nick said.

The deputy flicked his flashlight toward the water heater. "Your admirer hit the disconnect switch for your water heater. Guess he figured you'd investigate and plop into another kind of hot water."

Nick shifted his beam to his young protégé. "Carl, look around the water heater while I help Miz Reid to her feet."

Carl obeyed. When he reached the water heater, he pulled a string to activate the bare bulb overhead. Dust motes swirled in a yellow cone of light. He knelt to examine the disconnect switch.

"Should we ask the techs to dust for prints?" His attention shifted to the floor. "Hey, here's a button. Think her attacker lost it?"

Taking a handkerchief from his pocket, he lifted the stray object. Riley felt certain it came from one of Wolf's jackets. The manufactured evidence confirmed her faith in her lover. But it didn't solve her problem. How to prove Wolf's innocence and trap John Hunter and Deputy Monson?

I can't do it alone. And I can't let more people die.

FIFTY-ONE

Giant eagles swooped overhead; their beating wings hid the sun.

Wolf's head snapped up. His eyes blinked rapidly at the bright daylight. Remnants of the dream disoriented him. He remembered eating an energy bar and leaning against the warm boulder. His watch confirmed he'd dozed for half an hour.

The sun vanished, and a small engine sputtered. What the hell? It sounded like a lawnmower buzzing overhead. He searched the bank above, then the sky. The soaring object resembled a prehistoric bird. Its bright red wings, at least twelve feet across, rippled with the air turbulence.

An ultralight.

He'd seen them before, playing in the foothills' uncrowded skies. He smiled. The construction looked like an ill-advised marriage between a moped and a butterfly. When he quizzed a pilot friend, he learned ultralights were considered vehicles, not planes. No license required. The powers-that-be must figure a crash would only kill the attached daredevil.

He edged into the forest canopy's cover. Though certain the authorities hadn't commissioned an ultralight search, it seemed prudent to stay out of sight.

The blood-red craft rode an air current upward, then dipped and glided down the face of the mountain. The mewling of a second pint-sized motor startled him. Another ultralight? Golden wings floated into the airspace, answering his question.

He stretched. Time to get back to Ray. He'd left his uncle napping in a pup tent. "We need sleep," Ray advised. "Won't get any shuteye tonight." He expressed confidence the Jeep and his lean-to would remain undetected.

Wolf forsook sleep to hike to the petroglyphs and mark a path he could follow after dark. With no marked trail, he needed daylight to reconnoiter. As the visual reference points of ridges and outcroppings verified his position, he tied branches with reflective strips from a roll of neon flagging his uncle kept in his camping gear. The markers would guide him on the trek he hoped to make at midnight—if he was still alive.

His daytime sortie was a form of insurance. No matter what happened, he needed to warn Riley that Onward's threatened graduation attack was real. His pulse quickened as he pulled a pen and a scrap of paper from his backpack to scribble Tom's intel:

Onward has explosives. Trikes—motorcycles with sidecars?—may be used for delivery. An outsider is paying Onward to attack BRU's commencement. Threats against other colleges are decoys.

Wolf stuck the note in a plastic sandwich bag and wedged it beneath a flat stone. He looped neon tape around the rock to draw Riley's eye. Few people hiked here. He doubted an unsuspecting eco-tourist would uncover the parcel in the next twenty-four hours.

If all went well, he'd provide Riley with more details. Maybe even deliver the information in person. But a back-up plan was only prudent.

In case his nighttime vigil at the Onward camp was a bust.

In case he didn't live past midnight.

In case he never saw Riley again.

If she heeded his text, Riley or someone she trusted would visit the petroglyphs tomorrow—Friday. It buoyed his spirits to know that whatever happened, Tom's information would help protect BRU from these bloodthirsty cretins.

A motor buzzed. The golden-winged ultralight. Wolf slipped into the woods and retraced his steps along his trail of glow-in-the-dark breadcrumbs.

FIFTY-TWO

Riley followed the deputies out her front door and tailed Monson's police cruiser to the corner. When Monson turned right, she swung left, pulled to the curb, and checked for voicemails or text. Nothing.

A stab of regret. She'd never wanted, needed, to talk to anyone more. She scrolled through her contact list, found Gary's new entry, and hit Send. "Where are you?" she asked as soon as he answered.

"Sheriff's department," he said.

Not good. She needed to see Gary in private. Away from eavesdroppers. Her house was out. So was BRU. She racked her brain. Mom's. Her ex had visited her mother's condo while they were married. He wouldn't need directions.

"I have an important lead. We need to talk. In private. Meet me at Mom's condo."

When Gary didn't respond, she gritted her teeth. "Please."

"Okay, Riley. I need fifteen minutes." He paused. "Will your mother be there?"

She rolled her eyes. Gary feared the wrath of a frail woman on oxygen therapy. Smart man. Miz Pearl detested her former son-in-law for his unseemly behavior and her daughter's ensuing humiliation. "Don't worry. I'll make sure Mom doesn't throttle you."

She used her key to unlock her mother's front door. After her morning bombshell, she was uncertain of her welcome. Riley "yoo-hooed" to announce her arrival, then spotted her mother sprawled in a recliner. Her heartbeat picked up. Had her revelation about Wolf triggered a stroke?

She hurried to the chair. Her mother's chest rose and fell in a regular rhythm. Sound asleep. She sighed in relief and gently rubbed one of her mom's hands. Her fingers felt like popsicles, but her eyelids fluttered.

"Mom, are you okay?"

"Oh, it's you." The words came slowly, speech slurred. "I feel so groggy." Pearl raised her free hand to her head, and her bony fingers massaged her temple. "When John left, I suddenly felt tired. I barely made it to the couch before I collapsed."

Riley's pulse jumped. "John was here? Today?"

"Why, yes, honey. He dropped by for a few minutes. He's very concerned about you. And, well, our family."

She squeezed her mom's hand. A wince flitted across Pearl's face. She'd been rougher than she intended. "Mother, listen very carefully. I don't want you talking with John—"

Miz Pearl's eyes grew wide and her lips trembled. "Riley, what on earth has gotten into you? Even if you're not dating him, our families are friends. Why for generations—"

Riley interrupted. "Stop it, Mother, and listen. I can't explain everything just yet. You have to trust me. Trust my judgment. You know how to make excuses. If John comes by again, tell him you're on your way out. Say you're not feeling well. Just . . . avoid him."

Tears leaked from her mother's eyes. "You're scaring me." Her voice sounded tinny, distant. Yet she found the strength to lever herself upright.

Riley searched her mother's face. "I know this is baffling. I'm confused, too. But it's not a good idea for either of us to socialize with John right now."

"Fine. But we'll both see him tomorrow night. You can't ask your uncle to un-invite John. Or have you forgotten Jennie's graduation party? Six p.m."

"Good God, I did forget." She ignored her mother's scowl at her use of the Lord's name. "If you see John in public and there are people around, just behave normally."

"Normally? I'm not sure you know what that means, Riley."

She let the comment slide. No point picking a fight. Her mother still looked woozy. "Are you feeling all right? Do you need your oxygen?"

She shook her head. "No, I'm just old. All this recent"—she searched for a proper term—"excitement has tired me out."

Pearl paused and licked her lips. "John told me your Indian friend, this Wolf person, is wanted for murder. He said a deputy called to warn him. John is watching out for you."

Her eyes searched her daughter's face. "Tell me you're not in love with this killer. Are you trying to protect him?"

Riley didn't answer. "Mother, we have a guest coming. Please go down the hall and stay there till he leaves. I promised him privacy."

"Not this Wolf!" Pearl cried with alarm.

"No." Despite the seriousness of the situation, she wanted to laugh. Black humor. "It's Gary. Knowing how you feel about him, maybe you'd prefer a visit from Wolf."

* * * *

Gary's look said it all. He thought she was nuts. "You want me to get a warrant and look into John Hunter's life and finances based on a text message you refuse to show me from a fugitive? Hunter's a respected international businessman. Not to mention a big contributor to your uncle's political campaigns. Valdes's message said the murder was on Hunter's order, right? He didn't even give a complete name."

"You make this sound like I'm hallucinating." She paced, too agitated to sit still. "I saw Deputy Nick Monson plant evidence in my house."

"Oh, come on, Riley. You were lying on the cellar floor, dazed from taking a header down a flight of stairs. You think—*think*—you saw an object slip from Nick's hand? Can you be sure it was the button the other deputy picked up? Or do you just want to believe someone's framing your boyfriend?"

She tried another tack. "Okay, how about a compromise? Check out Nick Monson. Pinpoint the deputy's whereabouts when Smitty was killed."

"I suppose you want me to do it behind the sheriff's back? Not exactly how the Feds win friends with local law enforcement."

"Unfortunately, yes. How did Onward know to abandon that camp, to sweep it clean of evidence? Other than Wolf and our task force, who knew we'd located it? Who tipped off Onward? The leak had to come from the sheriff's office, one of his deputies."

She resumed her nervous pacing. "Sheriff Hendricks told his deputies what was going down, and Deputy Monson acted."

"Are you blaming this deputy and Hunter for the personal attacks on you as well?" Gary quirked an eyebrow, a familiar derisive gesture.

"Yes, God help me, I am. And don't think that admission doesn't cost. I dated John for three months. If he's behind this, how gullible does that make me?"

She glanced at Gary. He had the good grace to look sheepish. *Yes, you know exactly how gullible I can be.*

"John was in my house a dozen times. He could easily have peeked when I entered my alarm code or made an impression of my key. He had far more opportunities than Wolf to break my security."

Gary sighed and stood. "With just your say-so on a phone text, I'll give you this much and no more. I'll have an agent check for ties between Hunter and Deputy Monson. And, for the time being, I won't mention our conversation to the sheriff."

Riley didn't push. He'd given more than she'd expected.

They walked to the door. Gary reached out and gently stroked her cheek. "Promise, if you hear from Valdes, you'll call me. I won't send the sheriff. I'll bring him in myself. But swear you won't launch some solo crusade."

Riley swallowed. He seemed to care. A tear meandered down her cheek. She had no desire to go back with Gary—yet fifteen years of marriage couldn't be erased. The hurts and the highs.

She blinked to stymie fresh tears, struggled to regain control.

"Is it time to cancel graduation?" Her tone became businesslike, brisk. "We changed the venue—moved the ceremony to Clemson's Littlejohn Coliseum. Your task force has been great, helped us add extra layers of security. Bomb-sniffing dogs. Metal detectors. Monitors for nearby airports and private air fields. Even armored vehicles to stop a truck loaded with explosives from ramming any entrance. But is it enough?"

She bit her lip as she searched for words. "I love these kids. If there's even a one percent chance of danger, how can we gamble with their lives?"

Gary lifted her chin so their eyes met. "Life's a gamble. We can minimize risks, but we can't get rid of all the jokers in the deck."

The expressions that played across his face said he was talking about more than BRU's graduation. Losing a child had changed him.

"BRU should proceed with the ceremony. If you cancel, Onward will just shift the attack to another time, another place. Next week. Next month. The odds of catching—and preventing—the violence won't get any better than they are right now. We'll nail the bastards."

Riley watched him hustle toward his car.

"Thank you," she whispered. The conversation's unexpected twists provided a closure her divorce decree never delivered. Her ex was neither devil nor saint. She could acknowledge the qualities that made her love him and move on.

Of course, she had no intention of following Gary's advice. Her nighttime expedition would be a solo affair.

She found her mother. "Company's gone. You can come out of hiding. Mom—if it's okay—I'd like to stay here a few nights."

"Of course, it's fine. I'm sorry about this morning. Saying I wanted you to leave…"

"It's all right, Mom. We'll get through this. I love you." She gave her mother a gentle hug.

"I need to go to the office and run by my place to pack some clothes." She talked as she walked to the front door. "You don't mind entertaining Lucy, do you?"

"Of course not. Lucy and I will enjoy a little nap," Pearl said. "I can't fathom why I'm so tired."

"Want me to pick up Chinese? I'll be back by seven."

"No, don't you go picking up dinner. I have a container of vegetable soup in the freezer."

Riley considered saying something more about John. What did he have up his sleeve? Whatever it was, she didn't want the bastard paying social calls on her mother. But it was pointless to suggest John was a killer. She'd scare the woman silly. He had no reason to hurt her mother—his biggest fan. John's morning social call was probably harmless. He often dropped in when he visited his dad.

FIFTY-THREE

L.J. lounged in the room his late wife ridiculed as his man cave. Though it served as a home office, hunting trophies rather than diplomas lined the walls. The head of a giant polar bear snarled above his desk. Guests set their drinks on a glass coffee table mounted atop a rhino's stuffed gnarly legs—discreetly topped with ebony disks.

He'd informed his secretary he'd be out of the office and hadn't volunteered his whereabouts. The woman knew not to ask. A top secret clearance meant he often frequented Army war rooms where cell phones were verboten. Today he was concerned with his personal weapons program. He hunched forward in his executive chair. His fingers drummed on his desk as he waited for the man to answer his phone.

Two rings. Three.

L.J. pictured the giraffe-necked aide feeling the illicit cell phone's vibration. He was probably galumphing about in search of a private spot for their conversation.

"Hello." The aide whispered the greeting.

In the background, a toilet flushed, prompting L.J. to chuckle. "Charles, haven't you heard? These days the cops stake out men's rooms looking for queers."

The aide gasped.

"Relax, just kidding. Is our pigeon still on for commencement? You're flying down with him, right?"

"Yes, we arrive at the Greenville-Spartanburg airport at ten a.m."

"Dandy. Get my package?"

"Ah, yes." Charles' voice quavered. "You're sure it's safe."

"Absolutely. Take the pills after you deplane. In six hours you'll have full-blown flu symptoms. Low-grade fever, nausea.

Nothing serious, but no one will question your illness. A legit reason to stay in bed tomorrow."

L.J.'s voice took on a stern note. "Don't dick around. It's for your safety. Can't have someone puzzling over your absence at graduation."

For a moment, neither man said anything. Charles sighed. "All right."

"I assume Ben got his inheritance from a distant relative," L.J. said. "There were enough intervening lawyers to perform the Virginia reel."

It would take a genius to unravel the money trail, the payoff to Charles' lover.

"Yes, the money's in Ben's medical account."

"Good. Let's talk about your end of the bargain."

Yates' senior aide had agreed to destroy all correspondence between the reporter L.J. killed and the senator. Not too tough since Charles enjoyed unlimited access to the lawmaker's office. Not a trace of evidence or a whiff of speculation would remain to link L.J.'s company to a huge bribery scandal that would bankrupt the firm and put its top executives in jail.

"I shredded everything," Charles said. "When does Ben get the second installment?"

"After the senator's funeral. You'll be well enough to attend *that* ceremony."

L.J. snapped his cell phone closed.

FIFTY-FOUR

Ray shook him awake. "It's time, son."

Wolf felt groggy, drugged. "Give me a sec." He blinked. The tall pines cast long shadows. Dusk, not yet dark.

He made for the streambed, splashed water on his face, and gasped at the stinging wake-up call. Baptism. Born again into a world where nightmares and dreams interbred. The mountain brook felt as cold as the ice he'd used to tease Riley.

Will I see her again? He couldn't think about her now.

He returned to their makeshift camp. Ray opened a can of pork and beans.

Wolf chuckled. "Going gourmet, I see. Thought you warned me I didn't dare fart while we're sneaking up on these asswipes, and you decide to feed me beans?"

"Put a cork in it," Ray grinned. "Both ends."

They ate in companionable silence. He couldn't count the times he'd camped with his uncle. In many ways, the outing seemed normal. Except they might be the prey.

Even if just one of the Onward jokers carried a semi-automatic, they were seriously outgunned. Hunting skills and knowledge of the mountains were their only advantages. Using a bow and arrow or a single-shot muzzleloader forced a hunter to be stealthy, patient. They knew how to track, how to hide, how to wait for one clean, killing shot.

Wolf retrieved his digital camera from the glove compartment, while his uncle topped off his backpack with twin dynamite sticks.

Ray nodded at the camera. "Can it take pictures at night? No way to use flash."

He shrugged. "I'll override the flash. It does pretty well in low light. If we're lucky, they'll have a campfire."

Ray brushed away leaves on the forest floor to uncover a patch of black earth. He poured water from his canteen, then reached into the mini-mud hole to smear black goop on his face and hands.

He looked up at his nephew. "You, too."

Ray picked through his gear until he found a dozen fishing hooks strung on individual filament leaders and two rusty bear traps.

Wolf raised an eyebrow. "You planning a little fishing and hunting en route?"

"No. But I know how to dampen the enthusiasm of anyone who follows us if we need to hightail it out of there. Don't forget we'll have Tom with us. Things may get hairy."

Wolf's stomach dropped. His uncle had told him how crafty mountain outlaws strung fishhooks in tree branches with the barbs set to dangle around eye level. They threaded the invisible snares near illegal stills and marijuana patches. He glared at his uncle.

"Look, son, if we live through the night, I'll come back and remove all my little trinkets. First we need to keep breathing till dawn. If we're hunted, they'll be carrying semi-automatics. Think about Tom. Would you rather risk his life?"

Night tossed an inky quilt over the landscape as Ray led the way toward the mountain crest. They left their headlamps—ultra-slim, LED versions of the lamps coal miners wear—switched off to avoid alerting a guard with a dancing red pinpoint. They'd save the headlamps for their retreat. The focused beams would be invisible as they fled.

Once the waning three-quarter moon rose, it would allow some light to filter through the thick pine needle canopy. The blotchy darkness would be both enemy and friend.

Ray snaked silently through the trees. Wolf pretended he was his uncle's shadow, a mute condemned to faithfully trail his master wherever he led. *Wonder if there's a short story here?*

His color vision shrunk to a tunnel of blacks and grays. His sense of smell sharpened. Years ago, he'd picked wildflowers with his Cherokee grandmother. Tonight he felt her presence in the honey aroma of Sweet William and the clove scent of dianthus that floated above the sharp fragrance of pine.

He welcomed the drop in temperature. The chill air felt fresh, clean. He walked into a cobweb, and brushed uselessly at the sticky silk. *Too bad Ray's not taller.* Air stirred near his head—a bat swooping in for an insect?

In the distance, a canine chorus howled. Coyotes had cornered prey. A deer? Their urgent voices sounded musical, a cacophony of high howls, frantic yips, and menacing growls. The noise rose in pitch, faded away. As they walked, Ray set traps, and Wolf placed ground-level flags at each location to help them avoid their own invisible snares. As his uncle tied hooks to tree limbs, Wolf broke branches and stomped his boots to bait the path they wanted Onward to follow. The preparations added two hours to their trek.

Finally, his uncle signaled the camp lay ahead. Human voices. Like the coyotes, they sounded excited. Did they smell blood?

Wolf dropped to his knees and crawled beside Ray, taking cover behind the carcass of a once-massive oak. He positioned his bow, just in case. Arrows at the ready. They settled in to watch and wait.

* * * *

Half an hour after supper, Riley's mother yawned and excused herself. The bedtime seemed early, even for her frail mother. She hoped Miz Pearl wasn't headed for another pulmonary infection.

Riley stared at the TV set for another hour. Not a single line of sitcom dialogue penetrated. Her mind scripted its own scenarios. None made sense.

Certain her mother was asleep, she returned to the guest room and changed into jeans and a biking jersey, a high-tech number purchased for her last triathlon. The miracle fabric stopped wind, wicked away moisture.

From the nightstand, she retrieved the wristband GPS unit John had given her last month. He said the Army bought thousands of the snazzy devices from his company. Ironic. His gift might help her find Wolf.

As she laced her sneakers, Riley caught her reflection in the room's antique pedestal mirror. If it weren't for the gold trademark emblazoned over her breast, she could pass for a ninja. Her jeans and top were as black as Lucy, eyeing her suspiciously from a pillow-top perch.

The cat acted aloof—peeved at the shuttle to another foreign domain. Though Lucy and Riley had spent many a night in her mother's guest room—usually when Miz Pearl had a respiratory scare—her cat preferred the comforts of home.

Me, too. She stroked the cat's broad back, a promise of treats to come.

Unzipping the backpack flung on the bed's velvet duvet, she rummaged for her Foothills Trail map. Last fall her hiking club visited several sections of the trail, but never at night. While she had a fair notion of how to reach the petroglyphs, she wanted to fix the position in her mind. Her finger traced the route. Park at the Beaver Falls overlook. Take the spur trail north. Cross Trout Creek. Go straight for a quarter mile.

What would she find when she got there?

She hoped something more than inscrutable carvings etched in granite thousands of years before. Her goal was to reach the spot by midnight, keep vigil until morning. If Wolf didn't arrive by seven a.m., she had to trust Gary or contact a close friend with North Carolina's state police. Since the mountainous portion of Leeds County skirted the state border, Riley had a hunch her northern colleague would extend a neighborly hand.

Worry about that tomorrow.

She tiptoed to her mother's bedroom. Miz Pearl's chest rose and fell in a steady cadence. She lay on her back; sheets neatly tucked beneath her arms. Riley often wondered what had attracted her parents to one another. Her mom championed order and tradition; her dad had relished spontaneity and thrived amidst chaos.

No wonder I'm schizoid.

She headed to the kitchen sink, downed a glass of tap water. Time to go. She stopped at the back door.

What if Mom wakes? She'll panic. Call the sheriff or the FBI.

She glanced at the refrigerator where her mom kept a magnetic pad and pencil. She picked up the fat pencil.

Mom—Something came up. Had to leave. Don't worry. If I'm not back by ten a.m., I'll call. Love, Riley

Half an hour later, she parked in the Beaver Falls lot. It held only one other car—a vintage VW Beetle with Virginia plates. The trailhead wasn't a prime launch point for overnight hikers. She assembled her gear, shouldered her pack, and holstered her Glock.

The urgent play of rushing water drowned out other night sounds. The falls were less than one hundred feet below. Her route was up, the opposite direction.

She pressed a button, and her GPS unit glowed a greenish yellow. She marked a starting waypoint. Darkness hemmed her in. She flicked on her flashlight, an oblong light wand, and swung it at her side. She was tempted to whistle. The wavering beam offered little moral support in the spooky woods. Playing over hanging branches and jagged stumps, the light spawned contorted demons. Riley shivered. What waited down the path?

FIFTY-FIVE

"Hello." L.J.'s greeting was brusque. Any call after eleven p.m. meant someone had screwed the pooch.

"John?"

Even with the added quaver, he recognized Miz Pearl's well-modulated soprano.

"I'm so sorry to bother, but I'm very worried about Riley."

L.J. changed his tune from gruff to gracious. "Miz Pearl, don't you fret. I'm a night owl, and you're never a bother. What's wrong?"

This ought to be good.

"Something woke me half an hour ago. When I opened my eyes, Riley stood in my doorway dressed like a cat burglar. She wore that clunky watch-thing that acts like a compass. A few minutes later, her car started.

"I don't know why I didn't call out." She paused. "Riley hasn't been herself. So angry and upset. If I'd asked what she was doing, she'd have told me to mind my own p's and q's."

L.J. was all ears. "We both know Riley's under a lot of stress. Perhaps she couldn't sleep and decided to go into the office for a spell."

"Oh, no. Not dressed like that. She wouldn't take a backpack. She'd take her briefcase and laptop. The computer's still here. She left a note. Said she might not be home until ten tomorrow morning. What on earth is she planning to do all night?"

"You have no idea where she went?"

He heard Pearl suck in a toke of oxygen. Glad my substitute canister actually delivers air.

"I'm afraid she's trying to help this Wolf person. She has it in her head he's innocent."

242

"She didn't give any hint where he might be hiding?"

"Well, I overheard a snatch of conversation with her ex-husband. I wasn't trying to eavesdrop, but when they moved toward the door, their voices carried. Gary warned her not to go off on some solo crusade. Oh, John, she thinks this professor was framed. But what if she's wrong? What if he's a murderer?"

Pearl's voice climbed toward hysteria. "Should I call the sheriff? Have him search for Riley's car?"

"Now, Miz Pearl. Don't you worry. I have friends at the sheriff's office. I'll ask them to look for Riley on the QT. Wouldn't want to broadcast that your daughter might be helping a fugitive, now would we?"

He almost chuckled at the woman's relieved sigh.

"I knew you'd know how to handle this. I'd have called my brother, but he's not due home till morning. I hope your friends can find Riley before then."

"So do I. Now get some sleep. Good night."

Damn. What was the bitch up to? How could he find her? L.J. closed his eyes. *Think!*

A second later, he smiled. Who said generosity didn't pay?

He walked to the desk in his home office and rummaged through the top drawer.

"Time to see how well our products perform."

FIFTY-SIX

Wolf cupped his watch face to prevent light from leaking. 11:05 p.m. Less than half an hour until Tom jumped ship and joined them.

So far the stakeout disappointed. A dozen milling men had arrived in dribs and drabs and seemed to lack any sense of purpose. Since Wolf had never seen Nick Monson, he glanced at Ray after each arrival. His cocked eyebrow always triggered the same response—a shake of the head that said no, not him.

His jaw tightened as he watched Tom saunter over to Dark Hair, the guy who'd chewed out Smitty the day before. He'd witnessed the hulking man's short fuse, which seemed to be coupled with a measure of authority. Though Dark Hair didn't look like he itched to draw the pistol on his hip, worry tugged at Wolf.

If only he could hear the conversations. Occasional expletives proved loud enough for clear reception. Nothing more. Time was running out. He snapped a few photos. Even if they didn't identify Onward's leaders, they'd help the Feds round up players and chip away at the hate group's cell.

Ray nudged him and pointed his chin toward a swaggering newcomer. Deputy Nick Monson.

The man didn't look evil. Except for his cock-of-the-walk strut, he looked, well, ordinary. Under six feet, muscular build, thinning brown hair streaked with gray. His tan, weathered face might have belonged to a middle-aged farmer. Wolf couldn't see his eyes.

Monson wore civilian clothes—hunter's camouflage. While the man had jettisoned his uniform and badge, he'd brought two guns to the party, an AR-15 semi-automatic and a 9mm pistol. Wolf held his breath as Nick walked toward Dark Hair and Tom.

Move off, Tom! Time to disappear.

Wolf shot photos of Monson, Dark Hair, and Tom in the iffy lighting. Through the lens, he watched his student turn to leave. Then the boy stumbled and his hand dipped into the pack at Monson's feet. Dark Hair helped Tom recover his balance.

You idiot. What are you trying to pull? Get out of there.

Tom ambled away. Thank God. He tracked his graduate assistant's progress while he continued to monitor Monson and Dark Hair. Deep in conversation, the men paid no attention to the kid's departure.

Casual as you please, Tom sauntered to the edge of the woods. He playfully punched one of his new comrades in the arm. Hand gestures and laughter followed. Tom disappeared between two massive pines at a ninety-degree angle to their rendezvous site.

Smart. If anyone went after him, they'd start in the wrong direction.

Once the forest swallowed Tom, Wolf and Ray began their own withdrawal. They'd taken cover behind a moss-covered oak log with dead branches pulled over their heads to create a makeshift blind. As Wolf rose to a crouch, he retracted the surrounding twigs with silent precision.

Gaining his feet, he probed the forest floor with the balls of his feet before he committed to planting his boots. He held his breath. Sweat pooled under his armpits. A mosquito buzzed near his ear. His fine-tuned hearing made the pest sound like a Bell helicopter.

Not a single dry leaf crackled beneath his feet. *Thank you, Jesus.*

Linda Lovely

They'd agreed on a meeting spot about three hundred feet from the camp. As Wolf and his uncle crept toward it, they bent at the waist to shrink their profiles. They'd almost reached their destination when angry shouts erupted.

"Where'd that damned kid go? That blond boy in the gray T-shirt."

What the hell? A man who was still in Wolf's sightline yelled back. "Aw, calm down, Nick, he went to take a leak. I just passed him."

As the talker zipped up, the deputy stormed into Wolf's narrow field of vision. "Go after him. He's a thief! Everyone, and I mean now!"

The Onward men rushed to obey the order. They made so much racket Wolf quit worrying about acoustic cover and ran flat out. Time to snatch Tom and boogie out.

Wolf knew their one-time contingency had become their primary plan. They had to lure the pursuers to Ray's booby-trapped path and hope the unexpected hazards gelded any macho enthusiasm. If the traps slowed pursuers, the trio could gain separation, melt into the woods.

If the booby traps didn't shake Onward from their tail, they'd employ guerilla tactics. A necessity given their inferior firepower.

Ray signaled Wolf. He'd spotted Tom. The young man crashed through the brush like a wounded buck, looking back over his shoulder to see how fast the devil was closing on him. Wolf snagged the terrified kid and clamped a hand tightly over his mouth. A holler would draw the bubbas faster than free tickets to a stock car race.

A ragged burst of gunfire echoed on the hillside. Wolf guesstimated the trigger-happy shooter was five hundred feet to his right. He'd probably flushed an animal and mistook it for human quarry.

He took his hand from Tom's mouth. "What the hell did you do?"

"Palmed Nick's cell phone." Tom gulped air. He sounded proud. "Figured the Feds could check out who the deputy's been calling."

"Ah, crap," Ray said. "We gotta move. Fast. We're gonna turn on our headlamps. Don't have one for you. Stay between us. Keep low. Here. Grab hold."

Ray clamped Tom's hand around a rope he'd attached to the flap of his backpack.

The men switched on their headlamps. The red wavelengths safeguarded their night vision while helping them spot obstacles. They moved in single file. Shouts and grunts sounded behind them. Someone—Nick?—screamed orders to organize the ragtag band.

We know the mountains. We'll lose the beer guts. But maybe not Dark Hair or Nick.

Wolf's headlamp picked up the first neon flag warning of a dangling fishhook ahead. Ray pocketed the flag before the trio veered off the trail. Would the Onward boys take the false trail and fall prey to their improvised landmines?

Thirty feet down the road, his uncle swung back onto the planned escape corridor, and Tom's wheezes lessened. Then a scream echoed through the forest. The bleating cry seemed to vibrate the air.

Wolf sensed Tom's fall even before his arms windmilled. He struggled to put on the brakes, stop his forward motion. He didn't want to land on top of the kid.

Dammit. Wolf swerved sideways. The ground rushed up to meet him.

FIFTY-SEVEN

Riley could pick out the well-traveled trail with relative confidence, but the disorienting darkness slowed her to half her normal speed. Thirty minutes to hike the first quarter mile. In broad daylight, it was easy enough to get confused and wander off a poorly marked spur. In the darkness, she checked and rechecked her direction. The going would get tougher once she branched onto the lesser-used petroglyph side trail.

Her ears tuned to the forest's discordant night melody. She gave herself a silent pep talk. "You have a gun. Those noises are just creatures trying to get out of *your* way. You have a gun."

The mental mantra didn't erase her unease. Beetles, roaches, and other creepy crawlers scurried among desiccated leaves, creating a scratchy blanket of white noise. Rodents — bigger and less omnipresent than the multi-legged forest dwellers — rustled the woodland debris with more vigor. In her dark orbit, each unexpected noise made her flinch.

Nearing the bottom of a dell, her nose detected the creek before her flashlight speared the weathered footbridge. While the water smelled sweet, the oily creosote odor of the bridge's treated lumber dominated.

She stepped onto the wooden planks and slipped sideway on slimy wood as slick as black ice. She grabbed the handrail to brace herself. She slid one foot forward at a time, just like her first time on ice skates. Her pulse quickened. A frigid creek rushed below.

Gaining the far side of the bridge, she began a new ascent. Her ears picked up new sounds. *Things,* much larger than mice, moved parallel to her. Coyotes? Her heart thudded. Surely coyotes wouldn't attack a full-grown woman.

She splayed her light beam over the section of woods where the sounds seemed to originate. Nothing. The padding footsteps paused, too.

My overactive imagination?

She started walking again, and the cushioned footfalls resumed. She stopped abruptly, swiveled the flashlight. Silence. No red eyes glowing in the dark.

Just keep going!

She stepped up her pace, and her invisible four-legged companions matched her gait. She halted and they—whatever *they* were—froze.

"Just in case those coyotes aren't the friendly sort, how's about we keep our gun handy."

Good God, I'm talking to myself! She pinched the flashlight between her shoulder and neck, unholstered her gun, and quietly slid the slide back just far enough to see the chambered round. *Now let's remember to keep that finger off the trigger. The last thing I need is to take a tumble and shoot myself in the foot.*

Despite the chilly air, sweat beaded on her upper lip. Her light raked a section of woods again. Thousands of tiny blue dots sparked on the forest floor. *What the hell?*

She bent to investigate.

Ohmigod! The blue needlepoints were eyes. Millions of them. Spider eyes.

She ran. Sprinted for five minutes as fast as her legs would carry her. A stitch in her side forced her to stop. Gasping, she held her bruised ribs.

I was braver in a shootout with drug dealers. She laughed softly and resumed a hiker's measured pace. She cocked her head. No soundtrack of coyote paws falling softly on pine needles. Her four-legged companions had lost interest, moved on to check out something more interesting—or edible.

The metal sign gleamed in the flashlight's beam. The spur trail. Time for a break. She holstered her Glock, peeled off her backpack, and sat on a log. A long swig from her water bottle brought relief to her chapped lips. The cool liquid soothed her throat.

According to the maps, the spur led directly to the base of the petroglyphs. Less than a mile to go. Piece of cake. If she didn't let the bogeymen steal what was left of her mind.

A great horned owl hooted. The haunting bass hoo-hoo-hoo triggered a higher-pitched cry from its mate. The calls didn't unnerve her. That's what the woods were supposed to sound like at night. Lonely and somehow romantic.

Riley took a GPS reading and started up the spur trail. She stopped regularly to check her bearings and make sure she hadn't missed one of the blazes painted on trees to mark the way. The big toe on her right foot slammed into a tree root.

"Dammit!"

Visual feedback provided by the light wand wasn't three-dimensional. Images looked flattened—like cardboard cutouts. With no depth perception, she couldn't tell the shadow of a gnarled root from a hole in the ground.

Sunrise can't come soon enough.

When Riley entered the clearing, the three-quarter moon poured cold light from a clear sky. Granite outcroppings loomed like giant gray bubbles cascading down the hillside. She spotted her first petroglyph. The mark, a circle, had been chiseled into the rock thousands of years before. Rain, ice, and wind had weathered the marking, feathering the once sharp edges. Still the creator's intent remained clear. Her fingers traced the circle, feeling the rough indentations. Wolf was right. Magic lived here.

In the moonlight, she counted two-dozen marks before she quit trying to tally the symbols. How many boys had journeyed here and left as men?

Maybe I'll be braver on my return trip.

She checked her watch. Nearly one a.m. Did she dare nap? Exhaustion tugged at every nerve—her bruised body rebelling at the nonstop punishment. She looked for a hidden spot out of the wind, and a smooth surface to brace her stiff back.

She spied the perfect boulder configuration. Almost a cave. Then her flashlight illuminated a neon-ribboned rock. *Wolf! Had to be.*

Her damaged shoulder screamed in protest when she tried to lift the stone. She heaved and pushed. She finally levered it sideways and pried loose a plastic sandwich bag holding a lined piece of paper. She trained her flashlight on Wolf's neat cursive.

Her euphoria changed to bone-chilling dread. Dear Lord! BRU's graduation had to be stopped.

When had Wolf left the message? Did he plan to return? If there was even a slim chance he might come back, she wanted to be here. Yet her responsibility rested elsewhere. She needed to get to BRU, cancel the ceremony. She had to let the FBI task force know the Onward threat had weight. It was no hoax.

She rose to her feet, adjusted her backpack straps. That's when she spotted another neon tell. A fluttering scrap of fabric tied to a tree at the edge of the clearing. The flag marked a path that led deeper into the woods, in the direction opposite from her approach. Had Wolf tied the ribbons hoping she'd follow? Was he leading her to his hiding place?

She had to know. If she didn't find him by two a.m., she'd return to campus. Wolf left the message for a reason. He wanted her to cancel graduation. She couldn't fail BRU's students.

She took several deep calming breaths and set off at a brisk pace. Within moments, the moon's brilliance seemed a memory, extinguished by millions of pine needles swaying overhead. A great horned owl hooted. This time there was no answering cry.

Like the owl, she wanted to cry out, to see if someone answered. Instinct kept her quiet. It might not be Wolf who heard her call.

FIFTY-EIGHT

Thanks to his firm's technology, L.J. knew he could pinpoint Riley's location. Miz Pearl said her daughter was wearing his gift—a wristband GPS designed by Whitten Industries to locate missing soldiers with amazing accuracy, even if the grunts were injured and unable to activate distress signals.

He'd kept the gift's serial number. As soon as he entered it, the tracking system spit back the woman's location, a short hike from the Onward campsite. L.J. had no doubt the bitch was meeting her lover.

He dialed Nick. No answer. The deputy always answered his calls. Had to be out of satellite range. Frustrated, he threw his cell phone across the room.

Damn! The deputy was so close to Riley's signal. If only Nick would pick up, L.J. could order Valdes killed. Riley would be easy to control then. Boo-hoo. Losing her lover was bound to crack her composure. Hard to be an efficient security chief when you're blubbering.

He stomped across the room, picked up his cell, and hit redial. Nick's number rang, once, twice. The ringing stopped. He heard scratchy noise on the other end, but no voice.

"Hello," he shouted. "Hello!"

Dammit all to hell! Piss poor reception.

He pocketed the phone and walked to his gun safe. The outside resembled a bank's walk-in vault, but the six-foot-square interior was unique. Racks mounted on three inside walls displayed more than two hundred guns, mostly collector items—Old West six-shooters, a German machinegun captured in World War I, a baby Glock owned by a famous spy. He bypassed these collectibles to extract a Remington 700P from its place of honor. The unregistered sniper rifle was accurate to one-thousand yards in the hands of a pro. Though no pro, he could certainly down a target at fifty yards.

Unable to reach Nick, he'd handle things himself. He consulted a map, ran his fingers along latitude and longitude lines. Riley had to be right here. He stabbed the map. A spur trail in the middle of nowhere. Since this area was closed to hunters, he hadn't traveled the trail.

No roads, no nearby structures. A long hike from the nearest access point. But she had to come back to her car. Probably planned to drive her half-breed to some hideaway. Had the man found the Onward camp? Spied on it? All the more reason to kill him.

Only one logical spot for Riley to park—the Beaver Falls trailhead. No other access points were remotely close.

He locked up and headed to his garage. After his Mercedes purred its deep-throated welcome, he tossed the throwaway cell phone on the passenger seat. He'd try Nick periodically. If he couldn't reach him, L.J. would play janitor and sweep up the trash.

FIFTY-NINE

Wolf and Ray looped Tom's arms around their shoulders and carried him to a secluded spot a hundred feet off the trail. "Sorry. That scream startled me. I never saw the hole."

"Shit, your leg's broken."

A protruding bone made Ray's diagnosis superfluous. Wolf watched his uncle's fingers gingerly explore the break.

Ray shucked his backpack and rummaged inside. "I'll make a splint. Just keep quiet. Without dogs, they'll never find us."

"I'll play lookout, move closer to the trail," Wolf promised. "Let's see what Onward does before we push on."

With his headlamp switched off, he couldn't see Tom's face. "Hang tough." He squeezed the boy's hand. "We've made it this far. We'll beat the bastards."

He crept to high ground fifty feet above the path. Voices echoed in the distance. How far? He knew his ears played tricks on him in the dark. Without visual grounding, every noise seemed to boomerang. A new scream tore through the forest. One of Ray's fishhooks imbedded in another terrorist's cheek or eye. That or a bear trap's sharp teeth shredding a man's ankle. The images nauseated. But they were out manned, outgunned, and Tom was injured. Ray's guerrilla tactics evened the odds.

Five minutes passed, then ten. He cringed as another bellow of pain tore through the silent woods. While the booby traps slowed their pursuers, the men weren't turning back. He had no doubt who drove them—Deputy Nick Monson.

Fifteen minutes passed. No more screams, just muffled voices, snapping branches. The trackers had smartened up. He imagined their bodies bowed at half-mast, their eyes searching the ground for bear traps.

Linda Lovely

He heard movement. A lone man? Though the figure materialized as a faceless silhouette, He recognized his thick build and Australian bush hat. Monson.

Wolf held his breath. His pulse thundered in his neck as his heart pumped with a disturbing chaotic rhythm.

If Monson spotted Tom or Ray, they were done for. One burst from the deputy's AR-15 would mow them down. He didn't even need to aim.

Hunched forward, Monson's muscled body looked more like a bear than a human. He moved like a beast, too, with lumbering determination. He clutched the AR-15 in his right hand near his waist. Wolf figured the deputy knew how to bump fire the weapon, laying down a hail of bullets by jamming a thumb in his belt loop and forcing the recoil to constantly reset the trigger.

Sweat slicked Wolf's trembling fingers. Monson would be a good twenty feet past Wolf before he had any chance of detecting where Ray and Tom hid. Should he shoot him now? The deputy came even with him, moved on. Wolf's fingers flexed. He pulled the bowstring taut, sighted the arrow in the middle of Nick's back. *Keep going and you live.*

If Monson moved beyond Ray and Tom, he'd allow the deputy to keep trucking. Less risk. If he shot an arrow and missed, Monson would spray the woods with bullets. Smarter to let him go. They could hide in place a few hours longer, find a different route to the waiting Jeep.

Go on. Go, you bastard, Go.

Wolf's mental urgings seemed to work. The deputy was at a ninety-degree angle to Ray and Tom. Then he was past. Ten feet. Twenty.

The cell phone's singsong ring startled Wolf as much as it did Monson. He watched in horror as the deputy's head jerked

256

toward the source of the out-of-context noise. The phone trilled three times before it was silenced.

"Got you, you bastard!" Monson bellowed, whirling his AR-15 toward Tom and Ray.

Wolf processed the incoming data a second behind the deputy. Tom had Monson's phone. Someone called.

The barrel of Monson's AR-15 swiveled toward the cellular bulls-eye. With his arms raised, his torso was unprotected, vulnerable. Though Wolf had kept an arrow trained on him, his aim shifted a fraction when the cell ring startled him. No time to adjust, re-sight. The deputy would pump his bullets into the woods any second.

He released the arrow, willing it to find its mark. Half the shaft vanished, burrowed deep in the deputy's side. A scream tinged with outrage accompanied the man's collapse.

Wolf ran toward his uncle and Tom. He gulped air, trying to steady his nerves. "Move. Fast. No telling how many men are behind him. Soon as they see the deputy, their bullets will turn these pines into toothpicks."

"Give me a hand," Ray said.

"I'm so sorry," Tom sobbed. "Never thought to check the phone, turn it off."

"Water under the bridge," Ray said. "But we can't afford another mistake. It's off now, right?"

"Right."

Wolf reckoned the deputy was injured, not dead. Should he finish him?

Ray seemed to read his mind. "Leave him be. Help me with Tom."

They extracted a thermal blanket from Ray's pack and used it as a gurney. Tom was no lightweight. He swayed only a couple of feet off the ground as they hustled toward the waiting Jeep. Taking the lead, Wolf set a measured pace.

He felt under the spell of some weird psychedelic. His headlamp painted a narrow band of red light, coloring the surreal nightscape in a blood-red swath.

The firebreak road came into view. He sighed his relief. Sweat coated his body. Ray and Tom appeared in worse shape. His uncle staggered as he lowered his end of the makeshift stretcher. An agonizing chorus of soft moans suggested the young student had gone into shock.

"Listen, Dr. Wolfman, I may pass out—gotta tell you some things." Tom's fingers gripped his shirt.

He bent his head close to the boy. "I'm listening."

"Those trikes Onward talked about aren't motorcycles. They're ultralights. The bombs will drop from the sky."

"Damn," Ray swore.

Wolf put his arm under the grad student's shoulder, hoisted him to a sitting position, and bundled him into the passenger seat.

"Ray, take the Jeep. Drive Tom out of here. No one should shoot at you two if I'm not on board."

His uncle started to object. Wolf shook his head. He handed his uncle the camera holding pictures of the Onward assembly. "Take Tom to the highway patrol station on State 11. Ask the troopers to call the FBI. They'll believe Tom. The photos should help."

"Come with us," Ray protested. "Some of those goons may still be following our tracks."

He shook his head. "Without Monson giving orders, they're running for the hills. Regardless, this is our best shot to stop Onward. I'll head to the petroglyphs. If Riley sends someone to meet me in the morning, we double our chances of stopping this insanity. Now go!"

Ray lowered his backpack to extract his twin dynamite sticks. "Take these. A little extra firepower can't hurt. They're safe so long as they don't get overheated."

He pulled his nephew into a bear hug. "Good luck, son. I'll come back for you, soon as I deliver Tom to the state boys."

"No. Stay with Tom. After I leave a new message at the petroglyphs, I'll disappear for a spell."

When the Jeep drove out of sight, a cold loneliness gripped him. He was thankful his uncle listened. He prayed the two men reached the state police in one piece. Still he'd never felt so isolated. So alone.

He packed the dynamite carefully, separating the sticks in his pack with softer items. Kinks made his neck muscles feel like over-tightened guitar strings. He retrieved his bow and arrows.

Now I know. I can shoot a man.

The knowledge was burden, not gift. He switched on his headlamp. He reached the first neon flag, untied it, and stuffed it in a pocket. If any Onward men tracked the trio to the firebreak road, they'd see the missing Jeep's deep ruts. He hoped they'd assume they were all gone. But he'd leave no neon markers to raise their curiosity, make them wonder if someone remained.

He walked quickly, eager to reach the petroglyphs and try for a few hours' sleep. He'd discovered a small cave, an excellent hiding place. Exhausted, he needed sleep. His thoughts bore fuzzy edges.

His senses functioned absent conscious thought. He could smell—almost taste—acrid animal droppings deposited on the forest floor. He knew a freshly fallen tree decorated the path before his headlamp unveiled the log. The toppled pine oozed a sharp aroma as if blood drained from its body.

A wild creature cried in alarm. Adrenaline flooded his system. He fumbled with an arrow as he searched for the source of the din. A second later, a wild turkey ran for cover, making more noise than a combine as it thrashed in the brush.

He relaxed his fingers on the bowstring. Then a bright light shone in his eyes, destroying his night vision. Though nearly blind, he saw a human silhouette.

Don't shoot. It could be a hiker. No. It wasn't.

Though the bright light winked out quickly, the phantom image stayed on his retina. The shadow held a gun.

How did Onward get ahead of me?

He sighted the bow. Another human target.

SIXTY

A red pinprick danced on the path. Riley switched off her flashlight and drew her gun. Who was out there? Wolf? She wanted to call out. Considered the consequences if the light belonged to an Onward thug or the crooked deputy.

Frantically she searched for cover. She edged toward the trunk of a large tulip poplar.

An animal's anguished cry froze her in her tracks. Her body stopped; her heart didn't. It slammed into overdrive, thumping her bruised ribs in a cruel version of patty cake.

The creature's shriek accompanied its kamikaze departure. The bird crashed through the underbrush as if Lucifer himself breathed down its neck.

When she glanced back in the direction of the manmade light, Riley found herself lasered in the center of the red beam. *Oh, no!*

She threw the flashlight, hoping the noise would distract the interloper while she dove behind the poplar's ample trunk. As she fell toward the ground, she heard a whistling sound. Not a bullet. An arrow?

"Wolf! Wolf!" she screamed. "It's me!"

"Oh, my God. Riley?"

Recognizing his voice, she shook with relief.

In seconds, he reached her. A lethal hunter's bow still clutched to his chest.

"Dear God, I could have killed you." He reached down and touched her cheek as she rolled painfully from her side onto her back. At least she hadn't landed on her damaged shoulder.

"What the hell are you doing here?" The anger in his voice was palpable.

Riley bit off an answer, "You invited me, remember?"

"No, no. You weren't supposed to come until tomorrow, Friday."

"Look at your watch, genius." She was miffed. "The little hand is on the one. It's Friday morning."

She felt around for a sturdy branch, some handhold to lever herself upright. Wolf tossed down his bow. His strong hands found hers. A second later she tottered up.

"I'm so sorry," he murmured.

She retrieved the Glock knocked from her hand at impact. "If we're confessing, you're lucky to be breathing. I considered pulling the trigger, too." She holstered her gun.

He wrapped her in his arms and tilted her head up, his kiss fierce. He broke the embrace and lowered his voice. "I don't think anyone followed me, but we should play it safe. I know a hiding place."

"Let's find my flashlight first. I tossed it to distract you."

Wolf spotted it a few feet away, nestled in a pile of pine straw. He led Riley back the way she'd come, stopping occasionally to strip the tree branches of the neon confetti blazing the trail.

Once they exchanged the forest canopy for the moonlit field of granite boulders, they no longer needed to walk single file. Wolf pulled her against him, his arm tight around her waist. Her body soaked up his heat like a sponge.

"There's a cave just ahead," he whispered.

"Any inhabitants who might be grumpy about sharing?"

"Just a few hundred bats." He chuckled softly. "No, it's barely big enough for us."

The smallish opening proved a squeeze. Inside, the diminutive cavern formed a perfect circle, its radius less than six feet. A rock ceiling hovered about five feet off the ground. *No bats.*

They huddled at the back of the dark cocoon and traded stories. Wolf's fingers periodically danced over her face. Caressing her cheek, tucking a wayward curl behind her ears. Riley wondered if he thought she was a mirage—one that might vanish if not tethered by his touch.

"You had to shoot Monson," she said. "He would have killed you, Tom and your uncle given half a chance. He was Smitty's friend, and he slit the man's throat and scalped him."

She shivered. Wolf ran his hands up and down her arms.

"What now?" she asked. "I'm sure Onward's abandoned camp. Do we stay the rest of the night, head back to civilization at dawn?"

"You should go now," Wolf said. "I'll stay. It's safer. If anyone comes, I'll detain them."

"No." She shook her hand fiercely. "We're stronger together—"

"You're forgetting Smitty's cousin, Deputy Swihart. There's at least one officer out there—maybe more—planning to shoot me on sight for 'resisting arrest.' And I don't trust your damned ex-husband."

"There *is* someone I trust." Excitement tinged her voice. "My uncle."

Wolf's flinch reminded her. Uncle Ed was enemy number one to her lover's relatives. She rushed ahead before Wolf could interrupt. "His estate's near here. I'll throw a blanket over you in my backseat. No one's looking for a lone woman driver. I have a key to the guesthouse. We'll be safe there. My uncle's not home. But he'll listen when he does arrive. He flies in tomorrow just before noon."

Her uncle's absence was her only hole card. To lighten the mood, she pulled his head level with hers, bringing their lips millimeters apart.

"I can make a citizen's arrest. My gun trumps your bow."
Figuring a kiss would seal the deal she closed the gap between
them. They were both panting when they broke apart.

"I know two more reasons for hiding at Uncle Ed's." Her
voice slipped into seductive alto range. "A king bed in the
guesthouse and a very private hot tub. Nude bathing is
practically required."

He shook his head. "Sure you were with the FBI? You could
sell insurance any day."

Her smile faltered. "That's what I am selling. Life
insurance."

He insisted they walk single file with Riley in the lead so he
could protect their backs.

"How's the trail to the parking lot?" he asked.

"Not bad. If you don't mind coyotes and a billion spiders."

Bet he thinks I'm kidding.

* * * *

L.J.'s headlights swept the Beaver Falls parking lot. Only
two cars—a red VW Beetle and Riley's Honda. Good.

The vehicles looked like opposing bookends on an empty
shelf. The VW had pulled tight to the woods at the left, Riley's
Honda cozied up to trees right of the clearing. Between them
lay space for five cars.

L. J. made a U-turn at the end of the graveled clearing and
shut off the engine. His Mercedes faced out for a speedy exit.
Given the gravel, maybe he wouldn't try for zero to sixty miles
per hour in 4.2 seconds. But he wouldn't linger after he shot
Wolf. He had no doubt he'd find Wolf when he found Riley.
Why else would she traipse around these woods at night? She'd
come to help lover boy.

He muted his cell phone before pocketing it. Grabbing his
Remington, he attached a night scope, and chambered a round.

Excitement electrified his nerves. The hairs on his forearms lifted as if in a force field. A tiny voice inside his head whispered, "Aren't you glad Nick didn't answer his phone? Now *you* get to kill Valdes and watch Riley fall apart."

He'd shot bigger game—though polar bears lacked the wherewithal to shoot back. He assumed Valdes had a weapon. One he'd never have a chance to use. This wasn't a duel. Riley was a worry since he wanted her alive. Fortunately, her handgun lacked his rifle's range. *Don't get in her wheelhouse.* His plan was simple. He'd be the unseen sniper who killed the professor. He'd disappear while Riley blubbered her goodbye to a dying lover.

Decrepit wooden steps negotiated the steep rise from the trailhead to the start of the footpath. Scraggly brush and stunted trees hugged both sides of the stairs. Good. A funnel if he missed his shot in the woods.

L.J. climbed the steps and darted along the trail. He paused every few feet, using his night scope to search the tiered landscape for optimum position. He wanted a bead on his target across fifty feet of open ground. He'd kill the man, then hotfoot it to his car.

In his mind's eye, he choreographed the scene. With Riley sobbing over Valdes's corpse, he wouldn't need to break a sweat to beat her to the parking lot. He'd be tooling down the highway before she ever thought about staggering to her car.

* * * *

They tiptoed across the slick footbridge and returned to the main path. Riley's car at the Beaver Falls trailhead waited minutes away. Wolf grabbed her shoulder and spun her toward him. A finger pressed against his lips. Gunfire erupted. No warning shout. No angry cry. Just bullets shredding pines.

Bullets slammed into trees ten feet to their left. They crouched and ran further right where a swale provided a natural bunker. Could the mound of red clay absorb more rounds? No question more bullets would come.

Riley spared a glance at Wolf as she drew her Glock. His fingers pulled his bowstring taut, his arrow ready to fly. She trained her eyes on the dark hillside, waiting for a telltale muzzle flash. Where was the shooter? She didn't care who was firing or why. All that mattered was his location.

Another burst of gunfire. *There.* She had him. Maybe sixty yards away. Should she shoot? A flash from her gun would give the killer their location.

He'd keep reloading, sweeping the area until he ran out of clips.

Riley steadied her pistol. She held the Glock two-handed to brace for recoil. She fired. An instant later a man's roar preceded a new batch of bullets—bullets that shattered a branch high above the shooter's location.

"You hit him!" Wolf yelled.

Before she could object, he ran forward. She followed, but couldn't stay on Wolf's heels. By the time she caught up, Wolf kneeled beside the gunman. His fingers probed the man's neck for a pulse. He shook his head.

"It's Monson. He's dead. Got to give the son-of-a-bitch his due. See this hole?" He pointed at a bloody circle just below the deputy's rib cage. "My arrow entered here. Bastard broke it off. Hard to believe he had the strength to track us."

She looked at the corpse. Nick's strength rose from a powerful fuel—hate. She wasn't about to give him kudos. "I hope he's on track now, straight for hell."

Her shot had created a third eye, off to one side of his forehead. Purely accidental. She had aimed for the torso as trained, center mass, a bigger, surer target. But using muzzle flashes for target acquisition was dicey. This time close was good enough.

Looking at the dead body, she felt no regret—less than when she'd killed a drug dealer. Did taking a life come easier with repetition, or was it that Monson threatened someone she loved. *Loved?*

Wolf interrupted her thoughts. "There might be others. Let's get out of here."

She needed no further coaxing. As they ran, Wolf's synchronized footfalls comforted her. *We'll make it. We'll make it. We have to make it.*

* * * *

The climb to the ridgeline post winded L. J. He surveyed the field of fire with his night scope and settled in to wait, hoping his prey hadn't bedded down for the night. His mind wandered, picturing the prostitute he'd seen by the bus station.

Gunfire startled him. It sounded like firecrackers popping. L.J. knew his guns; the burst came from a rifle, medium bore, semi-automatic. Had to be Nick or one of his Onward cronies. He felt momentary regret. *Damn.* He'd wanted to kill the professor. Personally.

The murky light made it impossible to decipher what was happening. He'd never been good at visualizing off-screen action, even with the aid of a radio announcer's calls. A single gunshot punctuated the silence after that first hail of bullets. The sequence repeated. Another three blasts from a semi-automatic. Silence. A minute passed. Two. Three. Nothing.

He strained to hear—something, anything to suggest the outcome.

Raised voices. A woman and a man. Two words floated up to him—"Monson ... Dead."

Dammit. Hard to tell what the Onward clowns would do without Nick riding herd on them.

Linda Lovely

The gunplay hadn't compromised his ambush. The couple still had to come his way. Walk into his sights. In fact, the unsuccessful attack might make them less wary.

He watched the figures enter his kill zone. The smaller silhouette had to be Riley; Valdes the tall shadow. *Crap. They're running.*

His choreographed vision hadn't included targets zipping through his shooting gallery.

Hurry! Take a shot. Now.

He sighted the gun ahead of the bigger, running target, trying to judge where he'd be when the bullet arrived. He squeezed the trigger.

SIXTY-ONE

For a moment, the stinging confused Wolf. Had he snagged his arm on a briar? He glanced toward the ridge. Saw the shadowed figure in the moonlight.

"Take cover! Another shooter!"

Riley looked over her shoulder, perhaps hoping she'd misunderstood. Whatever she saw convinced her to run faster on the downslope.

Determined to protect her, Wolf raced ahead, closing in to shield her body. The bullet had barely grazed him. His arm burned, but there was nothing wrong with his feet.

The trees ahead would make the sniper's roost almost worthless. "Faster, Riley!"

A shot pinged. She didn't falter. He felt nothing. A miss. The protective canopy of pine boughs closed overhead.

Riley yelled, "There's no cover at the stairs. Follow me."

Stairs? What stairs?

She scrambled down a steep embankment, grabbing saplings and brush to prevent a precipitous freefall. Wolf hesitated, worried he'd crush her if he stumbled.

She skidded to a stop at the bottom of the hill. He launched himself, clutched at a bush and missed. He tried to jam the sides of his shoes into the dirt. His feet slithered over the slick pine straw. He picked up speed.

Careening down the slope, he snagged a sapling. It held a moment before snapping with a sharp crack under his weight. But it slowed his momentum, let him negotiate the final third of his descent without breaking any bones. The pummeling re-ignited pain in his banged-up shoulder.

A rolling three-point landing—foot, hip, right arm—spared his sore shoulder further trauma, but knocked the wind out of him. Panting, he lay still.

When he opened his eyes, he didn't see sky. Just swaying pine branches. *Good.* Protection. He turned toward Riley as she machine-gunned a full-clip of four-letter words. He followed her gaze. The sports car gleamed like a black diamond.

"That car is John Hunter's pride and joy." She spat out his name as she nodded at the Mercedes. "He's the shooter. Dammit, how did he find us?"

"Worry about that later. Run to your car. Stay low. Get it started."

"Why? What are you going to do?" Suspicion seeped into her voice. "I won't leave you."

"I certainly hope not. I just want to derail any plans John might have to follow. Now go!"

As she sprinted toward her Honda, Wolf removed one of Ray's dynamite sticks from his backpack. Rummaging in the pack's zippered compartments, his fingers closed around a pillbox holding a half-dozen waterproof chemical matches. Had Riley reached the Honda? Yes.

He ran to the Mercedes, placed a dynamite stick below the gas tank, and lit the fuse. He dashed for the Honda's open passenger door.

"Go! Go!" he yelled as he dove inside. "I don't know when it'll blow."

He turned to watch for the explosion. *How long?*

As the Honda reached the edge of the parking lot, Wolf saw the rifleman. He stood atop the stairs, took aim at them.

"Keep your head down," Wolf screamed as a bullet thudded into the car's metal trunk.

Riley stomped on the gas. Gravel spit out from the tires. The car whipsawed forward.

Come on dynamite. Explode already.

* * * *

L.J.'s anger fueled his scramble from the ridgeline.

What the hell? No one ran along the trail. Were they goddamn ghosts? He heard rocks tumbling. Trembling tree limbs marked their descent. The bitch realized the stairs were a trap. *Okay. Nail him in the parking lot.*

They scurried like jackrabbits. Before he gained a clear field of fire, they'd climbed in the Honda, motor running. *Take out their tires. Trap them.*

He pulled the trigger. A second later, he was deaf and blind.

The explosion rocked him on his heels. Pulsing white light, a fireball, destroyed his vision. His night scope intensified the explosion's leaping flames. His ears rang from the concussive blast.

When he regained his senses, the Honda was gone, and his beloved sports car was a heap of smoldering junk.

"Dammit!" His outraged scream rivaled the explosion.

He sank to a seat on the stairs, buried his head in his hands. He was screwed. Riley had seen the Mercedes. Hell, the cops would have no trouble proving the wrecked vehicle was his. He'd be tried for attempted murder—unless he killed the lovers before they talked.

He walked toward the area where Valdes had pronounced Nick dead. Might as well make certain of the verdict. L.J. found the corpse, kicked it once to make sure, then headed for the parking lot. He stared at the lowly red VW Beetle, the only vehicle left. Faster than walking. He'd put his undergraduate degree to use. Surely a one-time electrical engineer could hotwire a vintage VW bug.

Having found purpose, his mood improved. He tried the car door. Locked. He grabbed a sizeable rock and pounded it against the driver's side window. The excuse to beat something lifted his spirits. He pretended Riley's body absorbed the blows.

Thoughts of the woman consumed him. When they first dated, he thought her an attractive companion for social events. Pretty face. Excellent bloodline. Someone to escort to the symphony and corporate shindigs. He toyed with the notion of marrying her. He could do worse than have a senator for an uncle and unfettered access to the Yates family fortune. After a suitable period, he'd assume the role of grieving widower again.

It hadn't been long before Riley began to grate on him. Despite her mother's impeccable pedigree, the daughter was a damn know-it-all Yankee. She disagreed with him and said so— even when he entertained clients. She worked in a man's job and most of the time dressed like one.

Worst of all, she seemed immune to his charm. The more he gritted his teeth and labored to impress her, the more she backed away. Another whore like his mother who thought he wasn't good enough. He'd given up on wedding or even bedding Riley the bitch when her uncle stuck his nose in his business, forcing him to pretend he adored her just to stay close.

He slammed the rock against the window a fourth time. The spider web of cracks in the safety glass grew. With the fifth blow the glass caved.

He tricked the VW into life and took a deep breath. Time for a new plan. One that didn't involve jail. He could spin this. No one had seen his face. The gun he'd fired wasn't registered. He'd wipe it clean. Toss it in a creek. Nick—his only link to Onward—was dead.

He smiled. Hell, he'd make himself out to be a damned hero. Maybe even sue Valdes's estate for destroying his car. He patted his pocket. Good, he still had his cell phone. As soon as the damn satellites aligned, he'd call the sheriff. Better rehearse his story.

"Miz Pearl begged me to find her daughter. Once I figured out where Riley might be, I drove to Beaver Falls and started searching. I heard gunfire and an explosion. I stumbled across a body—Deputy Nick Monson. It was horrible!

"When I ran for help, I found my Mercedes blown to pieces. Desperate, I hotwired a car. Sheriff, I know it was wrong, but saving Riley was all that mattered to me."

L.J. laughed aloud, thinking of a closer to make the sheriff ready to lynch Valdes.

"Sheriff, I think that crazed professor shot your deputy and kidnapped Riley."

Flawless. Riley had zero proof to contradict him. Reviewing his plan, he discovered one tiny blemish. He couldn't use his throwaway cell. He'd exchanged calls with Nick on it. Forget the phone.

He drove toward the sheriff's office. He'd make his panicked report in person. Then he'd revisit the senator's funeral arrangements.

SIXTY-TWO

The Honda slewed around a sharp curve, skating on loose gravel near the ditch.

"I think you can slow down, Riley. Hunter can't walk this fast."

She glanced at Wolf. Even in the dashboard's dim light, she could read his satisfied expression. They'd beat John Hunter. Wolf's fingers pressed against the arm of his jacket.

"Are you hurt?"

"It's nothing. A bullet grazed my arm. Stings a bit, but I've had hangnails that hurt worse."

She saw a pull-off, swerved in, and slammed on the brakes. "Let's see this nothing. If it's more than that, I'm taking you to the hospital. Period."

She eased off his jacket. The bullet had barely grazed him. "Okay, you'll live." She cut him a stern look. "But next time you're shot, I expect you to mention it."

She rummaged in the storage console between the driver and passenger seats for tissues. "I'll clean it with alcohol when we get to Uncle Ed's. Ten minutes at most."

"Hmmm," Wolf said. "I have this recurring naughty nurse fantasy."

Riley shook her head. *Men!*

"We're near Highway 11. Get out and climb in the backseat. I'll cover you with a blanket. Don't want to take any chances when we're this close."

Though she could no longer see her passenger's face, she kept talking. "I should have cell service now. I'll phone Gary, tell him what we learned about Onward and John Hunter."

Her brief call was productive. Gary agreed that a change of venue couldn't erase all risk. He promised to see to it that graduation ceremonies were canceled. Riley let the breath she'd been holding escape. Thank the Lord! BRU would accept the FBI's advice. The students would be safe.

When Gary demanded her location, she stonewalled and refused to say if she was with Wolf. She knew her silence frustrated the hell out of her ex.

Once the call ended, she pitched her costly smart phone out the window. "Can't risk Gary tracking us. He's ticked. He'll turn over every rock looking for us."

"Did your ex have any news?"

"Yeah, all good. The state police took your uncle and Tom into protective custody. They're headed to a Greenville hospital to treat Tom. Gary's sending agents to guard the two of them until the mess at the sheriff's office gets ironed out."

"Thank God," came a muffled response from the backseat.

She left the scenic highway for a stretch of asphalt marked "Private Drive." A mile later the Honda pulled up to a decorative but no-nonsense iron gate. She rolled down her window and punched in a code at an unmanned security box.

The gates creaked open. "You can get up. It's another mile to the house, but we're on the grounds. No one will see you. My aunt and uncle have more than a hundred acres."

Adjusting her rearview mirror, she watched Wolf throw off the blanket.

"There's nobody here? What about the senator's daughter? Doesn't a spread like this mean fulltime staff?"

She smiled. "I promise we have the place to ourselves. Jennie told me she wouldn't arrive until minutes before tonight's party. Didn't want her fussbudget mom bugging her about clothes and makeup.

"As far as staff goes, it's the middle of the freakin' night. There are no live-ins, and the gardener doesn't arrive until seven. If I park behind the guesthouse, no one will see the car. We're fine. Trust me."

She drove past the main house—a stately mansion reminiscent of Scarlett O'Hara's Tara. A glance at the empty staff parking spots behind the plantation-style home assured that her assumptions were good.

She pulled behind the guesthouse and shut off the car. Exhausted and filthy, she let herself slump against the steering wheel.

"You okay?" Wolf's voice vibrated with worry as he extricated himself from the backseat.

"Yeah. I feel like I was strapped in an electric chair and got a pardon at one minute to midnight."

She opened the car door, swung her legs out, and slapped her forehead. "What was I thinking? I threw away my cell, and I need to make one more call. Guess I can use the phone in the guest house as long as no one's monitoring the number I call."

Inside, Riley walked to the telephone on the hall table and lifted the receiver. She'd memorized her BRU communications officer's home phone number when this mess started. His groggy response indicated he'd been sound asleep. Once he gathered his wits, she asked him to notify all staff that graduation ceremonies would be postponed indefinitely.

"Tell Alan to take charge until I can make it in—sometime after noon," she added. "One last favor. Have Patty ring my mother at eight a.m. and tell her I'm fine, my assignment just took longer than expected. I'll phone later."

She hung up. "I'm officially off the grid. Nobody knows where we are, and Uncle Ed's not due for eight hours. I can't think of bigger blessings."

"You look ready to collapse."

"Yeah." She studied Wolf. He looked beat, too. Exhaustion had erased the flush of victory from his face. "I guess we're both bone tired."

Glancing across the living room to the winding staircase, she groaned. "There are stairs involved. But I guess it's worth the climb. A soft bed. Clean sheets."

"Promises. Promises. Looking at those stairs makes curling up on the floor sound fine to me."

Riley dragged her battered body up the staircase. The sound of Wolf staggering in her wake reminded her of the last time they'd climbed stairs together. Her house. A frisky prelude to a romp in the hay. This night couldn't be more different. They barely had enough energy to make it to the second floor much less engage in nude horseplay on the stairs. There would be no playful banter. No teasing laughs. Just bed and, hopefully, sleep.

Neither of them spoke. Fear and death, horror and fatigue had been their steady companions for too many hours, too many days. Hard to laugh when you wake from a nightmare, terrified it will replay the moment you shut your eyes.

I'm alive. Wolf's alive. That counts for something, right?

Riley barely waited until she stepped across the bedroom threshold to begin shucking her clothes. She discarded her shirt first. Her throbbing shoulder stabbed with pain as she tossed it aside. She felt as if she were shedding an old, soiled skin, peeling away a stink that had nothing to do with her filthy clothes. She needed to escape the horror, to separate herself from death's door.

In her haste to strip away the remnants of this night of terror, she momentarily forgot Wolf. She turned toward him. His hungry gaze roved over her naked body. She'd never seen this look. His untamed lust—pure animal desire—triggered her own.

"I want you." His words came out closer to demand than plea. Fierce, fiery.

"Yes." She didn't recognize her own graveled voice.

Wolf grabbed her, crushed her naked body against the length of him. He found her mouth. Claimed her lips, drove his tongue against hers. The coarse edges of his dirt-caked clothes sandpapered her flesh as they grappled and tumbled onto the bed. Her below. Him on top. Questing hands. Harsh, frantic. Nothing gentle. What she needed. *Take me!*

His mouth found her neck, a new trophy. Moist, hot. The sharp pain in her shoulder melded with the sharp pleasure. Her face scrubbed against the bristle of unshaven cheek. Her lips skimmed a patch of skin on his chin where prickly briars had etched a tiny rivulet. Her tongue flicked over the crevice, tasting the tang of salt and dried blood.

The sharp musky odor of his sweat heightened her need. She fumbled with Wolf's zipper. Panting, she grabbed his waistband and yanked with new-found strength. He moaned, wriggled free.

Hot, fevered skin. Writhing muscles. His calloused fingers pushed against the inside of her thighs. Opening. Claiming. She arched to meet him. He shuddered as she found him, guided him.

"Don't stop!"

He pounded into her. Pulled free. Thrust deeper. The fury of their coupling cauterized the pain in her shoulder, the ache of her ribs. She lost herself in the white-hot need.

Riley gasped. "Ohmigod. Don't stop!"

Each time Wolf retreated, she bucked against him. Demanding.

"Harder."

The precipice felt near. Explosive light tinged with dark oblivion.

Live and forget, block out the death. Hold it at bay.
"Harder." Her nails dug into flesh. She screamed. "Yes!"

SIXTY-THREE

What fun, riding with the sheriff. Lights strobing, siren wailing. The car led a parade of official vehicles; L.J. serving as the grand master.

As they entered the Beaver Falls lot, he pointed toward a smoldering heap. "My Mercedes." No need to feign the misery in his voice.

"Good Lord," Sheriff Hendricks swore.

The lawman told L.J. he'd been fast asleep when his office advised him a distraught civilian had stumbled in to report the murder of one of his deputies. The sheriff's jutting jaw and tight-fisted grip on the wheel said he was wide awake now.

Hendricks parked, and they climbed from the car. The night filled with the echoes of slamming car doors.

"You two," the sheriff yelled at the officers parked nearest the Mercedes scrap heap. "Secure the area around the car."

He turned back to L.J. "Where did you see the deputy's body?"

L .J. pointed left of the trail. "Not exactly sure. Two hundred feet past the stairs. On the left side. Have to admit I was scared. Not thinking straight."

"Understandable," Hendricks said. "Stay here. You can sit in the car while we search."

L.J. declined the offer, preferring to lounge against the vehicle for a better view. He sucked in the cool night air and watched dispassionately as the deputies swarmed.

"We found Monson!"

The shout came shortly after the rotund sheriff huffed his way up the stairs. Fifteen minutes later, the coroner arrived, and white floodlights flickered in the forest like swarms of giant lighting bugs. L.J. watched crime scene techs take impressions of the tire tracks left by Riley's Honda. Of course, they also had the portion of an arrow still buried in Monson. *Gotcha!*

The sweating sheriff grunted as he descended the stairs. L.J. was mildly surprised at Hendricks' competence. The man lumbered among the knots of investigators, clearly in charge.

Gradually, the level of activity ebbed along with the initial rush of adrenaline. It was late; everyone tired. The lawmen would find no more bodies in the dark.

The sheriff returned to his car. "Want me to drive you home?"

"Could you give me a lift to the Whitten building? Thought I'd pick up a company car so I'll have a ride come morning."

"Sure." Hendricks turned onto Highway 11. "Looks like that professor's gone postal. I'm real worried about Riley."

At his office building, L.J. shook Hendricks' hand. "Thanks for the ride."

The sheriff's double chins danced as he shook his head. "For the life of me, I can't imagine what got into Riley. Why'd she go out alone in the dead of night? She seemed cool as a cucumber when we talked. Had me convinced this professor was nothing more than a colleague. You suppose he spun her a sob story, saying he'd only turn himself in if she came along?"

L.J. faked a frown. "I'm as baffled as you are, Sheriff."

Hendricks sighed. "Don't know which I'd rather believe— Riley as accomplice or kidnap victim. Either way I'm afraid it won't end well. I put out a BOLO for Riley, too."

The sheriff looked L.J. squarely in the eye. "You did all you could. Now it's up to us to find them. Hope we get a hit on Riley's Honda. If they hide out in the woods, it'll be a bitch to find them."

Not for me. I'll know as soon as I get a fix on Riley's GPS.

L.J. walked across the corporate lobby, startling the man at the security desk. The guard dropped his magazine to greet the

big boss as he signed in—protocol for everyone, even top
honchos. After all, there were secrets—some legal, some not—
inside these walls.

"Who's doing the rounds?" L.J. asked. Two men shared
night duty. One manned the front desk; one roved the building.

"Harve," the guard answered.

"Radio him to get a company car gassed and ready to roll at
the front entrance."

"Yes, sir, Mr. Hunter."

L.J. strode to the elevator and jabbed the up button. The
ascent seemed interminable. As soon as the doors pinged open,
he made a beeline for his office, powered on his computer, and
accessed the GPS tracking system. When he entered Riley's
serial number, a world map appeared. With successive zooms,
the image tightened on the United States . . . South Carolina . . .
Leeds County . . . and Senator Yates' spread off Highway 11.
The locator beacon for her GPS pulsed steady as a heartbeat in
the middle of the estate.

"Should have guessed. Senator Edwin Yates. Tsk. Tsk. How
could you harbor fugitives?"

Technically the senator was innocent. Yates was still tucked
in his Capitol Hill bed. L.J. leaned back in his chair. Did Riley
plan to drag her uncle into the fray? That could complicate
matters big time.

He balled his fists. He wanted to rush over. Kill Riley and
Valdes in bed—the slut was probably screwing him right now.
He unclenched his hands. Couldn't afford to act rashly.

He walked into his executive suite's bathroom, stripped,
and dumped his filthy hunting clothes in a hamper. Turning the
water on full force, he shoved the temperature lever deep into
the red zone. He stood in the shower for long minutes under the
punishing, scalding spray. Finally he soaped up, rinsed, and
toweled dry.

He kept a spare wardrobe at the office so he could change into fresh clothes if he played a game of handball in Whitten's fitness center. Dressed in a clean nylon running suit, he felt better. But a plan eluded him.

It'll come. It'll come.

He nodded to the guard manning the lobby desk.

"Your car's ready, Mr. Hunter."

Of course it is. The beige Camry would do nicely. Comfortable. Nondescript.

He turned his car radio to a station that played oldies into the wee hours. He listened to Andy Williams croon "Moon River." Mid-song, a reporter broke in with a news bulletin. L.J. turned up the volume, hoping to hear BOLOs for Riley and Wolf. A description of the fugitives as armed and dangerous would be a nice bonus.

"A new development in the Blue Ridge University threat story," the reporter began. "Informed sources tell us the university has canceled graduation ceremonies. WUTC Radio also has learned the FBI has at least six Onward suspects in custody."

L.J.'s smile died. "Shit! Damn! Son of a bitch!"

His fist beat the steering wheel. There went any chance to blow up the senator at commencement with the added bonus of flipping the bird at BRU.

Calm down. The senator's coming home. You still have a weapon. Just the where needs to change.

His mind circled to the party for the senator's daughter. Miz Pearl would be there, and L.J. was on the guest list. Perhaps he could use Riley's mother and her handy dandy bomb-on-wheels at that bash. Step outside the mansion, make a phone call, and KA-BOOM! A merciful God would allow him to be one of the few surviving party-goers.

Was there a way to hang *that* on Onward? Perhaps a fake note could say Onward targeted Yates for harboring Valdes, the man who murdered and scalped old Smitty.

No, wouldn't work. How could Onward know Valdes had found refuge at the estate? Time for a new scapegoat.

He nosed the borrowed car into his garage and retrieved another throwaway cell. Two rings later the senator's aide picked up.

"What's wrong?" Charles asked. No groggy hello. The sleepless man had degenerated into a nervous jellyfish.

"Get a grip," L.J. said. "Slight change of plans. Forget the pills. Graduation's canceled so there's no need to play sick. I want you alert. Able to follow instructions."

"But—"

"I can't talk now. I'll be in touch. Do as I say and everything will work out fine."

SIXTY-FOUR

As Wolf climbed from his dream, his hands quested for Riley's soft skin. Sun streamed in the window, sparking red dots on his closed eyelids. His fingers slid over the satiny sheets. Smooth—and cold. He was alone.

His eyes popped open. Where was she?

Had he hurt her last night? What had come over him? She was injured. He'd been a rutting animal. Not his style. Had he scared her?

His thudding heartbeat slowed to normal when he spotted her at the corner desk, chewing on a pencil. Wearing a baggy purple-and-gold BRU sweatshirt and gray sweatpants, she looked more like a schoolgirl than an FBI veteran. Her curly hair was shower damp. Bare ankles poked above a pair of purple Crocs decorated with gold flowers.

He sat up in bed. "I see we're wearing school colors."

Her smile flickered and vanished. "I woke up early. Walked over to the main house and scrounged clothes from Jennie's closet."

She nodded to a man's jogging suit folded on a chair. "You fared better. You're taller and thinner than my uncle, but the elastic waist should keep the pants up."

"I'd better be long gone before he discovers someone pilfered his clothes."

"That's the least of our worries," she mumbled.

He climbed out of bed and pulled on briefs. Riley didn't look up. He walked over and lifted her chin, forcing eye contact. "What's wrong?"

She looked down. "Why don't you shower and get dressed. Then we can talk."

She seemed cool, distant. Some bizarre "off again" bounce?

"Sure." He snatched the borrowed clothes and headed for the bath. "Guess you'll tell me what's on your mind when you're good and ready."

He didn't exactly slam the bathroom door but he didn't close it gently either.

Take a shower. Don't throw a fit until you know it's warranted.

He completed his bathroom routine in record time. When he returned to the bedroom, he caught Riley pacing.

"My mood has nothing to do with you," she said. "Last night all the news seemed good. Graduation's canceled. Tom and your uncle are safe. Monson's dead and the FBI rounded up the Onward members you photographed."

"So why the gloom and doom?" Too keyed to sit, he leaned against a doorjamb.

Riley's pacing opened more distance between them. "Uncle Ed's the only person I know with enough clout to push for Hunter's arrest. This morning I realized he won't help me. I was dreaming."

She shot a quick look at him. "I'm sorry, Wolf. Once he learns who you are, who Ray is, I doubt he'll listen to anything. Especially since I haven't a shred of evidence against John Hunter."

"What are you saying?" Wolf's volume notched up. "Ray saw Hunter order Smitty's death. He heard the man admit he bankrolled Onward. Hunter shot at both of us last night. That fact alone should convince your uncle to overlook the small matter that he considers Ray and me to be slime."

She slumped into a chair. "He'll ask if I actually *saw* Hunter fire a weapon. I have to say no. Neither of us can identify the sniper. The only thing incriminating John is his car. I'm sure John will dream up a logical explanation for why it was parked at Beaver Falls."

"This is insane," Wolf said.

"I know," she said. "But it's reality. Then there's your uncle—an alcoholic who suffers from combat stress." Her voice softened. "Only Ray can connect Hunter to Onward. Authorities can't coax Monson to roll over on him. He's dead. So it's Ray's word against a man who holds a top-secret clearance. Guess who my uncle will believe. He'll decide you've brainwashed me. My mother will second that opinion."

She combed her fingers through her hair. "Hunter's a successful businessman. No trouble with the law, not even a traffic ticket. If my uncle convinced someone to arrest him, he'd be out on bail in fifteen minutes. John has clout—and power—here and in D.C. When John goes to the White House, it's not on a public tour."

Wolf unclenched his jaw. Pain pounded behind his eyes.

"What then? We wait and see if your old family friend screws up his next murder? Should I turn myself in now? There's lots of physical evidence against me—my knife, my jacket. I had motive and opportunity. Then, of course, I write smut, and no one trusts *me* with top secrets. Will your uncle push for my execution like he did for Cousin Hank?"

Riley's defeated expression punched him in the gut.

"My God, that *is* what you think. Have you called the sheriff to pick me up? Or do you have the power to arrest me off-campus?"

"Don't be ridiculous," she snapped. "We have to face facts, be prepared. I'm not sure the FBI can do any more than Gary's already agreed to do. He'll try to link John with the dirty deputy and look at his finances."

Wolf felt he'd fallen down something deeper than a rabbit hole. He *knew* Hunter was guilty. Riley did too. Yet he was the better candidate to be fitted for handcuffs. His immediate future seemed clear. He'd disappear. He knew the woods. How long did that abortion clinic bomber evade the Feds? Five years? Maybe by then there'd be proof Hunter was the killer.

If Wolf were charged with murder, hell would freeze over before a judge gave him bail. In jail, he'd be a target for any Onward scumbag assigned to his cellblock.

He took a deep breath. *Calm down.* Riley's not your enemy—even if her family is. She's thinking logically. Still an extended vacation looked mighty appealing. Ray and Tom were fine. The BRU threat ended. He could and would vanish.

He walked to the nightstand to retrieve his watch and wallet. They sat beside her GPS watch. He spun to face her.

"How did John Hunter know to go to Beaver Falls? How did he find us?"

"I ... I don't know," she stammered.

He plucked her electronic toy off the nightstand. "You told no one where you were going. Hunter must have tracked you electronically—maybe with this. He knows where we are this very minute."

She snatched the GPS unit from his hand. "He gave me this. God, I'm an idiot. You're right. He knows where we are."

"Can we use that? Will he come here?"

"No. Or he'd be here. He must have decided it was too risky. He doesn't know we're alone. But he does know we're armed. He may think he'll have an opportunity tonight. He's invited to Jennie's bash—along with two hundred others."

Wolf's mind churned. "Let's go back to Hunter's motive. Why did he want Onward to bomb the graduation ceremonies? According to my secretary, he has a chip on his shoulder about his dad giving so much money to BRU before his bankruptcy."

Her forehead creased. "I didn't know that. But I can't see an old grudge as motive. The man's no zealot. The bombing had to offer personal gain. But how? He's a defense contractor. BRU has squat to do with the military, not even research. We're a liberal arts college."

Wolf ran through scenarios as if he were crafting a plot for a novel. "It's not what." He stared at Riley. "It's who. Hunter needs to eliminate someone he was certain would attend graduation. He wanted the death to look like collateral damage."

Riley finished his thought. "Uncle Ed. It has to be. John wants the Chairman of the Senate Armed Forces Committee dead. But why?"

She collapsed onto the bed.

He sat beside her, took her hand. "Think our hypothesis might nudge your uncle to open his eyes, see things your way?"

Riley squeezed his hand. "It sounds so preposterous. I'm not sure Uncle Ed will buy it. But I may know how to light a fire under John Hunter. Force his hand. God help me, we'll break a dozen laws."

SIXTY-FIVE

Riley arrived at the Greenville-Spartanburg airport a few moments before her uncle's flight was scheduled to land. As she pulled up to the terminal, a silver-topped Rolls disgorged Doris Hillman and Reverend Jimmy, who played chauffeur. She bet the Rolls wasn't the only engine Jimmy cranked for Doris.

She watched the Rolls' famous ornament sink into the hood like a shy mermaid diving into the depths. A deterrent against vandals intent on stealing the coveted winged artwork from unattended vehicles.

Jimmy offered his arm to the heiress, who kept a firm grip on her mink stole with her free hand. Doris knew how to play up her best feature—the scent of old money. The preacher's silver hair shone as brightly as the Rolls' burnished hood. As they walked toward the airport entrance, Jimmy dropped his companion's arm to embrace a young lady, probably a parishioner.

Riley focused on Doris's face—a savage mask of rage. "I truly think she's insane. If Doris had a knife, she'd sink it into that young lady's chest."

Riley's hands tightened on the steering wheel. "Oh, my God, Doris *did* use a knife."

That's what had bugged her about the police reports. An eyewitness saw a well-to-do couple leave Amanda's apartment building around the coed's time of death. The witness claimed the top of their car gleamed like a stainless steel refrigerator. But she was confused about a hood ornament. First she told the police it had a fancy one. Later the car she remembered had none. The sheriff chalked the discrepancy up to witness confusion.

But what if she wasn't confused? Maybe the car had a peek-a-boo hood ornament.

Riley vowed to revisit the file on Amanda's murder once the current crisis ended. She entered the terminal and spotted her uncle and Nancy, wife number two, on the escalator. The plane had landed early.

She waved. Nancy responded with a frown—probably provoked by Riley's chosen attire. A former beauty queen, Nancy always dressed as if she were about to crown the next Miss South Carolina. *Wonder if she realizes these are Jennie's clothes?*

"Why, Riley, what an unexpected surprise." Her aunt's air hug had no chance of disturbing her sprayed hairdo. "Is everything okay with your mama? We've had enough bad news. I'm *so* disappointed the graduation ceremony's been canceled."

Riley disengaged from the limp embrace. "No bad news. Mom is looking forward to tonight's party. I just need a few words with your husband."

Ed greeted his niece with his usual rib-crushing hug. "Riley. I've been worried." He frowned as he released her.

"I assume your driver's waiting to whisk you home," Riley said. "But I'm hoping to shanghai you. If I give you a lift, we can talk en route."

"Of course." Ed's eyebrows knitted together.

Nancy's mouth shaped itself into a displeased moue. "Now, Ed honey, we have all kinds of last-minute party preparations. Don't you dare disappear. You promised."

"I swear I won't borrow him for long. Heck, we might even beat you home."

The senator clasped the shoulder of his gangly aide. "Charles, will you see Nancy home?" He winked at the hovering minion. "You're one of the few men I trust alone with my bride in the backseat of a car."

Though it seemed impossible, given Charles' pasty skin, he paled even more. Her uncle was the only one to chuckle at his joke. It startled Riley to realize Uncle Ed had never figured out his aide was gay.

Riley didn't care for Charles. Sexual orientation had zip to do with it. Charles was pompous and wound way too tight. Today he seemed unable to still his fidgeting hands.

"Uh, maybe I should ride with you two," Charles stammered. "I studied the FBI reports on Onward. Perhaps I can offer assistance."

The man usually didn't speak unless spoken to. *Way out of character.*

"Thank you, Charles." She tried a smile to ease her dismissal. "But I want to discuss a personal matter. I'm sure you understand."

"Of course." He grimaced and twitched like he'd just been diagnosed with a terminal illness.

Was he averse to spending time alone with Nancy?

The senator kissed his wife's cheek. "See you at the house, darling. Charles, don't worry about the luggage, let the driver handle it."

Ed turned and took Riley's arm. "Shall we?"

Once they were out of earshot, her uncle dropped the cheery bonhomie. "Riley, what in hell are you up to? The FBI and the locals are steamed. Director Stewart phoned to tell me the Leeds County Sheriff's Office has a be-on-the-lookout for *you* along with some fugitive professor suspected of murdering two men—one of them a deputy."

"Old news." She kept her tone light. "No one's looking for me. I talked to Gary an hour ago, promised to give the FBI a full report after I spoke with you. The professor—Dr. Valdes—has been framed. He's no murderer. And I told Gary I didn't know Dr. Valdes's whereabouts."

Her comment wasn't precisely a lie. While she knew her lover's itinerary, she had no idea where Wolf might be at any given moment.

When they reached her illegally parked Honda, she sighed in relief. No ticket. Maybe her luck was changing. They climbed in, and she pulled away from the curb.

"How to begin?" She chewed on her lip. "I'm convinced you're the reason Onward threatened to bomb BRU."

"Say what?" Uncle Ed practically strangled on the words.

"I know it sounds far-fetched, but I believe John Hunter wants to kill you. He planned to make your death look like collateral damage. Onward was misdirection, a distraction."

The senator barked a laugh. "Far-fetched? It's preposterous. Hunter's been one of my staunchest supporters. He's contributed tens of thousands of dollars to my campaigns. Hell, you've been dating the man. What have you been smoking?"

She filled her uncle in on Smitty's death and her first-hand knowledge of the dirty deputy's efforts to frame the professor for the break-in at her house. She sidestepped naming Wolf and Ray. She described Monson's ties to Onward and Hunter's appearance at Beaver Falls.

The senator had long since stopped laughing.

"But your only evidence against Hunter is some hermit's word that Hunter ordered the deputy to kill Smitty?"

The man knew how to skip to the bottom line.

"Correct. But I think we can trap the SOB. If—and I admit it's a big one—if we can figure out *why* he wants you dead. Any ideas?"

The senator let out a long sigh. Out of the corner of her eye, she read his body language. Slumped shoulders. Head bowed. Defeat.

They drove in silence. Riley wanted to give her uncle time to assimilate everything she'd said.

The Honda chewed up five miles before her uncle re-engaged. He took off his glasses, pinched the bridge of his nose, and tilted his head back against the car's headrest.

"That day you visited me in Washington I met with Carl Oldfield, that *Washington Post* reporter who died of a heart attack. Carl claimed he'd latched onto a bribery scandal. A DoD contractor making huge payoffs to obtain military contracts. Said the bribery had been going on for years and the sums were staggering. Carl asked me to pursue a parallel investigation. Oldfield was damn nervous. Only gave me one name, a dirty DoD official named Beck."

Riley swallowed hard. "And Oldfield died minutes after he spoke with you."

The senator nodded. "The DoD official, this Beck fellow, died the day before. That's why Carl came to me. He suspected Beck's death was no accident. I asked Charles to launch an investigation. If we had a renegade contractor, I figured it was one of the beltway bandits. Never dreamed it might be a South Carolina-based company—Hunter's firm."

"What did Charles find out? Did he comb through Beck's finances?"

The senator frowned. "I asked Charles for an update last week. He put me off. Said he'd made progress but needed till this coming Monday to finish."

"Next week?" Riley stole another glance at her uncle. "After your untimely death?"

"Oh, no. You can't be suggesting Charles is involved?"

She winced, knowing the pain of disloyalty, of betrayal by someone you trust. "You have to consider the possibility."

They'd reached the highway exit to the senator's estate. After making the turn, Riley coasted to a stop. She turned in her seat to study her uncle. Folks usually pegged the athletic and distinguished-looking Yates as late fifties. With his slumped shoulders and dejected expression, he looked his age—seventy.

He met her gaze, touched her arm. "How do we find out if Hunter and Charles are really traitors?"

When she didn't answer, his jaw jutted forward. His bulldog face. "You already have a plan, don't you? Whatever you're thinking, it better not put my wife or daughter at risk. If it does, I'm out."

Riley wondered again if she'd gone loco, engaging in criminal conduct to trap John Hunter. No. If she stuck with her principles, the bastard would get away with murder, and Wolf might go to jail.

SIXTY-SIX

Wolf bounced over the rutted track, swerving occasionally to avoid horse manure. Riley had offered a choice—stallion or dirt bike. He hadn't mounted a horse for a decade, and he'd never ridden a dirt bike. He figured a hunk of metal wouldn't sense his amateur status and use his body to de-bark a tree.

The trail linked the Yates estate and seven neighboring properties. Back in the 1970s, the owners signed an easement granting common access to this stretch of woodland border to ensure fences never barricaded a bridle path shared for generations. Now younger family members, including Riley's cousin Jennie, exercised a different kind of horsepower on the trail.

The bridle path ran past Hunter's property. Too narrow for cars, it intersected with no public roads. Zilch chance of encountering a sheriff's patrol. Nonetheless Wolf's blood pressure soared as he left the path crossed into enemy territory –Hunter's estate.

He skidded to a stop at a maintenance shed Riley had told him about and pulled on a pair of the senator's gloves. Luckily, he had big hands, too.

A simple wooden hasp secured the shed door. No lock. *Good.* The inside gloom didn't deter his search for a usable tool. He rested the axe on his shoulder and walked toward the historic main house. Lifeless, a relic. He hoped the unoccupied vibe wasn't wishful thinking.

He left the visor of his borrowed motorcycle helmet down. From a distance, the tinted shield assured anonymity. His heart beat faster as he climbed the stairs to a back veranda where mullioned windows offered a framed view of any intruder.

He unstrapped Riley's GPS from his wrist and tossed it in one of the patio's potted plants before checking his own watch. Hunter's silent alarm would trigger the moment he broke in. Given the property's remoteness, Riley estimated deputies would need ten minutes to reach the house—even if they happened to be patrolling this section of the county.

"Don't stay longer than eight minutes," she'd cautioned. "My guess might be wrong."

Armed with an interior diagram, Wolf figured he needed five minutes tops. He took a deep breath, hefted the axe, and swung at the center French door. A mighty crash sprayed shards of glass across a colorful Persian carpet.

Inside, he hustled to Hunter's office. The computer sat exactly where Riley said it would. He unplugged it and placed his remaining dynamite stick in the mouth of the polar bear guarding the desk. He'd already lit the fuse when he spotted the stuffed wolf. The taxidermist had preserved the lupine predator in attack mode. The power of its bared teeth and angry snarl survived the beast's death.

He couldn't resist. Wolf tucked the computer under one arm, the wolf under the other, and ran like hell. The wolf's spirit would make a return.

This time Hunter would be stuffed.

He deposited the trophy wolf on the patio and sprinted to his dirt bike. An explosion erupted with a satisfying whomp as he roared over the enemy's property line.

He hadn't mentioned the dynamite to Riley. He doubted she'd approve, but an arson charge was peanuts compared to the murder rap dangling over his head. And he owed Hunter.

Leaving the wolf was stupid. *Childish. But satisfying.*

Three miles away he coasted to a stop and pulled out the cell Tom had stolen from the Deputy Nick Monson. Wolf pocketed the phone when he bundled his injured grad student into his Jeep. *Kismet?*

With a few button pushes, he redialed the last number Monson called.

Come on, answer the phone. I know it's you, Hunter.

* * * *

The intercom's insect buzz set L.J.'s teeth in grind mode. Was his secretary going senile? He'd told her to hold all calls.

"Who is it?"

"I'm so sorry, Mr. Hunter. I was certain you'd want to take this. It's Safe-Guard Security. There's been a break-in at your home."

L.J. snatched up the receiver. "This is Hunter."

He listened. "No. I live alone. No one should be there. . . Yes. Call the sheriff immediately. I'm on my way."

Damn! Was Riley still hunkered down at the senator's? He powered up his computer to check the GPS unit's beacon. The software performed its usual zoom-in magic, moving from the United States to South Carolina. A final zoom. The tracker beacon beeped steadily. Its location seven miles south of the senator's estate—his own home.

His throwaway cell rang. He flipped it open and bellowed: "Charles, you nervous little dickhead, I told you I'd deal with this—"

"So sorry," a smooth-as-silk baritone interrupted. "Not Charles. Killing Smitty is one thing, but did you really think you'd get away with murdering Senator Yates? We know you paid Onward. Now you'll pay us."

"Who is this?" He heard the roar of his own pulse. "You're talking nonsense. I'm hanging up."

But he didn't.

Had to be that pornographer pretending to be a novelist. Valdes. Any proof for the accusation? No. They'd need more than cheap theatrics to get him to blubber a confession.

"I hear you breathing." The caller laughed. "Bet you're wondering how we figured it out. Thanks for confirming Charles's involvement. Bad form. Didn't your mother teach you not to curse when you answer a phone? Miss Manners would not be amused."

L.J. wanted to beat the man to death, squeeze the life out of him with his bare hands. "What do you want?" he snarled.

"Something you understand—money. Five million wired to an offshore account. We have your computer, a nice top-of-the-line HP. I hear sirens. Gotta run. We'll be back in touch. Keep your cell phone handy."

L.J. heard a click. Cold sweat trickled down his back. Fire burned the length of his esophagus as his churning stomach pumped acid like an erupting volcano.

Money? Blackmail? Not Miss Straight-Arrow Security Director. Had to be a scam.

But maybe he didn't know her as well as he thought. She met loverboy last night. Didn't tell a soul, even though she knew he was wanted for murder. 'Course Valdes could be striking out on his own.

Damn. Even if they have no proof, I'm screwed. Charles. The slightest pressure and the little wimp would confess. That would give Yates enough ammunition to call in the Feds. A goddamn Senate probe.

I'm out of here. Forget my freakin' computer.

All the files he needed resided on his back-up thumb drive. Still, he'd play along with Riley and Valdes. Keep them busy while he disappeared.

As L.J. hurried past his secretary, he barked an order. "Tell Art I had to leave before I could take my coat off. A burglar hit my house. I'll call as soon as I can."

One final visit to his elegant house—home to the Hunter family for five generations until his father lost everything. L.J. bought it back to erase the family disgrace. Too bad his dad's mind was too far gone to appreciate the gesture.

He'd never see his father again. Though Lewis John Hunter was little more than a breathing husk, the idea of cutting that final cord made L.J.'s gut ache, even though the old man wouldn't know the difference. L.J. had made financial arrangements to ensure his father always had the best of care. No matter how long he lived. No matter what catastrophe befell his son.

L.J. shook off the sadness, straightened his shoulders. He would start anew—with lots of cash. He'd be free. In a third-world hideaway, he'd treat himself to a different female every day. Hell, for the right price, locals would line up to sell their ripe little daughters.

He'd keep his visit to his ancestral home brief. Just long enough to appear outraged while he grabbed the thumb drive and a counterfeit passport from his gun vault.

An icy knot cramped his stomach. By now, Art must know he'd cocked up their plan. His partner would be ready to stuff him in his oversized paper shredder. The ruthless CEO might just arrange a convenient accident for his former brother-in-law.

Sweat pooled beneath his armpits. No time to lose. He'd transfer Whitten's bribery slush fund to his well-endowed offshore account immediately. Another ten-million dollars would double his nest egg and provide a nice severance package. He just needed to steer clear of Art until he skipped the country. Fail and he'd be dead.

SIXTY-SEVEN

"Your ex parked his butt in your office," Patty whispered as Riley approached her desk.

"Thanks, I figured he'd be here."

Lifting her head high, she walked through the door. Gary stood when she entered. His dark look and aggressive stance suggested he could breathe fire.

A wonder my eyebrows aren't singed.

Riley held her hands palms out in a placating gesture. "I know. I have a lot of explaining to do. I also have new information. We're very close to unraveling this mess. My theories might not stand up in court, but Senator Yates agrees with my logic."

She figured the senator's imprimatur would prompt the man to listen. It did. He waved her into her own visitor's chair. She decided not to press her luck by arguing seating arrangements. She talked for fifteen minutes straight. Gary seldom interrupted. He asked a few questions then nodded.

"Riley, you shot a man and didn't report it for what, twelve hours? True, there were extenuating circumstances, but you know better." He looked more hurt than angry. "You could have called me, trusted me."

She shook her head. "I couldn't compromise Wolf's safety. There's still a deputy on the loose who thinks the professor scalped his cousin, and I don't know how many other deputies might be dirty."

"Valdes is no longer a suspect in Smitty's murder," Gary admitted. "Two of the Onward suspects rolled on Monson. Said the deputy told them he killed Smitty to demonstrate what happens when knights—that's what they call each other— disobey orders."

Her shoulders sagged in relief. "So Sheriff Hendricks knows Wolf is innocent? That'll make it easier for the sheriff to buy what I saw—Monson planting evidence at my house. It also gives credence to eyewitness testimony from Wolf's uncle."

"Yes, but the old coot is still the only one who can tie John Hunter to Monson and Onward. We need more concrete evidence to move."

"The senator's hoping Charles will fess up," she said. "He plans to talk with him this afternoon. Uncle Ed says he knows his aide better than anyone. He thinks he can get him to open up if the conversation's private."

"I can't allow that," Gary interrupted, his alarm evident. "If his aide's involved in a murder plot, any confession to the senator would be tossed. It's damned dangerous, too. What if he attacks your uncle? I need to bring Charles in for questioning."

She nodded, her eyes troubled. "Believe me, I made the same arguments. Uncle Ed told me to stuff it. Said he might be seventy, but he wasn't senile, and he knew how to shoot a gun if it came to that."

She chewed on her lip. "The senator's too worried about his wife and daughter to be concerned with legal niceties. He doesn't care if Charles goes free if it lets him protect his family. The bomb plot proves Hunter's capable of slaughtering innocents. That makes everyone near and dear to Uncle Ed vulnerable."

Gary sat up straighter. "I'll send agents this minute. The director will approve around-the-clock protection for the senator and his family. We'll locate Hunter and initiate surveillance."

Though Riley had a hunch about Hunter's whereabouts, she didn't volunteer the information.

"Thanks, Gary."

Her ex-husband leaned forward and locked eyes with her. "You're not the only one who's been working. We found Onward's explosives stash and the ultralight craft they planned to use for delivery. They were hidden in an abandoned barn near Cougar Mountain."

"I don't get it." Her brows knitted in confusion. "Are ultralights capable of delivering the explosives Hunter needed to make the senator's murder fool-proof? It's not like they're precision-controlled guided missiles."

"That bothers me, too," he admitted. "Our experts say Onward might have killed a couple hundred people if all went well. However, if the goal was to murder a specific person, the plan seems seriously flawed."

Her ex frowned. "In fact, given the size of the audience, the odds favored the senator's survival. You're certain killing Yates was Hunter's motive?"

"I'm positive. We're missing a puzzle piece. Maybe he planned to smuggle an additional bomb inside. But how?"

"He could have paid off one of your security officers."

Her shoulders slumped. "I hope not, though it's a possibility."

Gary used her desk phone to contact Director Stewart, who promptly agreed the FBI should provide security for the entire Yates family. He also gave the go-ahead to obtain a search warrant for Charles' home and office.

"Gary, I need to check on Mom. She's been disoriented and weak. Will you buy me a little time with the sheriff? Give him the overview on Monson's death. I'll make an official statement as soon as I escort Mom over to Uncle Ed's place."

"Okay, Riley. But you need to give me your gun. You shot a deputy. It will be evidence in the justifiable homicide investigation. I'll take it to the sheriff."

She hesitated. Her Glock had been a leveler in last night's nightmare. Of course her uncle had a well-stocked gun cabinet.

"Come on, Riley. I'm giving more than I'm asking. With the FBI providing security at your uncle's estate, you don't need a weapon."

Reluctantly she unholstered her Glock and handed it butt first to Gary.

SIXTY-EIGHT

"It's me," Riley called as she opened the door to her mother's house.

"Riley?" Her mom's frigid tone put a world of rebuke in those two syllables.

Pearl struggled up from her recliner and tottered toward her daughter. "I've been frantic. You snuck out in the middle of the night dressed like Batwoman. I presume you went off to meet that killer. I got so worried I called John Hunter. Where have you been?"

One mystery solved.

Her own mother sent the real killer after her. Would the woman never listen?

Riley bottled up her anger. A screaming match wouldn't help. "Mother, I left a note, and I had Patty call you first thing this morning. I'm not a child."

"Did John find you?"

Gee, how should I answer that one?

"Mom, please listen. Some people want to kill your brother. I just left Uncle Ed, and he agrees with my take. The whole point of bombing the graduation was to kill him—"

"Oh, my God!" Miz Pearl's breathing inched toward staccato. She pressed a hand against her chest.

"There's no immediate danger," Riley continued, her tone soothing. "Let's sit." She helped her mom to her favorite chair and gently stroked her hand.

"I talked with Gary. The FBI will provide around-the-clock protection for Uncle Ed and his family—including you. I'll help you pack enough clothes for a few days."

Linda Lovely

"What about Jennie's graduation party?" Pearl frowned. She seemed as concerned about her niece missing out on the festivities as she was about the death threat.

"The party is on," Riley answered. "FBI agents will screen the guests. However, one invitee won't be admitted. Mother, I know you love John Hunter, but he's up to his eyeballs in this."

She caught her mom's exasperated eye roll.

"If you don't believe me, listen to your brother. Please. I'm begging you. Don't talk with John again until this mess is straightened out."

Pearl shook her head sadly. "Fine. If that's what you and Ed want. But I'm certain you'll be eating crow. John is a gentleman. I know character. This is a big mistake."

It took Riley half an hour to pack her mother's "necessities" in two suitcases and load the car with her oxygen concentrator and hypoallergenic pillow. Then Riley corralled her cat for another relocation. "Sorry, Lucy. We'll be home before you know it."

Her cat acted as peeved as her mother. *Nice to be popular.*

Twenty minutes later, Riley pulled up to the senator's gated entrance. She was glad to see an armed guard. After showing ID, she drove to the main house where another gun-toting sentry protected the front door.

Ed greeted his sister and ushered her into the house. "I'll take care of Pearl," he told Riley. "The gate just called to say you have a visitor. A Steven Wingate? What aren't you telling me? Should the guard direct him to the guest house?"

"Yes. Thanks, Uncle Ed. I promise I'll tell you everything later today—after I talk to Steve. Have you, uh, made any progress on your end?"

"Still getting my ducks in a row. I want to be fully prepared for my *interview*."

* * * *

Hearing two cars pull up outside, one right after the other, Wolf separated the guesthouse blinds to spy on the arrivals. Riley and Steve Wingate, Ellen's father. Fine. He didn't need to hide in the damn closet.

It chafed to play stowaway just so Riley's uncle didn't discover he was harboring a relative of his son's "killer" on his estate. After all, he was trying to save the old bigot's life.

Though Wolf didn't want Hunter to kill the senator—and hundreds more in the process—he had no use for the man. Riley's affection for her uncle was beyond irritating.

He walked downstairs to greet the new arrivals. As soon as Steve spotted him, he flashed a nervous smile. "I know I said to call if I could ever do anything for you. I just didn't expect you to phone so soon."

Wolf waved a hand at the man's case. "You have everything you need?"

"Yep, my daughter's a bit of a geek, too. Ellen had most of the stuff I needed in her dorm room. We picked up the rest at a computer store. Show me to our patient."

Wolf led the way upstairs. "Sorry to drag you into this. But we needed a computer security expert. Glad you decided to stay in town a few days. How's Ellen doing?"

"Great. She'll be very proud if her dad can help her favorite professor stymie some bad dudes." He nodded at Riley. "At the request of the campus security director, of course."

If they were caught, Riley would be lucky if she just lost her job. Wolf knew the decision cost her big time. A law-enforcement officer, she believed in due process. But time was short, and they hadn't figured any legit way to ferret out Hunter's secrets. They needed leverage—fast. Riley was gambling with her reputation and career to prevent more murders.

Steve took a seat at the desk, ready to tackle Hunter's pilfered hard drive.

"Can I get you something to drink?" Wolf asked. "The fridge and bar are well stocked."

"A Coke now, scotch if I succeed. You might as well relax. This may take some time."

Wolf touched Riley's arm. "Let's leave Steve to it. He doesn't need an audience, and we need to talk."

They headed downstairs. "When do you plan to tell your uncle I'm tucked away in his guesthouse? It's only a matter of time until he finds out. Your mother is bound to mention who you ran off to meet last night. Your uncle's not dumb. What'll happen when he finds out?"

Riley gnawed on her lip. "I know, I know. I need to tell him."

He studied her face. The forlorn look, the wobble in her speech. Deceiving her family tore her up. He had no right to ask more when she'd already risked her life for him.

"Don't worry. I've decided to leave with Steve."

* * * *

"Hey, you two, I did it," Steve yelled as he leaned over the banister. His smile looked a mile wide.

Riley and Wolf raced upstairs.

"Hunter has a bank account in the Caymans with a balance just over ten million dollars." Steve beamed. "I sent all the files to your friend, Nexi Ketts. She's on speaker phone, waiting for your instructions."

"Nexi, can you hear us?" Riley asked.

"Wow. I never dreamed Miss FBI would ever ask me to use my forensic accounting skills to steal money." Nexi chuckled. "But I'm more than glad to return the favors you did me in Jamaica. I just hope we don't end up sharing a jail cell. I've already set up the new offshore account Steve told me you needed."

"Great," Riley said. "Can you transfer ten-million dollars out of Hunter's Cayman account and stash it in the new account? I'm hoping you can pass the funds through enough channels to make it extremely difficult, and, at the very least, time consuming to track. We can't let our villain get his greedy mitts on that cash for at least twenty-four hours."

Nexi laughed. "Easy peasy. I just transferred out all but one dollar. Didn't want to close Hunter's account. Figured you might want to tell him to check his balance."

"Perfect, Nexi. Can't begin to thank you," Riley said.

"Okay, call if you need anything more," Nexi answered. "Nice working with you Steve. Hope we get to meet sometime. Good luck, you guys. Keep me posted."

After Nexi hung up, Steve rocked back in the executive style chair, hands laced behind his head. "Playing the hacker was kind of fun for a change. Nexi said the same about doing a little reverse engineering. Need anything else?"

Riley hugged Steve.

My God, I just helped embezzle ten-million dollars.

She massaged her forehead and reminded herself that lives mattered more than legalities. "This is bound to unhinge John. While I want to force his hand, I'd feel a whole lot better if I knew how he'd planned to kill Uncle Ed."

"What do you mean?" Wolf asked. "Weren't Onward bombs supposed to take him out?"

She shook her head. "Doesn't look that way." She shared the FBI's opinion that the Onward explosives and ultralights lacked sufficient firepower and accuracy. "John wouldn't leave the outcome to chance. He must have found a way to detonate a bomb inside at the same time the ultralights dropped theirs."

Steve looked thoughtful. "Technical magazines talk a lot about using cell phones to trigger bombs. Engineers are trying to tweak the technology. Eliminate a tactic that allows terrorists to kill without risking their own skins."

"Killing by remote control sounds like Hunter," Riley said. "How does it work? He calls another cell phone?"

"Sort of," Steve answered. "Circuitry stripped from a cell becomes a detonator. When that number's dialed, the connection creates a spark and boom!"

A shiver ran down her spine. "Gary suggested John might have bought a BRU security officer. Someone to smuggle a bomb inside."

Steve put his elbows on the desk. "The bomb would have to be bigger than, say, a breadbox, and positioned near the senator. I'd think even a security guard would have a hard time depositing a mysterious item of that size near the senator."

She nodded. "Yeah, it would. How in blazes could John smuggle a bomb inside?"

Nobody had an answer.

Wolf stood. "Fantastic job, Steve. Can I ask one more favor? A ride out of here. The trunk will do."

Riley swallowed. *No.* "What are you thinking? You can't go. The charges against you have been dropped, but we still don't know which deputies are dirty. Monson wasn't alone. You could be shot on sight."

"I'll take my chances. I'm not sure my odds are any better here—on enemy ground."

Steve's gaze pin-balled between them. "Sure I'll give you a ride." He licked his lips. "Where to?"

"It's better if Riley doesn't know. Then she can quit lying to her family."

Wolf hustled Steve to the front door, ignoring Riley's plea to stop.

"Don't worry. I'm not quitting. I'll keep the phone, play Hunter along. I'll call you with his response."

SIXTY-NINE

A mile from his house, L.J. spotted a balloon of dense smoke. When he heard sirens, he punched the accelerator. He whipped into his driveway then stood on his brakes to keep from rear-ending a fire engine slewed across the pavement. Men scurried over and around emergency vehicles like a colony of fire ants.

Before he could shut off his engine, a gaunt-faced man in fire gear rapped his knuckles on the car window and ordered him to back up.

"It's my house!" he yelled.

"Okay, don't back up. If you won't give us room to work, your house will be cinders."

He jammed the car into reverse, creating a cloud of dust as his wheels bumped over the curb and spun across tinder-dry grass. Exiting the car, he spotted Sheriff Hendricks and stormed toward him.

"What's going on?" he demanded.

"Take it easy," Hendricks cautioned. "We responded to a burglar alarm and discovered a fire in progress. These guys are optimistic they can contain it."

"I have valuables inside." L.J. licked his lips. "Irreplaceable. I have to get in, make sure they're safe."

Dammit, he needed his backup drive and fake passport.

"You can't go in until these guys say it's safe," Hendricks countered. "It's not as bad as it looks. The chief thinks they can limit structural damage to the room where the fire started."

Hellfire! L.J. bit the inside of his cheek to keep from screaming. He wanted to punch the sheriff in his oversized gut. Tell Hendricks that either Riley or her porno lover had stolen his computer and set the fire. However, the portion of his brain still sending sane impulses warned him to keep his trap shut. How could he *know* Riley or her lover had visited? Just a few hours ago, he'd pretended the woman's kidnapping was a crushing blow.

"Any idea who's responsible? Any leads? Any evidence?"

The sheriff shrugged and led him to his back patio. When L.J. saw his trophy wolf crouched on a lawn chair, he couldn't stifle a scream of rage—"Wolf!"

"I gather that stuffed critter doesn't belong there," Hendricks drawled.

L.J. was getting bad vibes. The sheriff wasn't showing his usual deference. His tone held a hint of sarcasm. Had someone talked to him, turned him?

"If this isn't evidence, I don't know what is," L.J. barked. "That murderer, the one who killed Smitty, his first name's Wolf, isn't it? He left a calling card. This shows how dangerous—and crazy—he is. The man should be shot on sight."

"Now, L.J.," the sheriff cajoled, "we already have a BOLO out on the professor and Miz Reid. There's no real proof he's been here. Why would he come after you? His beef's with Onward, right? Could be a prank. A kid breaks in, steals your wolf on a lark then decides it's too heavy to carry. Fire might be an accident, too. Who knows?

"And you won't let me inside?"

Hendricks pursed his lips. "'Fraid not. Too dangerous. Probably be two, three hours before the house is determined safe." He checked his watch. "How's about you come back mid-afternoon?"

"Fine." He spun on his heel, stomped to his car. When he cast one last glance in the sheriff's direction, he didn't like the sly expression on Hendricks' face. Not one bit.

He swore under his breath. "Riley and Valdes are dead."

Linda Lovely

L.J. kept his speed to a crawl as the billowing smoke shrunk in his rearview mirror. Valdes had his computer, and he couldn't lay his hands on his backup drive. He had no counterfeit travel documents to help him skip the country.

They figured they had him. They thought wrong. All he needed was an Internet connection. He maintained an anonymous account, emailed copies of critical files to it once a week. This wasn't a catastrophe.

Thirty minutes later a well-endowed waitress handed him a large cappuccino. He scanned the Internet café's available computers, spotted a free one near the door, and pulled up a chair. He typed in his fake user name and password, took a sip of his fresh brew. L.J. called up his financial files, jotted down his Cayman bank account number and the complex password—a lengthy jumble of letters and numbers he'd devised for hacker protection. He'd buried the sensitive data in an innocuous document. L.J. could never remember the damned password. He downed half his cappuccino before he accessed his account.

Balance—one dollar.

He bit his lip so hard he tasted blood. He wanted to scream obscenities. Only one logical conclusion. Goddamn you, Riley! I'll force you to put every penny back. Then I'll kill you and Valdes, and it won't be quick. You'll suffer.

His throwaway cell rang. Charles or Valdes? If Charles didn't know he'd been exposed, he might have uncovered some helpful information.

L.J. answered as though he hadn't a care. "Hello."

"Why, hello," a cheerful baritone sang out. "Forget the ransom we discussed. You can have your computer back. We helped ourselves to a little cash. In case you haven't checked your bank balance, you really should make a deposit. You're under the minimum."

"You bastard," he growled. The heads of patrons at nearby tables swiveled his way. He threw a two-dollar tip on the table and hustled outside. "Put every penny back, or you can say goodbye to your girlfriend—forever."

"Big talk for someone without a pot to pee in. No money, no home, no future. Oh, and no sporty little Mercedes. Plus a number of your best Onward pals are in jail or dead. The FBI has their explosives under lock and key. I doubt your military cronies will call down an air strike on Senator Yates. You're finished."

L.J. barely controlled his urge to smash the phone on the pavement. *Don't let him egg you into saying something stupid.*

"You have no idea who you're messing with." He paused, choosing his words with care in case he was being recorded. "Onward is colorful theater, of no importance. I'm giving you a deadline. Nine o'clock. Tonight. Return the money or the consequences won't be pretty."

L.J. hung up, a signal he was in the game, a player with chips. He'd turn Yates, Riley and Valdes into bloody confetti. The senator would go ahead with tonight's soiree. Wasn't his style to hide. Pearl and her ever-present oxygen concentrator were bound to be in the thick of things.

Never before had he wanted to murder anyone more than he wanted to kill Riley and Valdes. Yet his priority was survival—and not as some penniless expatriate. He needed money, and there was no way to siphon more from Whitten's treasure chest. No time.

Riley was the key. Valdes would put the money back if he put the squeeze on his little squaw.

SEVENTY

Riley closed the library door. Time for an unpleasant conversation with Uncle Ed. She couldn't believe Wolf had left, his life at risk because she'd been too cowardly to confront her uncle about a decades' old vendetta.

"We need to talk."

"Not now," her uncle replied. "My dear friend Charles will knock any minute. It's time for him to spill his guts."

Footsteps echoed in the marble hallway. "Wait," Riley pleaded. "Please leave Charles to the FBI. A confession extracted under duress will be thrown out."

"I don't give a damn. If he sold me out, he was willing to murder my wife and daughter, sacrifice hundreds of people. Before I'm finished, he'll tell me exactly what's going on and if he played a part in it. I need to know if my family's still in danger."

The senator brandished his old Army service pistol, a 1911 model, semi-automatic. Riley's throat tightened. "Do you even have bullets for that thing? If it's loaded, I wish you'd quit using it as a pointer."

The senator set the pistol on a coffee table and ran his fingers through his hair. His hands trembled. "I'm beyond angry. I can handle death threats. But Hunter planned to wipe out my family. I lost one child. I'm not about to lose another. I want you to leave. Now. This is my show. That little prick is about to enter the lion's den."

"I'm staying." Riley folded her arms over her chest. "You want to talk with Charles, fine. I won't leave you alone with him."

Uncle Ed glared at his niece. "Don't interfere."

After a tentative knock, Charles poked his head inside like a frightened turtle.

"Come in and shut the door," the senator barked.

Charles jumped. His gaze slid over Riley. "What, um, what's wrong?" His Adams' apple bobbed. "Can I help with something?"

"You bet you will," Senator Yates answered through clenched teeth.

The aide's face blanched to the shade of bleached flour. When he spotted the gun sitting on the coffee table, he tried to crawfish out of the room.

Riley sprang up behind him and locked the door. "Hands up." She patted down the aide's bony body and confiscated the cell phone secreted in his jacket's inner pocket.

"What's the meaning of this?" Charles sputtered.

She held up her prize. "We know you're in contact with John Hunter. Want me to prove it? His cell is 555-9876. We've been eavesdropping. His number will show up a dozen times on your phone. Help us nail him, and maybe, just maybe, we can help you."

She hoped reeling off John's illicit phone number would give credence to the eavesdropping bluff. No dice. Charles clamped his mouth shut and stared at the floor.

She glanced at her uncle. The senator's jaw jutted forward aggressively. He wasn't happy she'd taken over the interview. If Charles didn't start talking soon, the bad cop would explode.

"You're way off base," the aide wheezed. "I've been talking with Hunter about a job offer. Didn't want the senator to know I was considering a position at Whitten."

* * * *

Once firefighters allowed him inside his house, L.J. salvaged his travel documents and a semi-automatic pistol. He took the ten thousand dollars cash he kept in his vault and put all but one thousand in his briefcase. He saved ten crisp hundred dollar bills to fatten his wallet.

One more fast errand. A visit to a Whitten warehouse where his company stored C-4 and keyed remote firing ignition systems—the kind used to blow up everything from buildings to bridges.

Then he'd troll for a hooker with an off-the-radar pad, a pro who wouldn't call the cops. He drove to the dingy side street where the whore he'd once used as a punching bag worked, confident some new slut had taken over her franchise.

Half an hour later, he eyed Tiffany's one-room hovel. He gave the hooker two hundred bucks. Promised eight hundred more if she kept her ass inside the apartment, and did whatever he asked, for six hours.

Tiffany laughed. "Why not? Think you're man enough to last a day?"

He backhanded her. The woman's eyes went wide. Her surprise fleeting. She licked her lips. Her expression hinted she might even enjoy rough trade.

"One more thing. You don't talk to me—or anyone else. Just do as I say."

"Okay, mister." She made a show of zipping her lips.

"On your knees."

The skinny bitch bore no resemblance to Riley. Dyed red hair, needle tracks on her arms. Didn't matter. He pictured Riley's full lips as he pulled on a condom, clamped Tiffany's head between his hands, and pumped away.

The explosion built. "You're mine, you bitch," he screamed.

He turned his back on the whore as he tucked his dick back in his boxers. He didn't want to see Tiffany. Wanted to leave with his fantasy intact.

"I'll be back soon. Have an errand to run. Sit tight if you want the rest of your money."

* * * *

After Steve dropped him near the entrance to Oconee Station State Park, Wolf melted into the woods. Budget cuts had whittled staff to a single park ranger—his buddy Tim. He knew it was Jim's day to run errands, buy groceries. To lessen the odds of encountering hikers, Wolf avoided the popular trails.

He picked Oconee Station for its good cell reception. At higher elevations he might miss Hunter's call. He knew the bastard would phone as soon as he dreamed up some threat to get his money back.

Thank God Riley was safe, locked away inside the senator's estate. She was ex-FBI and could handle herself, but who knew what move a desperate Hunter might try. By now, Wolf was sure FBI agents guarded the Yates family. Riley's ex might be an asswipe, but he had real feelings for her.

Sitting beside a fast-flowing stream, Wolf listened to the water's soothing gurgle and the rustle of forest creatures. He lifted his face. Dappled sun warmed him. Maybe he'd become a hermit like Ray. Solitude offered peace.

The corrupt deputy's cell phone trilled its distinctive ring. Wolf answered. "Hello. Lonesome and calling to chat?"

A high-pitched sob startled Wolf. "Who—who is this?"

"Jennie—Jennifer Yates. Please . . . please, let me talk to Riley." The girl's voice quaked. Her cries communicated near hysteria.

"Sweetheart, stay calm," he pleaded. "Are you alone? Can you talk?"

"Of course, she's not alone," a gruff male voice said. "Her favorite Dutch uncle's escorting her."

Hunter. "You son of a bitch."

"Temper, temper. Put Riley on. I know she's with you."

"Guess again. She's safe with the senator. I took off. I'm the only one you have to worry about. Riley's history." Wolf ad-libbed. "We parted. She didn't care about the money. I do."

"That's a real shame for Jennie here. Riley's rather fond of our perky graduate. You give the security director a message. Tell her to borrow her uncle's Hummer and park it in front of her own house. I left a radio transmitter, a cooler, and a roll of duct tape by her back door. She'll need all three items for our ransom exchange. I figure little Jennie is worth ten million in negotiable securities."

"You think Riley's stupid enough to believe you'll just let her and Jennie go free?" Wolf interrupted.

"Stupid, no. But I gain nothing if I kill Jennie. It's not like she's the only one who can tell who kidnapped her. If Riley delivers the certificates, I'm out of here. Murdering Jennie would only increase how much effort's put into finding me."

Hunter chuckled. "I'm counting on Riley's Superwoman complex. It would kill her to let Jennie die and know she didn't try to save her. Oh, and she'd better not gossip about our exchange with any of her old FBI pals. I have a mole there, too. And I'll retaliate."

"Okay," Wolf said. "Why the cooler, radio and duct tape?"

"The cooler's small, sized for a six-pack, and easy to carry on her hike. The senator should ask for the ransom in hundred-thousand dollar bearer bonds. They'll fit nicely inside the cooler. Tell Riley to seal the cooler with duct tape and make damn sure it's waterproof. If the securities get wet, Jennie dies."

"Why the senator's Hummer?" Wolf asked.

"It'll make it easier to reach my starting point—where Cane Brake Road dead ends. She needs to be there by seven p.m., and she'd better be alone. I'll radio instructions for the next leg of her journey. If you or your bitch try anything stupid, I'll blow

Jennie to bits. After all, she's part of the wired generation, right?"

Wolf heard a rustling noise. A pain-filled scream filled the air.

"Tell him I'm serious, honey," Hunter said.

"He'll—he'll kill me..." Jennie gasped. Her words dissolved into sobs.

"Oh, and no more calls. I'm trashing this phone. You lovebirds do as I say or Jennie dies."

The line went dead. Wolf snapped the cell phone shut. Dammit! He hadn't seen this coming. Neither had Riley. Both assumed the FBI had all members of the Yates family protected.

Did Hunter really have a mole in the FBI or was he bluffing? He had sheriff's deputies, DoD officials, and the senator's own aide in his pocket. Was an FBI agent a big leap? Could they take the chance?

Riley would trade her life for her young cousin. Despite Hunter's claim that he wouldn't murder Riley or Jennie, Wolf knew with icy certainty he'd kill them both. No way would that mad man let Riley go once he had her alone and vulnerable.

I have to go back, have to find a way to keep Riley alive.

* * * *

The handle on the library door rattled. "Honey, how come the door's locked?"

Riley recognized Nancy's whiny voice. The woman sounded panicked.

"Nancy, I'm in the middle of a private conversation. Give us a few minutes."

The door rattled harder. "Ed, you open this door now. I want to see who's in there. Pearl thinks that Indian hooligan who's wanted for murder is holding you against your will."

Ed lasered his niece with a glare. "I assure you. The only people in this room are Riley, Charles, and me. Now go."

Nancy battered the solid mahogany barrier. "I won't. Not till I see you with my own eyes."

The woman's tenacity shocked Riley. She'd only seen Nancy's public face—eyelash-batting and submissive.

"Fine," the senator grumbled. "I'll open the door. Take a look inside. Then I insist you leave us alone."

Ed whispered, "Make sure the scumbag doesn't run."

The senator cracked open the door. Nancy stood erect and red-faced. Pearl tottered beside her. Riley kept a close watch on Charles. The aide's breathing hitched. Two frail women seemed to frighten him more than the senator's gun. If Charles sprinted for the door, she'd tackle him.

The aide made no move toward the women. His eyes looked like they belonged in a cartoon, saucer-like with fright. Tremors shook his body.

Charles pointed at her mother. "The old woman's the bomb—Hunter's bomb," he screamed. "You've cornered him. He'll use her to kill us. She's his weapon."

Charles' chest heaved as his eyes raked the room. Before Riley could react, the aide dived for the senator's gun, stuck it in his mouth, and pulled the trigger.

Nancy and Pearl screamed in unison.

SEVENTY-ONE

L.J. pounded on the whore's door. Tiffany answered, and he shoved Jennie inside. The frightened girl almost knocked the hooker over. He waved his gun at Tiffany. "Not a peep."

He focused on his prisoner. Jennie Yates wouldn't say a word. He'd duct-taped her mouth and tied her hands after luring her into his car and phoning Valdes.

He pushed his hostage into a chair, pulled several lengths of rope from the bag he carried, and bound the girl where she'd have a good view of the festivities.

He turned to Tiffany. "Don't worry. She's playacting. This excites her. She likes to watch. Likes to pretend she's a captive and she'll be next."

Tiffany shrugged. Her eyes said she didn't believe him. Her shrug said his gun and the promise of eight hundred dollars made him king for the day.

His hand snaked into her open robe and fastened on one of her sagging breasts. He smashed and twisted the tit as if juicing an orange. The hooker sucked in a breath but bowed her head in supplication. She spoke, though he'd told her to stay quiet. "I've been bad. I deserve to be punished."

L.J. glanced at Jennie. *I like her watching.*

An hour later, he lay back on the bed, sated. Tiffany curled in a tight, whimpering ball. Angry red welts crisscrossed her snowy ass cheeks. She flinched when he traced the crimson ridges with his fingers. Bruises already purpled her arms. Though he couldn't see her breasts, he knew he'd branded them. Her left breast would bear a clear impression of his teeth.

Playtime somewhat restored his good humor. He even felt kindly toward Jennie. Her muffled cries and pleading eyes were a turn on. While pounding into Tiffany doggie-style, he positioned himself to watch his bound princess. He winked at her, bounded off the bed, and stood over Tiffany.

"Sorry, whore. Can't risk you running your mouth." He stretched her out, one limb at a time, and tied her to the bed then slapped duct-tape over her lips. He searched the grimy flat. No land line. Her purse yielded a cell phone. "Afraid I have to take this with me."

She watched, eyes wide. Should he kill her? No, it would make Jennie tougher to handle. She'd know what was in store. Using the butt of his pistol, he knocked the prostitute unconscious and threw eight hundred-dollar bills on the bed.

He pocketed the handcuffs and key sitting on the bedside table and nailed Jennie with a cold stare. "See. I could've killed her, but I'm a man of my word. Remember that and I might let you live."

Jennie's terror amused him. "Time for another ride. Afraid you won't have much chance to enjoy the scenery."

How he wished Jennie looked like her cousin. If there'd been any resemblance, he'd have had his way with her. He wished he could do Riley. Bang her until she begged him to kill her. But the way things set up he'd have to be kind to the bitch, kill her long distance.

He herded Jennie to the alleyway where he'd parked the car—a classic Nick Monson had been restoring. He'd let the deputy keep the unlicensed Mustang in a barn on his estate. No one else knew about it.

He smiled. It wouldn't help Riley if she found some way to track his company car. He'd parked the Camry in front of his smoldering home. No car rental to track. No report of a stolen car to fret over. Magic. His kind. The bitch would soon discover she wasn't as smart as she thought. Definitely not as smart as Lewis John Hunter the Fourth.

SEVENTY-TWO

Riley checked Charles' pulse. "He's dead."

She raised her hands and stood as two FBI agents, guns drawn, charged through the door almost knocking over Nancy and Pearl.

"We're fine." The senator sounded calm. "It's over. My aide shot himself. Before he pulled the trigger, he claimed John Hunter had turned my sister into a bomb. Check Pearl's belongings. If Charles wasn't raving mad, her oxygen concentrator may be rigged. It's the only thing Hunter could be certain she'd take to Jennie's graduation."

Pearl gasped and staggered back from the concentrator at her side. Attached to a light-weight cart similar to a flight attendant's, the compact machine looked harmless. The design allowed it to be hand-carried or wheeled. Since carrying its ten-pound weight tired her, Pearl wheeled the unit around the house.

The senator hurried toward the women. It looked as if Pearl would collapse if his wife loosened the grip on her arm. "Let me get the ladies settled. I'll be right back."

Riley's cell vibrated. She checked the screen. Wolf. "I need to take this."

She unlocked the French doors and stepped onto a bricked patio.

Wolf dropped his verbal bomb about Jennie, and she staggered to a lounge chair.

"Will you bring in the FBI?" Wolf asked.

"It's not my call. She's Uncle Ed's daughter. Hunter may be telling the truth about a mole. It's a risk."

Her voice lowered a notch. "You've done what you can, Wolf. Stay out of this now."

"Like hell I will. I'll be at your house by five. That gives us plenty of time to reach the gate where Cane Brake Road ends. Hunter's right. A Hummer will have no problems with the fire road."

"Listen, please. The sheriff doesn't know if he's corralled all the deputies Monson corrupted. Even if he has, some may believe you framed Monson for murder, not the other way around. I can take care of myself. Wherever you are, sit tight and stay out of sight."

"Not a chance," Wolf said. "I'm coming."

The line went dead.

Fifteen minutes passed before Riley could separate her uncle from the FBI.

He immediately ripped into her. "How dare you! You think I don't know who Wolf Valdes is? How could you hide the fact you've been helping that pornographer and his lying uncle. Hank Youngblood killed my boy. But that wasn't enough. Ray Youngblood destroyed Will's reputation at the trial."

Spittle flew from his lips. Riley let the waves of hatred wash over her. No time for this stupidity now. "Stop. Listen to me. Hunter has Jennie."

Instant silence. Taking advantage of the shocked lull, she rushed to finish the story. Her uncle collapsed into a chair, battered by images no father can bear.

"Oh, my God, not Jennie." His face seemed to age a decade, feverish eyes burning in a papier-mâché mask. "Jennie's cell was off. I left messages, told her to hurry. I should have ordered the FBI to collect her."

He raked his hands through his hair. "Jesus, it's my fault. I never dreamed Hunter would go to her apartment."

"We'll get her back, unharmed." Riley willed herself to sound calm. "I know about hostage situations. But you must decide—do we tell Gary, bring in the FBI? I wish I could say

Hunter's claim of an FBI mole is bogus. I can't. Given what we know about his reach, I'd put the odds at fifty-fifty."

* * * *

Wolf knew where Tim hid the spare key to his cabin. He unlocked the park ranger's house, walked to his gun cabinet, and helped himself to Tim's Winchester lever action 30-06, and ammo. He zipped the Winchester into a padded case with a shoulder strap. Using a salt shaker, he propped a note on the kitchen table before heading to collect his buddy's Harley.

Would Tim keep quiet until morning? He hoped so. By then, someone would be dead. Whatever happened, it would end.

He had to stay out of sight until he met Riley. A hiding place, one ideal for a motorcycle, popped into his mind. The bridle path connecting the Yates and Hunter estates was too narrow for cars. No curious passersby. Who'd look for him there?

He kept the bike just under the fifty-five-miles-per-hour speed limit. Only a short patch of highway before he reached a field that offered a cut through to the path.

He estimated he was two miles from Hunter's property when he stopped. Middle of nowhere. A great place to hide. But, with two hours to kill before he met Riley, curiosity gripped him. How much damage had his dynamite caused? Maybe he'd take a quick look-see. What could it hurt? The firemen should be gone. He fired up the Harley.

His mind kept circling back to Hunter's demands. The Foothills area selected by the kidnapper offered certain advantages. Once he radioed Riley with instructions, she'd be unable to tell anyone. No cell phone reception. That's why Hunter provided the radio. But the radio also provided a clue. The mountains made radios as useless as cell phones at any distance. At seven o'clock, the monster would be within a few miles of the Cane Brake terminus.

What orders would Hunter radio? The Foothills Trail swung both north and south where it crossed Cane Brake Road. Or he could tell Riley to climb in the Hummer and drive to the intersection with Jackie's Ridge Road. Too damn many options. Regardless, the final destination for the ransom exchange couldn't be too far away if he stayed in radio range.

Wolf stashed his borrowed bike behind five-foot-tall azaleas just short of Hunter's property line. He'd sneak in, stay out of sight. Someone might still be there. An arson investigator. FBI agents.

The place looked deserted. What the…? A tan Camry sat in the front drive. Riley said Hunter was driving a tan Camry when last seen by the sheriff. Could he be so lucky? Have the chance to take the bastard by surprise before he harmed Jennie or Riley?

A half hour of searching convinced him the owner wasn't on the grounds. Neither was Jennie. But the firefighters had turned the rear lawn into a sea of mud, making the telltale car tracks coming from the old barn as distinct as Armstrong's footprints on the moon.

Wolf peered into the drafty, canted structure. While the barn hadn't received any TLC, it had been used. Recently. Tools littered a workbench. Fresh oil puddled on the dirt floor. Had the bastard tinkered with cars? Didn't seem his style.

He studied the work bench. Bits of electrical wire. He noticed some discarded packaging on the floor, stooped to examine it. He pieced a torn label together. It touted the virtues of a remote firing ignition system. *Crap.* He rose and examined the bench again. A wrench rested atop a map folded to the Laurel Fork section of the Foothills Trail. He'd hiked that section from Laurel Fork Falls to the Cane Brake gate. At most, the distance was two miles.

Wolf stared at the map dominated by the blue of Lake Jocassee. An idea clicked. The lake's serpentine shoreline allowed boats to swing close to both the Cane Brake gate and Laurel Fork Falls.

He phoned Riley. Didn't let her say more than "Hello" before he peppered her with questions. "Does Hunter have a boat?... Lake Jocassee, right?...Where's his dock?"

The more Wolf thought about the gamble, the more certain he became. Hunter would want a fast escape. Hoofing it over mountain trails didn't compute.

There was a high cliff just south of Laurel Fork Falls. Boats could anchor nearby. If Hunter came by boat and Riley walked to the cliff, something like one hundred vertical feet would separate them. If she tossed the cooler into the water below, he'd have a nice head start on a getaway. He could be a mile away before Riley could scramble down the embankment.

He shared his theory. "I'll find a boat, stake out the area. Hope to hell I'm not wrong."

"Whatever you do, keep him alive," Riley pleaded. "We have to find out where he's holding Jennie. He won't kill her. He gains nothing if he murders her. He told that part straight."

"I'll wait. But you're wrong. The bastard does have something to gain from killing Jennie. He knows what her death would do to you and the senator. I heard it in his voice. It's personal. You and Senator Yates ruined his plans. He wants revenge."

SEVENTY-THREE

Gravel sprayed as Riley sped away in her uncle's Hummer. The high seat offered a catbird's view. The machine's girth lent a feeling of strength. If only Hunter would cross some street in front of her, she'd squash him like a bug.

Hang tough, Jennie.

No FBI. Uncle Ed's decision. His aide's betrayal inclined him to trust no one. That made his acceptance of Wolf's help all the more ironic. Love for his daughter trumped his mindless hatred of any Hank Youngblood kin.

Can the three of us outwit Hunter?

Wolf could be wrong about a boat. Hunter tracked and killed game. He was no stranger to the woods in Jocassee Gorges. Based on Wolf's intel, he had a set of wheels. Maybe he planned to drive to the Cane Brake gate, watch her climb from the Hummer, and shoot her. Bang, bang, and he'd be on his way.

No. Her gut agreed with Wolf. Hunter would use his kick-ass speedboat. He'd taken Riley for a ride. Boasted about it ad nauseam. Claimed he pushed it to ninety miles per hour on a calm day. He'd stash his car somewhere south on the lake. By boat, he'd reach it much faster than by car. The braggart was forever faulting his military customers for a lack of contingency plans. A boat provided options—even if the senator brought in the FBI and helicopter support. Lake Jocassee had over seventy miles of shoreline—most undeveloped woodland. He could ditch the boat, vanish beneath the virgin forest canopy.

Riley sighed. No sense over analyzing. Their strategy was set. She pulled into the carport behind her house and hurried to her small back stoop. The promised objects waited under the roof overhang. A two-way radio, duct tape, a six-pack cooler.

She picked up the items, went inside. She expected her uncle at six p.m. His personal banker claimed he'd need until five-thirty to ready the bearer bonds. She had time to shop for her own supplies.

* * * *

A side road looped past the rental cabins at Devils Fork State Park. Posted speed: ten-miles-per-hour. Wolf scouted each log cabin as he crept past. No one paid any attention.

Stealing a boat could prove trickier. It was five-thirty. Sunset was three hours away. Though a north wind warned a storm was coming, campers still puttered outdoors, enjoying unobstructed views of the lake and their boats, whether beached or moored off shore.

As he approached the end of the paved loop, a couple locked their cabin door and walked toward a black SUV. The woman tottered on high heels. Not out for a hike.

"Is the Downtown Greenville map in the car?" she asked. "You know how lost we got the last time we tried to find a four-star restaurant."

Wolf didn't pause, drove right by. He couldn't see behind the cabin. He hoped this couple hadn't come strictly to sightsee. He needed water transport.

Ten minutes later, he found a muscular jet ski—the kind that seats three and can tow a skier—beached behind the cabin. Ignition key missing. Had they left it in the cabin? He had no idea how to hotwire a jet ski.

Making sure no one watched, he shoved his rifle case through an open window at the back of the cabin and shimmied in after it. The ignition key sat in plain view. Its oversized key-ring float made it impossible to mistake.

He hadn't considered boosting a jet ski, but thieves can't be choosy. It would be one freakin' frigid ride. Fed by mountain streams, Lake Jocassee evoked goose bumps even in summer.

What he'd give for a wet suit. Hmm. The man who left looked close to his size.

A full-body wetsuit hung in the closet. Wolf shucked his jeans and sweater, tugged it on. Tight but serviceable. He'd repay the vacationers and his buddy Tim for their unknowing generosity later—if he wasn't dead or in jail.

He exited through the front door, hoping nearby campers would assume he belonged. With his rifle case slung over his shoulder, he ambled toward shore. He checked the gas tank. Almost full. Perfect. Except for the noise factor. Hard to sneak up on anyone in a machine that made more noise than a wounded moose.

He waded into the frigid water. The deep lake's icy tendrils penetrated the wetsuit. *Initial shock. I'll warm up.* Positive thoughts didn't stop his teeth from chattering.

SEVENTY-FOUR

L.J. parked Nick's restored Mustang in front of Art Whitten's lake house. Only a handful of homes had been built before most of the land surrounding Lake Jocassee became protected forest or parkland. Bless those bloody-minded conservationists. No nosy neighbors to watch him haul Miss Jennie from the car and perp-shuffle her to the house.

He popped the trunk. His hostage squirmed and squinted at the sudden light. He'd taped her mouth shut, kept her hands tied. No blindfold, no need. He grabbed her upper arm, grunted as he hoisted the top half of her body over the lip of the trunk. Didn't attempt to lift her. Why get a hernia? Let gravity do its work. She plopped onto the gravel drive. A noisy wheeze snuck through the loosened edges of her taped gag.

He yanked her upright. She tottered, then collapsed. A little too long playing pretzel.

"Walk, crawl, or I'll drag you. I don't give a damn."

Hunter stood her up, steadied her. As she shuffled forward, he retrieved the house key from its fake rock cubbyhole. He wondered why Art bothered to lock the door. The hideaway was damned hard to find even if you knew its location.

Inside, he looped a rope around the girl's waist and tied her to a chair. He ripped the tape from her mouth, leaving a gummy red slash.

"Wa…ter." She had trouble forming the word.

"Why not?" He headed to the kitchen. "I may have a little tipple myself."

Hunter poured himself a scotch neat, drew tap water, and placed a glass in the girl's bound hands. She gulped like a pup lapping at a water dish.

He was glad she didn't speak. Quiet helped him think. He stared out the window. The lake's distinctive blue-green hue barely registered, though the dark clouds on the horizon were a bit worrisome.

Might Riley remember this place? Make a connection with the Foothills Trail? Even over water—the most direct route— Art's house was seven miles from the area he'd selected for the ransom drop.

He'd brought Riley here once, took her out in his boat. What a joy. She whined the whole trip. "Slow down. We're going too fast to enjoy the scenery."

Hunter sipped his scotch. Breathed rhythmically in and out. Riley might think he'd hole up here. He'd limit his time at the house, wouldn't return to it.

He walked to the house phone, dialed a number. "Hi, is this Andy? Hey, glad you're home, son. Out of college already for the summer, huh? I have a little job. Can you find a friend and come over? Some buddies and I are hiking tomorrow. We want a ride parked at the end of our route. You can drive my car there, ride back with your buddy. … Good, I'll meet you out front in thirty minutes."

He took the empty water glass from Jennie's hands. "Sorry, sweetheart, but I need to tape your mouth again. A boy is coming over. His folks own a place a cove away. He runs errands for Art and me. Can't let him hear you scream. I like the kid. Don't want to shoot him."

* * * *

Riley set her purchase on the counter and checked her watch. Lucky that Radio Shack was only a couple of miles down the road. She cursed the packaging's impenetrable plastic, clawed at the tough cardboard surround, pulled out the radio. Identical to Hunter's "gift." She carefully followed the clerk's directions to set it to the same frequency.

The doorbell rang. She raced to the living room, parted the plantation slats covering the front bay window. Her uncle. He looked hunched, old. Raindrops freckled the shoulders of his coat. It had begun to drizzle.

She opened the door. He clutched a briefcase to his chest. The bearer bonds.

"I'm going with you," he said. "I can't just sit here. What difference can it make? Would Hunter do anything differently if I'm there?"

Riley nodded. "Yes, I want you to come. But I need you to make a side trip first."

Her uncle's puzzled look said he'd expected a fight. He followed her to the kitchen where two radios sat alongside the cooler. "What's your plan?" he asked.

* * * *

The Jet Ski rocketed across the waves. Heading north, Wolf saw two boats bobbing on the water. Both dull gray-green, no match for Hunter's big boy toy. Riley said the killer's boat looked like a red-and-black striped hornet.

Rain began to pelt Wolf's face. His uncle believed rain brought anglers good fortune. Something about a downpour triggered fish appetites. He gave the fishermen and their anchored runabouts a wide berth. Given his speed, he'd drown in curses if he ventured near the anglers.

Just about full throttle. Any faster and he risked losing his seat. A freshening wind churned the lake. White-capped waves periodically flung his stolen machine skyward and tossed it down with punishing force. Wind scoured his cheeks, his eyes watered. Wind slanted the icy raindrops, stinging his cheeks. *Should have stolen a pair of goggles.*

He zoomed up a foaming monster wave, slammed against the seat as the Jet Ski crashed into the water's trough. A sound. *What?* A heavy gust tore at the borrowed rifle case. The strap snapped. He looked back, watched in horror as his case disappeared. He swung in a wide circle, frantically searching for some sign of the camouflaged carryall. Nothing. *Dammit!*

Though his eyes stung and the shore looked blurry through the curtain of rain, he sensed he was close. Squinting, he searched for landmarks. Pine trees and more pine trees. Ridges and cliffs. Sandbars and coves. He'd tramped the surrounding trails his whole life, yet the landscape looked foreign. Point of view mattered. He couldn't afford to miss the Laurel Fork cove. Finally a familiar rock formation, a place where teens pretended to be cliff-divers. He'd arrived.

He poked along at idle speed, carefully skirting rocks and the jagged branch tentacles of storm-felled trees. The roar of the falls overrode the sighs of wind in the swaying pines. He searched for cover. The Jet Ski weighed too much to drag more than a few feet up the muddy red clay beach.

He spied a thicket of sweet shrub and mountain laurel growing almost at the water's edge. Promising. Looking through them, he'd see any boat that ventured up this finger of the lake. Shrubbery coupled with rain would help hide him from view.

Six-thirty. Setting up his stakeout took less time than expected. For something to do, he looked in the Jet Ski's waterproof storage compartment. Band-Aids, a candy bar, a package of chewing gum. What did he think he'd find—a spare bazooka? He tucked the package of gum inside one of his wetsuit's sleeves. Maybe a stick would keep him from breaking a tooth. Not an unlikely development the way his teeth chattered.

What he'd give for a blazing fire.

Not as much as he'd give to have the Winchester back.

Not as much as he'd give to take Riley's place on point.

SEVENTY-FIVE

L.J. rummaged in Art's closet and found a hooded, waterproof poncho. Much too big for Jennie. Ideal. He slipped the poncho over her head. It completely hid the homemade homicide vest. If he encountered any busybodies—doubtful with the rain—the vest was invisible. They'd think she was simply bundled up, trying to keep warm and dry.

He patted her cheek. "Good girl. No sudden movements. Wouldn't want you to blow, now would we?"

Shallow breaths said she was afraid to even breathe. His docile captive believed any struggle might cause her to explode like a dandelion blown apart and scattered by the wind. Did she think he was insane? There was zero chance of an explosion unless he wanted one.

The stable C-4 blocks and companion ignition system strapped to her chest were harmless until he decided otherwise. Contrary to movie myth, you can shoot a bullet into C-4, drop it, even set it on fire, and it won't blow up. Takes both extreme heat and a shockwave to trigger. In his case, that combo required inserting a key in the ignition box before he pushed the button on the firing system's remote. The key was tucked safely in his zippered pocket.

He wished the remote had a pressure switch. But what the hell did Riley know? He'd claim it did. Say if he stopped applying pressure Riley's little niece would blow sky-high.

He pulled up Jennie's hood, cinched the drawstring tight. Only a small oval remained. Her wide, frightened eyes were visible, but not her duct-taped mouth. He'd save the handcuffs he'd liberated from the whore for later.

He left her feet untied. She needed to walk to the funicular, a most appreciated Whitten home improvement project. It connected the house, perched high on a cliff, to the dock. *Thank you, partner.* It would have been a hassle to bundle Jennie down the embankment's forever-and-amen set of stairs, especially after they'd been slicked by rain.

The miniature cog railcar moved with glacial speed. Ample time. When the car shuddered to a stop at the bottom, he maneuvered Jennie onto the dock and into his boat's front passenger seat. After starting the motor, he untied the dock cleats and checked the sky. Dark clouds had turned the scene twilight. He'd arrive about quarter to seven. Plenty of time to walk a short way up the closed fire road to ensure good radio reception. Would rain interfere?

Riley had better be on time. He wasn't eager to negotiate the lake after dark, especially if the storm worsened. Too many rocks near shore. He needed the ransom to go like clockwork.

* * * *

Riley parked the Hummer. One car sat vacant near the gate. Virginia plates. She prayed the owner was hiking miles away and not hustling back to get out of the rain. She didn't want to endanger another innocent. She jumped down from the vehicle, opened the rear door, and set the duct-taped cooler on the ground. She patted her jacket. The shoulder holster and gun— more loaners from her uncle—felt odd. She missed the familiar comfort of her own Glock.

Her watch confirmed fifteen minutes to go. She thumbed on the radio and hoped its batteries proved in better shape than her nerves. The raindrops fell closer together. Cold water trickled from her hair down her collar. But she didn't climb back in the Hummer.

She prayed Uncle Ed would radio and say he'd found his daughter. She'd sent him to Art Whitten's lake house to search for Jennie. If Hunter no longer had a hostage, Riley could handle the bastard any way she chose. As the radio silence lengthened, hope dimmed that her uncle would find Jennie unharmed before her scheduled rendezvous with Hunter.

Too bad she couldn't contact her uncle. Was he nearby? If the lake house proved empty, he would be heading her way. He might even have started down Cane Brake Road. However, since she'd turned her radio into a party line, she couldn't talk to him. Hunter might be in the neighborhood by now. He'd hear anything she said.

Where was Wolf? She tuned her senses, willing her mind to register his presence. While she'd never shown any telepathic talent, she closed her eyes, concentrated on a single message. Over and over again, she repeated her mental mantra. *Stay safe. I love you, Wolf. Stay safe. I love you.*

* * * *

Wolf watched the red-and-black boat bomb across the water. Hunter. Couldn't be anyone else. Two silhouettes. Had he brought Jennie? As soon as the boat shot past, Wolf walked his jet ski into deeper water and revved the engine. No way the kidnapper could hear him over his own boat's roar and the whistling wind. Yet it would be dicey to keep tabs on the bastard. To stay invisible, Wolf doddered along, hugging the shore.

Ahead the sleek boat slowed and slipped into a shallow cove where a spur trail joined the Foothills Trail. Was Hunter meeting Riley on foot?

Though he itched to gun his Jet Ski, he idled near the mouth of the cove, giving Hunter time to exit the boat.

Betting the bastard wouldn't travel farther up this narrowing finger of the lake, Wolf stashed his watercraft just north of the cove. On foot, he doubled back, silently cursing the slick mud at water's edge as it sucked at his feet.

~~L.J. rummaged in Art's closet and found a hooded, waterproof poncho. Much too big for Jennie. Ideal. He slipped~~

the poncho over her head. It completely hid the homemade homicide vest. If he encountered any busybodies—doubtful with the rain—the vest was invisible. They'd think she was simply bundled up, trying to keep warm and dry.

He patted her cheek. "Good girl. No sudden movements. Wouldn't want you to blow, now would we?"

Shallow breaths said she was afraid to even breathe. His docile captive believed any struggle might cause her to explode like a dandelion blown apart and scattered by the wind. Did she think he was insane? There was zero chance of an explosion unless he wanted one.

The stable C-4 blocks and companion ignition system strapped to her chest were harmless until he decided otherwise. Contrary to movie myth, you can shoot a bullet into C-4, drop it, even set it on fire, and it won't blow up. Takes both extreme heat and a shockwave to trigger. In his case, that combo required inserting a key in the ignition box before he pushed the button on the firing system's remote. The key was tucked safely in his zippered pocket.

He wished the remote had a pressure switch. But what the hell did Riley know? He'd claim it did. Say if he stopped applying pressure Riley's little niece would blow sky-high.

He pulled up Jennie's hood, cinched the drawstring tight. Only a small oval remained. Her wide, frightened eyes were visible, but not her duct-taped mouth. He'd save the handcuffs he'd liberated from the whore for later.

He left her feet untied. She needed to walk to the funicular, a most appreciated Whitten home improvement project. It connected the house, perched high on a cliff, to the dock. *Thank you, partner.* It would have been a hassle to bundle Jennie down the embankment's forever-and-amen set of stairs, especially after they'd been slicked by rain.

The miniature cog railcar moved with glacial speed. Ample time. When the car shuddered to a stop at the bottom, he maneuvered Jennie onto the dock and into his boat's front passenger seat. After starting the motor, he untied the dock cleats and checked the sky. Dark clouds had turned the scene twilight. He'd arrive about quarter to seven. Plenty of time to walk a short way up the closed fire road to ensure good radio reception. Would rain interfere?

Riley had better be on time. He wasn't eager to negotiate the lake after dark, especially if the storm worsened. Too many rocks near shore. He needed the ransom to go like clockwork.

* * * *

Riley parked the Hummer. One car sat vacant near the gate. Virginia plates. She prayed the owner was hiking miles away and not hustling back to get out of the rain. She didn't want to endanger another innocent. She jumped down from the vehicle, opened the rear door, and set the duct-taped cooler on the ground. She patted her jacket. The shoulder holster and gun — more loaners from her uncle — felt odd. She missed the familiar comfort of her own Glock.

Her watch confirmed fifteen minutes to go. She thumbed on the radio and hoped its batteries proved in better shape than her nerves. The raindrops fell closer together. Cold water trickled from her hair down her collar. But she didn't climb back in the Hummer.

She prayed Uncle Ed would radio and say he'd found his daughter. She'd sent him to Art Whitten's lake house to search for Jennie. If Hunter no longer had a hostage, Riley could handle the bastard any way she chose. As the radio silence lengthened, hope dimmed that her uncle would find Jennie unharmed before her scheduled rendezvous with Hunter.

Too bad she couldn't contact her uncle. Was he nearby? If the lake house proved empty, he would be heading her way. He might even have started down Cane Brake Road. However, since she'd turned her radio into a party line, she couldn't talk to him. Hunter might be in the neighborhood by now. He'd hear anything she said.

Where was Wolf? She tuned her senses, willing her mind to register his presence. While she'd never shown any telepathic talent, she closed her eyes, concentrated on a single message. Over and over again, she repeated her mental mantra. *Stay safe. I love you, Wolf. Stay safe. I love you.*

* * * *

Wolf watched the red-and-black boat bomb across the water. Hunter. Couldn't be anyone else. Two silhouettes. Had he brought Jennie? As soon as the boat shot past, Wolf walked his jet ski into deeper water and revved the engine. No way the kidnapper could hear him over his own boat's roar and the whistling wind. Yet it would be dicey to keep tabs on the bastard. To stay invisible, Wolf doddered along, hugging the shore.

Ahead the sleek boat slowed and slipped into a shallow cove where a spur trail joined the Foothills Trail. Was Hunter meeting Riley on foot?

Though he itched to gun his Jet Ski, he idled near the mouth of the cove, giving Hunter time to exit the boat.

Betting the bastard wouldn't travel farther up this narrowing finger of the lake, Wolf stashed his watercraft just north of the cove. On foot, he doubled back, silently cursing the slick mud at water's edge as it sucked at his feet.

Only one person inside the boat. Jennie. Panting, Wolf held the boat's gunnels as he tried to catch his breath from his sprint. His anger and frustration soared when he saw the handcuffs. One bracelet encased the girl's slender left ankle; the other was fastened securely to the boat's steering column. No key in the ignition. Hopes of quickly freeing Jennie crashed.

Placing a finger to his lips, he warned the girl to stay quiet as he loosened the duct tape covering her mouth.

She sobbed. "He's coming right back. Please help me. Hurry." Jennie ducked her chin toward her poncho. "I'm wired to blow up. Get it off me."

He lifted the hem of the oversized rain gear. Blocks of C-4 covered her ribs, held securely in place by what looked like an acre of crisscrossed duct tape. Wires ran from the C-4 to a bright yellow case taped just below the blocks of explosives. The bastard had transformed a terrorist's suicide vest into a murder weapon.

Wolf remembered the discarded packaging he spotted on the floor in Hunter's barn. The remote firing system wouldn't operate unless a key was inserted. He opened the bright yellow plastic case. The slot for a key was empty. Good and bad news. Good because he could fool with the wiring without blowing them both up. Bad because he couldn't just throw away the key.

Though he had no personal experience with such devices, he'd researched explosives for the plot of his next novel. He knew just enough to be dangerous. The missing key gave him confidence.

"Get it off me," Jennie sobbed. Her whole body shook. "Get me out of here."

"It would take too long to hack through all that duct tape. So I'm going to make certain the bastard can't ignite this," Wolf whispered. "Then we'll figure out how to escape."

He knew the wires inserted in the C-4 dead-ended in blasting caps. He yanked the assemblies free. Unzipping the sleeve of his wetsuit, he salvaged the Swiss Army knife tucked inside the neoprene covering his wrist. He sawed through the wires, separating them from the metal sheathing that encased the detonators.

Linda Lovely

No explosion. Air escaped his lungs with an audible whoosh. He started to throw the blasting caps into the shallow water, then thought better of it. Hunter might notice, know what he'd done. Wolf decided to take them, wait to trash them until he was well away from the boat.

"Jennie, listen to me. Hunter can't make this stuff blow up now. But we can't let him know that, to know I've been here. I need to surprise him. So I'm going to stick these wires back in the C-4. They're harmless without blasting caps. I'll come back for you. Promise."

Okay. Now, how the hell do I get the damn handcuff off the steering column?

* * * *

The radio crackled. "Hello, answer me. Have you arrived?"

Riley hit the talk button. "Where's Jennie? Did you bring her?"

"I'll do the talking. Limit your answers to yes and no. Our agreement called for an exchange. I get the money. Then and only then do I tell you about Jennie." He paused. "Get back in the Hummer, drive to Jackie's Ridge Road, park at the Laurel Fork campground, and walk down the path to the falls overlook. You can't see me, but I'm watching. I'll know when you arrive. We'll talk then. Bring the cooler."

Was he watching her now? Had to be close for the radio to work. Would he trail her to the overlook?

No, she'd bet anything he'd come by boat. Hunter would play it safe, scoot in by water, hunker down at the base of the falls, tell her to toss the cooler in the lake. Did he hope to shoot her the instant she complied?

If she died, at least her uncle and Wolf would know. Hunter wouldn't escape. They'd capture him, force him to take them to Jennie.

She drove to the camping area, jumped out of the Hummer. Gripping the cooler handle with her left hand, she walked at a fast clip, frightened but eager to end the drama. Tall pines lining the trail swayed like grass in the wind. While rain reached her, the pines feathered it, softening its force. The damp intensified the tangy pine scent wafting up from the pine needles littering the forest floor. As she neared the cliff overlook, wind-stunted shrubs replaced the pines, opening a view of the falls and the lake. The steady rain showed no sign of let up. A curtain of drenching rain appeared on the horizon. Sinister clouds, an evil black, swirled above. Lightning flashed, skim-coating the turbulent waters below. Thunder sounded a few seconds after the flash.

Maybe God will strike him dead. Fry him with a lightning bolt. A second later, she canceled the mental wish. Not till they had Jennie safe and sound.

Wolf was on the water, too. In danger. The storm wasn't helping matters.

* * * *

Wolf's ears pricked at the sound of crackling branches and a shouted curse. Someone headed down the trail. His guess— less than two-hundred feet. Hunter? How he wished he could sight the Winchester, shoot the scumbag as he emerged from the woods. Wishing wouldn't help.

"He can't blow you up now." He zipped Jennie's jacket and gently tapped the duct tape over her mouth. "I have to hide before he sees me. I promise I won't leave you. Keep as far away from Hunter as you can. I'll take him out first chance."

He jumped from the boat, ran uphill, and crouched behind a thicket of mountain laurel.

The panicked look in Jennie's eyes clawed at his gut. Could he do something else? Something that wouldn't put Jennie's life at greater risk? He had to assume Hunter had a gun. If the kidnapper saw him, he was bound to shoot. Jennie could be hit.

Hunter stumbled out of the woods. One side of his body was covered with red mud. He must have slipped and fallen, prompting the curse that warned Wolf.

He watched the kidnapper push the boat off the muddy sandbar, jump in, and turn south. The driving rain was Wolf's friend. Hunter wouldn't be able to see more than thirty feet if he glanced over his shoulder. *I can follow closer, make my move at the falls.*

* * * *

"Stop where you are."

The radioed command arrived as a sibilant whisper in Riley's ear. The howling winds had coalesced into a high-pitched shriek. Riley's breath hitched as her gaze raked the banks one hundred feet below. A silhouette materialized in the raucous gloom. Hunter.

Damn! His arm crushed Jennie to his body. A human shield. He held the radio in one hand, something else she couldn't make out in the other hand. Okay, no gun. He couldn't shoot. At least for a minute or three.

The radio squawked again. "Toss the cooler down. Don't even think about any funny business. Or Jennie will blow sky high."

Hunter's head scrunched to the side to cradle the radio between his neck and shoulder. With his newly freed hand, he lifted Jennie's poncho above her waist.

Riley squinted, trying to pick up details through the curtain of rain.

"I'm good with electronics." Hunter chuckled. "Changed the button on this here remote firing system to make it a pressure switch. If my finger stops applying pressure, the circuit opens. Goodbye Jennie. If I were you, I wouldn't upset me. Throw down the damn cooler. Now."

Riley caught movement behind Hunter. A muscular figure rose like a black sea monster from the boiling water. Rain pummeled the figure, and water swirled around his calves. He stood perhaps twenty-five feet behind Hunter. A flash of lightning served as a fiery strobe.

Wolf!

Oh, my God! Does he plan to tackle Hunter? He must not know about Jennie. If he attacked, he'd blow up all three of them. Wolf had no radio. Could she scream loud enough?

Her rapid heartbeats crowded one another. They seemed almost to merge, an audible thrum, the distress of an overworked motor. She swallowed, fought down her panic.

She threw the radio to the ground, then heaved the cooler over the cliff. Watched it tumble through the air. She sucked oxygen into her lungs to bellow a warning.

"Keep your finger on the damn switch, Hunter," she shouted. "I'd love to see you blow up, but you know I won't sacrifice Jennie."

A clap of thunder harmonized with her vow. Had Wolf heard her over its deep growl? Did he understand?

Hunter edged sideways to collect the cooler. Jennie doubled over and leaned away from her captor.

Wolf sprinted forward, rapidly closing on captor and captive.

No. No. Oh, God, no.

They were dead.

"No!" Riley's scream echoed in her ears.

The kidnapper's head snapped up at her strangled cry. Wolf's arms rose. A large object loomed above his head.

* * * *

Wolf understood Riley's warning, felt her anguish. He wished he could yell back, tell her Hunter's threats were hollow. He couldn't. Couldn't chance Hunter turning, looking behind him. He lifted the heavy rock higher. His arms shook from the strain. Tremors raced down his arms, sentries of pain shot through his shoulders. Five more steps.

He tripped on a tree root hidden below the water. Fought for balance. Staggered to right himself. His limbs trembled. He couldn't last much longer. Keep moving. Three more steps.

Hunter pivoted. The storm's noise had failed to mask Wolf's stuttering approach. Hunter's eyes flashed with rage.

Wolf smashed the rock into Hunter's skull. Heard the crack and the curdling scream. Blood streamed down the kidnapper's face. Jennie toppled as her captor totally lost his grip on her.

Hunter tottered but didn't fall. Wild eyes glared behind the curtain of blood. "Go to hell!" he yelled as he pushed the button to detonate Jennie's vest. The madman closed his eyes, a faint smile on his lips anticipating the explosion.

"You screwed up again, asshole. Jennie's safe." Wolf's right arm shot out, punching Hunter dead center in his chest.

The man's arms windmilled. A second later he lay spread-eagled in the mud. Wolf dropped a knee into his abdomen, pinning him. He socked him in the jaw, knocking him out cold. Then, he rose and gathered Jennie in his arms. He looked up, searching the cliff for Riley. He couldn't see her, but he heard her voice.

"Uncle Ed, we have Jennie," she yelled. "She's safe. Drive until you can get a cell signal. Call the FBI."

The voice seemed so close. Was he hearing it on Hunter's radio. No. Riley was coming down the embankment beside the cliff, sliding in the mud, grabbing branches for handholds to slow her descent.

She reached the bottom and ran to hug Wolf and then wrap her arms around her cousin. "Thank God. Thank God."

The rain and winds slackened as if the heavens knew the curtain had come down on the drama. Wolf leaned down and kissed Riley. "I love you."

EPILOGUE—SIX WEEKS LATER

"Lu-cee, I'm home."

The ebony cat jumped from her perch and ambled forth offering herself to be paid the homage she was due. She seemed pleased a new subject had embraced the singsong greeting. Wolf scooped up the feline and combed her fur with his graceful fingers. Lucy purred like an idling racecar.

"Sometimes I think she likes you better than me." Riley pretended huffy indignation.

Wolf grinned and deposited the kitty on a chair. "She knows I love all the women in this abode, even though we'd both rather be in your home. I'd rather be just about anywhere except Senator Yates' guest house."

"It'll be fine," Riley said. "Don't pout. We didn't get to enjoy all the guest house amenities on our last stay. Remember, there's a big Jacuzzi on the balcony, right outside the bedroom."

"Hmmm. As I recall, nudity is required."

"Yes, a *hard* and fast requirement." Riley winked as she sauntered past him, heading for the stairs. "I passed on the family get together tonight since you were flying in from a meeting with your editor and would arrive late."

Wolf smiled. "A welcome reprieve."

Riley wiggled free of her exercise top on the second stair tread. Jettisoned her bra on step three. She swiveled to face Wolf two steps behind her. He licked his lips as his gaze slid over her swaying breasts.

"You coming?" she asked.

"Can I expect this welcome every time I walk in? If so, I think I'll invest in a revolving door once we find a home so I can walk in again and again." His deep rumble of laughter triggered a rush of warmth. He grabbed for her, and she skipped out of reach.

At the threshold to the balcony, she stripped off everything. She poked a finger in the Jacuzzi. "Temperature's perfect. I like it hot."

"I like *you* hot," Wolf replied. He'd already stripped to his briefs.

His right hand snaked out to cup one of her breasts. His thumb lazily circled her nipple. A tiny gasp of pleasure escaped her lips before she firmly grabbed his wrist. The erection poking at his briefs made her chuckle. She forced her smile to morph into a mock frown.

"I've been thinking about that naughty nurse fantasy you mentioned. We never explored where that might take us."

He laughed and nodded at his woody. "I'm hoping for hands-on healing."

And you'll get it—no doubt about it.

She slipped into the bubbling water as he tore off his briefs. Moonlight burnished his sculpted body. It seemed to glow in the soft light. Her nipples tightened.

Time to indulge his nurse fantasy.

"Get in here this minute. Your nurse has scheduled you for physical therapy."

"Yes, ma'am." He answered meekly and slid into the water. He sank beneath the surface, disappearing completely, before he flew upward like a frolicking dolphin. He felt frisky, too.

Water beaded on his broad shoulders. She wanted to lick those drops away, then crush her body against his. With great willpower, she slowed down. No need to rush tonight. Time to play. They needed to love—and laugh.

There'd been no laughter in her marriage. Sex was serious. Gary's exclusive business. It wasn't that Riley failed to have orgasms—her ex attempted to satisfy her. But her husband decided the when, the where, the how. Perfectly scripted. Riley playing supporting cast.

With Wolf, lovemaking had many moods. Feverish. Life affirming. Yes. But it could be fun, too—even funny. Playful anticipation intensified pleasure.

"Where do we start, Nurse? Might I suggest finger exercises?" He waggled his digits in slow motion.

She closed the gap between them. A cool breeze caressed her nude breasts, but the banked furnace inside kept goose bumps at bay.

"Yes, I want to see all those fingers engaged. No slackers."

"Nurse, ma'am, if you'll lie back, I promise I'll demonstrate that all my fingers work."

She swallowed. "They'd better. If they don't, I'll schedule you for another hour of therapy." Even to her ear, her words sounded more like lusty pleas than stern orders.

Floating on the sea of bubbles, she let her thighs drift apart.

Their eyes locked. Wolf flexed his fingers as if limbering up to play piano scales. His index finger began the calisthenics, skimming a fingernail along one thigh, tracing lazy circles that became smaller and smaller.

"Why Nurse, you're all wet."

"We're in the water," she panted. "No mystery."

His finger waggled playfully. She closed her eyes as her body convulsed. Another finger opted for play time. She writhed with desire. The fingers skipped away, revisited. All the while his thumb rhythmically stroked her.

She pressed against his hand. His fingers perfected an infuriatingly lazy dance, and Riley was ready to tango. She gasped when he stopped the siege and cupped her bottom. She'd clearly lost control. The patient was calling all the shots.

She reached for him, and he dunked her. Though her head only bobbed beneath the water for a second, she came up sputtering and swearing. She slicked wet curls back from her forehead. "You're begging for a shot with a big, fat hypodermic."

"I couldn't resist." He grinned. "Guess I didn't tell you everything about my nurse fantasy. Any more orders, ma'am? If not, I'd like to play doctor now."

He stood, and water foamed around his waist. His green eyes turned dark with desire. He looked like a god sprung from an angry sea. He pulled her to him. Their bodies joined. He bent forward, brought his lips to her breast. While one nipple enjoyed his teasing tongue and gentle nips, the other tightened as his nimble fingers twirled and tugged.

"Ohmigod. Ohmigod. Ohmigod." Riley called as she climbed the precipice. Alone in the night, it felt wonderful to give raucous voice to her pleasure. To let Wolf know how his touch ignited her body.

Wolf was her personal dynamite.

He cradled her on the water's surface until the tiny aftershocks abated. She gazed at his face, then at the moon, bright overhead. She remembered the woods and the owl crying for its mate.

"Hoo-hooo-hoo!" she hooted.

"Is that a compliment?" His eyebrow lifted.

"You betcha."

* * * *

Wolf and Riley woke to sunshine. Jennie joined them on a hike to the petroglyphs. Something they'd all wanted to do with bright sunlight chasing away old shadows. The day had sped by. Wolf was delighted it involved no contact with other members of Riley's family.

He straightened his tie. "You're sure about this." He drew her into his arms. "I can't get enough of you. But your family? Will you be my food taster?"

She kissed his cheek. "You saved Jennie. Uncle Ed suggested this weekend to honor our engagement. They want to make amends." She smiled. "I love you. They will, too."

"Jennie will be at dinner, right?" he asked. "I'm happy that she's doing so well."

Riley smiled. "She's a remarkable and resilient young lady. I think the counselor she's seeing has helped her handle the ordeal. She insisted her dad find the prostitute Hunter abused and get her into a drug program."

Riley tugged him toward the bed. "Sit a minute. I have more news. Since we're combining our honeymoon with research for your next novel, I called my friend Kate Johnson yesterday. She spent two years in Jamaica with the Peace Corps. Gave me the inside scoop on things to see and do."

"Terrific." Wolf smiled. "Can't wait."

Riley chewed her lip. "We talked about Amanda's death, too. Kate was a senior at BRU when Amanda arrived as a freshman. They came from the same town, so Kate took her under her wing. They emailed frequently after Kate left campus."

Wolf squeezed her hand. "I'm guessing you shared your suspicions about Amanda's killer."

"Yeah. I told Kate about the car with a here-you-see-it, now-you-don't hood ornament and my hunch that it was Doris's Rolls Royce with Reverend Jimmy playing chauffeur. Kate got excited. Turns out Amanda told her the reverend kept pestering her after she volunteered at a soup kitchen."

Wolf shrugged. "Not exactly a smoking gun."

"No, but we didn't need one. Sheriff Hendricks called while you were in the shower. The preacher confessed. A combination of guilt and fear prompted him to sing as soon as he was brought in for questioning."

Wolf frowned. "Really? The televangelist killed Amanda?"

Riley shook her head. "It's even more bizarre. Reverend Jimmy used some sort of religious guise to call on Amanda. When he put the moves on her, they tussled. Amanda fell and hit her head."

"So he claims her death was accidental—with all those stab wounds?"

"Yeah, he says he panicked and called Doris. It was her idea to make it look like a violent crime scene. Doris stripped so she wouldn't get bodily fluids on her clothes as she stabbed the girl—again and again and again. A nude, knife-wielding Doris scared Jimmy so badly he didn't say boo. Went along because he worried he'd be next."

"And the post-mortem rape?" Wolf's tone telegraphed his horror.

Riley shuddered. "Doris. I didn't ask for details."

Wolf pulled Riley into his arms. "At least Amanda was past suffering. My God, where's the boundary between crazy and plain evil?"

She returned his fierce hug. "Damned if I know. I'm convinced John Hunter is both—evil and crazy. The sheriff says Hunter's recovered enough to stand trial. Of course, his attorney will plead insanity."

Wolf shook his head. "We're lucky. If Charles hadn't told us your mother could blow us all up, I doubt we'd have figured out that Hunter rigged her oxygen concentrator."

Riley smiled. "Speaking of Miz Pearl, she really does want to make peace with her future son-in-law. Can you forgive her?"

Wolf held her gaze. "She's your mother. How could I hate her and love you? It's time to look forward, not back. I'm looking forward to loving you for a very long time."

"Ah, Wolf, you do know how to write dialogue."

BOOKS BY LINDA LOVELY

Smart Women, Dumb Luck Series
Dead Line (Previously titled Final Accounting, 2012)
Dead Hunt (2014)
Dead Cure (Coming 4th Quarter, 2015)

Marley Clark Mystery Series
Dear Killer (2011)
No Wake Zone (2012)
With Neighbors Like These (Coming late 2014)

Please check for the availability of audiobooks. Dear Killer, No Wake Zone and Dead Line are available now. The audio version of Dead Hunt will be available late 2014.

About the Author

Linda Lovely's romantic thrillers serve up a main course of suspense along with generous helpings of romance and humor. Her manuscripts have earned final spots in 15 contests, including RWA Golden Heart and Daphne du Maurier contests. *Dear Killer*, the first in Lovely's Marley Clark Mystery Series, was a finalist in the RWA Golden Quill published novel competition, while ***Dead Line*** (previously titled *Final Accounting*) made the finals of the National Readers' Choice Awards for Romantic Suspense.

A journalism major, Lovely pursued a career in PR. One of her clients—the investigative firm that served as a prototype for the heroine's employer in ***Dead Line***—introduced her to forensic accounting and other techniques for catching savvy criminals.

During five terms as president of the Upstate SC Chapter of Sisters in Crime, she established ties with many law enforcement experts willing to share expertise with authors. In 2014, she attended her third Writers' Police Academy—this time as volunteer staff.

She also belongs to Romance Writers of America, International Thriller Writers, and the South Carolina Writers Workshop. A popular speaker, Lovely teaches genre fiction classes through Clemson University's Osher Lifelong Learning Institute, participates in panels at writers' conferences, and often visits with book clubs.

To learn more, visit: www.lindalovely.com.